First published by Amazon

Version 2

Text copyright © Ian McLean

The moral rights of Ian McLean are asserted

To my late Mum, Nola May, nee Stephens Howard, who encouraged my sisters and I to read. Also to my elder sister Vanessa, who encouraged me to put "pen to paper" and to stop prevaricating. Finally to myself, without whom, none of this would have been possible.

Table of Contents

FaceDead

Phillip Anderson

I love you to the moon and back x 5, I love you more than the moon and the stars, more than infinity. You are my heartbeat. I love you Francis.

Phillip Anderson stared at these words. As he did, he felt his heart thump, like the drum intro at the start of Diana Ross' song, I'm Coming Out. His temporal artery began to throb like the bass speaker at a house party. The words were not music to his ears, more akin to the constant whine of tinnitus.

I love you to the moon and back x 5.

He read that, and the whole sentence again.

Ricki Finn, who wrote the post on Facebook was a former school friend and work colleague. He was a devious little toad with a nose as brown as horse shit, but that was not the main issue for Phillip. That Ricki had left his sweet natured wife, a fellow colleague, was also not an issue, or the fact that Ricki was now openly out of the closet as a gay man changing his name from Ricky Finnegan in the process.

Ricki had once asked the hypothetical question of whether were he gay, would Phillip be top or bottom, but no offence was meant and none taken. Ricki liked to shock. The main issues for Phillip were that primarily, Ricki now lived out his life on Facebook and flooded his pages with inane, vacuous, meaningless, self-gratifying, shallow and self-obsessed posts. On an almost daily basis he professed his love for Francis, his boyfriend for the past two years.

The second issue was that despite Ricki using social media to advertise his true love he was often staying behind at work in the evening to have sex with the Cuban cleaner, Antonio.

Phillip knew this because Antonio had told him.

"Senor Phillip, I am having, what you can say jiggy jig, with your amigo, Senor Ricki, we do it twice a week in the room where I keep my broom. Do you think I am important to him or do you think he is using me just for pumper?"

Phillip had looked at the swarthy young man, short, around 5 foot two, dressed in skinny jeans and dainty flower coloured converse trainers. His black tee shirt had fun fun fun written in writing that resembled a Warhol scrawl. Antonio's angular face was not manly but not too effeminate as he had a scar that ran down from below his left ear that made him look slightly menacing. Any menace disappeared at the sound of his voice, which was camp and heavily Latino and matched his eyes which were large round and had a constant look of surprise. Antonio's faint hint of woody cologne was offset by the smell of disinfectant that was in the bucket that seemed to accompany him around the building like a loyal but damp dog.

Phillip replied, "Antonio, you should decide whether what you are doing is just fun or whether you want a relationship with Mr Finn. I am not the best person to ask."

"But you know him, you are his friend, does he not talk about me?"

"No I am not his friend, I work with him. That's all."

"He told me you were his friend. That you like men and women."

"Neither is true Antonio. You should talk to him."

Phillip had breezed away from the diminutive South American wondering whether to raise the issue with his erstwhile colleague but had thought against it, knowing that Ricki was likely to react either like a petulant child caught with his hands on the cookie jar or a prostitute caught soliciting but with the audacity to claim tax concessions. It didn't really matter to him that Antonio thought he was bisexual, the effeminate South American had an endearing innocence about him. It was a shame that once Ricki was bored with him he would have him sacked on a trumped up charge of incompetence, just as he had done with the Filipino cleaner before him.

For Phillip, the expression "I love you to the moon and stars and back x 5," ranked alongside "a cheeky pint/wine/bet/night out," or "it would

2

be rude not to," as an insult to the intelligence of anyone with an IQ higher than a pair of fish.

Phillip's sensible self said circumnavigate the incessant drivel about nights out at Freedom Bar in Soho or Revenge Club in Brighton or OMG in Plymouth. The constant appeals for attention with a post, "I can't believe what's just happened," "OMG this is unbelievable," or "Ricki is feeling sad."

Why did Ricki need to check in at the hospital when he was going for a routine eye test or voice a concern about an irritating cough that would turn out to be just that? The detail of his visit was never stated, leaving the one would assume, avid reader, in a state of internet intrigue, given the possibility of there being an ailment that could only be discussed behind a closed door.

Each of these posts would be followed by the inevitable, "What's up babe?" "Are you okay Hon?" "I'm there for you Ricki love" or "PM me if you need to."

There were posts about Ricki's perceived discrimination as if he were the only gay in the Westcliffe-One-Sea where he lived. "I can't believe the look that bitch in Asda gave me." "Pub landlords are such homophobes." "Why do I get the feeling I am being judged for what I am?"

Phillip's rational self, told him to ignore the missives about lovers, relationships and break-ups but he was drawn to Ricki's postings like a gambler on benefits to a scratch card. Like that gambler he needed to remove the silver coating and be disappointed at the result.

His hatred of Ricki was visceral.

The list of Ricki's Facebook transgressions were endless. His friends were semi-literate, opinionated buffoons.

He read the sentence again. I love you to the moon and back x 5.

He wished Ricki Finn met with misfortune, perhaps expiring during a sex game gone wrong or better still, having a household or workplace accident and losing his fingers and the ability to type.

Phillip knew this thoughts were cockeyed and sometimes wondered whether it was due to his own life being quite mundane. He wondered whether his lack of female company, bar his mother, meant that Ricki's sexual successes rankled, but he knew that amongst the Facebook or other contacts he detested, envy was not an overriding factor.

He knew this because he had an overwhelming desire to drive a poker between the eyes of his mother, Christine, and she had no love life, was not fabulously wealthy, no children to boast about, no dog, and wasn't forever checking in at an airport to publicise her latest trip abroad.

Phillip eyed himself in the mirror. At 54 he was hardly in his prime. The once prominent chiselled features were now slack and saggy. Cheeks, full and pliant, he could have doubled for a bloodhound eyeing a juicy bone. The bags under his eyes, red and veiny, resembled the protuberance at the back end of a primate. He looked at his hands, hairy knuckles, with concert pianist long fingers, crowned by nails as jagged as an iron file. The thick bushy eyebrows, inherited from his mother, were the bane of his life. She had had hers lasered off, he felt stuck with his. He looked down at his belly, once washboard flat now there was a distinct paunch. Too much cake, too many sweets, too much Guinness and lager. The bulge of fat around his waist had grown from a spare tyre to a full set of four and not low profile. At five foot seven Phillip was not the tallest but then neither was he short enough to ever be accused of having small man syndrome.

He came in at around thirteen stones and eleven pounds. Overweight according to his own subjective eye but obese according to his BMI of 30.2. He had black hair that was very well cut for a 54 year old man. He had managed to keep his mane and was glad of that. He could see without glasses but did need them for reading. His teeth were British crooked. When he was young anyone with braces was mercilessly mocked and for that reason, as well as it not being a standard practise, his overcrowded teeth resembled tombstones sitting on the subsided earth that were his gums. Phillip's teeth were however, pearly white, having paid £350 for a bleaching kit which consisted of bespoke gum shields and tubes of Polanight gel which he had applied religiously every day for two weeks forsaking red wine, curry, coffee, and corsadyl anti-gingivitis mouthwash. A fairly nondescript man who wore chinos, a shirt and shoes to work and at home lounged around in loose jeans, trainers and a tee shirt. Not at the height of fashion but not a dinosaur would be how he would describe himself.

He wished he had aged well, like George Clooney or Jeff Goldblum. If he only had half their money. He knew he shouldn't compare his life with that of the rich or famous because that was another pet hate of his. People who knew about the lives of minor celebrities but did not know what was going on in the world around them, locally, nationally or internationally. People who knew which celebrity was dating or married to who. Who was pregnant, who had babies, what they were called. All gormless piffle. These same people did not know what countries made up the United Kingdom, the name of their local MP or the opening time of the library.

He still however wished he had aged as well as George Clooney or Jeff Goldblum.

Phillip mused. If only he had kept up his gym membership. An uncomfortable incident had occurred which forced him to stop his training regime.

It came about because, whilst in the gym he had kept glancing at an extremely fit and busty girl who was on the cross trainer adjacent to him She was dressed in a matching top and leggings and had iPod in-earphones attached to her head. Phillip had been mesmerised at how someone with such a small waist could have such a large chest which bounced hypnotically with the girl's every stride. Her hips were, as his mother would have said, child bearing and her legs looked firm and taut as though she could have kneaded dough with them.

The girl had said shrilly, "For fuck sake do you want to take a picture? Do you like to screw out 16 year old girlies then? Wish you could have some you peado-perv?"

Phillip had blanched, the girl's voice had rattled him. She had an accent, somewhere below common but above white trash that he immediately found repellent.

She had called to her friend who was a number of cross trainer machines down the row and said, "Chelsea, this old creep is giving me the shivers man."

Chelsea had come over with her mobile phone in her hand, she had pointed it at Phillip, and obviously filming what she hoped might be a fracas that could be loaded onto a social media platform. She was similarly dressed to her friend, matching Nike top and leggings with fluorescent trainers. On her head she wore a headset. It was surprising, given their size, she could still hear her friend speak.

Phillip had wished the ground had swallowed him whole, like Jonah's whale. He had stepped off his cross trainer and looked into the phone camera lens Chelsea had in front of her.

"Don't worry Tanya," Chelsea had said, "I'm gonna get this all on film. Weirdo alert, this is going on Facebook man."

Tanya had stepped off her cross trainer too and waved her arms in Phillip face so enthusiastically her breasts had once again became too prominent for him not to notice or for his eyes to be drawn to.

"Got him Tanya, got him, he is proper perving you man. He can't help himself looking at your babylons," Chelsea had whined.

"I can't believe it Chelsea I am getting so upset." Tanya had said, this with her arms outstretched which caused her Lycra top to strain to bursting point. She began flapping her hands around her eyes as if fanning herself but this only resulted in her bosoms jumping around even more, replicating a training session at LA Lakers.

Tanya's outburst had attracted the attention of two other girls. These two were in their mid-twenties, standing by a thigh flexor. Ebony and Misha, normally spent their gym session gossiping to each other and doing little in the way of a workout.

Phillip prided himself on recognising most of those who trained. He wasn't outgoing, therefore he rarely spoke to anyone but he silently watched everyone, making a mental note of how long they spent on each machine and whether they wiped them down with tissues soaked in anti-bacteria wash.

Misha and Ebony were on Phillip's angry radar, he knew their names because they couldn't go two minutes without one referring to the other, be it to offer encouragement or to point out someone they knew. They would follow each other around the gym making feeble efforts to take turns to use the machines, their favourites being those that afforded seats. They would spend 15 minutes on the running machines, intermittently jogging, but walk whilst chatting for 25 of those minutes and have the bare faced cheek to press the cool down button. Every five minutes they would slurp hungrily at their bottled water, as if chatting needed hydration. Often this pair would monopolise the mats used for stretching, sit ups, plank position or curls. They would just lay there yakking. Phillip often eyed them with growing fury but never verbally gave vent to his anger. At regular intervals one or the other would take her hair out of whatever clip or scrunchy that was holding it and toss a long mane back and re-apply said tie. Such hair re-arrangement seemed to take place whenever a reasonable looking lad was within view.

Part of these girls gym routine would be to look at each other's phones and social media content. Phillip was aware of this because he had furtively peeked at their screen displays when he walked past. It had filled him with ire because in his opinion, gyms were for working out and if you couldn't put your phone down for 45 minutes whilst working out you were a moron. His indignation was exacerbated by the fact that when he brought his own smart phone down the gym to track the sale of a Dr Who Dalek toy on eBay, he couldn't get a signal via Vodafone and there was no Wi-Fi access.

Ebony and Misha, with some other distraction to take them away from each other, began fuelling the tirade adding their own. Each of them began to record the indignant 16 year olds and Phillip on their smartphones, as if they were at a concert, festival or party.

*Yeah he's always staring at us mate," Misha had said to the young girl, adding more cordite to an already explosive situation.

"His creepy eyes are always following us around the gym, he wants locking up," Chelsea had replied.

Tanya had said nothing at this point, she had moved stealthily, as if armed with a grenade, switching the camera feature focus of her smartphone from herself to Phillip to the girl to her friend.

7

Aware that most of the people in the gym were now no longer pumping iron or burning calories on bike, cross trainer or stepper, Phillip made a decision that flight was the best option.

He held his hand up, hoping to silence Chelsea, and also to shield his face from being stabbed with the edge of Tanya's iPhone. "I don't know what you're going on about but I am going to complain to the manager about this. Your harassing me and you shouldn't be videoing me without my permission. None of you." he said, with authority.

Phillip had marched toward the gym door with the sound of all three banshees screeching after him, "Jog on paedo." "I've got it all on film Tanya, that weirdo," Chelsea shouted.

Tanya's retort was menacing, loud, and delivered with conviction, "My old man's going to do you, you bastard."

Phillip was on his toes and exited the gym, his heart racing. Some women made him uncomfortable. If he were twenty years older he would probably have had a coronary. There was the smell of stale odour behind him, his own with him, and an even sourer smell of embarrassment as he bounded up the stairs head down. He leapt two stairs at a time, arms pumping and lifting his thighs as if he were preparing for an Olympic long or triple jump.

As he reached the top stair he tripped, just as a middle aged woman appeared and whose chest collided with his outstretched hand. Today was breasts day.

The woman gave him a startled look and stifled a scream as he groped for his balance and only managed to knead at one of her ample bosoms and tweak a now pert nipple. When he had finally righted himself he recognised her, or more so her décolletage.

Chloe, a very stand offish gym junkie who did a 30 minute session before work and a two hour session post. Spinning twice a week, insanity classes twice a week and boxercise on a Wednesday evening. She was the wrong side of 40, nearer 50 if truth be told, with a reasonable figure but a lined face that looked as though her life had been full or not easy. It was more the former, Chloe had in her time snorted enough lines of cocaine to fund a large village in a third world country.

Chloe had crow's feet around her eyes that lay atop darkened rings that betrayed a lack of sleep, her addiction to Xanax was the primary cause of this. Worrying about being over 40 and not a size 10 was the cause of her anxiety. Chloe was six foot, one inch tall, a size 16. Her leggings, matching top and expensive trainers screamed out the desire to be recognised as a serious gym buff. Whenever Phillip saw her, the Commodore song, Brick House sprang to mind and the lyric "Built like an Amazon." Currently however the only song Phillip could think of was Jailhouse Rock, which was where he might find himself.

Phillip always assumed that Chloe wore training tops that were as low as Belgium and the Netherlands, in order to give the men, and perhaps the lesbians, something to think about when she worked out, other than her aging looks.

Chloe did like to get admiring glances from the boys, unfortunately for him, Phillip was not one of the boys. Time stood still momentarily.

Phillip said, "Sorry, I slipped." Sweat cascaded from his brow like an outside pipe that had burst having not survived sub-zero temperatures. With his quite naturally large eyes the vision confronting Chloe could not have been less attractive. Alarming was a more apt description. She uttered nothing initially, but looked at him with horror. "If I was more cynical I would say you did that on purpose," she said. "You really got off on that didn't you."

It wasn't a question.

"No, not at all," was all Phillip could muster and he tried to ease past her, being careful not to make any further contact. As misfortune would have it, his sweatshirt snagged on a protruding fine splinter of wood that framed the noticeboard at the top of the stairs. Tugging at his top he over compensated thinking his polypropylene Nike running vest was as strong as advertised. It wasn't. He propelled backward faster than anticipated and his arse collided with Chloe's.

Phillip heard her take a sharp intake of breath and as he turned toward her she placed a hand firmly on his shoulder. "Don't do that again," she said, her eyes fixed on his, and then added, "you fucking cunt."

Once again, time stood still.

The impasse was broken by the sound of voices approaching, high pitched ladies voices. Some women were talking about the class they were about to do and how they hoped Bridget was going to go easy tonight. Phillip used the distraction to break away from Chloe's death glare and he shot along the corridor to the bank of lockers that were opposite the changing rooms. He quickly extracted his kit from his locker. He was in such a rush he forgot to take his pound from the locking mechanism. His normal routine post workout would be for a 15 minute sauna, followed by a 10 minute steam, and a 15 minute jacuzzi,but not that day.

He had considered popping into the office and explaining to Bernard the manager what had happened with the 16 year old. Knowing that Chloe was on speaking terms with the female pair he guessed that by the time he had got to his car the three women and the 16 year old girl would be filling each other in on events and then debating whether to form a vigilante group to tar and feather him or the more likely event, out him as a pervert via the gyms Facebook page.

As he drove home, anxiously peering into his rear view mirror at times looking for the blue and white tell-tale sign that a warrant had already been issued for this arrest, he decided that the gym was no longer for him. He would purchase some dumb bells and do a daily routine in the comfort and safety of his own home.

Now, in the present day, in his bedroom, as he stared at the cardboard boxes in which the said dumb bells had been delivered, and back to himself in his full-size mirror he wished he had got into the habit of a fitness routine.

He looked around his bedroom. It was as if it had been decorated in his image. A wardrobe with a sagging shelf, the MDF chipped in places to reveal the grainy pressed wood substitute. The headboard to his bed was a beige velour more suited to the 80s. A golden age of funk and soul but now in need of some update. Phillip sat on his office swivel chair at his MDF desk that housed his laptop and filing tray.

10

Phillip's domesticity was not averse to some of the practises that he encountered at work therefore he adopted a clear desk policy at home. Apart from the laptop and filing tray there was a gold coloured desk lamp, a pen holder and a picture frame with a photo of him smiling aged 16 year old when he had one of his best days out. The picture was with his Dad, Oliver, just before going to Brisbane Road, the home of Leyton Orient. Both wore red and white scarves and bobble hats and Oliver had his arm lovingly around his son like a high quality protective layer of cladding around a building housing professionals and the tenants of foreign investors.

Oliver was an amazing father. When he was five Phillip had in his class at infants school a boy, Matthew Mullane, who would take great delight in digging children in the ribs with the tips of his fingers or stamping his heels onto their feet. Matthew had behavioural problems as well as being in a single parent family, raised by his father, who was aggressive and ignorant and thought that all issues were to be resolved using fists.

As Phillip and Oliver were walking home from school one day Oliver had asked his son why one of the boys, who had been close by to the school gates, was crying. Phillip told his Dad about Matthew and his violent tendencies. Oliver, knowing that his son could be sensitive, enrolled him at ju-jitsu classes.

Eight years later and Phillip was a junior black belt. As he was a very placid person during his school years he never once used the martial art he had been taught. For a lad growing up in Essex through the sixties and seventies, he was fortunate never to have had a violent confrontation. As an adult the closest he came to threatening behaviour was being given the V sign by irate motorists. Once he was threatened by a male pedestrian who had walked out into the road, phone in hand, without regard for vehicles or other road users. Phillip had no inclination to leave his car and wreak havoc. Phillip was a very controlled person, he internalised all his aggression.

In his room, anything that he didn't need was stuffed in a drawer which meant that the three of these, his desk afforded, were full of receipts, paper clips, installation manuals, sweets, plugs, cables, old phones envelopes, paper and four cameras.

Phillip mused over the many misgivings he had about himself but decided that the nature and behaviour of others were far more insidious. At this precise moment in time Ricki Finn was the person least deserving of a right to be happy.

Before Phillip had a chance to contemplate the many ways Ricki could become less of an irritant, one of the other objects of his ire, his mother, called from the downstairs of the mid-terraced semi-detached they shared in Seven Kings, Essex.

 "Phillip Sebastian," Christine Anderson called, in a stern tone, "your dinner will be ready in five minutes."

Phillip and Christine Anderson.

His mother's voice aroused him from his trance-like state and, Phillip looked around him to concentrate more on the place he was in rather than the place he would like to be, which was by Ricki Finn's hospital bed offering fake sympathy, his funeral offering even less sincere condolences or, failing Ricki's misfortune, a beach in the Bahamas.

His negative energy now transferred to his mother Christine. When all else failed and he had none of his internet loathing's to increase the risk of him experiencing an aneurism, there was always his mother. Without a doubt, to Phillip this was the most irksome person in his life and he had to deal with her every day. He felt like an innocent man, fitted up for a murder he did not commit but serving a life sentence with no chance of an action group or tenacious lawyer coming up with the evidence to free him. Returning to the same cell to look at the same four walls, the same rock solid bed, the same blood and urine stained linen, the same rickety table, the same plastic chair and the same chiselled graffiti on the wall by the same barred window that read, "see you tomorrow con, same time, same place."

Christine insisted on calling Phillip, Phillip Sebastian, even though she knew how much he detested the pretentious name she had tried to foist upon him.

He dreaded dinner with her, where once it was a pleasant experience, now it was a chore. She was showing signs of dementia, repeating the same conversations over and over again. Giving him the same

12

information she gave him yesterday which often led to the same arguments. Being cantankerous and argumentative and grating on his nerves because she knew his tolerance level was as low as the belly of a lizard.

Phillip wished he were able to ignore her or at least not get into the same battle that he had before, that made every day seem like Groundhog day but Phillip was not built of such stern stuff, he had the vertebrae of a narrow minded lumbricus terrestris.

Christine often used this phrase to describe her son instead of saying the backbone of a common earthworm. Where narrow minded fitted into the description Phillip neither knew nor cared. Christine had enjoyed the period when the mad cows disease had taken over salmonella as the health scare of the nations and was eager to say bovine spongiform encephalitis whenever the opportunity arose and even when it didn't.

Phillip was pedantic, critical, argumentative, cold, sceptical and inflexible, all Virgo characteristics according to Christine.

Christine was a Pisces. According to her star signs book they were incompatible. On this matter Phillip fully agreed.

"I called you five minutes ago what were you doing?" she said as he entered the large kitchen. Christine had a motherly figure, plump like a happy Italian housewife but as miserable as a Yorkshire one. She was around five foot two and dressed in a blue shirt and skirt. On her nose was a pair of horn rimmed glasses. She looked like her son except for her pencil drawn eyebrows. Christine had thick black shoulder length hair, a dumpy brown eyed face and a saggy neck that would fool a cockerel. Her teeth were a mix of her own and dentures, with one gold crown which she said was 21 carat and could be melted down when she passed and used to pay for her coffin. Christine dressed well and was an aficionado of Chanel No 5 which was not unusual for women of her age but was a smell that made Phillip shudder, so cloying and over fragrant.

Phillip was of the opinion that not only should this event be sooner rather than later but that once dead he would seek permission to dump his mother's body in the River Lea.

Christine's kitchen, her pride and joy, was fitted with top of the range NEFF hob, double oven, extractor, integrated microwave, dishwasher, washing machine and tumble dryer. The hob and oven were the latest in design and cutting edge technology. Unfortunately Christine's cooking was as basic as a 14 year old with a fondness for a gravy drenched roast every Sunday. The kitchen fitting included an Italian granite work surface which had almost doubled the price of the installation and a heated ceramic flooring and mahogany dinging table. The granite work surface was so exquisite and delicate that it had to be polished daily with an imported cleaning agent as it was prone to staining, even if a droplet of water lay on it for more than three hours. The magnificent mahogany table seated eight but consistently was used for two. Christine's favourite utterances were, "You can't scrimp on quality," "You can always trust a person who drives a top of the range Mercedes or BMW," "A person with good breeding turns left at the top of the stairs of an aeroplane," and "Why holiday with the proles? Do not vacate in an abode that has less than 5 stars."

The number of times Christine Anderson started a sentence with "I'm not a snob but….." were incalculable, and another reason for Phillip wishing she would have a fatal heart attack.

"I don't think it was five minutes ago," Phillip replied. He had a thing about food being served hot so was fully aware that between his mother's call and him getting to the kitchen was approximately one minute. She knew he had this hot food thing but she also knew how to press his buttons.

"Your dinner will be cold and you know how you like your dinner to be served up at 100 degrees so you scald your tongue trying to eat it," she said acidly. "Remember how you burned the roof of your mouth trying to eat my delightful home-made pizza that came straight out of the oven? I can still see the melted cheese dripping down your mouth like sputum out of the mouth of a dribbling imbecile."

"I came straight down Mum, probably within 30 seconds of you saying Sebastian," he said, sarcastically emphasizing the name. It sounded like he was referring to the government official who abolished free school milk.

"I know you don't like your name. Your father behaved most appallingly and treacherously recording your birth certificate as Phillip Sebastian and not Sebastian Phillip. It was a callous and cruel act and I'll never forgive him."

"Dad is dead. He is beyond whatever vilification you have for him, and, as well, Sebastian isn't a name for people like me."

"People like you. People like you!" Christine shrilled, what sort of person are you lives with their mother, 56 years of age, unmarried, with no heirs and still can't afford to drive a decent car?"

When you're dead the first thing I will do when I get your money is buy a Bentley. You don't even know how old I am you batty cow, Phillip thought to himself.

"Don't think you're going to hang around until I am dead then spend my money like the prodigal son," she said, "I'd sooner leave my money to Battersea Dogs Home."

Christine hated animals and small children who didn't sit up straight and still, call her Madam or keep their mouths firmly shut when not being spoken to, Battersea was no more likely to get her money than the RSPCA or the NSPCC. She could be quite a vindictive woman and was more likely to turn her capital into fluid assets, withdraw the money and burn it on a bonfire the day before she died were it possible to predict a date of death.

"What's for dinner?" Phillip said, hoping a subject change might rid him of this tiresome estate conversation that he had at least twice a week.

He looked at her, with her now ample bottom and ever increasing waistline and her jowly face that housed a mouth out of which seemed to constantly emit venom like a cagey rattlesnake.

There was a picture of Christine in the hallway, with his father, Oliver, 40 years ago. That picture was committed to Phillip's memory like the route to a stash of nuts, cached by a hibernating squirrel. He tried to think of this rather than the dervish that stood before him.

15

In the picture, Oliver looked dashing in a pale blue three piece suit, grey trilby, explosive white shirt and yellow polka dot bow tie, set off by black and white brogues. He had slicked hair with a side parting and a pencil thin moustache. From the corner of his mouth snaked a woodbine. He looked as if he were a danger to women and teenage girls alike.

Christine, looking like a debutante in a real fur stole, off the shoulders Coco Chanel evening dress, sheer stockings and patent leather Christian Dior high heel. Smiles as wide as stepladders are long. Such a happy and gay looking couple. How it had all changed.

He looked at his mother now and thought of his ample pear shaped bottom that he had lost when he started to work out but had returned. He remembered vividly how he was ribbed at school for being shaped like a woman. Phillip ArseSirSon, Big Phil, Big Butt, Fatso Phil. When, in his first year at Warren Secondary School in Chadwell Heath, a teacher inadvertently revealed Phillip's middle name to the class, Sebarstian, pronounced, Seb Arse Tee Un, became a nickname Phillip had to endure for the remaining five years of senior school.

Christine's hands were the softest part of her, delicate little things with long finger nails that were kept immaculately. Phillip too always remembered what his PE teacher, John McKellan, had said to him when he had fallen over trying to kick a football and cut his knee. "Christ, Sebarsetian, your hands are like a young girls. I bet you enjoy wanking."

All Phillip could do was slope off with a note to the school nurse to get a dressing as the rest of the class rolled around in mirth.

Having had no answer to his question Phillip repeated, "What's for dinner mother?"

"Pan fried calves liver with a balsamic drizzle, sautéed Brussel sprouts and pancetta, cous-cous surprise," Christine said.

Phillip recoiled at this response to his question. Apart from the fact his mother was a hopeless cook, could not follow a recipe but had ideas of being a Masterchef contestant, she knew he wasn't over keen on offal, abhorred brussel sprouts and deigned that cous-cous was no substitute for pasta, rice or potatoes..

16

He had forgotten how many times he had told his mother that he disliked the aforementioned food items but her apparent senility made him wonder whether she had simply forgotten. Was it worth moving from one argument to another he pondered? On a positive note at least she wasn't serving quinoa.

"That sounds nice," he said, through gritted teeth and added, "I'm not going to be able to eat loads because when I went out at lunch time I met Helen Tyler from school and we grabbed a bite and a coffee."

This was a lie he hadn't seen Helen, if he had he would have avoided her and her three pugs and the French poodle dogs she treated like children. This he knew from her Facebook posts about her four beautiful fur babies. Before he had time to wonder what Helen was doing that day Christine replied.

"I'll dish some out, what you don't eat you can finish off tomorrow but I know once you've tasted it you'll be positively relishing extra helpings."

"Mother," Phillip said dryly, "I don't particularly like liver, brussels or cous-cous, having it once will be the limit of my yearly intake. What is cous-cous surprise?"

Christine ignored him and ladled ample portions of each food item onto one of the oversized plates she used for dinner. She gave herself a much smaller portion and brought both plates over to the dining table, placing them on the mats already equipped with knives, forks and spoons. The surprise about the cous-cous was it had been coloured with turmeric therefore resembled a babies diarrhoea.

"Are we having dessert?" Phillip asked, trying to lighten his mood at the thought that his overweight sweet toothed mother might have had a temporary mental aberration bought some Hagen Das or Ben and Jerrys ice cream, or a Millionaires cheesecake.

Hot fruit for dessert was also a no-no therefore baked pears or apples were not for him unless the apples were under a crumble. He detested rhubarb with a vengeance.

"No Phillip Sebastian, there's no dessert, we can't have you getting fat can we, girls don't like porky boys," Christine said, as if addressing a ten year old.

Phillip glared at his mother. He could ask why she had laid spoons out but decided once again that this irksome woman was not worth entering a debate with. Besides this, eating dessert would mean spending more time at the dinner table with her, something he did not relish. He sighed and began to eat. He wanted to kill this woman badly but he needed to know that he wasn't the only suspect.

"I went into that nice lady's house next door but one today," Christine said.

"That nice lady who wouldn't take in your parcel last week?"

"She explained that. I told you. She wasn't sure of our name and she didn't want to get caught up in any funny business."

"Funny business. Taking in a parcel for a neighbour?"

"We're not neighbours, she doesn't live next door."

"She's in our neighbourhood."

"Yes but we're not neighbours. She gave me a drink of orange juice."

"Freshly squeezed was it?"

"No she poured it out of a carton. Why are you being so obtuse?"

"She is as much a snob as you are. She looks down her nose at me because I drive a Focus. I was going out the other day and she shouted over, are you going out in your old jalopy?"

"Nothing wrong with having class. She has a top of the range BMW 8 series. Black leather seats with red trim. It's an automatic."

"How do you know it's an automatic? Did she take you for a spin?"

"No. She gave me some orange juice. The glass was Dartington Crystal."

How do you know that? Since when have you been an expert on cut glass?"

"She told me. She said, have some juice. Her exact words were, I'll give it to you in a Dartington Crystal glass. I can see you are wearing a Chanel jumper so you must have taste."

Christine smiled as if reliving the memory of an encounter with a kindred spirit and then frowned when she looked to see her son was looking at her as if she were some sort of simpleton. She sneered at him.

"Her name is Alice Keppel, such an aristocratic name don't you think?"

You got your Chanel jumper from the charity shop. Her name is Alison Caple."

"How do you know?"

I took a parcel in for her on Saturday. Are you going senile? Please leave me in peace so I can eat my dinner Mother"

"Why did you take in her parcel if you thought I didn't like her and yes I think I must be going senile? I think I spend too much time with you and not getting any stimulating conversation. Alice is such a well-travelled lady. She used to be a travel representative you know, going around assessing the finest hotels. She was telling me about all the exciting places she has been to. I was in there for hours. The registration on her car is almost personalised"

"Her registration is personalised if her name was ELI 45 N, and I would think her being a travel agent you would expect her to have travelled extensively Mother. Why don't you pop over now and give her a plate of food, there is enough for another share. I am sure she will love your cous-cous surprise."

"No, I am sure she will be eating just as well as you are, she's probably picked herself something up from Waitrose or the local butcher. Anyway, if I give her any of this what will you have tomorrow?"

She smiled as she said this, she knew that Phillip was likely to get up in the middle of the night and spoon the plated up leftovers in the bin. He didn't do the same cooked meal two days running just in case it upset his sensitive digestive system. His only refined quality she thought.

Her Times newspaper was on the table, she drew her son's attention to it by pointing at it.

"There's a big write-up in the Times about the murder of that schoolgirl, you know the one who went to a party and took drugs and died."

"Not exactly murder then was it?" said Phillip.

"She was underage, giving her drugs was illegal."

"I would have thought no-one forced her to take ecstasy tablets."

"In the paper the reporter said there was some lovely comments on Facebook."

"Not much of a reporter if he had to go to Facebook for information. The same people commenting on Facebook are probably posting pictures of their dinner now."

"The girl's mother said something on Facebook too."

"What did she say? That it was the first time her daughter had taken drugs and she was a regular church goer?"

"Such a cynic. She said that her daughters Facebook page would remind her how loved her daughter was."

"Why didn't she just ask people? Facebook, Facebook, Facebook. What a load of shit."

"You're on it you hypocrite."

She eyed her son as she slowly ate her food. She loved him dearly once. She had loved him since the first time she laid eyes on him.

When the midwife gave him to her she had cried. She knew that she would keep him. The first boy she had given birth to have been taken away from her hours after he had been born and she never saw him again and she had lost her daughter.

Christine had no time for her son any more, he was past his best by date, and she wished he was out of her house. If he wasn't going to make his way, find a girl, hopefully one with children of her own or one young enough to give her children then she would drive him mad. She did want to leave her legacy to someone, someone cultured and ambitious, but who? Alice would have been a catch. With her top of the range car and history of travel and high powered job as a marketing representative for a pharmaceutical company.

Christine had hatched a plan, she would feign dementia and get under Phillip's very thin skin. She would drive him mad and he would have to kill himself or move out. He didn't have the backbone to do anything to her. Inwardly she smiled as he picked at his cous-cous.

Phillip looked back at his mother, and wished she were dead.

Christine Venables

Christine Venables was born in March 1943 while her father Clement was serving with the British Eighth Army in Tunisia.

Her mother Doris had had a lucky escape. Whilst Clement had been in away on the front in mid-1942 she had bedded her brother in law Alfie Venables. Alfie was a womaniser of some repute in Bethnal Green. He had escaped conscription due to being a police constable. Rumour had it several women, whose husbands were away fighting for King and country had borne children by him. Some were unfortunate to have fiancé or husbands who had been away for a year or more prior to the birth of a child and the children had either been put into homes or the wives abandoned. Some of these cuckolded men had lain in hospitals, bodies broken by enemy gunfire and mortar, torpedo or shrapnel. Men who had seen friends and comrades fall like broken flowers never to bloom again while the seed of Alfie Venables lay inside their wives.

Where Doris had some fortune smile on her was that Clement had been sent home on leave five weeks after she had shared a bed with his brother, she knew she was already pregnant when she had slept with her husband, her monthly, normally as regular as the toll of the church bell, had not arrived. Clement would be none the wiser when he finally returned home to see his daughter Christine, whom Doris had written to him about while he saw action.

Doris was not wholly averse to extra-curricular marital activities during the war, Alfie was not the only man to whom she had succumbed. A trip to the West End with her friend Florence and a drunken session in a Soho bar led to an encounter with a black American soldier, Henry Crockett, and a knee trembler in an alleyway. The soldier, aware of the likelihood of a venereal disease from the local girls, had the presence of mind to insist on donning a thick prophylactic. His fortitude did ensure that Doris was able to keep Alfie's baby as it was highly unlikely any offspring out of the union with the American could have passed as Clément's.

Christine's life as a war time baby was uneventful. The Venables house escaped being struck by German bombs, but only just. Doris took to motherhood and living in the two up two down with Clement's parents. With friends and neighbours in similar positions, husbands at war, rationing, the imminent fear of death. Doris had a job in the Singer factory on Commercial Street repairing uniforms. She did this leading up to the birth and soon her parents in law Myrtle and Albert were willing babysitters for their adorable first grandchild as ignorant as thy were about the son who had been the sire.

Clement would never know there was a cuckoo in the nest.

In 1947, twelve months after Clément's demob from the army he took over running the local pub. It was being managed by the parents of Bernie Tanner and Bernie's wife Gladys. On the day before the war was declared over Bernie was hit by sniper fire and fatally wounded. His parents and Gladys lasted nearly a year before deciding they would move out of the area and back to Methwold, Norfolk from where they had originated.

Clement and Doris proved to be naturals in the field of publicans. A fondness for beer and bawdy conversation helped, given the clients they served and the area in which they were located. Rough and ready would be the most apposite description. Clément's army training instilled a no nonsense approach to any shenanigans or inappropriate behaviour before it exceeded the boundaries of a quite low bar of acceptance.

The Red Lion was a large pub with a saloon and public bar. The former had a leather seat that covered the length of two walls. Round tables and leather chairs were adjacent and groups of the less raucous clientele would gather in groups to play shove ha' penny or dominoes. The older ladies of the area preferred this bar and often some of their husbands. Spinsters, widows and widowers were evident, often other younger family members would join for a gathering. The wall against which did not house the leather seat was occupied by a less than magnificent piano.

Pre karaoke days the musical accompaniment to a sing song would need an accomplished pianist or one who was either drunk or thick skinned. Woe betide anyone who stepped up but could not tinkle the ivories with suitable flourish. The bar faced the longest stretch of leather and it was here that Doris took charge with the two or three barmaids. There were less beer and ale pumps in this bar than in the public. Just two choices of each but there was a large selection of gins, whiskies, rums and brandy together with liqueurs and wines. The wines were of a fortified variety as Merlots, Chardonnays, Sauvignon Blanc and Pinot Grigio had yet to reach this less sophisticated outpost of London.

Clement had prided himself in his ability to source the widest range of sprits and had cabinets where the alcohol were too rare or too good for his clientele to serve. These were for display purposes only. Doris would often stand by the beer pumps, in her element and gaze around, priding herself in what her and her husband had achieved.

The public bar was a more rags affair. No leather here or fancy decoration and this gave the room a less formal character which was why Clement was the lord of this internal manor. The seat that was once a proud gold and red fabric but was now more a kaleidoscope of dried stains, beer, food and the odd spot of blood. The blood stains a hazard of being drunk and falling over rather than the result of any physical confrontation. As base as the customers were, they were 95% regulars and it did not pay to brawl with your neighbour or the person you might be working alongside the next morning.

Rectangular tables were dotted around and stools by them were once covered in the same gold and red fabric now frayed and as tatty looking as the suit on a jobless war veteran. A cloud of smoke created a haze above the patron's heads and clung to the chandeliers like a colony of grey bats.

This bar was more for the younger working man and woman and Doris knew if she was a punter this is where she would drink. The conversation was louder and the laughter brayed and hummed. The clothing factory workers usually congregated nearer to the bar whilst those from the few offices and who were in non-manual labour found their spot by the far wall near the jukebox.

There was always ample custom from the clothing factory that had during the war produced and repaired uniforms. There were Friday and Saturday night sing songs in the saloon bar when the place was at its busiest. On a Sunday afternoon there was a meat raffle and on a Sunday evening there was a less rumbustious session as the clientele wound themselves up for Monday morning blues.

Doris was, if nothing else, a shrewd business woman. The younger or better looking barmaids, worked in the public bar where more of the younger and thirstier customers congregated. The girls acted like magnets to the men who did most of the buying, Even men who were in attendance with girlfriends or wives enjoyed being served by a pretty barmaid and were more likely to offer "One for yourself?" to their order. With Clement in charge with his brother Gordon there was plenty of banter where the bar was as wide as a Cunard liner but rarely did the behaviour go beyond the line of impropriety.

The more homely, chubbier or older barmaids worked in the saloon bar. There was a hint of a, them and us situation with those from the public bar, in the main there was harmony amongst the staff.

Such an arrangement could not happen seventy years on where the remotest hint of body shaming would result in outrage, protests, tears and unreserved apologies. How times change.

As demand ebbed and flowed most were satisfied with their lot and familiarity with customers ensured the tills rattled like the collection box of St Barnabas Church further up the street. Throats were lubricated with a production line efficiency the foremen at the factory would have been proud of.

Christine was 15 when she started serving in the public bar and she did this most weekends. Fridays were one of the busiest evenings.

On this particular Friday Christine looked around at the usual throng of faces most of whom sat in the same places with the same crowds. She, like her mother would feel the same pride at the Venables place in the East End world of hospitality.

Over by the Wurlitzer jukebox Ronnie and Buster Phelps would hold court with their rockabilly style cronies. The brothers monopolised the machine selecting the latest hits when the machine was powered on. Clement had managed to acquire the box from an American soldier, Jack Crockett, who himself had managed to snaffle it from the army base when it was replaced by a more up to date Seeberg model.

Ted Baxter and his wife Margaret and their group of friends were nearest the rockabillies. Young Frank Gough, the bank manager's son was with his group of friends, strategically nearest Gail Connor, from the chemist and three of her shop assistant friends each with the standard look of the time, bleach blonde beehive, blood red lipstick, blouse and pencil skirt with high heel shoes and fishnet stockings.

The factory crowd, around twenty of them were by a set of tables nearest the bar and Kenny Phillips, the union man held a large group of them in his thrall, probably complaining about the management and a need for better pay and more humane conditions.

As Christine poured a pint for one of the factory workers she glanced up and saw that he was making no effort to hide his hypnotic stare at her developing cleavage. She smiled at him, tantalisingly running her tongue around her lips, as she put the pint on the beer mat on the bar with the other five he had ordered and was pleased that he invited her to keep the change out of the he had seven shillings he had given her. Doris wasn't the only business woman in the pub.

Christine loved the atmosphere of the family business, especially the smell of tobacco and beer. She was at that time a girl with basic tastes and outlook. As common as a sewer rat lurking next to a floating crust but no different from any other East End teenager. Whilst Doris and Clement were non-smokers but enjoyed a whisky with customers Christine was fond of an illicit cigarette, mischievously scrounged from a willing punter, borrowed from an unguarded packet or, if she was lucky, a discarded packet dropped or lost.

Christine loved to hear people singing in the pub and her passion was the music she listened to on the wireless. The music of the late 50s was moving away from the more formal music of the 40s, and rock and roll was king. Of course Christine loved Elvis and Bill Haley and the Comets, Gene Vincent and Frankie Lymon but she especially loved the black singers Clyde McPhatter, James Brown, Ray Charles, Sarah Vaughan and Ella Fitzgerald. The soulful voices that made her close her eyes and think what it would be like to have such rich voices and no doubt rich lifestyles. She imagined these singers driving around in big cars, living in big houses and playing in halls being appreciated my vast crowds. Little did she know that across the Atlantic, as talented as these black artists were their lives were limited by Jim Crow, especially those unfortunate enough to live below the Mason-Dixie line.

Christine could, it was said, carry a tune. Songs were dear to her and her harmonious voice could often be heard in the bathroom or in her room singing her favourite song of the time, Yakety Yak by the Coasters, Sweet Sixteen by Chuck Berry, Fever by Peggy Lee, The Book of Love by The Monotones, Tears on My Pillow by Little Antony and the Imperials. There were so many more that were enjoyed not only by her, also by her family and her best friend Kathleen McGuiness.

For Christine her teens were an idyllic time and when she turned 16 she left school and worked full time in the pub. Her social life revolved around this typically East End working class life. Occasionally Bethnal Green Town hall or York Hall would host an event. A barn dance, bizarrely popular, or a rock and roll night, even more popular. All the "with it" teenagers would attend and more from the adjacent areas of Stepney, Stratford or Bow. Christine and Kathy would be dressed in their full skirt dresses with lots of crinoline and bobby socks and would bop the night away. Christine and Kathy thought they were the height of cool each puffing their way through a pack of Peter Stuyvesant cigarettes. "The scent of the big wide world" was how this brand of cigarettes were marketed and Chrissy, as she referred herself to now, and Kathy were two streetwise, internationally aware hip ladies who not only liked rock and roll but blues, boogie woogie and jump. Each had hair like Elizabeth Taylor, dark, curly and luxuriant. Although without the same smouldering looks each applied make up that accentuated eyelashes and pumped up lips.

Fortunately for Christine, Doris and Clement were easy going about the lads that came calling for their daughter and her love of life and fashion was a matter of pride for a couple for whom academia and formal clothing were an unknown quantity and an unrequired asset.

Kathy's parents, Brian and Maureen or Mo as she was referred to, were regular punters at the pub and were equally acquiescent to the frenetic life their daughter, one of seven children, enjoyed as a teenager.

The seasons came and went. Christine and Kathy enjoyed casual relationships but more so the thrill of the pub, the nights out and for the former, the mornings in.

Oliver Anderson started coming into the pub in 1959. Although he lived locally and had a job as a clerk at Barclays Bank in Holborn, he had few friends who frequented the pub. He came in alone and although initially he drank in the saloon bar he soon gravitated to the public bar as his face became common amongst the bar staff and the clientele who also flitted from room to room dependant on who was around.

Christine found 26 year old Oliver polite, friendly and generous. When his face became more recognised and widely accepted and if he was in a group he would stand his round and always asked her if she wanted, "one for herself." He wasn't an unattractive lad. Not really her type she had told Kathy. His hair wasn't designed to be slicked back or to the side with brylcreem and it was neither blonde nor smoulderingly dark, he looked a bit like Glen Campbell and she preferred her lads to look more like Tony Curtis or James Dean. He wasn't one for fashion but he was, what her Grandparents would have called "steady."

Christine looked at Oliver after she had served him his latest drink. He always looked as though he was on the verge of asking her out and she often wondered what his reaction would be when she turned him down. She had often rehearsed the scenario with Kathy. Oliver asking her if she wanted to go to the flicks or, in an attempt to be glamourous to see a show up West. She would respond depending on whether she wanted to be a bitch or a lady and say "Not in a month of Sundays." or "That's really nice of you to offer Ollie but I'm not interested in dating at the moment, I just want to be free."

Kathy and Christine would collapse in giggles as they played out each scenario, especially when Kathy pretended to burst into tears, fall theatrically to her knees and beg for a date, offering the moon and the stars, to be with the most beautiful girl in the whole of the East End.

Around six months after Oliver began his drinking in the Red Lion, Ken Harris arrived on the scene. Ken was a Rock Hudson lookalike and jaws dropped when he first visited the pub although his looks did not match his attire. He was about 29, he dressed very smartly, always in a collar and tie. If not wearing a suit then a pair of trousers with a jacket dependant on the weather. His shoes were spotless as were his nails which were also short and stubby like his hands. Ken's hair was fashioned with a side parting and was lightly greased finished off his clean cut look, and made even more debonair by a neat moustache. He had a dimple on his chin and a winning smile. He had unusual green eyes that made Christine, and most of the women in the pub, look at him slightly longer than necessary.

What also set Ken apart from the clientele in the pub was his broad Wolverhampton accent. It was rare in the pub to hear any accent apart from broad Cockney in the pub. There were a few Irish as the need for labourers to work on the ever increasing motorway network was evident in the period. Later in the 50s and early 60s West Indian immigrants would join the throng and the pub became quite cosmopolitan. Kens utterings of yeows and yams and calling everyone Babs was as exotic as the linguistics were in the pub would be in 1959.

Ken never discussed what he did for a living but insinuated on more than one occasion that his work was of a transient nature and that when his business in one area was completed he would move to the next. He seemed solvent enough to drink from 8pm till closing time, he was good for a round and for offering a barmaid a drink. For three months he lodged in a boarding house near the underground station and initially spoke highly of the land lord and his wife and the friendliness, cleanliness and homely nature of the two. After three months however, following Ken's landlords running off with one of his lodgers Ken complained to Doris that his current situation had become less than satisfactory. The newly single landlady began to entertain several men per day in her ground floor flat and the comings and goings were a source of embarrassment to him he had said.

Ken was delighted to be offered a room above the pub that hitherto had been used by Uncle Gordon but was now vacant as he had moved with his new wife, Connie, to manage a pub in neighbouring Whitechapel.

Ken went out round the same time each day, about 8.00 am and returned about 6.00pm. He had, apart from the dark grey suit he wore to work, two pairs of black trousers, one blue, four white shirts, one pair of shoes and a four sets of vests and pants. Christine knew the contents of Ken's wardrobe because she often went into his room and had a look around. .

Apart from the clothes that were in the room, in his brown suitcase Ken had what appeared to be his travel companions. A camera, a lock knife, a passport, a cosh, silver lighter, playing cards, a cloths brush, a flute and a large thick photo album.

It was the photo album that Christine found most beguiling it was heavily populated with pictures on women aged between 20 and 35. The photo on the first page was one on which was written "us at a wedding."

The six people in the photograph looked like they had been forced to eat each other's regurgitated breakfast prior to the snap being taken. All were dressed in standard wedding apparel. The flowers, in the lapels of the older men, and posies for the two women and the small girl were an indication of the occasion. Matching grey suits with waistcoats for the males, white dresses with for the women. The girl also had a posy in her hair which would have made her look angelic were it not for the scowl on her face. The much older couple were obviously the Grandfather and Grandmother as the former and Ken's dad were like two peas from the same pod. Wiry and short, about five foot six inches, with thin faces, moustaches and dark furious eyes. The Grandmother looked tense and the mother looked like she was

29

about to burst into tears. Both children looked like they were about to be taken to an orphanage.

If Christine had ever seen a picture of an Amish family this would be the self-same. Matching clothes and expressions that gave no insight to the characters of those displayed. Christine would occasionally sit on Ken's bed wondering what the names of his family were and decided on Grandad Cuthbert, Grandmother Edith, Father Stanley, mother Olive and sister Patricia.

Christine's imagination would run riot. Whose wedding were they going to? Did the women share the same scent, were the men doused in an inexpensive cologne? Did they drink beer or whisky? Did they dance wildly or sit conservatively in a corner nibbling at the buffet? Had there been a family argument before the photograph was taken? What had been the cause? Did either of the men tell either of the women how beautiful they looked, if not in earnest but out of duty?

Christine imagined herself at the wedding, aged about eight going up to Ken and asking him if he wanted to dance. She would have got the whole family up to dance and they would have all had a grand time and turned frowns into smiles.

When Christine looked at the other pictures, again she imagined herself to be a part of the action. There were the odd picture of an older Ken with groups of men or in mixed groups, in his early and mid-twenties. He must have had a fondness for having his picture taken but he rarely smiled. He had a look of a man with a burden, a secret that no-one knew but he. His smouldering, dark good looks made up for his lack of gaiety

In his collection of snaps, with the vast array single portrait pictures of women, Christine surmised that Ken's job might have been loosely connected to being an agent of some sort. Perhaps for a theatre or to find girls to model on cigarette packets or billboards. The pictures were varied some blonde, some brunette, one or two red heads, defined by the freckled skin, and one a curly haired mixed race woman with high cheekbones and full lips and the most beautiful curly hair. The photographs being black and white Christine could not make out with certainty the colour of this woman's hair but it seemed to have a light and dark tone which were quite exotic. Christine decided this woman was from South America, she had heard that the Brazilian and Colombian women were amongst the most beautiful and fashionable in the world and here was confirmation.

Over the course of about 25 pages were around 80 pictures of a woman who in particular fascinated Christine. The woman was incredibly beautiful, a female version of Ken, with milk white skin, eyes as bewitching as a cobra and hair that cascaded around her shoulders like a Hollywood siren. She wore pearl earrings and a dress with a ruched lace neck line that sat low exposing her throat and a matching pearl brooch sat amid her chest, perfect bone structure and flawless skin.

Christine wanted to be this woman, elegant, beautiful and classy. She wondered if the woman also had a Midlands accent or whether she was as noble as she looked, perhaps with a clipped tone that might have read the news on BBC radio. She wondered if this woman was a lover or a relative. Maybe a sister or a girlfriend who looked like his sister. She was certainly attractive enough and had the same smouldering dark looks that Ken also possessed. Christine thought of Sophia Lauren, Shirley McLaine, Audrey Hepburn and Jane Russell and imagined that this woman had modelled herself on one of these.

It was hard to tell from the family picture whether the girl and the woman were the same. Christine decided they were not. Why would Ken have so many pictures of his sister?

A call from her father roused her from her musing and she drifted back into the here and now.

One spring day, two months into Ken's occupancy at the pub, Christine found herself once again, in his room. She smelt his clothes, even his underwear and wondered what sort of lover he would be. She was at that age where men were defined by whether they would want or she would allow, carnal knowledge of her.

Would he be passionate, as she was told Italians or French men would be, would he be typical of men from up North, no nonsense, non- romantic, no frills? Would he be all action like American soldiers? According her friend, Frances Westhall. The American soldiers, black and white, were excellent lovers, generous with compliments and presents, fun-loving but non-committal. Frances,

31

had spent a seven months in Attlebridge, Norfolk during the war and had had flings with at least six of the soldiers stationed at the USAAF base near there. Frances had been evacuated to Norfolk during the war but she was so wanton her Grandparents felt she was safer with her parents under the threat of doodle bugs than beneath a GI or two.

Christine doubted Ken's lovemaking would be as hurried as John Gilmartin, with whom she had lost her virginity. It was over in a matter of seconds. It had taken John less time to put on the rubber than make love. He had fumbled over getting the rubber out of its foil wrapper and struggled to pull it over his member as Christine had watched him, sweating and panting heavily. The act of actual intercourse had been preceded by 50 seconds of him kneading her breasts and making loud groaning noises in the back seat of his Ford Cambridge. Once inside her and two thrusts later and it was over. Hardly spent, they had both lit up cigarettes and sat there, he was smiling thinking he had added another notch to his lamp post she was wondering what the fuss was about and whether Frances had been lying.

Johns only attraction had been that he had access to his Dads car and when he wrote it off a week later Christine had summarily dismissed him. She wasn't the type of girl who would be doing it standing up in an alleyway after a night at the flicks.

Since John, Christine had had sex with four lads with whom she had short relationships. The quality had varied, her enjoyment was determined by the length of time the activity took and the attentiveness of her partner,

Christine sat in Ken's room and lifted the photo album out of the suitcase and started to go through it once more. She hadn't noticed a set of pictures after the glut of the women in striking portrait poses.

Once more in her active and vivid imagination she made up a story for each person in the snap. The picture of the man and the lady in their 50s, Very Victorian looking, very stern, with starched white collars and matching black uniforms that identified them as staff, either the house of a rich man or perhaps a small hotel. This must have been the other set of grandparents, or even the great grandparents, the picture must have been taken 50 years ago. The couple in their 20s thru to their 50s. A more jovial looking man but a woman with the stern look of a harridan who had endured her spouses roaming ways. There were pictures of the man dancing and carousing. Photographs of them under billboards and posters of jive and jazz bands. Pictures of her, more austere, knitting and holding up loaves of bread in the kitchen. Pictures together, he smiled and flashed teeth as large as a lion and as ferocious looking, that could probably eat a chicken whole, the woman, her mouth pursed, as if she could only imbibe through a straw. As ill-suited a couple as one could find. Christine wondered what brought these two together and what made them remain so.

Husband and wife and Ken's parents. Ken and his sister. One picture with a lady who looked like their mother, an Aunt perhaps, smiling and goofing around, gurning for the camera. There was a picture with Ken's father, he had his arm around his sister in law. He sneered at the camera in a way that made Christine shudder. The children though looked happy enough in another picture, covered in mud with chocolate circling their lips like wagons around campfires.

As Christine was always drawn to the 80 pictures of the beautiful woman. She dove into the woman's imagined life of glamour and privilege she created an illusion of herself looking confidently and seductively as Ken took the picture, inspiring her to make love to the camera with her eyes, to pout and lick her lips and flare her nostrils like a race horse that had just won the Grand National was now soaking up the adulation.

As Christine gazed intently at the album Ken walked into his room.

His face was flustered and he was panting slightly. There was a bruise below his left eye and as his caught hers there was a look of bewilderment and what Christine took to be his guilt not hers. His lips quivered and she could see that his forehead was glistening with sweat. Time stood still he stared at her quizzically and she at him. From his quivering jaw to his forehead where his hair lay limp and damp like a cleaners mop, she stared. An age passed before the spell was broken because his eyes moved from her to the album in her hands. She had subconsciously moved the book from a position where she could look at it comfortably to press it against her chest like a shield. As if by covering herself with it she would become invisible. She had meanwhile continued to stare at him like a recently born deer, caught in the headlights of a large truck.

When he saw the album she feared his reaction would be rage. The book was a private thing, the people in it were his people, his past, his secrets, his family and she had entered his most personal space, and Christine believed knew who all these people were but she had not been invited to the party. She had gate crashed and was drinking wine from his own glass.

Ken outwardly did not react with fury however, instead his face broke into a smile. Not a comforting smile that said, "You nosey mare I hope you haven't been laughing at pictures of me when I were a lad." No. It was a smile that said, "You have taken away my privacy. I can take something from you now Christine."

Without uttering either sentence Ken casually walked across the room, his eyes held hers and his jackal-like smile never left his lips. He knelt down before her and gently took the album from her grasp. Christine felt mesmerised, like a mouse within range of a snake she knelt, transfixed. Without the book she felt naked. Not just visible but vulnerable, as if she was as naked as a child sitting in a nuclear reactor without a protective suit.

Supporting himself on his left hand and bottom Ken put his right hand on her left shoulder and, very gently, eased her back on to the bedroom floor. Here legs were still bent underneath her but instinctively she unfolded them and they were now stretched out underneath his shoulder as he leaned across her and now supported himself on his right hand. Christine made a deliberate gesture of putting her left foot above her right, as if this action would send a message that there would be no entry to her most intimate of private parts unless she gave consent by uncrossing her legs.

Christine looked at him now, less mesmerised but more in hope that he would stop before things went too far.

Her mind raced. Did she want this to happen or did she not? Could she become the girl in the photograph, Ken's favourite.

The now faint smile became a frown when Ken slipped his hand on one of her knees and he felt her tense slightly. "You shouldn't be here." He said, his voice was flat and very controlled and Christine felt confused. Her hearing became more acute and she listened out for voices downstairs but instead she heard the ticking of the grandfather clock that stood on the landing. She knew the place would be empty for another two hours at least as there was weekly farmers market in town and Doris and Clement had gone to pick up meat for Sundays raffle.

Ken lifted her bottom off the beige carpet of her bedroom floor, and gave her a look that told her not to move, he then roll her skirt up to her waist and pushed her legs apart wedging one of his own between.

"Please don't." She said as he fumbled with his belt and she heard the familiar sound of a zip. That same sound she had heard before John Gilmartin had reached inside his trousers, that and the heavy, almost laboured breathing.

Either Ken hadn't heard what she had said but more likely he had chosen not to listen. He had moved into a mode that Christine could only describe as robotic. Like a determined zombie in the movie Zombie Is Shot she had seen with Kathy. She had covered her eyes for most of that film and she wanted to now. Ken's eyes, that she had once thought were hypnotic in beauty seemed to translucent covered in a clear film like an alligator about to devour the solitary wildebeest that had decided to take that one extra sip of water whilst the remainder of the herd had departed.

It took an instance and he was inside her, riding her energetically. He grunted every time he thrust into her, one palm was on one of her shoulders the other on her head holding a handful of hair pulling it painfully and giving her something else to think about and not the more foul deed that was being carried out.

Christine knew about rape but she lay there wondering whether she was being raped. There was no pain. All she could smell was the peppermint on his breath as he breathed heavily atop her. Although John Gilmartin had not taken long she knew he had been inside her. For all the time Ken was taking she did not feel the same sensation and she counted this as a relief.

This wasn't how she thought her relationship with Ken would turn into. She closed her eyes and thought of the photos he had. As she turned the pages, instead of the beautiful woman there were pictures of her. She wondered whether he would stand up, reach for his camera and

35

ask her to pose for a photo or whether he would ask her to be his girl. Thoughts whirled around her head as Ken thrust away and then she gasped as she felt the sensation of liquid filling her like a jet like a small pump watering a bud with a large reservoir behind it to replenish the load.

He rolled off her and lay on his back. Spent. Christine lay there too, her eyes fixed on a spider that was crawling across the ceiling. Busy in its own way and oblivious to what had gone on below it.

This wasn't how she had envisaged them lying together but she liked sex, she liked the thought of sex with an experienced man and even though Ken was looking at her but he wasn't looking at her she had a feeling of accomplishment. He could have had sex with any number of the woman in the pub but he was having sex with her. She was confused.

Although he was taking what he wanted and he was doing it out of revenge perhaps because she had invaded his privacy he was a successful man. If he had offered her £100 to sleep with him she would have told him he could have her for free so now he was having her. For a an uneducated girl from the East End who was never going to amount to much except getting married to a local lad and perhaps taking over her parents pub life was never going to be one of coronets and kings.

Perhaps Ken would take her out a few times, perhaps he might be the one she would marry and she would be the only woman in his photo album. Perhaps Ken had liked her all along and thought a young but pretty girl was out of his league but now he had taken her this could be the start of something good.

Christine came out of her thoughts with a start as Ken started to groan as his climax took hold. He made a sound from deep in his throat like a bear who had found honeycomb and was calling his mate. His thrusts became less rhythmic and more punctuated by pauses as his seed split into her and temporarily caused him paralysis. His thighs, seemed to lock and she sensed them now, strong like two thick trunks of wood making sure the entrance to her sex remained open.

He gasped and Christine felt his hot breath against her face. She looked into his eyes and they seem to re-focus because now he was looking at her. He looked at her intently and she felt her eyes water because he seemed so mesmerised and so enchanted by something that he saw in her face that she knew that it wasn't just lust that made him do what he had done so forcibly. He licked his lips and swallowed and Christine knew he was going to say something profound. She took a deep breath and felt her nostrils flare. She covered her bottom lip with her top teeth because she had read somewhere that it made a woman look coy and quizzical.

Ken spoke.

"That will teach you to pry in other people's business." He said.

These were the last words Ken Harris ever spoke to Christine again.

He stood up and put his member back into his pants and fastened his trousers and belt without looking at her. Christine had pulled up her knickers as she lay on the floor and pushed her skirt down while standing up. She was going to say something to him before she walked out of the room but he had moved to the window and was looking out of it, probably looking at nothing but definitely not looking at her.

At 11.00 the next morning after an evening working in the pub on its quietest night of the week she ambled into the parlour to hear her Mum say,

"I'm really surprised Clement. His room was so neat you would have thought he had never been there. There was £10 on the dresser and a note to say he had been called away on urgent business and wouldn't be able to stay and that I should give Christine a drink."

Christine walked into the room and both her parents looked up, quizzically. Her Mum held up the £10 as if it were a declaration of world peace.

"So what's Ken doing, pissing off in the middle of the night and leaving a tenner for you to have a drink?" Clement asked.

"I told him I was going to run the pub one day and I would stand the first round of drinks on my opening night. He said I would need a few quid the amount of freeloaders would that would stampede you. I guess you owe me at least a fiver Dad" Christine said. Her business head was quick to react and this wasn't a lie, Ken had said that to her once but he had also added that he'd have wanted to be her head barman and that she could give him a Xmas bonus in kind. He had been joking at the time, now she wasn't so sure.

"When you take over the pub we'll give you a fiver Chrissy but I think your Mum and I will keep this beauty on account we have lost our lodger."

Mindful that she paid no rent and that Ken hadn't mentioned her snooping Christine gave a dismissive wave of her hand as if to say she wasn't too bothered about the money and turned on her heels and went back to her room while Clement and Doris began bickering about what the £10 should be spent on. Doris favoured a new sofa and Clement, a day at Ascot.

Pub life chugged merrily along the steam from the factory workers releasing periodically as alcohol stoked their bellies and money greased the palms of barmaid and barmen alike.

Christine wasn't too alarmed when she missed her next monthly. She had been regular since she was 14 but she knew that Kathy had missed hers the first time she had unprotected sex but as her subsequent period was on time the two girls concluded that you couldn't get pregnant the first time.

Christine began to have feelings of nostalgia and would often stare at the door to the bar hoping that Ken would walk in with a posh camera, take a few snaps of her and then ask her to go out. Instead of feeling like the victim of a rape she felt like she was a lover scorned. If only Ken would come back and ask her if she wanted to go to the Odeon or to Ilford Palais.

Some mornings she felt quite nauseous but she decided that her taste buds were beginning to mature and the smell of the new Alsatian dog Barney had bought with its dog breath and dog smell fur that were toxic to her.

After missing her second period Christine did become more anxious. She didn't think she had a baby inside her. What did it feel like? She didn't think she was any fatter, all her clothes still fitted the same and she was still able to go out and have a good drink every once in a while.

Missing a third period alarm bells started to ring but she knew she couldn't go to the family doctor Mr Phillips for a test. He was, not only a regular in the pub but a family friend. It was he who had delivered her when her Mums waters broke in while she was walking down the Bethnal Green Road with a bag of shopping.

She didn't tell Kathy immediately because, as good a friend as she was, she was a blabber mouth who couldn't keep a secret. Christine had heard about 10 Rillington Place and what had happened there. Women who had visited John Christie for an abortion ended up dead and sealed behind walls. She wasn't up to stick a knitting needle inside herself in the hope she would pierce the foetus. Christine had a moral code that told her that self-abortion was an activity carried out only be the lowest dregs of female society. All though she had a narrow view of religion and Christianity all she could do was pray for a miscarriage.

Each morning Christine got up, she knelt by the side of the bed and prayed to God that the baby inside her would not survive the full term. She pledged that if the baby died when she did have a relationship she would commit her first born to the Lord to be a priest or a nun. She promised that she would do charitable work twice a week and go to church herself every Sunday. She swore that she would not allow anyone to use profanities in her house or to blaspheme or drink to excess. She would honour the father, son and the Holy Ghost.

Christine did manage to hide her pregnancy. She eventually shared the information with Kathy who swore to take the news to her grave. Her bump was unnaturally small and she was able to conceal it under some less than flattering clothes. She drank and smoked as much as she could hoping this would lead to a miscarriage. Christine woke up and prayed as fervently as ever but still the baby lived on inside her, a child pickled with whisky and cured with tobacco.

Camilla Adams hurried to Bethnal Green station cursing her husband Percy for not waking her up before he had gone off to his job as a

39

milkman. She marched along her normal route, almost trotting such was the urgency. She knew she had better be at Leicester Square and the construction companies typing pool in time because Mrs Fraser, department head, had warned her already in the last two weeks about her tardiness. As she took the short cut through the alleyway she saw, a few yards off, a bundle of rags on the pavement, propped up against a lamp post. It wasn't unusual for the odd blanket or even item of clothing to be seen along this path. Kids or mothers dropping or purposely dumping unwanted bed linen.

As Camilla became adjacent to the bundle it moved and the unmistakable sound of a baby's cry could be heard. It was quite a damp April morning and the sky looked ominous, rain was imminent. Camilla faced the choice of walking on briskly, leaving the baby to whoever might follow her down this route or stopping. She would be late and her excuse was likely to be poo pooed. It was a chance she would have to take.

Oliver Anderson

Oliver Anderson noticed that Christine hadn't been her bubbly self for a few weeks. Ken Harris, who always seemed to be sniffing around the young barmaid had disappeared nearly a year previously and in that time Christine's carefree and blithe spirit was somewhat faded.

Whenever Oliver said to Christine, "have one yourself," she had refused. For months Christine was less flirtatious or engaging with the lads than usual.

On this particular day however she seemed less frosty she had actually looked at him when he handed over his money. He hoped she was looking at him. Her eyes did seem to flit between him and the new Voigtlander Vito C 35 mm camera he had hanging from his neck.

He had bought the camera that morning as he had had the day off and went shopping in Tottenham Court Road. He took the camera into the pub to try it out and Christine seemed to over the moon when he took a picture of her. "When I get it developed I can give you a copy." he had said. Christine was genuinely interested as he told her about the features the camera had and he was happy to let her take a couple of shots with it.

A few weeks after buying the camera and with it being a topic of conversation for the pair Oliver finally plucked up the courage to ask Christine for a date, or rather whether she wanted to come with him for a walk to Ilford and Valentines Park he would take some snaps with his new camera.

When Christine could manage an afternoon off it became a routine that Oliver and her would go for walks taking photographs of buildings or people or animals. The relationship went from friends, they became fond of each other. Oliver started to come out of himself and began to dress like the film stars the two would see when they went for their trips to the Odeon at Ilford. So it was that Oliver and Christine became an item.

Oliver prided himself on reading the Times, and not the less informative Mirror, he liked to keep himself abreast of current affairs including politics. Oliver now had a partner to take to functions and charitable events arranged by the middle class colleagues he worked with and they no longer saw him as the offspring of working class inferiors who was socially out of his depth. Much of this was due to Christine's chameleon like change from a semi boorish, hard drinking working class girl to a more refined and sophisticated lady who looked down on the patrons of the pub she still worked in and no longer found delight in nights out with Kathy who was dropped with as little compunction as a vulture discarding rotten meat.

Christine loved to be amongst Oliver's colleagues. Whenever there was an event she would say little about her own life pulling pints but would enjoy to hear about the lives of her new social group who would later come to invite Oliver and her to their house to play card games drinking sherry. If they had a night out it would be in a bar in Soho, full of well-spoken city types or the idle rich. None of these colleagues were from the East End, they commuted from Surrey, West or North London. The female clerks, of whom there were many, as it was a very large bank tended to have boyfriends who were blue collar workers. It was a far cry from her world.

The married women amongst the set spoke of their children who attended grammar schools and were earmarked for University and careers as doctors, lawyers or school teachers. This was all a distinct difference to the parents 's who frequented the pub and were lucky if

41

their children attended school regularly but were happy to see them find a labouring job at the docks or local factory.

When she reached the grand age of 20 she felt proud of what she had done in the three years since she had first started to date Oliver. She saw and described herself as manageress of the pub. She had set her stall out when she was 19. During the exceptionally busy weekends she paid particular attention to the money changing hands and began to notice that some of the bar staff were not charging friends for rounds or worse still she had spotted Amy Riley twice give her brother George, change for one pound when he twice paid with a ten shilling note. The behaviour of Amy was quite blatant and for the other staff generally, seemed to be accepted as a perk of the job or thinking, it was "good for business."

On the night of the second instance as the staff were clearing up she asked her Mum and Dad to come into the bar and in front of the gobsmacked barmaids told Amy what she had seen and told her that the family couldn't afford to lose money on ne'er do wells like George Riley.

Amy was sacked on the spot, before she had a chance to offer an explanation. Thereafter the staff knew that instead of the now lackadaisical Doris and Ken, who were surprised but pleased, they were now dealing with Christine, courting Oliver Anderson head clerk at Barclays Bank, Holborn branch. Christine's ambitions were to build the reputation of the Red Lion and expand into ownership of two or three other pubs. She would be the overall area supremo, installing competent managers whose remit would be to maximise profits and create a chain that would have a reputation for not only oiling the throats of thirsty worked but provide good wholesome food, mainly at weekends, to those who liked the homely ambiance of a public house without the formal constraints of a restaurant of which there were relatively few.

Oliver was ambitious and worked hard to be rewarded to the position of senior clerk and it was, on the day he received his new improved salary that he laid out his plan for the future. Christine and he would be married and they would get a mortgage to buy a house in Seven Kings, Essex, it wasn't quite as upmarket at Epsom, Chelsea or Highgate but it would be a start and they preferred to move east, than to any other point of Greater London. They would have a couple of children who would attend the local grammar school and then University and follow the paths of the middle class friends they had joined.

In June 1963 when she was 20 and Oliver 30 they were wed at St Peters Church, Bethnal Green. The plan was for the couple to live in the pub for a while until they were settled and then move to Essex. Christine would continue in the pub with the view to take over when Clement and Doris retired.

In January 1964 Christine found she was pregnant, before she had to the doctor for confirmation she knew it was an experience she had had three years ago.

The couple got their mortgage and with financial help from Clement and Doris and Oliver's parents, David and Vanessa, for £3,000 were able to buy a house in Seven Kings. Christine decided that working in a pub was no longer appropriate for the pregnant wife of a bank official and that she would from now stay home and look after the house.

When Christine went to the maternity unit of King Georges Hospital in Newbury Park she would meet with women who were from the area and they would tell her what to expect given she told everyone it was her first time. The women she met here were a far cry from the women who frequented the pub in Bethnal Green and Christine quickly forgot where she had come from and her East End accent was replaced with a refined lilt more suited to Edenbridge or Effingham.

In September 1964 Christine, with the baby imminent sat in the house contemplating the life she had now to the one she had left. She looked round at her living room with deep satisfaction. Her deep red Axminster carpet with Persian styled design. She sat on her three seater matching red velvet Chesterfield style sofa and looked at the Phillips television that stood proudly beside the Queen Anne sideboard. The oak effect finish of the television gave the room a modern edge and fitted nicely with the period features. The dining table and chairs were also Queen Anne. There were red velvet curtains to match the sofa and the embossed wallpaper a regal gold and red stripe

That she had furnished her house on mainly taking advantage of hire purchase was of no consequence... They had scrimped and saved to bring their ideas together. So far they had decorated their bedroom with a

"We shall call our child Sebastian Phillip if it's a boy, Penelope Rose if a girl." Christine had stated when she was four months pregnant. Oliver wasn't keen on Sebastian but held his counsel knowing that in pregnancy Christine was volatile and when her temper came out her voice reverted back to its shrill and coarse East End roots.

Often, during her pregnancy Christine wondered what had become of the son she had to give away. Whether he was having a happy life. Whether he had older or younger siblings and an extended family of cousins, uncles and aunts, and whether he knew that his real mother was almost a child herself who had abandoned him.

The birth of the baby, two weeks late, 11th September was navigated without complications, Catherine had after all given birth to a baby on her own and went into the hospital with a self-assurance that both surprised Oliver, her mother and maternity staff alike. As she lay in the bed cradling her new born Christine once more contemplated the life that her abandoned son. She looked at her new baby and the face of her first baby came into vision. They had similar round faces and full lips. Sebastian had a shock of straight black hair and his eyebrows were not as dark but prominent. His eyes danced as if he were busy trying to focus trying to bond with the mother who cooed and purred at him.

The first baby had a red face and even redder hair. Neither baby had cried too much but where Sebastian looked content Catherine had been puzzled by the countenance of the first child. He had had a shape to those full lips that made it look like he was scowling and eyes that were defiant. She had felt haunted by them as she placed him in the woollen blanket and even more so when she place him gently by the lamp post in the alley, gave him one last look and walked away. AS she had scurried up the path she felt his young eyes bore into her back like a red hot poker dabbing at the embers of a cooling, soon to be dead, fire. Ashes caught by the wind, floating skyward to dissipate in the harsh world above the chimney breasts, lost forever in the cruel and harsh world.

Whilst Christine was in hospital Oliver took the opportunity to register the birth of his child at Redbridge Town Hall. As he had marched purposely from the house he convinced himself over and over again that his child could not have a first name of Sebastian. Whilst he had the same aspirations of his wife that the child would get a good education and a rewarding career he remained sceptical whether such a name would seem pretentious and would mark his son out for ridicule amongst friends. Seven Kings and Chelsea were a world apart and Christine appeared oblivious of this...

Oliver deliberately completed on the forms provided, child's first, name. Oliver carefully wrote Phillip. Child's surname, Oliver wrote, continuing his swirling handwriting, Anderson. For other names, Oliver had an inkling to choose Steven but decided that he would not enrage Christine even more than so wrote, Sebastian. On receipt of the birth certificate he wondered how he would disseminate this information to his wife but decided that it could wait for a time when she was less likely to ignite.

After several weeks of Oliver calling his child Phillip, Christine snapped

"Why don't you ever call him Sebastian? I know you hate the name." she said.

"Why do you call him Sebastian, his name is Phillip" Oliver countered.
.
Colour draining from her cheeks Christine said, "His name is Sebastian Phillip, as we agreed."

"No, we agreed to no such thing and his name is Phillip Sebastian, or at least that what it says on his birth certificate."

"You had one job to do Oliver, register the birth of our child with the name we had both agreed on and you maliciously and wilfully went against my wishes. You're not the man I married and your son will not go to a good grammar, then Oxford or Cambridge as we have planned but to that Beal School which is full of working classes. He'll get no qualifications and then on to shovel cement on a building site."

"I don't think the name of our child will determine his eventual path but I thought we had agreed on Phillip Sebastian." Oliver lied. "Change his name by deed poll if you must." He added and with Christine seething he went into his garden and pottered about in his shed away from his once sweet and demure wife turned into an insufferable snob during the course of a pregnancy.

Twenty two months after Phillip was born Penelope Rose arrived

Although Christine had had ambitions for herself she had no such illusions for her daughter. She did not want to saddle her child with a name that proved to be too big a shoe to fill. Prunella, Constance, Verity, Tabitha. All lovely names but they belonged to girls who belonged and the likelihood was that her daughter would marry a solid hard working man, preferably blue collar and would settle down and by her mid-twenties have at least one child and a nice house. The child became known as Penny. Whilst Christine liked the ring of Penelope. Marjorie Davenish, the pregnant bank manager's wife, sent a new baby card which read,

Dear Christine and Ollie, Congratulations on the birth of Penelope Rose We have decided we are going to call our child Penny if its girl. So wonderful choice of name!

Christine decided then that Penny had a nice ring to it and decided it was suitable for the middle class Davenish's then so it would be for the equally middle class Andersons.

In an ideal world Penny would have had had the opportunity to meet a nice man and to settle down and perhaps work as a typist or secretary each putting money together to bring about a deposit for a house where they would raise their family. It would have been nice if Penny had called a son Sebastian, Farquar or Lindley and had aspirations for him to go to Oxford or Cambridge. Ideal things sometimes do not happen.

When Penny was five she was raped and murdered.

It came about because Christine and Oliver had been invited to a black tie event at the Grand Connaught Rooms, Holborn. Usually Oliver's parents or sister babysat but his Vanessa Anderson was ill and his sister, Anne had recently given birth to her own child who was born with health problems that necessitated impromptu visits to the hospital due to it fitting...

Although she was not estranged from her parents Christine spent less time with Clement and Doris and in consequence the pub was not a place she would often take the babies. Most of her visits were timed when the pub was closed, which wasn't often or on the rare occasion when her mother wasn't working.

Doris had insisted that she would take the night off and care for Phillip and Penny. She didn't need to go into the pub because the full quota of staff were in and it being January things weren't too busy after the Christmas festivities.

Despite Christine's reservations that her mother would be able to sit upstairs all night caring for her grandchildren she was glad to be going out. The inability to accept invitations for an evening with the bank crowd was beginning to become a drain and the negative side of being twenty three and having two small children was something Christine felt, especially when babysitters had other commitments.

Christine was pleased that her figure restored to its pre baby size 10 glory. She was able to go Oxford Street and buy herself an elegant black dress, fur wrap and sling back heels.

Oliver's and Christine's relationship, after a hiccup after the birth of Phillip had taken a turn for the better, and mainly because the birth of Penny. Oliver adored his daughter and was even more pleased that Phillip had taken a shine to his sister and was very protective of her even though he was only six.

If loving someone to the moon and back times five had been a phrase used back in the 1970s Oliver and Christine would certainly have used it with gusto.

Doris heard the sound of loud laughter coming from the rooms of the pub below and cursed her ill fortune. Her cousin Peggy was celebrating her 50th birthday and had bought in a large crowd of friends and some of the family. Most of these were half cut before they had crossed the threshold of the pub having been out in the West End beforehand. One of their number was a dab hand on the joanna and accompanied the raucous singing and even more riotous drinking. The vibrant atmosphere in both bars could be felt before the doors to either was opened.

A crowd had come in from the Kings Head due to a leaked pipe in the toilets which had left the pub floor swimming in waste. This misfortune for the rival pub, had swelled the numbers in the Red Lion, so much so that some of the closer members of the Venables clan had popped up to see Doris and were using the family convenience and facilities for freshening up or just having a breather.

Phillip was asleep but Penny was wide wake at 9pm but Doris popped downstairs for 5 minutes left her in the capable hands of slightly drunk Connie who was having a quiet 10 away from her completely inebriated husband Gordon Venables, and enjoying her woodbine and large whisky, as she cooed over the .

Connie felt no compunction, being when she too left, the five year old child playing with a doll 30 minutes after Doris had gone downstairs.

When the Doris returned at 10.30 to the upstairs living room, it was later said the scream she emitted could be heard by those imbibing the smell of shit with their alcohol, the diehards still left in the Kings Head, which was a good half a mile away.

Penny lay on her back, legs askew beside the velvet chaise lounge. The child's bloody knickers were stuffed in her mouth. Clement was the next in the room and when he had pulled up Penny's eyelids her cornea was spotted with red veiny lines that zig zagged like bloody rivers, her eyeballs were like two planets on which no life existed.. The whole of Penny's small neck was covered in a bruise that could only have been caused by someone squeezing at her throat and throttling the life, the little life that she had had, out of her.

In an instant the pub became eerily quiet. Hushed whispers interspersed with the sound of men and women weeping. Doris was sobbing hysterically, she had collapsed on the floor by the baby and was now lying on her be. Most of the people in the pub had seen death before. The war had made them accustomed to its visit, knocking on the door, literally when an Army officer imparted news of the loss of loved one somewhere in France or Turkey or Asia or closer to home, here in the East End, a V2 bomb dropped by the Luftwaffe during the Blitz.

48

While the police took statements, who had seen what, who had ventured upstairs, how long exactly Doris and Connie were absent. Everyone knew that the hardest part of what was to follow was to explain to Oliver and Christine that their daughter was gone.

Doris and Clement rarely saw Oliver and Christine again after that night.

Christine had looked her mother full in the face at the funeral, when all the facts were known and spat, "We're done." That was all that was said, the fury Christine felt, seared through her body like the pain from an inadvertently touched hot iron.

Doris and Clement never saw their daughter, son-in-law or Grandson again.

Oliver was emotionally spent, his grief sent his body into a catatonic shock. Whatever energy remained he channelled into supporting his son, who was told his sister had gone to live with the angels. While Oliver's relationship with his son became strong Christine's relationship with everyone became fraught. Where she had aspirations for her son these disappeared and she became withdrawn and melancholy she sought arguments where there was a case for tranquillity and conflict where there was a case for harmony.

Christine did eventually snap out of her torpor when Phillip was in full time education. She took a computing course and got a job in IT with British Telecomm and then moved to the Civil Service until retirement.

Phillip Anderson

Phillip attended Seven Kings High School, which became the new name of Beal Grammar in 1974. He did not go to Oxford or Cambridge, or any University for that matter. He left school at 16 and went straight to work. He never married but not for the lack of romantic trysts, starting when he was 15.

Helen Tyler's mother, Cassandra, became chairperson of the PTA shortly after both her child and Oliver's enrolled at the school. On the Friday, the day before the first school fete Oliver got a call asking for help from Cassandra because she needed someone to help set up the stalls. Oliver obliged, he had after all offered his services as a standby. Oliver helped in the evening, him, the janitor and the deputy head, clearing classrooms and setting up displays and come back at 0700 in the morning to apply the finishing touches. At 10.00, when the opening klaxon was sounded by the headmaster, the event was flooded with parents wearing PTA Member badges, much to Oliver's dismay, strutting around as if they had each personally put the event together.

Every year since then though, Oliver was on hand to help on Friday and Saturday morning. Cassandra and he would organise and prepare together and it wasn't uncommon for the two to leave on the Friday, one car following the other, to Wanstead Flats in Forest Gate East London, where lines of other vehicles would be parked like fairground ride, some of them bouncing rhythmically to the motion of illicit love making.

Phillip knew Helen through seeing her mother flirting with Oliver at the school fete whilst both teenagers stood by in embarrassment. Ever since he was 12 Phillip had a crush on Helen but never had the courage to ask her out. It was something of a surprise when on November 3rd eight months before her 16th birthday she accepted his invitation for a meal at the Golden Egg restaurant. A chance meeting in the hallway as each sped to separate classes Phillip asked the question and she had said yes, they were both on cloud nine having just been given positive mock CSE exam results.

After accepting his offer of a date Phillip and Helen went to the pictures once a week on a Saturday afternoon and to the Golden Egg once a week on a Thursday after school. Both were aware of the consequences to go beyond French kissing. Phillip's hand once ventured North to grope manically at Helen's left breast but she violently elbowed him in the ribs which put him in no doubt she was not that type of girl, yet. In school, as the two were never in the same form group or dong the same options they saw little of each other and during breaks boys and girls tended to do separate things. Outside school the rest of the time Helen would be at home or hang around with her in crowd of friends.

The courtship was a boon for Oliver because he now had a reason to see Cassandra at her home on the occasions that he picked Oliver up. Cassandra's husband was a captain, serving in the Navy so was often away. Whilst Helen and Phillip were upstairs Cassandra and Phillip would be in the kitchen, blinds shut, tearing at each other's clothes like sex starved teenagers. With an absent husband and a forlorn wife respectively Cassandra and Oliver were 16 again.

Phillip's best friend was Ricky Finnegan. Ricky was bucktoothed, geeky looking, bookish, snobbish and effete. They were drawn together initially because of their thick eyebrows. Ricky's mother was extremely highly strung, she would screech at her son if his tie wasn't straight or if he walked too slowly to the car or if she saw a spider. Phillip having grown up with a mother whose behaviour had been erratic since the loss of her daughter was sympathetic to the foibles of Ricky and his mother. Whilst Phillip was generally well-liked he didn't have a large crowd of friends, possibly due to the fact that Ricky hung around him like a limpet to a ship's hull.

Helen's 16th birthday was in June. Cassandra and her daughter started planning the party in January. The event warranted a mention in the PTA Newsletter as Cassandra had, in five years, quadrupled the profit from the PTA with a mix of schmoozing local sponsors and parents alike. With a detached house in Hainault with a football sized garden even the teachers were vying for an invite. The party was the most talked about event in 5th form, more so than the impending CSEs.

In the weeks before the birthday party approach Phillip started to notice that Perry Simons, captain of the football, cricket and rugby team was spending a lot of time with Helen and her group of friends. Helen's already cloud high stock had risen stratospherically and she was attracting both male and female attention like gastropods to lettuce.

Phillip found the situation quite alarming and he was finding it difficult to concentrate during lessons but anxious not to create a scene when out of them. Perry and often his sidekick Jason Penn were constantly goofing around with Helen and the girls. The members of the Five Blind Boys from Alabama could tell there was chemistry between the school's sports leader and the good looking daughter of the chairperson of the PTA. Helen giggled loudest at Perry's jokes and tossed her mane of blonde locks to and fro so vigorously she risked scratching the pupils of his eyes.

On Saturday 6th June the day of the party Phillip and Helen didn't see each other, till the evening, for the first time since they had started going out. One of the presents Helen got from her parents was a hairdo at Vidal Sassoon in Regent Street and then to pick up her pre-ordered dress from Harrods in Knightsbridge.

Phillip spent his day doing chores as usual, sweeping the stairs, dusting and polishing. Saturday morning was when Phillip and Oliver did chores while Christine did the weekly shop. Without his normal Saturday afternoon with Helen he rang Ricky to ask if he wanted to accompany him to Granditers in the High Street to get a pair of trousers, shirt and shoes for the party. Ricky was as eccentric as ever and while Phillip settled on navy high waistband trousers, a pale blue wing collar shirt and shiny black solatio crossover shoes his erstwhile friend picked out lime green drain pipes, a canary yellow silk shirt and patent black winkle pickers, an outfit set off with a blood red cravat for his throat.

Together that evening Phillip and Ricky went to the party, the former walked solidly hands in pockets, one of which contained Helen's present, a gold plated bracelet from Ratners, the latter flounced along with a card that contained a £5 gift voucher for HMV record store. Phillip had posted Helen a card the day before and it too contained a £5 gift voucher for HMV but he thought he would deliver the main present personally.

Helen's father opened the door and, surprisingly to Phillip gave him a quizzical look but broke into a smile when Phillip greeted him warmly with one hand for shaking and the other brandishing the fondly wrapped present.

The party was in full swing, it transpired there had been a bit of a pre party with family and Helen's close friends one of whom appeared to be Perry Simon with whom she was in deep conversation in the kitchen. Perry looked up and appeared furtive when he glanced at Phillip and Helen looked at him balefully then said flatly "I got your card and your voucher Phillip, look what Perry bought me." She held out her hand to display a solid 9 carat gold bracelet that sparked with what looked to be real diamonds.

52

"I bought you fine trinket too." Phillip replied, as jovially as he could, holding out the box in which lay a much less spectacular piece of jewellery.

"Oh," said Helen, in an offhand way. "I thought the vouchers were my present."

"Didn't you read the card? The lion said to the lioness, I hope you can wait for the mane event. The mane event is this present. Do you get it?" Phillip was floundering.

Helen looked at him as though he had just poured a bucket of his urine over her birthday cake.

"Can you put it on the lounge please Phillip and help yourself to a drink. So what were you saying Perry?" Helen said, and turned away from both Phillip and Ricki, who was holding out his card forlornly...

Thus was Phillip dismissed, Helen spent the evening surrounded by her acolytes no doubt anxious to be with her when she spent her newly acquired wealth. £405 in cash and around £200 in vouchers ranging from Top Shop, Virgin Record Stores, Our Price and Woolworths. Together with an array of new outfits and a party with a DJ, Helen had become the alpha female in Bale School.

When Phillip went to the upstairs lavatory about three hours into what for him was the worst party ever he saw the door to Helen's bedroom door was shut but giggling coming from it. He poked his head through the crack and saw Helen and Perry lying on the bed, he was astride her and had one hand down her bra cupping her breast. Phillip wasn't sure whether they were actually having sex but Helen's dress was hitched up round her waist, her legs were wide open and Perry's hips were thrusting up and down the top of his trousers were below his bottom which was covered by red underpants.

Phillip took one step into the room, the floorboard cracked and both Helen and Perry looked up at him. There was a momentary silence and then both burst out laughing, it was obvious they were both drunk as the laughing was maniacal and their eyes unfocussed. Phillip backed up only to find Ricky was standing behind him looking at the scene over his shoulder.

"Shall we go? Ricky said.

"Yes I think we'd better." Phillip replied, and they did.

In May 2017 Phillip decided that Facebook was becoming even more of an insult to his intelligence. If not the service then the people who used it. For all his faults Phillip prided himself on being open to different cultures considering it a sign of his superior intelligence. He sat in his room looking at the latest Facebook posts it was awash with discussion regarding Brexit. Suddenly all his associates had graduated from Oxford or Cambridge with a degree in Politics. For most of the Brexit voters their views were mainly right wing.

Stephen Grimley wrote,

"Getting so pissed off with these people saying stay in the EU not one of them has mentioned immigration and saying stay in vote for more jobs what a load of bollocks send them foreign cunts back and we would have jobs simple

Sorry rant over"

Phillip despaired at the lack of punctuation but felt equally as despondent at both the content of the post and immediate responses.

Andrea Holdsworth wrote,

We all need to vote out n get Britain to be independent. We're being overrun with immigrants n its getting worse….thing is we're getting thieves. Rapist. U name it. Out out I say x

Chrissie Westlake wrote,

"Its all our laws as well ther are plenty of Australians who would like to get in but cant"

Andrea Holdsworth replied,

"Kick all the immigrants out…send them back I say…sorry if it sounds bad but its getting bad for bout future kids….x"

Stephen Grimley said,

"Totally Andrea clear them out and maybe I wont have to wait for a doctors appointment until 3 months"

Stephen had then shared a post,

"I am shocked and disgusted at what I found out/saw! I really can't believe it. Immigrants get £26 a day for food in Tesco vouchers from our government. Which means each person gets £182 a week, therefore each family of four gets £728 a week or £2912 a month just for food that's without their free housing and other benefits for clothes, shoes etc etc. So I am in Tescos and surprise surprise the immigrants are spending their money on crates of beer and bottles of spirits!!!!!! They are being treated better than our old people that have paid into the system and have every right tho the money the government are giving away when they are struggling on their measly pension and freezing and starving! So pissed off with this! Rant over...copied from a friend"

Phillip sat, with his head in his hands. Stephen Grimley was a guy he knew, who had grown up amongst black and Asian kids and never showed a hint of racists. In fact one of his best friends was a black guy Orville Smith Phillip had often seen them together as teens, in their baggy jeans, tee shirts, white socks and loafers. Stephen with a massive wedge haircut and Orville with a tight curly perm. Off to some soul weekend or festival.

Phillip scrolled down and his mood was brightened by the following post by Sophie Aston. Sophie was not a "friend" of Phillips but he wished she were, even though her name pointed towards someone in their late teens or twenties.

Sophie posted,

"I don't mean to get too involved in your post Stephen but people can get a docs appointment because the government made cuts to the nhs, not because of immigration. Without immigration the nhs would be much worse, we would lack doctors and nurses at the very least!! By voting out you are voting for a party that have always wanted to privatise healthcare, now how will the poor and disadvantaged pay for this?

Phillip mused. Sophie Aston. He wondered what she looked like. No point wondering he thought. He typed her name into the search field and her picture popped up. She was very attractive, long blonde hair and grey eyes. She was, as he expected, quite young. Graduating from Plymouth University in 2015. There were lackadaisical security settings on her account therefore Phillip was able to browse through all her profile photos and the two albums she had created for trips to Athens and Berlin. Cultural, Phillip thought as he browsed through pictures of the Acropolis, The Parthenon, back streets, Greek fare, Graffiti that said Grow Trees Not Armies, plants, Road signs, tortoises. She seemed to have a thing about tortoises. The ocean. He moved to the Berlin folder. A number of the photos were of more graffiti one of which Phillip found hit the spot, and he was a naysayer when it came to anything too hippy it stated, in capitals,

"SAY YES TO FREEDOM, PEACE, DIGINITY AND RESPECT FOR ALL. SAY NO TO TERROR AND REPRESSION TOWARDS ALL LIVING BEINGS. IN THE BEGINNING WAS FREEDOM. JOLLY KUNJAPPU 1990, 2000, 2009"

There were photos of what left of the Berlin wall, the Brandenburg Gate, The Holocaust Memorial, The German Historical Museum and the Berlin Cathedral.

Phillip thought, why couldn't more people on Facebook be like Sophie? He fantasised wishing he was in his mid-twenties, taking Sophia to London museums and holidaying in Cambodia and Costa Rica not Marbella or Magaluf like all the atypical British lout.

He pondered on what he should do next and decided on a direct personal message.

Hi Sophia read your post to Stephen Grimley with interest. I have a friend called Linford McDonald who's Mum was a nurse in the late 50s and some of the old patients would tell her they didn't want her black hands on them. Most people who post these views read the Mail which has an anti-immigration agenda. Have known Stephen years and I don't even think he is racist that's the worrying thing he believes what the papers say. Blame immigrants for everything!

Equally worrying is the support his views get. Hope you educated someone on that thread. BW Phil

Sophia responded almost immediately,

Hey Phil, Ah gosh that's absolutely horrible :-(it's honestly a crazy crazy world. I can't believe in the 21st century people still believe / listen / post these types of things, it honestly blows my mind. I really just want to open their eyes to all the good immigration has done, not just in the uk but across the world! And why should certain people only live in one place forever anyway?! Maybe one day we'll live in a fairer world hey!

Phillip was elated. This beautiful thoughtful girl and intelligent girl was also non-discriminatory against sad middle aged men.

He replied,

"No worries Sophia hopefully you gave people something to think about. My friends 23 year old daughter is travelling in Asia heading for New Zealand in Aug and his son 25 went to Portsmouth uni, Gabe McFarlane, he did History and is set to travel in Sep, My friend and I had some good times with him at Gunwharf and Pompey FC not so good in any of his accommodation in Southsea. Both are world friendly. Best wishes to you and God bless you for being so thoughtful."

Sophia came back with,

I hope so but looks like no one bothered to respond I'm afraid...Never mind :-) ahh amazing! I went to Portsmouth uni too, I graduated last year. Best wishes to you and your friends as well :-)

Phillip decided to leave it there. Linford McFarlane did exist, he was an old school friend but that was a true as it was. Linford was a proud father who although divorced from his wife hadn't abandoned his children. All the information Phillip had provided came from Linford's Facebook posts. It had its positive uses sometimes, if you needed to make something up, some else had done that thing and posted it online.

Phillip mulled over whether had he met Sophia in his prime they would have had children. The children would have learnt French or Spanish from an early age and played at least one musical instrument. He caught sight of himself in the mirror and frowned. He only spoke English, attempts at learning even the basic French, Spanish, Italian or German, courtesy of free audio CDs from the Sunday Times, had ended in a failure to master anything apart from elementary knowledge. Ordering beer in four different languages was no great feat and it was a few associate he knew thought was a sign of great culture. Not Phillip, if he wasn't going to be fluent he wasn't going to be Del Trotter with his pigeon Spanish.

He had read another Brexit thread.

Charlie Bestwhich was putting her tuppence worth in,

"Vote out I say all we are getting is thieves, rapists paedos and ponces in our country getting benefits and not putting anything in"

Phillip had met Charlie when he had been on a work trip to Norwich she had asked him to take a picture of her and her five year old daughter as they were all in Wetherspoons waiting for their burger and chip meals. Phillip had told Charlie it would be a lovely picture and she had insisted he friend her on Facebook in order she could tag him as the photographer. Whilst Phillip had reservations about adding someone he hardly knew he could hardly refuse. Some of Charlies subsequent postings were so bizarre he did not unfriend her for the amusement value of her poor spelling and parenting skills.

The responses to Charlies, Brexit posts were typical,

"Well said Cha Cha ….most of them get more benefits than me and they have only been here five minutes"

"Yeah I am voting Brexit too mate, fed up with them raping our women then claiming asylum"

Her brother Kevin Bestwhich responded with,

"Our Uncle Bobby was a paratrooper in the war and jumped out of planes fighting for Grate Britten. I am voting out I don't think any of those Eastern Europeans would jump out of a plane like our Bobby"

Charlie was buoyed by the approval and posted,

"I am just thinking of my baby and making sure that when she is old enough she can get a job instead of someone giving it to some mangey pikey from Romania"

Charlie was a single parent who worked in Lidl, chances are her daughter would follow the same path. This didn't stop her from venting her spleen,

"The government always put immigrants first we need to look after our own"

"Totally agree with that one Charlie we need to take a stand and look after our kids future or there will be no council houses left when my four little ones fly the nest"

Phillip recalled his visit to Norwich. On the way to the Wetherspoons pub from the hotel on every street corner was a homeless person, with local accents asking for some spare change. The ones that didn't ask stared into space, grey and gaunt faces with hollow sockets in which sat vacant eyes. Spare change needed for the next fix. Immigration did not appear to be a problem for the city, he passed one or two Polski Skleps and that morning whilst in Costa most of the very polite, very efficient staff seemed to speak with European accents. All contributing to the economy of Norwich rather than taking from it unlike the indigenous drop out that plagued the country.

Phillip was also well aware that during World War 2 the RAF had squadrons with Polish fighter pilots and it was a well-known fact, to anyone with a minimum level of intelligence that Polish paratroopers fought alongside the British. Operation Market, Montgomery's attempt to spearhead an advance into the German Reich in the autumn of 1944, being one such campaign where Polish and British paratroopers, with Americans, stood shoulder to shoulder.

Charlie's child was mixed race, quite a lovely little face with enquiring eyes and a cherubic smile. When her mother had asked her if she wanted some salad she had said, "Piss off." Charlie shrieked with laughter and after setting her phone to record asked again, got the same response and promptly uploaded the video to Facebook with the comment,

"When you know your kid aint going to be one of those skinny veggie eating wankers lol. #nosalad #lovemyjunkfood #jog_onlettuce #givemechips

In the here and now of spring 2017 Phillip's life of mundane drudgery continued. His weeks followed the same path. Monday to Friday he would get up for work, he didn't need an alarm. When he was 13 Phillip took a paper round at Albert Collins newsagent, the shop was a 10 minute walk away. These were days before personal phones therefore an alarm would need to be set on a ticking clock, or at least they did in the Anderson household. As Phillip had an aversion to the sound of a ticking clock in his bedroom he had to rely on his innate ability to wake up at 5:45 each morning which he found easy enough. The routine became a habit and now, around 42 years later Phillip's body clock would wake him up any time between 5 and 6 am. Alcohol inhibited this on occasions, although a leaving do at work was the only social function to which he was invited these days.

Phillip's job was fairly well paid but fairly mundane. He was a system support manager. This involved maintaining a number of in-house computer systems for a telecommunication and systems solutions company, PriZSolutions. Phillip would manage upgrades, conduct weekly status meetings, pore over progress on outstanding issues, produce reports for senior managers and "go the extra mile" by investigating ways to make the systems he managed, more efficient, less labour intensive and generate more income or cheaper to maintain.

Phillip's colleagues did much the same jobs within the IT sphere. Phillip would sometimes drift off thinking to himself about the odd moments of excitement in the office.

There was the time when Rhonda Blackman, the wife of Tony Blackman strode in to the open plan area, just as the department were assembling for a briefing from the director, demanding to know who the whore in the office was her husband was seeing. Tony having had a dalliance with Rachel Maloney from accounts.

A contractor was summarily dismissed, again in full view of the office, for downloading porn. There was the mortifying incident when John Prentice, another of the Support team broke down in tears when a system he was managing crashed in the middle of the day. The overseas Technical Support team hadn't been monitoring high user usage. Two of the three servers the system used had deteriorated to make them unrecoverable. Senior management had implemented a no back up system no system rule shortly after this episode but unfortunately too late for John who had the weekend to ponder over being called inept by Barry Flanaghan the senior director. John spent Sunday afternoon and early evening hanging by his neck via a rope tied to the banister rail of the house he had lived in with his wife and three children. It was a scene his 12 year old son Joe, who would regret asking his mother for the key in order he could rush in and get onto his X box, could ever forget.

Phillip's weekend routine was an advertisement for Mundane and Boring if ever a book with that title was published. He wouldn't sleep in as his view was that the more time you are in bed the less life you could have. Phillip often came to the conclusion that with a life as dull as his it would need to be extended, perhaps it would change when his mother died. He would normally read a book, an autobiography or historical tome. He enjoyed books on wars, religion but not politics. For someone non-sporting he enjoyed tales that recounted a rise from tenement block, council estate or favela to a gated mansion with the trappings that came with great ability.

He would read with his headphones and iPod plugged in and volume turned as high as possible to drown out his mother's voice or the sound of the Dyson which was Christine seemed to use at every opportunity.

"I am going to Dyson she would say,"

"You are going to hoover." he would respond.

"A hoover is a hoover and a Dyson is a Dyson. It's like calling Iceland prawn flavoured prawns, langoustine. To Dyson is so much more sophisticated."

Why that infernal woman cleaned the house on a weekend he never knew. She shopped on a weekend when she had Monday to Friday when the house was empty and the shops were less busy. She was such as cantankerous as a cat in bath water.

She would come home and let him know exactly what she thought of those who shopped in Lidl or Aldi. The fat people who were in Greggs the bakers. The pimply, track suited in Birthday's card shop and about the homeless that sullied the streets begging for money for drugs.

She would wax lyrical about the higher class of person in Marks and Spencer and Waitrose, how polite the staff were, how wonderful the displays were and how the smell of the fresh olive and honey made her as giddy as a young child on a carousel.

On this particular weekend Sunday in June 2017 Phillip had abandoned his book and was trawling through the latest Facebook updates. He noticed that Sophia Aston had spent the night working at a homeless shelter and a feeling of warmth, like a radiator filling with hot water, flooded over him.

Helen Tyler

Helen Tyler had posted a picture on Facebook of her dogs, or fur children as she referred to them. In the days when her contacts were having and boasting about their offspring she had posted:

"If you can drone on about how wonderful your children are then I can do the same about my dogs."

And so she did. Her dogs, three pugs and a French bulldog each had names where you would expect children to answer. They were called, Chelsea, Jess, Billy and Dave. The dogs had more clothes than the children's section in Debenhams.

There was a picture of the four dogs in school uniform outfits, accompanied by the comment,

"So proud of my kids, first day at school."

Phillip had chuckled at that one.

Later she wrote,

"I am grateful for pawprints on my floor, slobbery kisses on my face, nose prints on my window, dog hair on my clothes, BECAUSE THERE WILL BE A DAY WHERE THESE THINGS ARE MISSED."

Phillip wondered how things would have turned out if they had ended up together. Would he have to contend with the affections of her canines?

One December Helen had posted a picture of 12 pugs in Christmas jumpers with the caption,

"When your parents insist on taking a Christmas photo."

Phillip felt not an ounce of sympathy one day when Helen posted,

"I'm heartbroken to announce that I had to make the unbearable decision to put My Little Buggly to sleep yesterday. Walking Bug and Chelsea last Thursday evenin we were attacked by a staff running off lead. It got Chelsea by the throat & I managed 2 punch it 2 release her but then it turned on me biting in2 my leg & Peter managed 2 get it 2 let go. The very sick individual wiv the dog kicked Bug in the head as we were retreating. Bug boy was very sick in the vets & I was heartbroken 2 have 2 make the heartwrenching decision. I know many of you met the strange looking little terror or have seen photos of him growing up on here. He has left a very big hole in my life x"

While Phillip was a dog lover he was much of the view that most pets died before their owners and if one did die you could simply go and buy another. The posts that followed reminded him of when Princess Diana died and people who didn't know her personally were traumatised and acted irrationally.

"Aw Aunty Hels hope ur ok."

"So sorry Hels, bless the little fellow."

"Awe Helen. Im so sorry to hear that. So tragic and sad. My thoughts are with you. Rest in peace Peter x x x."

"I'm so sorry for your loss Hels. Bless little Petie for doing his best to protect you. Have you involved the police ....I hope?

"Sorry for your loss Hels. Have you been in touch with the dog warden? If not do so, they will prosecute and are very serious about owners who can't control their dogs!"

Hugs and love coming your way that's dreadful. I hope you are able to persue the attack with the police and get that monster prosecuted."

"That's so sad, I hope the dick gets what he deserves!!x"

"ahhhh that's so sad Helen. I hope your ok xxxxxxxx"

"Sorry to hear that Hels. Other than that, hope all is well."

"Oh how awful, sorry to hear that, hope you are ok xx."

"omg sweetie that is so horrific. I hope you're ok and I hope that bloke gets done for kickinh Peter what an arsehole some people shouldn't be allowed to have animals"

"so sorry Hels – I hope they get the twat with the dog that did that x."

"I'm really sorry to hear that. What happened to the other jerk with the other dog? Thinking of you"

Phillip had been on the verge of leaving the page and its pitiful thread but then decided that he would add to the online book of condolences. Just in case there was a smidgeon of a chance of meeting her, her feeling vulnerable, and inviting him into her bed,

"Sorry Hels, Sorry to hear about your dog. Hope things otherwise ok."

Short and sweet without referring to the hound by its name.

Now Phillip then went to one of Helen's posts which showed a video was available. Frozen on the screen was a minute pug with the bold capitalized headline,

THIS IS THE WORLDS SMALLEST PUG

The accompanying text said,

"If you're into small dogs, then you're gonna love this one! A woman claims to have Britain's smallest Pug. The puppy is so small that she stands less than four inches tall!
Everyone, meet Pip! Pip is so cute and so small that she's smaller than a soda can! Pip is four months old and she is the runt of the litter. Her owner is Joanne Astley, a 54-year-old woman who started breeding Pugs last year. One of Joanne's Pugs gave birth to four puppies, and she was surprised to see that one of the puppies was half the size of the others. Check out the video below and learn more about Pip!"

Helen had tagged her friend Marty Jones in the post with a row of hearts to which he responded,

"Everyone go home this dog has just won the internet today"

Helens response was,

"Poor little sod, hair lip, cleft palette, internal problems with lungs & heart he does look sweet & cute but just shows how bad breeding turns out. Unfortunately he'd be the one I'd end up taking home & loving"

Helen's next animal associated post was accompanied by the exclamation,

"Oh my god! Kylie Dawn Spencer have you seen this!"

This was followed by heart and dog emojis aplenty.

"I love this video & like this judge I also often have to tell people that Polly is blind but most never even realise. Like this little one she rarely bumps into..."

The caption read,

"Blind Pug Enters A Courtroom And Sits On The Judge's Lap, What He Does There Is Too Cute
Read more at http://www.reshareworthy.com/blind-rescue-pug-mikey/#C47Mz41UiTBpIIVI.99"

Watching the video Sabrina L Johnson the judge in question spoke about Mikey her blind pug. Phillip noticed that there was three minutes and 14 seconds of video to watch but he persevered. The video went through problems Mikey had when found, glaucoma, mistreatment and mange. The initial problem necessitated an operation for the removal of his eyes Judge Johnson went through the adoption process for Mikey and how easily he adapted to home living and also the love the staff at the court had for him.

Phillip, with his often stone cold, heart, found the story not in the remotest endearing and wondered how it would end.

With Mike sitting on the judge's lap Sabrina started to sing. Very good, thought Phillip, a string to her bow. She had a soulful voice that reminded him of Roberta Flack. Momentarily Phillips heart began to thaw, he was swaying to the music as the Sabrina belted out her vocals. She was a good looking woman His warm heart shrank as quickly as the Titanic's sister ship, the Britannic, and harden like water tossed into a freezer. The hound started to howl, it was a high pitched whine that cut through Phillips head like an angry chainsaw through an ancient oak.

Phillip mused over another of Helen's comments,

"I have no words…… :-("

The screen said,

We've blurred this image as its so distressing. Be aware report contains distressing images

Phillip clicked on the link and read on,

"Warning: We've now received some distressing images from the RSPCA of the two dogs. We thought twice about showing them, but in an attempt to stop neglect of this level happening again, they are shown at the bottom of the article"

The article read,

"Isle of Wight residents Tony and Kaye Toogood have been banned for life from keeping dogs after appearing in court this week.

Tony Toogood, a town councillor in Brading, and his estranged wife, Kaye Toogood, both admitted neglecting their two dogs, Minnie and Daisy.

RSPCA inspectors discovered the neglect after the older dog, Daisy, was found as a stray. A visit to the couple's home in Brading revealed similar neglect of the other dog, Minnie."

Phillip scrolled to the bottom of the page and there were pictures of, in his opinion, two dogs that seemed well fed but had matted fur. He went back to Facebook and saw that Kenwyn Belmont responded,

"I have words "f@cking bastards"!!!!"

To which Dorothea Tyler replied,

Should have locked them up and neglected them for months or years. Selfish bastards!

Phillip sighed. So many drama queens and kings using social media.

He looked at an earlier post. It was a video of a baby elephant struggling to get out of a waterhole. The creature made several attempts to negotiate the muddy bank and each time slipped back into the water. After five minutes the elephant was clearly in distress and getting exhausted. Two mature elephants eventually came to the rescue. Using their trunks and heads they manoeuvred and hoisted and pushed and finally hefted the baby onto firm ground. One of Helen's friends, Heather Cable posted,

"If those adult elephants were humans, they would just stand round on their phones taking pictures and videos. Oh wait ...... x"

Helen responded with,

"Yeah Chick, it goes to show how the animal kingdom are so much more living and caring than the human one and we would best to learn from them to get on with peace and kindness x

Facebook took Phillip to the next video which showed a crocodile dragging a baby elephant into the depths of a river. He felt no compunction to read the inevitable comments about how cruel crocodiles were because he was sure they would be likened to ISIS or Boko Haram. He was quite stunned because most rational people would know that animals were instinctive, they did not kill for sport but to survive. He was sure that Helen would love to lead a campaign to turn crocodiles, cheetahs, lions, hyenas, vultures and the like to the promise land of veganism.

He wondered what had happened to the callous bitch who had so ruthlessly dumped him.

Phillip wondered why people were not as realistic about life as he was. Animals and humans were so different. He did agree on one thing that Helen had written when she had lambasted a dog walker on her page because he had the temerity to allow his canine to playfully chase after ducks at the local park.

"Some people don't deserve to breathe."

She had said.

Phillip went to YouTube from Facebook and typed "crocodile attacks elephant" in the search field.

He amused himself over the next 30 or so minutes watching When Prey fights back 2017, Wild Animals Fighting, Smart Monkey v Tiger, Baboons save Impala from Cheetah and Most Spectacular Big Cats Compilation. Some of the videos included narration either by the person shooting or posting and he wondered whether these people had anything better to do, although he guessed it might be related to an insatiable delight at viewing bloodletting.

 He opened his drawer and withdrew from its sheath the nine inch hunting blade he had purchased when he had been to Morocco and visited the Marrakesh Souk. It was a red deer real Moroccan genuine animal bone handle hunting knife. The tip of the handle was metal with a hole which seemed to serve no purpose whatsoever but Phillip concluded it might be in order it could be hung to the wall by hook or nail. The said handle, oak in colour was riveted together with smooth curves to accommodate a hand grip. From its base, headed by gold trim was a ferocious looking steel blade. The edge was so sharp Phillip shuddered to think of the damage it could do were it to encounter flesh.

Maybe, Phillip thought, he could carve "idiot" on Helen's forehead or cut a rabbit in half and leave it on her doorstep. She was after all only 20 minutes away in the car as she had moved only a mile from her parents in Hainault. He laughed to himself and then decided to look at more videos of crocodiles grabbing prey, and taking them on a death roll to the bottom of rivers. He enjoyed seeing the startled look on the faces of zebra or antelope as they disappeared beneath the murky waters...

Late on that same Sunday evening Chelsea, Jess, Billy and Dave anxiously stood wait by their bowls for supper. Each bowl was identical in style, made of tin with alternating paw and bone prints. Yellow and pink for the girls, blue and brown for the boys. Each bowl had its owners name scribed in a flowery swirl of Helen's best Lucida style handwriting. The bowls were currently as empty as the dogs felt their stomachs were and as shiny as a bald man's pate where each dog had licked at the plates hard enough to take off a layer of coating. They always got a roast on Sunday, it was a tradition. Chicken smothered in Bisto gravy, baked potatoes and carrots. Helen had tried cabbage once but the dogs had become flatulent. It was funny for about an hour but the smell became nauseating and so unbearable the dogs were exiled to the garden like incontinent pensioners. Having not seen their owner since mid-afternoon one by one they each proceeded to climb the stairs and took it in turn or concurrently to yelp at Helens bedroom door.

Helen lay on her bed. Her eyes were wide open as she lay on her back with the artexed ceiling above her. A skittish brown spider moved across the ceiling, the vast expanse of white plaster, a snow covered expanse, while a small fly moved jerkily around the lightbulb like a lightweight champion circling the challenger.

Helen's eyes did not move, neither did she notice the tiny fellow occupants of her room. She could not hear her fur children whining at the door. Billy, the more mischievous of the four had decided that whining was a futile exercise and took to scratching frantically at the door pulling the carpet away from the grips. With the old fashioned pattern coming away the pile lay on the backing like droplets of blood on straw.

It wasn't until Wednesday morning that Helen's body was found. Her throat had been cut, Cassandra had been calling for two days and having had no reply let herself in with the spare key. A clean and very deep slice that severed her windpipe and almost decapitated her. The room had been ransacked, drawers were open and clothes strewn on the floor. It looked like robbery that turned into murder.

The dogs by then had been frantic with hunger but not too worse for wear. 70 hours without food was hardly a fast but routine had been broken and for Cassandra, also a dog lover getting Chelsea, Jess, Billy and Dave back into a routine was imperative now their mother was dead. She would focus on the dogs, her own beloved cockapoo had been run over three weeks previously. She had been grieving since then and had even contemplated taking her own life but now she had four new fur children of her own and she was going to give them the best home ever and leave the police to find out who had murdered her daughter.

Phillip Anderson

It was July, it was a Monday and a single sun beam shone through the office window, a disco ball spotlighting a dance floor. Phillip looked out of the window and sighed and cast his mind back 24 hours previously as he had looked out of his bedroom window. Then, the sky was grey and as angry as a soiled baby. Rain had come down in buckets, horizontal. Diagonal, vertical and at times was so hard it had bounced off the path. How ironic, his planned day for cleaning the car was shelved and yet here, back now in the present, sat in his office, the heat was intense enough to fry eggs, mushrooms and bacon on the steel roof of the annexe to the building that housed the new backup servers.

Phillips's thoughts were broken by the notification of an email that popped up in his taskbar. Emails were common and getting to be a cause of irritation, Phillip getting approximately eighty a day. He used his office email for personal correspondence too therefore fifty of those emails were from companies from which he had purchased clothes, books, CDs. tools, white goods and the like. He needed to get round to unsubscribing to these newsletters as soon as he could be bothered.

This particular email jumped out at him because it was from Sheila Hastwick, Senior Director, Barry Flanagan's PA. The email asked him to accept an invitation to a meeting in Barry's office at 12:30 regarding training. It was now 11:57. Phillip had lunch at 12:00 on the dot every day and had at one stage blocked out his diary for 60 minutes to ensure he did as the company advised, took a break and wasn't shackled to his PC and desk for the whole working day. Other staff members had done the same but there was then an edict vetoing this practise issued by the top level management team t as it was not practical.

Please be advised that there are going to be occasions when it was essential to be available during "unsociable day time hours. Please be prepared."

Phillips proposed lunch hour was to be interrupted and his despondent mood became even more so.

Phillip responded to the email, grudgingly accepted the invite, he had no choice. He could have ignored the email but Sheila was astute enough to send the invite with a read receipt therefore would have known it had been seen. In Phillip's response he included a note asking Sheila whether he should bring any paperwork. As she hadn't responded by 12:10 he rang her number only for the phone to remain unanswered. He rang Sandra Benson, PA to one of the other directors and who sat next to Sheila. Sandra answered and told Phillip that Sheila had gone to lunch.

At 12:25 Phillip made his way out of his office down the corridor and up the lift to the top floor of the building where, proceeding along a well decorated corridor, he stood outside Barry Flanagan's office, cleared his throat and rapped on the door.

Hearing nothing Phillip rapped on the door again, louder this time.

"Why don't you just come in." a voice boomed from the inner sanctums Phillip felt sure he was walking into a hornets nest. It was more an order than a question and Phillip felt his stomach drop past his waist, through his thighs, grind past his knees and land with a thud on his feet which made walking through the door as easy as if he were wading through melted tarmac.

Barry Flanagan peered over his glasses and gestured to his guest he should sit down in the leather swivel chair that was opposite his. An oak table served as a buffer between senior manager and corporate drone. As Phillip sat he caught more than a hint of what he expected was a very expensive aftershave emanating from the man opposite him. It made his eyes water and he had to dab them with the crisp white handkerchief Christine insisted he carry alongside his organ donor card.

"Phil Anderson," Barry said affably, "how are things going?

Before Phillip had a chance to answer Barry continued,

"I hope you aren't too busy in two weeks' time there's been a bit of a pickle over the way the application team in Miami have been supporting the Venus. You know the one that has been going up and down like a brasses' draws?"

Phillip stuttered, "Well I."

Barry ignored him and continued,

"Rhetorical question I know you know it, you supported it for two years, Ricki Finn told me. Now I know Ricki supports it now but he can't make it out to Miami because he has some personal issues that require him to be this side of the pond. I need someone to go out there and give the Yanks a three day upskilling session Monday 24 to Wednesday 26th July on the latest support practices, do a bit of schmoozing, drink plenty of Budweiser, maybe get laid by a couple of broads and be back home in time for breakfast. I don't mean that literally obviously. The bit about the broads that is…..don't want to get the clap do you?"

Barry chuckled, somewhere in that delivery there was a joke which Phillip did not find amusing but he nervously joined Barry with a fake laugh of his own.

Phillip's mind whirred, three days in Miami sounded great but he knew from experience that it would be less glamourous than Barry had suggested.

"Good to go on Sunday week?" again this wasn't a question from Barry.

"Yes I think I can be away from the office for a week. The Apollo application upgrade is…….." Phillip started.

"Great stuff Phil," Barry said, obviously not wanting to know what else was going on in Phillip's world, "get the travel details off Sheila and Ricki will give you a heads up on what needs doing. Cheers mate. Ricki can cover whatever is urgent."

Barry picked up his phone and began to dial, which obviously meant Phillip's audience with him was over so he got up and left.

As Phillip walked, quite shell shocked, from Barry's office his mind began to work overtime, which was something else the senior management team had vetoed. He gave some thought to Ricki Finn turning down a trip to Miami. Although for most it would be a case of travelling on the Sunday going to the office on Monday morning, doing whatever needed doing until close play Wednesday and flying back Thursday. Ricki was the type who would spend Sunday afternoon finding a local drug dealer for cannabis and ecstasy and spend the night partying, as he would Monday night Tuesday night and Wednesday night. Doing as little as possible during the day and coming back to work on Friday with tales of debauchery with young American boys as he had done on the three previous times he had been to Miami.

Phillip ducked into the next available lavatory, went to a cubicle, sat down and opened up Facebook on his iPhone6. He typed Ricki Finn in the search field and clicked on the first entry which was his erstwhile colleague dressed in a skin-tight cat suit wearing what seemed to be a Mardi Gras mask in the guise of a devil.

Without looking at the diary entries Ricki had made about his romance with Francis, Phillip scrolled down until he found what he was looking for.

Malachi Cavendish, one of Ricki's 2071 friends had posted,

"41 sleeps before Trashy and Nasty Weekend at Bognor. Can't wait xxxxxxxx"

Ricki had made several of the 73 comments to this post including,

"What date is that Hun? Xxxxxxxx"

Sean KissmyBooty Evans had replied,

"21-23 July babe and there are still some tickets left but be quick…….."

Ricki had responded with,

"On it now precious"

So there it was. Ricki's personal reasons for not wanting to go to Miami were that on the Sunday that he would have travelled he would have been in Bognor with his gay friends. Drink, drugs and mis-behaviour and probably too shitfaced to get to Heathrow or Gatwick for a flight.

Phillip seethed. He had a mind to go back to Barry's office and tell him that he realised he couldn't go to Miami on Sunday 23rd because he was going to be partying with Ricki that weekend but he knew how ridiculous that was and he knew that Ricki was a golden boy with the senior management team.

Ricki's sexuality was not an issue for anyone in the company because he was a technical genius when it came to computers. Years spent alone while Phillip was with Helen, struggling with the demons that told him he was gay but compelling him to be seen as heterosexual he had absorbed computing systems, architecture and practise with both hands.

A Straight A student and a first class IT honours degree from Brunel. If there were any problems with any application that required a quick fix and a long term solution then Ricki was the go to guy at the company He used his knowledge of the systems to his advantage, always attending emergency meetings to provide an input and always in the ear of one of the seniors at group or department indoctrination sessions. Ricki could not be any more visible if he had a penis growing out of his ear.

Phillip on the other hand was a plodder, conscientious and diligent but lacked the flair and personality to be anything except another hamster on the wheel.

74

"Might as well get one with it," he said that afternoon when he sat down with Ricki to go through the requirements of the three day stay in "The good ole U S of A" as Ricki flamboyantly described it.

Briefing over. Ricki hated even more now than ever, Phillip saw out the rest of the day in the office doing some prep work then ambling off home.

During dinner, in which his mother wittered on again about the low class of person she had seen going into Birthdays card shop and how refreshing the selection of cards were in Clintons, Phillip took a quick look at the Facebook application on his iPhone. The red spot on the Facebook icon signified he had been mentioned in a post. Phillip had adjusted his settings so that he wasn't notified if a post was made that didn't explicitly mentioned him. He did find it tedious when he was tagged in a post until he had removed himself. How was it possible for thirty people to comment on whether milk or hot water should be added to a tea bag first?

He was hardly surprised to see that Ricki had posted,

"Happy days....was wondering whether I would miss Trash and Nasty to go to some corporate gig but thanks to the wonderful and gorgeous Phillip Anderson coming to my rescue………. Cinderella shall go to the ball"

The post was followed by 20 heart signs and 20 kisses. These were in turn followed by 44 comments from Ricki's friends and included an exchange between him and Malachi,

"Can I be your Prince Charming Sugarlump. What you dressing up in xxxx!"

"Now that would be telling but you can rest assured there will be some fine ass booty on display and Francis might not let you get near it"

"Cant wait to see that fine thing RickaDickaLickaLaLaLaLa"

"Pre gig at mine on the Thursday night Hon…can you make it"

"I can make it and your gon try to break it big boy. Hope you r getting loads of bubbles in"

"In the bath you scrummy little soldier lol"

"Teasy weasy lemon squeezy your such a bad boy"

"Maybe you can invite Phillip he looks nice and cuddly"

At which point Phillip decided he would read no more and glanced at the newsfeed. Nothing of interest except a share by Keith Huntsman.

"The Daily Mail suggested that the country was horrified that a blonde British Airways hostess from Essex was to be incarcerated in the Central Prison in Al Aweer alongside prostitutes and drug smugglers. The stewardess' crime was to have given the pilot of the plane she had flown to Dubai with, a blow job on the Jumeirah beach. The pilot had escaped punishment as he was had some influential contacts at Dubai Marina Yacht Club but once outed in the newspaper was thrown out of the house by his pregnant wife."

Phillip moved from Facebook to Twitter as he needed to fire off a tweet to the journalist at the Daily Mail who had reported the Dubai story but decided that he would keep his spleen unvented.

Keith Huntsman

The days leading up to the flight to Miami were as uneventful as the ride itself.

Phillip had noticed he wasn't the only one going abroad on Sunday 23rd July. Lisa Prentice, a girl he had met when she did a work placement with the personnel department, and friended as many people in the company on Facebook as was humanly possible in two weeks, had checked into Gatwick Airport at 0600 and posted a picture of a glass of wine with the caption,

"It would be rude not to. Cheeky vino before take-off"

Having 1721 friends all who seemed to have the Facebook application hardwired to their hands meant that by 0800 Lisa had 71 likes and 23 comments which said more or less the same thing,

"Have a good time. Where are you going?"

If only it were that straightforward for the Facebook junkies. Phillip read through each posting and became more and more piqued.

"You trying to outdo me. Didn't you just come back from Magaluf Leesy Peesy Where to now Hunnnybun…come on spill the beaneroonies"

No question marks he thought, and this was one of the more literate postings. Phillip looked at the picture of the culprit and could see from the woman's profile picture she was probably in her late 30s. Not possible Phillip thought. The post was more akin to that one would expect from a 14 year old. He clicked on the ladies name. Marie Armitage and to his surprise the profile picture matched the other photos that had been uploaded and she was indeed middle aged. Wading through Marie's posts he saw that every day she posted a number of inspirational quotes, the theme seemed to be around how strong she was and how weak and unsuitable most men were,

"I am waiting for Mr Right, not Mr Right Now"
"Love Yourself Before You Learn To Love Someone Who Will Hurt You"
"A Successful Woman is one who can build a foundation with the Bricks others have thrown at her"
"No I'm not single I am in a long distance relationship because my boyfriend lives in the future"

Phillip looked at Marie's pictures again. Very plain quite a plump woman. Described in the old singles pages as "bubbly." There was usually a cigarette hanging out of the corner of her mouth.

He looked at the previous days posts,

"You are not fat, You have fat, You have fingernails, You are not fingernails"
"Is fat the worst thing a human being can be? IS fat worse than vindictive, jealous, shallow, vain, boring, evil or cruel? Not to me"

"The only reason I am fat is because a tiny body couldn't store this personality"
"I try to avoid things that make me fat, like mirrors, scales and photographs"

He laughed out loud at the last one. If he had been Marie's friend on Facebook he might have posted LMAO or LOL but many of her friends had already done that.

Bar the quotes Marie had been on holiday for a week in Cyprus and Phillip browsed through her pictures. There were a group of five girls, two of them were quite pleasing on the eye and Phillip searched for pictures of them on the beach.

Marie seemed more self-conscious than he would have liked and most the pictures were of the girls in restaurants or bars. Marie obviously liked her food because of the five girls she was the only one who could be seen to be tucking into the highest stack burger, thickest steak, voluminous chip bowl or heftiest ice cream dish. The only hint of fruit that Lisa was pictured with was a hair clip shaped like a banana.

Marie's posts soon bored Phillip so he went back to Lisa.

On the day of travel Lisa posted 23 times. Phillip didn't need to wonder why he counted each entry. He knew it was because he took an abnormal liking to be irritated by Facebook and by counting Lisa's posts it justified the angst that he felt.

Phillip kept a mental note as he went through the posts,

0415 "Silly o' clock got to turn this alarm off"
0430 "What is this lady doing up so early in the morning, Can anyone guess"
0440 "Am I the only one excited. Havent heard a peep from my partners in crime yet"
0441 "Another 4 hours and it will be wine o clock"
0459 "Better get out of bed spose"
0515 "Love standing under the shower and thinking about nothing. It's the best feeling. Think Mum is going to be complaining about the water bill again lol"

0550 "I love the smell of my new conditioner. Who else loves that just showered just hair washed feeling. Come on peeps time to get up ha ha"

0605 "Just making myself look beautiful. Had to get up two hours early lol"

0620 "Don't you just hate it when you have made your mind up to use your Mums spray tan and she's used it all. Come on Mum get a grip lol

0810 "Think I have done a great job time for breakfast"

0900 "Cab has arrived its time to round up the gang"

0910 "Lisa Prentice has checked into Clifton Road with Gabby Reiner"

0915 "Lisa Prentice has checked into Deaconshire Street with Gabby Reiner, Sylvie Carter and Rene Carter

0930 "Lisa Prentice has checked into Penley Road with Gabby Reiner, Sylvie Cater, Rene Carter and Grace Farnsworth

1030 "Lisa Prentice has checked into Gatwick Airport with Gabby Reiner, Sylvie Cater, Rene Carter and Grace Farnsworth

Lisa's posts were awash with comments from friends asking where the girls were all going but were being kept in suspense

1045 "Lisa Prentice drinking wine with Gabby Reiner, Sylvie Cater, Rene Carter and Grace Farnsworth in the Red Lion Gatwick Airport

1145 "Just going through customs

1148 "OMG Rene had a bottle of water in her handbag so they are searching her

1205 "Hate waiting for our flight to come up its been such a long day just want to get there now"

1220 "More wine"

1259 "Feel pissed"

1310 "Boarding now"

1350 "On the plane"

1415 "Its taking off!!!! Its taking off!!!!!"

At 1845 UK time Lisa and her friends checked into the Hotel Atlantica Sancta Napa in Ayia Napa.

Phillip smiled. He had always felt superior to most people that used Facebook, none more so than now. On the morning of his flight he had no inclination to let people know what his progress was because he was 100% certain no-one would be interested. He had the good fortune that the plane was not full and with no passenger adjacent to him was able to lay out his two novels and his two iPods, lift up his arm rest and recline his seat without the ignominy of being castigated by an irate fellow passenger in economy.

Once at his destination hotel Phillip unpacked and hung up or put into drawers his clothes, he hated living out of suitcases. He flicked through the countless TV stations and then opening up Facebook on his phone and did a CHECK IN to the hotel, he couldn't resist. He would check the responses over dinner.

The tranquillity of the journey from London to the Holiday Inn in Miami was.as sods law dictates the total opposite in terms of incident to the journey from the hotel to the nearby Sponderosa Restaurant which was laying on its usual Sunday eat as much as you want buffet. As usual, for the Sponderosa, the menu displayed in the local newsletter Phillip picked up, advertised,

Lobster tails for crunchin..........when you come a lunchin.

The accompanying picture of a cartoon lobster without a tail, eyes full of tears, sold the restaurant to Phillip, the crustacean feast being a big favourite with him.

Having visited the Sponderosa chain on many occasions on trips to the States he was pleased that Sheila had booked him into a hotel that was within walking distance. Although the drink driving laws in the States were not as harsh as back home Phillip was keen to get a few beers in after his long journey and as he had to pick up the hire car from the airport was morally unable to avail himself too freely when the drinks cart came along the aisle of the plane.

Having locked the Sponderosa in on google maps the tool confirmed that the restaurant was but 20 minutes along Le Mardi Avenue and on the junction of Flagpole. Confident that he was heading in the right direction Phillip purposefully strode toward lobster heaven and a few well-earned budweisers knowing that the next intersection was Biscayne, After 10 minutes power walking, lost in thoughts of what he would be eating, he noticed that there was a large area of rundown offices and apartments to his right where it seemed that this block had been left to decay. He walked on to the road junction that was 20 feet away and it wasn't Biscayne but Sistone. He took out his phone, opened up the google maps application and it confirmed, to his dismay, that his journey time was now 30 minutes.

"Fucking google maps," he said out loud. He had considered him a google map expert. He should have remembered that junctions in American cities could be 10 sometimes 15 minutes apart as opposed to England where they were generally around five times smaller. Everything is on a bigger scale in America. "Fucking America," he said, again aloud.

Phillip took a deep breath and decided to focus his mind on what he would be eating once he got to the restaurant. Perhaps mentally he wasn't with it. He should have kept the app open as he walked but a spate of iPhone muggings in London had indoctrinated him into keeping his in his jacket pocket for as long as possible. His focus was short-lived.

"Fucking google maps, fucking America, fucking idiot Phillip Anderson," he said again, frustrated at having to turn back and retrace his steps.

"Fucking motherfucker."

Phillip didn't say that but he heard it and he wasn't dreaming it. Neither was he dreaming that something rather sharp was digging into the back of his neck.

"Hand over your pocketbook motherfucker," the voice said again. There was a drawl to the voice, like Cletus Delroy Spuckler, the hillbilly from the Simpsons. The delivery was slightly highly pitched with suggested to Phillip as his head quickly cleared and his heart started to thump that the owner was in his teens.

"Aint gonna tell you again motherfucker."

"Ok friend I'm from England I don't want any trouble I'll give you my wallet," Phillip said trying to remain calm but he felt his heart pound loud enough to be heard in England.

"Don't give a hoot where ya'all from motherfucker, don't want no wallet, just give me your pocketbook and your phone."

81

Wallet was pronounced Whoaa-let and had become even more high pitched as the person got excited, Phillip was now more convinced he was being robbed by a younger person than an older one...

Phillip held his phone out to one side with his back still to his assailant who reached out grabbed it and, Phillip could sense the person was stuffing the item into a pocket.

"Now your pocketbook motherfucker."

Phillip reached inside his jacket pocket and took out his wallet, he held it out in the same way he had his phone but this time, as a hand reached out Phillip let the wallet drop to the floor. He felt the knife move from his neck and in an instant took a step to get out of range spun round and delivered a karate kick to the solar plexus of the white lad who was skinny and around five foot seven inches tall. As the lad began to fold double a flat handed jab with the heel of Phillip's left hand was delivered to a jaw that sent him crashing to the seat of his pants. The knife that had been used also landed, this with a metallic clatter, his was followed by a loud groan from Phillips assailant as he sat on his bottom rubbing his chin.

Finally Phillip's ju-jitsu classes had proved useful.

The would-be robber remained seated. He now supported himself with one of his hands while still rubbing his jaw with another. Winded and dazed with eyes that were slowly getting focus back he spoke,

"You fucking motherfucker, damn near broke my jaw."

The lad was around 16, scrawny as a hungry rat and dressed like he had just stepped away from the eye of Hurricane Katrina in New Orleans. He wore ragged blue jeans and a mud splashed, what looked to be aqua marine tee shirt that had Go Dolphins emblazoned in black writing. On the boys feet were high top Nike trainers that had holes in the toes, frayed laces and scuffs on what was once white synthetic leather. Phillip caught a slight whiff of body odour that teenage boys seem to acquire alongside pubescent acne.

"Give me my phone," Phillip said as he went over and picked up the knife.

"Damn near broke my jaw motherfucker," the boy repeated.

"Give me my phone or I'll slit your throat," Phillip said. He wanted to sound menacing because the boy seemed to be oblivious to the fact that he wasn't in a position to be speaking to him with anything but reverence.

"Fuck you motherfucker," the boy said pathetically, this time the bravado had gone out of his voice but not enough to satisfy Phillip that there was any genuine remorse.

Phillip grabbed the boy's thick curly yellow, afro-like hair and held the knife to his throat.

"Call me motherfucker again. I dare you. I double dare you," Phillip said this and hoped the boy had seen Pulp Fiction and the line delivered by Samuel L Jackson's character Jules Winnfield.

He watched as the boy's Adams apple rose and fell, he felt the boys shoulders slump. The boy let out a sigh that seemed to release a lifetime of misery from his open mouth and flooded into Phillip like an intravenous feed filling a vein. Tears filled the boy's eyes and he sobbed. The slumped shoulders heaved and the boy's body shook as he emptied out his emotion on that cold, harsh unyielding tarmac floor of his shit life so far.

"What's your name son? Phillip asked, when the tears had subsided.

"I'm just a lowdown motherfucker sir, you don't need to know my name," came the reply.

"How old are you?"

"18"

"Where are you from?"

"Motherfuckin Jacksonville sir."

"Where are your family?"

"Who knows sir. I got thrown out on account I stuck up for my sister when my Pa was molestin' her. My Ma said it was none of my damn motherfucking business what my Pa was doing to his own kin."

"Do you always swear like that son?"

"What do you mean sir?"

"You say motherfucker a lot."

"Cussin sir.......that's how we talk on the street sir, I been educated and I ain't done nuthin with my readin' and writin' so now I'm a street boy and all those cats that hustle, the ones that have got fancy clothes and fancy house and stuff. I want to be like one of them."

"Educated by whom?"

"Lived with ma Grandma and Grandpa for eight years on account my folks had nine children. Went to a good school till I was twelve years old then there was a fire at the house and they died and I ended up back with my folks and it turned to shit."

Phillip laughed, not at the boy but at his hang dog look and his angst. Eminem came into his mind, the only rapper he was aware of. Looking at the boy he reminded him a bit of the rapping superstar. He had a similar shaped head and his semi-permanent scowl. A real Slim Shady.

Phillip's stomach growled and it reminded him that if he didn't get to the Sponderosa in the next 30 minutes the lobster might not be so freely available.

"You hungry?" Phillip said to the boy.

"You bet"

"What's your name?"

"Marshall, everybody calls me Mathers," was the reply.

Phillip looked at the boy quizzically, and then smiled, but didn't ask the next obvious question.

"If you can keep from swearing..........cussing I mean, I'll get you some dinner."

"That's mighty motherfucking agreeable," the boy said, and then added mischievously, "I'm only fooling with ya, I'd like that very much sir."

And so the unlikely couple entered the Sponderosa and dined on lobster tails, chicken wings, baked tilapia, shrimp, pork chops and ribs, collard greens, mash potato and spicy gumbo.

They talked about Marshall's life and dreams and by the time they had spent an hour at the table the seed of charity Phillip had in him had expanded like a grain of rice. Whilst Mathers tucked into a dessert of ice cream Phillip approached, Florence, the round-faced, motherly looking lady who had shown them to their table and asked whether she could give his young companion a job in response to the sign on the window that said STAFF WANTED – APPLY WITHIN. He gave her $200 dollars and said that if she could get the boy somewhere to stay and some clothes and if he was still working in two weeks' time there would be another $200 just for her. When he left Marshall, after telling him he was now a working man he gave him $20 "holding money" and advised he should work hard and put his old life behind him. As he walked back to his hotel he ruminated on whether he had just wasted his $220 dollars plus the additional $25 for food. With a belly full of food and a brain befuddled by jet lag and 4 pitchers of beer and four whisky chasers, he reached his room, flopped still clothed on his bed and woke up punctually at 0600 on Monday morning.

He was still slightly hungover, he reached over and flipped open his wallet. The single ten dollar bill shocked him and he sprang out of bed thinking he had been robbed by the bug eyed bell boy who had shown him to his room and been given two single dollar bills as a tip but his memory of the previous night flooded back. Part of him have a warm feeling like he had, for once in his life done something spontaneous and charitable the other part made him feel slightly perturbed that he had been taken for a fool. As he showered and the life came back flooding through him he cursed his benevolence and thought that if he could turn back time he would have stabbed the boy, taken back his phone and gone for his meal alone.

Ablutions complete he quickly opened up Facebook on his phone. He had 47 likes and eleven comments to his check in at the hotel.

Ricki had commented at what was UK time Sunday evening by saying "Enjoy Phillip. I've had a great weekend in Bugger Bognor LMFAO."

He was able to respond to nine of the comments which were in effect "Lucky bastard you on holiday," by saying "Boring work trip won't have much time for sightseeing."

After Phillip's boring work trip comment Ricki had proceeded to provide a list of the best clubs and bars to visit and annotated the list with,

#dont be boring#live a little#Miami is the bomb#wish I as there#you lucky devil#hate being in England.

It was 0830 in Miami therefore it was about 0330 in the UK. Ricki was probably still off his face on drugs after Trashy and Nasty.

The other comment was from Keith Huntsman, an ex-work colleague, and said. "Hey Mr A what you doing in Miami, got time to hook up?"

Phillips initial thoughts were he would rather have burning pins put in his eyes, he had to be at the office at 930 and without time to reply left the hotel and went off to deliver the first days training.

The day went as expected. The American staff were affable, they complained about the way they were being treated and said that it was they who had raised the issue of training with the CEO Conrad Finklestein III 4 months ago and been told there was no budget to facilitate this. Phillip took delight in telling them that Conrad had recently taken delivery of a seventy foot yacht therefore money to keep his staff abreast of the latest best practises was in short supply.

Ideally Phillip might have had an invite for dinner from one of the more attractive female members of staff, one of whom had the figure of a model and breasts which stood to attention like trained pointy faced daschunds up on their haunches. Phillip turned down an offer of an evening with Conrad Brady who sported a God Is Love tee shirt, wore white socks, sandals and khaki shorts. Conrad had said his wife,

Philomena was making a delicious nut roast with assorted vegetables to be washed down with homemade lemonade or sarsaparilla. Phillip said he had made other arrangements.

Once in his hotel Phillip opened up his laptop and went on Facebook.

He could quite easily have met up with Keith, he wasn't doing anything that evening, or any other. It was only that having looked at Keith's posts since he joined Facebook a year ago he was pretty certain that the bloke was a complete arsehole.

Keith had moved from the UK branch of the company in 2003 for the warmer climes of Miami. The warmer climate was going to suit him because his hereditary rheumatism was already causing him great discomfort in the winter months of Kent where he lived.

After two years of being ran into the ground from afar by Barry Flanaghan, Keith had resigned. He was aided in his decision by the death of his wife Julie's, father, her sole surviving, and extremely rich, relative. The expected demise gave the Huntsman's access to a reasonably sized estate and they were able to buy a large villa complete with swimming pool, blue and pink Cadillacs and a Mercedes SUV. After six months of profligate spending they decided to open an Internet café in 2006. The business flourished in the years before smartphones ruled and they were able to expand the businesses, several franchise shops were opened. With someone to take on running the initial café both Keith and Julie now enjoy a life of leisure.

When Keith opened an account on Facebook, at the behest of his daughter still in England with her husband and two children Keith picked up on the fact that he could use the application to crow about his lifestyle.

Keith and Julie had a daily routine of walking to the café that sat on South beach, order respectively a mini white chocolate mocha frappucino and latte with turmeric and while away an hour or two before a stroll along the Ocean Drive.

In Keith's first Facebook week he took before and after pictures of the cups in which the beverages were made. If they bought a panini or a cake or croissant or any such delight these would also make the shot with a before accompanied by,

 "It would be rude not to"

And a shot after, with empty crumb dotted plate, accompanied by the comment,

 "All gone," or "didn't touch the sides," or "nom nom nom"

Comments that made Phillip cringe but he was drawn to read every post. The fortnightly trips to the same diner where Keith had a T bone steak with fries and two beers followed by a cocktail while Julie, who posted the same pictures on her Facebook page, would check in,

"Julie Huntsman is feeling loved, eating food at the 11th Street Diner with Keith Huntsman"

After the eighth time the Huntsman's had posted their visits to the diner and Phillip had analysed the picture enough to know they sat at the same table, were served by the same waitress, who would often be in the picture with one or other of the couple at the same time.

At regular intervals the pair would be joined by the daughter who had followed them to Miami and then the posts would be of the family meals with a picture taken of the table, then each plate, then each drink, then each family member of which there were a total of seven. Phillip wondered whether the Huntsman's spent any time talking to each other or whether they actually had time to eat their meals such was the volume of photos that were taken during the family visit.

When the Huntsman's were not posting breakfast, lunch or dinner pictures they were in the shops, or beside their cars, or in the pool or at the golf course. They didn't do anything that had not become routine. They didn't visit foreign countries, take in architecture or meet fascinating people, they didn't seem to have a life outside family gatherings but, for some reason, they shared this very mundane but very opulent life style with their social media contacts.

The Huntsman's use of childish words and phrases, to Phillip anyway, at every opportunity were a cause of irritation. He would add them to his mental list that added to his mental angst,

"Hubsta, Wifesta, Bubbsta, Grandbubsta, Holibobs, Famalam, fabfuntabulpous, huggles and cuggles, chillaxing in the hotness,"

Phillip had long decided that the couple were amongst several he knew that had rules of Facebook engagement, evident in the following short public discussion that was removed quickly, but not before Phillip had taken a screen shot,

Keith,

"Hey Wifesta, I notice you didn't wish Haley Croker a happy birthday or like her comment Happy Birthday Me"

Julie Huntsman,

"No"

Keith Huntsman,

"Unlike you!!!"

Julie Huntsman,

"Not going to wish comment or like she only goes on Facebook on her birthday to see how many comments she gets. She doesn't like any of our posts"

Keith Huntsman,

"Totally agree Sweetcheeks xx"

Haley Croker posted at the end of the thread,

"Fuck off"

Whenever there was a shooting spree that side of the Atlantic, in America or as far away as Canada, be it California, New York, Florida, Chicago or Toronto Keith would mark each of his family members safe on Facebook but then would like or agree with any social media comment made by a native American advocating the right of American citizens to bear arms. He would sign any comment made off with the footnote,

"It is people that kill people NOT guns."

Huntsman's visits to the hospital were a drama also played out on Facebook, evidenced by,

Keith Huntsman is at The Jackson Memorial Hospital.

18 February at 13:00 · Miami ·

"Wife taken in by ambulance"

The inevitable hand wringing comments followed along the lines of how concerned everyone was and that they hoped Mrs H would be ok. Keith had liked all the comments and thanked the individual for their kind thoughts.

Phillip had been slightly surprised at Keith's comment,

"Just trying to find her now"

which was posted in response to Pat Kilty's,

"What ward is she in?"

Phillip had kneaded the vein in his temple when he read this. Keith had found out his wife had been taken into hospital via ambulance and one of his first actions was to post this on Facebook and respond to any feedback. Phillip's hand scratched at his chin, surely this could not be the actions of a person in control of his senses.

Seventy or so comments followed bearing the same message of concern. Phillip was convinced that Julie was not in a critical condition because that surely would have necessitated full attention to her welfare than interaction with the distant users of social media.

The answer to the severity of Julie's illness came,

"Hello friends, just back from hospital.
Julie has been kept in tonight and probably has an infection of some sort, must have been the prawns she had last night. Doctors unclear

90

as of type yet. The poor girl has certainly gone through the grinder these last 11 months. Thank you from both of us for your kind words and support."

A series of heart emojis followed.

Around 100 comments followed after this, wishing Julie and Keith well. Phillip could imagine Keith and his wife sitting in the hospital, drinking a mini white chocolate mocha frappucino and latte with turmeric, going through the buzz that had been created by this routine incident...

Phillip was under no illusions without a doubt these were a couple truly at one, encapsulated in Julies birthday message to Keith,

"Wishing my amazing husband Keith Huntsman
A fantabulous birthday
I couldn't love you any more
But I can and it seems I do every day
Thank you darling for everything"

This was followed by a post from one of their three daughters,

"A long time ago, a woman stood alone with her 2 children, she did the odd jobs and had a truly wonderful family that helped and made sure we never went without.

It was us 3 verse the world, but also knew there was a massive hole in all our hearts, we saw other families and looked upon with subtle heartache, that deep down we longed for an extra member in our family, we longed for a daddy and a husband.

Well mummy Julie Huntsman did kiss a few frogs but then found someone who was completely different.
He made her laugh and knew from day one that she come with 2 little troops behind her, we was and always will be a team she told this man.....
Charlotte Huntsman and I instantly fell in love with this man, although we had a hero our grandad but something was different about this other man.

He made us laugh and made mummy really laugh, and that was a lottery win within itself.
As the years went by not only did we gain a daddy we gained a new

born little sister Britney Huntsman.

A marriage proposal came, a magical wedding came after as well. This man out up with some our stroppy teenage years, cuddled us when sad, made us laugh.

He walked me down the isle to the man of my dreams Sean Knott, gave the father of the bride speech, had a dance with me, told me he was proud of me.

He become one of the world's best grandads too, James idolizes him and even holds a Millwall flag for a pic lol.

To the man that changed our world
Happy Birthday to Our Daddy and Granda.
Thank you for everything you do and more, our father and daughter adventure still isn't over and cannot wait for more memories to be made and laugh about.

You really are our hero. Love you you so much xxx"

This post made Phillip realise that the two of the girls were not Keith's by birth but by marriage. Not that he cared, he responded to Keith's message,

"Hi Keith, how's life in Miami. Definitely not going to be able to meet up with you because I have daily training to deliver and each night I have to prepare reports and do an analysis for the next day. PriZSolutions hasn't changed as a company, dedicated and proper slave drivers now lol"

As Phillip stepped out of the shower he glanced at his laptop and saw that he had a message. Drying off his hands he read the incoming missive, it was from Keith,

"Hey Daddyo what a shame we can't hook up. We've just moved into a new place and its only 20 minutes from your hotel. Wifey is over at bambino number two Grandbubba sitting and I am here alone, drinking a 30 year mature bottle of bourbon. I might have a swim later, we have a 50 meter pool or go to the games room and shoot some pool ha ha. Are you still useless with a cue lol. Julie cant be bothered to cook these days and the Latina housekeeper has just left and made me the some sweet potato mash with greens and the tenderest piece of lamb this side of DIxy I paid $40 bucks for it so I guess it is going to be as easy to eat as one of those wafers the catholics suck. Heres my address and my number every night is a party at Gazza's night. Toodlepiperoony"

As Phillip reached for his roll-on something shiny caught his eye in a half opened drawer where he had stowed his socks and pants. At first he thought it was a coin or a part of a belt but on investigation seen that it was Mathers's knife. The blade was quite thick and its point was murderously sharp. The name of the manufacturer was written on the blade just below where silver met the wooden handle. He wasn't sure why he did but he did. Phillip took his reading glasses from their case and looked at the name on the blade. It said Huntsman in small capital letters.

What is it about Miami and coincidental names Phillip thought 15 minutes later when he had dressed and was ready to eat. He had the knife in his inside jacket pocket. Just in case.

When Keith Huntsman was found by Albera, the Puerto Rican housemaid, he wasn't completely naked as he was the first morning that Julie was away. Erection in his hand looking at Albera with eyes that betrayed the previous night had was alcohol fuelled. He was asking whether she wanted to earn herself some extra housekeeping. Mortified at his request and in her broken English she had gesticulated at her wedding band and said repeatedly, "No Signor Huntsman, no es posseebley." Keith had followed her round the large house, swollen member in his hand, tugging at it furiously until he had ejaculated.

This time Keith was not completely naked but totally dead. His throat had been cut and he lay by the pool, half in and half out of one of the expensive deck chairs now ruined by the blood that had gushed from his neck to lay between his legs. Once more Keith had emptied his load in front of his housekeeper but this was red and not a foamy off-white.

The police that investigated the murder might have considered Phillip a suspect, given the Facebook messages that had been sent out that previous night but a neighbour had reported seeing a young mixed race man acting suspiciously that evening. When the police pulled in Rodney Braithwaite, the brown skinned, a petty thief was in possession of a sharp knife.

Earlier that day Rodney had been detained briefly and let off with a caution by the security guard at Penneys for stealing razors. With fatal crime investigation and solution at an all-time low and Rodney without a watertight alibi, the mistakes of Brenton Butler's trumped up charge by Miami's finest were again repeated.

Despite the Huntsman house not being burgled. The doors leading out to the garden were open, there was every opportunity for the killer to ransack it. Although Rodney had an approximate four minute window to get in and out of the house but did not do so. His 27 year old girlfriend Sholanda was deemed not a reliable source, when she claimed Rodney had been with her for most of the evening except for the twenty minutes he when he went out on his push bike to get pizza. Sholanda had had a brush with the law when she was 18 as her brother was involved in a fist fight and she had whaled in with some blows of her own. She was now a very reliable English teacher at the local High School. Rodney had a driving license but no car but was seen 45 minutes before the estimated time of the death in the pizza house and would have needed 90 minutes to drive to the Huntsman's.

The killer was left handed and Rodney was right handed and had eight stiches in that right hand where he had cut himself in a fit of pique whilst arguing with Sholanda. The knife Rodney had had a one inch wide blade and bereft of blood stains as opposed to the two inch wide blade that severed Keith's windpipe. Despite all evidence pointing to Rodney Brathwaite not being the killer after a week of questioning he was charged with the murder and it would months of incarceration awaiting trial before the truth come out.

Keri Young

Phillip sat opposite his mother and took another bite out of his steak. It was one of Waitrose's 30 day matured cuts of sirloin.

"I really missed you while you were away," Christine said.

"This is really good steak Mum," Phillip replied.

"Whenever you go away I always cook you a steak as your return meal."

Christine had never cooked Phillip a steak on his return from anywhere but she had always told him how his father, on his return from a company trip that extended to an overnight stay would breezily say,

"The food at the hotel was awful. You are the only person who can cook for me. Now have you got me a nice steak my dear wife?"

It became a standard joke between Oliver and Christine and was one of the few times since their daughter had been killed that they were able to share a time of merriment. Christine, because she needed to feel her husband needed her and Oliver, for a peaceful life.

"I bet the food in your hotel wasn't up to scratch again. Poor service, got the wrong order, tepid meat, under or overcooked vegetables. Not like what you get at home with everything piping hot, all the trimmings and your home comforts." Christine said.

Now, Christine looked at her son coquettishly, and ran her tongue around her lips, cherry red and full which gave her the look like one of the bottom end Eastern European girls who now plied their trade between Manor Park and Ilford in the small hours.

Phillip glared at his mother. If the steak wasn't so tender, the chips so fat and crispy courtesy of the Delonghi Multifry Cooker, the mushrooms so perfectly cut and fried and the blue stilton sauce immaculately flavoured and presented he would have got up and left the table. As it was he decided to stay and humour the senile old bat.

"How did you know?" he asked. "If I was served food like this every day I wouldn't have come home. This is absolutely delicious Mother."

"The way to a man's heart is through his stomach."

"Well you are the love of my life, Mother." Phillip gushed but kept his eyes firmly on his plate. Better his Mother was kept in a good mood, she might less inclined to antagonise him.

"I had my hair done on Tuesday, Keri asked when you were coming in?"

"I'll probably go in Monday morning, in a couple of weeks, I have a day off."

"You better book an appointment you know she only works till 2 on a Monday. Why book Monday you could go in the evening anytime?"

"It gets too busy in the evening and I much rather go in on a Monday morning when there are less people around."

"I don't know why you don't go to the barber it must be much cheaper. I bet you only go there so you can dig your elbows into her privates. Typical man. Copping a feel like a lusty sailor. Disgusting. They should bring back the stocks."

Phillip ignored his mother's jibe.

"It's much better at the salon, much more organised and that barber insisted on trimming my hairline with a dirty razor. I kept telling him I was getting a rash. "

"You just want to eye up those young girls you old fox, there's life in the young vixen you have here you know Oliver."

Phillip winced visibly, and sighed. His mother referring to him by his father's name was becoming more commonplace. That was bad enough without the innuendo. Philip sighed again, then took in a deep breath as if trying to calm himself but only succeeded in taking a mouthful of his mother's Chanel No 5 and felt its fragrance cloying his nostrils. Christine smiled. She knew she was getting under his skin. She continued,

"I just don't know why to go all the way to Wanstead when you can get a perfectly good and cheaper haircut round the corner."

"Why do you go all the way to Wanstead, I am sure there are salons closer by for you too."

"Yes but you know I often go and see meet some of the ladies on my Facebook group. We love Wanstead, it's become so chic and becoming quite gentrified, not like here. No-one with any class apart from Alice. I don't know why I put up with it."

As Phillip wiped the last remnants of sauce with his final chip he heard Christine's chair scrape against the flooring as she stood up. The sound was as high pitched as the cry of a baby seagull and it cut through him. He knew his mother had done this on purpose.

"I've made you're favourite for dessert"

There was a pause for dramatic effect

"Steamed rhubarb and custard."

Christine watched him her eyes narrowed because she hoped he would break and he would acknowledge that she had been having a conversation with Oliver for the last hour.

"Mother. I am not your husband you crazy old woman you need to get to the doctors before I have you put in a home. I detest rhubarb."

Phillip stood up, he was sated and his normal self-control had gone as the last morsel from his plate slipped down into his stomach and ire simultaneously rose like a fairground bell.

Phillip left the kitchen his heavy footfall and muttering under his breath highlighted his discontent. Christine calmly went round the table and picked up his plate. She was laughing, not inside but audibly. She just could not keep it in as the door had slammed shut. She laughed so much her ample belly started to wobble and she felt herself getting a stitch. She placed her hands on her hips and could all but keep herself from collapsing in a heap on the floor. Tears welled in her eyes, her plan was working. She was going to send him mad and he would leave her in peace so that she didn't have to look at him anymore and see his sister's eyes. Eyes that had haunted her every day for the past 40 odd years.

While the kitchen door had slammed it did not catch so remained slightly ajar. As he walked toward the stair Phillip heard a sound coming from the kitchen that sounded like the gurgle of a drain. It was only when he stood stock still that he realised it was the sound of his mother's laughter. It took a second or two for him to realise that she was laughing uncontrollably and a further second or two to realise what she was laughing at. She was intentionally engineering these situations. He smiled to himself. So that was her game, she was enjoying annoying him. Whether it was his mother's insecurity, bullying or some other dastardly plan he wasn't sure. It didn't matter he thought. He was going to put an end to it. He who laughs last laughs longest he said to himself as he mounted the stairs stealthily and planned what to do next.

At 10.10 on the appointed Monday morning Phillip sat in Keri Young's chair at Gaston and Browns hairdressers on Wanstead High Street. He had been there since 09:40. Why he turned up early was beyond him because nine times out of 10 Keri was late. Sometimes only by five minutes, once by 45. She always had a different excuse. The car wouldn't start, the traffic was bad, one of her parents wasn't well, her appointment application hadn't shown she had someone in, she thought he had cancelled.

The actual reason for Keri's tardiness was that whatever time she set her alarm for she snoozed for an hour until it no longer sounded, then fell into a sleep until instinct or the sound of traffic, voices or birdsong woke her up. Amongst her colleagues it was a source of amusement and banter. For clients it was less of a joke and they would generally ensure they booked with her after 11.00am as she was more likely to make that time. Her lack of ability to get to her job on time was offset by the fact she was an exceptional hairdresser. A client need only come in with a photo or an idea and Keri would deliver the cut with as much precision as a robot driven laser.

Whilst delivering a head-turning cut Keri had the ability to talk about any subject however banal. Her listening skills were as finally honed as her hairdressing and she could offer an opinion that would often lack rationality but be high in conviction. Her clients loved tell the latest dramas in their lives or of the rich and famous. A situation between warring couples could be dissected and analysed and Keri could usually come up with a solution, however random.

Born and named Kerry Young she insisted her name was spelt Keri as this made her feel this gave her relatively common name a more unique twist. It was also generally fashionable for anyone with a name ending in a "y" to replace this with an "i", hence Becky/Beci, Kerry/Keri and Nicky/Niki, Terry, Teri Not having the capacity, desire or knowledge to make the change by deed poll, Keri with an 'i' was how she signed up to social media.

Keri was five foot five inches tall, a size 10. Dressed in designer jeans, shirts and shoes for work and the same socially. Her father was Iranian, her mother English and she had taken on the paternal dark hair and eyes as well as flawless skin that had a hue of light mahogany and was a face that was as striking as Selma Kayak's.

At Wanstead High School she had been nicknamed KY after the lubricant but she took that in good humour insisted that a good looking man made her moist and she didn't need any such assistance. Being 12 at the time was a slight concern for anyone more mature who was within earshot. Keri's crowd were mostly sexually active by the time they were 13 and innuendo and was standard banter.

Keri was Mark Zuckerberg's dream user. As she was an avid fan of reality TV, documentaries, the national news or reading a newspaper were strictly off limits. Strictly Come Dancing was on limits, as was Celebrity Big Brother, Big Brother, I'm A Celebrity, Blind Date, Don't Tell the Bride, Gypsy Anything, Real Housewives of Chelsea, Beverley Hills and Cheshire.

These programmes generated comment on Facebook and other social media and Keri would, whilst watching use her smartphone to make comments as each program was broadcast.

Keri was a selfie addict, she created an album with that name and unashamedly posted pictures of her pouting like a freshly caught trout, tongue out like a panting grouper and with her middle fingers lowered, outer raised as if she were a white Lil Kim but looking more like a complete buffoon. Selfies with any minor celebrity she might encounter plus any non-celebrity, the postman, the dustbin man, the girl at the checkout of Morrisons, the doorman at Faces nightclub and the toilet attendant at the same. At one stage her friends stopped saying they were having a selfie but they were having a Keri. The selfie stick was made for her and was as much a part of her every day kit which did not include her knickers as she had a penchant not to wear any.

Keri relied on Facebook for news and as she was convinced that all the articles on this were genuinely true she shared any post that said a company was giving away free flights, free money, free merchandise, free tickets and free holidays. If she received a post that said share with ten friends to get good luck she immediately did. The most tenuous positive would validate her actions. A decent tip, not getting the wrong dish when ordering a meal, getting home without there being a traffic jam, remembering to tape Strictly Come Dancing. Keri believed in fairies, ghosts, the preaching of shaman, Jesus, Duppy, leprechauns, astrology and the powers of holistic therapy.

Keri would instantly share if there was a post to say a husband, wife, child or pet had gone missing.

Where will you live in five years' time? What will you look like on Facebook in five years' time? What would your name be if you were a cat? Which celebrity should be your spouse?

All these Keri bought into because she was a social media junkie.

For every challenge she committed to, she threw herself in wholeheartedly. Her donation jar was always rattling under the noses of her clients. Cancer, animal, children and victim abuse charities received numerous cheques from her, a quality she had inherited from her mother who had over twenty years raised £117,000 for the hospice that cared for her cancer stricken father whilst he received respite.

Keri had done the ice bucket challenge and the press-up challenge. She signed up and took part in Sleep Walk, Pyjama walk and Race for Life. She set up a birthday fundraiser that enabled her to denote £213.47 to the Brain Tumour Charity.

 Phillip, not being of a charitable nature, was irritated by the frequent Facebook requests for a visit to one of Keri's Justgiving links but was more irritated by her posts asking what time Primark or Next or Iceland or the swimming baths opened. Knowing how easy women could switch Phillip was desperate to tell Keri not to ask whether New Look had a sale on but to simply google or visit the appropriate official website.

Phillip had lost count of the times, embarrassingly, he had watched one of Keri's video shares which were headlined with:

"Funniest things ever". "This will make you cry with laughter." "Watch what happens when this girl sees what her boyfriend has done" or "This is absolutely amazing."

On one of Phillips Facebook stalking evenings he went through a string of Keri's posts, the first was a video and Keri had added the comment,

"OMG what a horrendous woman"

Phillip played the video, not expecting anything great but willing to be surprised. The scene was set in a bookstore,

Assistant: Paul Sheldon? I am not familiar with that author
Chubby Lady: He wrote the Misery books
Assistant: Let me see if I can find it on our system
Chubby Lady: Yep, you better
Assistant: Alright, give me one second, let me look on the system back here
Chubby Lady: Ok
The assistant leaves the desk to go to the computer terminal whilst the chubby lady looks at him quizzically
Chubby Lady: S-H-E-L-D-O-N. Paul, his first name
The assistant is looking on his computer terminal
Chubby Lady: Do you have it?
The assistant returns to the desk
Assistant: I have looked it up on my system unfortunately I am not coming across any, any of Paul Sheldon's book that we have here in the store. Do you want me to see if I could order one for you possibly?
Chubby Lady: You should have it here, he's very popular. Paul Sheldon
Assistant: We probably just sold…..
Chubby Lady: Misery, have you ever read the Misery novels, they are very good
Assistant: I'm not familiar with the Misery novels I'm more of a history kind of guy
Chubby Lady: How can you not know Misery you work here? How can you not know? Paul Sheldon writes the Misery novels, they're very good, I'm looking for the latest one, Misery's Child. I really need that to complete my collection and I really think you need to have that here

She raps on the desk in frustration

Assistant: I don't have that in the store. I can probably order it for you
Chubby Lady: I'm not interested in waiting. I've already waited a long
time for the paperback to come out. Mis...Paul Sheldon
She raps on the desk, harder this time
Chubby Lady: Misery, Misery's Child, Misery In France Misery
Betrayed, Misery in Love. You don't know any of these books. What
kind of cockadoody bookstore is this that you don't even know Paul
Sheldon. Paul Sheldon.....let me tell you something. I am Paul
Sheldon's number one fan. His number one fan"

Phillip paused the video and put his hands to his head. The video was
a spoof. He was a Stephen King fan enjoying numerous novels
including Misery, IT, Salems Lot, The Shining, Rita Hayworth and the
Shawshank Redemption, Cujo and many more. He recalled that the
line "I am your number one fan" was attributed to the crazy fan Annie
Wilkes in the Misery novel and that Paul Sheldon was author
character.

Paul looks at the comments made by Keri and her friends,

Sadie Ambrose:
"I think that woman needs locking up"
Keri Young:
"She is proper skank. If I was the shop assistant I would tell her to
fuck off."
Mandy Kingston:
"The shop assistant deserves a medal"
Grace Henderson:
"That woman doesn't need the book called Misery she is a misery"
Greg Vallence:
"Why don't any of the other customers go over and tell her to stop
making a scene she is an embarrassment"
Tilly Chester
"Ha ha if that fat cow came in my shop she would get chinned"

Rather than continue watching the video he scrolled further down
Keri's page.

The next post from her was:

"I never post these but it rings so true to me and many i know.
How often do you sit at home and wish someone would ring you and
suggest, well anything rather than these 4 walls? How many of you
have had a night out planned, or arranged coffee with friends and
suddenly "these 4 walls" seem the only safe haven because it's the
only place you don't have to pretend you are ok, so you cancel. Or
when you are invited out you tell them how terribly sorry you are but
you're already booked up that weekend, when you are actually just
really busy holding it together in your safe box. And so the first
problem starts, all by itself. People stop asking you and the isolation
that at first wasn't true becomes your only truth.
Please don't give up on your friends. Ring them, go round, even when
they don't want you to. Because they really do they just don't know
how to say it.

Everyone says: "If you need anything, don't hesitate. I'll be there for
you ".

I'm going to make a bet, without being pessimistic, that out of my
Facebook friends that less than 5 will take the time to put this on their
wall to help raise awareness of and for those who have mental health
difficulties. You just have to copy it from my wall and paste it to yours
(hold down on my post and you will be given the option to copy... then
go to your status and hold down to paste).

Who will be my 5 I wonder?

Mental Health Awareness"

Within 17 minutes of this post three Facebook friends had
commented,

"Done"

The fourth post was from Mandy Kingston and read,

"What friends? I don't have any! Worked in same place as my
ex...when we divorced he stayed in the office and I had the kids to
care for....lost all my friends back then - they remained friends with
him through work, not me.. My 4 walls are my sanctuary AND my
prison, such is life! Xx"

Phillip was surprised that Mandy received no responses to her post
therefore he clicked on her name to see what her activity was like. He

was surprised to discover she either had a reasonable level of security or little activity because he could not access any of her posts. He went back to Keri's wall and the next item,

She had posted a video with the comment

"Watch this, I know you'll love it, made me cry xxxx"

The comment under video was:

"Moms across the world are labelling this song as the best song ever. Listen for yourself."

Phillip listened to 20 seconds out of 3 minutes of a mush video that was about a mother and her children and moved on.

Keri postings about going for a walk and what she was having for dinner, pictures of her with her seemingly endless number of nieces and nephews, Phillip counted 17 leaving him was numb with boredom. He ploughed on regardless.

Phillip sat through the least funny, most cringe worthy, hardly worth any effort, bottom of the amazing list cinematography. Like a heroin addict in rehab with his dealer friend paying a visit Phillip would often find himself looking the videos and the following stream. This obsession with Facebook would eat away up to six hours that could have been better spent. After each session Phillip would rue what he had done and the time he would never get back.

Phillip became almost obsessed with Keri's postings.

He started at the top again and reviewed Keri's activity again. He created a word document and named it FacebookCrap_KeriVideos.

He created a four column table and in the first row first column he input the date and time of the first video shared 27 January 10:38. In the next column he put the title of the video

 "If dogs could talk"

In the next, Keri's comment,

"Byrony Fraser I nearly cried"

The only thing that was flooded about Byrony's posts were the number of emojis, smiling or laughing faces. About 60 of them.

In the next column he put down the number of views,

22.687,331

In the next column he copied and pasted the comments,

"Byrony Fraser That is hilarious
Keri Young I can't stop watching it xx"

He did this with the next,

Keri Young shared It's Gone Viral's video.

Genna Martins hilarious

Official List of worst drivers

11.451,869 Views

Most people would think this was behaviour one might think would be confined those on the autistic spectrum. To Phillip he was being normal. The accompanying video was a list of fifteen names in white letters with black background, snowfall was the only animation. The names were a standard set and oddly enough Phillip was not surprised that his name did not appear,

James, Jacob, Zack, Nick, Chris, Noah, Emily, Ryan, Ellie, Josh, Dan, Lauren, Hannah, Sarah, Alex, Nathan, Genna, Nicole

Genna Martins commented,

"why have you tagged me I cant drive! LMAO"

Phillip's didn't have to wonder why Keri activity got under his skin. She used Facebook like a diary and he wasn't interested but it was there, in his face and he couldn't miss it when he went on line.

The,

"Good morning Facebookers"

"Goodnight Facebook friends"

had stopped after 4 months.

What Phillip hoped would stop were the details and pictures of at least one meal per day. Every course at a restaurant both hers and whoever accompanied her would be posted. Every shopping trip, even if it was a supermarket was noted. Keri had once posted that she had nicked her leg while shaving and almost prompted Phillip to reply saying if only it was the finger she used for typing or her carotid artery but he didn't want to upset her because, she was innocent enough in her naivety and she cut his hair so well.

"Oh my god Phil" Keri exclaimed as she put the protective bib around his shoulders to stop his hair falling down his collar.

"What is it?" Phillip asked, he was quite alarmed because looking at Keri in the mirror of the hairdressing salon, even though she boasted an all year round tan, she was quite ashen.

"McDonalds are injecting their burgers with ammonia, that's disgusting."

"that might be an old post I think McDonalds have come out with a statement saying it is untrue, didn't you once tell me that Kentucky were using artificial chickens?" he added light heartedly.

"McDonalds are bound to say it's not true and I don't know how Kentucky can sell that much chicken and it all be real meat." Keri said petulantly. "It's like the Chinese restaurants serving us cats and dogs. They aren't going to put special fried Persian or sweet and sour cockapoo on the menu are they?" she added, her face set with as intelligent a look as she could muster.

Phillip frowned, he didn't want to upset Keri because he didn't want her going onto Facebook and being tagged in a post detailing the conversation so he changed the subject.

106

"Talking of food I saw your pictures about you eating at the Wagamuma's in Stratford yesterday, it looked really nice."

Keri's countenance changed, she loved having a post of hers noted and the more comments and likes the better, a verbal ratification was almost as good.

"It was lush Phil I had chicken steamed gyoza and lollipop prawn kushiyaki to start, seafood ramen for main and white chocolate ginger cheesecake for dessert it was proper lushmans"

Phillip was on the verge of saying politely he knew what she had when Keri held her fore-finger up to signify she hadn't finished speaking.

"Come on Edgeways" she said "I can't get a word in edgeways with you can I?" she laughed.

"Linzi is a veggie so she shared my lollipop prawns then she had teriyaki salmon soba and finished off with banana katsu. I can't remember what Verity had. Hang on."

She went to her phone and began scrolling through her Facebook posts for the entry from the restaurant visit.

Phillip wished he hadn't asked but he knew Keri was in full flow and nothing was going to make her stop until she had done.

"Oh yeah," she said, "Verity had a pad Thai salad then grilled duck donburi. She wasn't going to have a dessert because she's been on a diet for her wedding but when she saw ours she just couldn't keep her gob shut and ordered a chocolate and schichimi ice cream. Can you believe it?"

Phillip couldn't believe Keri was accusing someone of not being able to keep their gobs shut. She still hadn't finished telling him what he knew because it was all been posted.

"We started off on beers and we had a couple of Asahi's. Verity was drinking water because of her diet and then as me and Linz had two each then she said bugger that I am having one and she ordered a large bottle, and we was just drinking regulars so we changed our order to large ones too, so we have two of those each. Then Verity said that it was too much liquid so then we went on to the wine and then me and Linz fell out a bit because me and Verity like Pinot and Linz likes Sauvignon and wouldn't share one bottle so we bought one of each and then Linz wouldn't let Verity have any of hers and wanted to drink her bottle herself. How bad is that? Anyway we had words and Linz got in a right strop threw down a twenty pound note and walked off. Unbelievable."

Phillip was trying to switch off. He didn't find gossip too interesting because Ricki Finn was one of the worst offenders of this and two faced people were unattractive. It was difficult to ignore Keri because she was standing in front of him with her hands on her hips and he knew that changing the subject was not an option. During her rant she had continued cutting his hair and it was as ever, cut to perfection. The flyaway bits and straggly ends were now the same length where required and tapered to meet his ears at the optimum angle

Phillip forearms usual starting position for his haircut was the armrest on his seat but as soon as Keri pressed her pubis onto one of his elbows he would move his arms within the boundary of the chair. He wasn't sure why he did this every time he had his haircut because he always thought Keri was capable of cutting his hair without pressing against him but he did feel a tingle as he pictured what lay on the other side of her clothing. He was glad that he didn't come into the salon with his mother.

His mop of unruly grey flecked locks were now looking almost George Clooney like in sophistication and style.

Phillip smiled and said "Brilliant Keri."

His heart sunk when Keri replied "Almost done."

She meant almost done with his head and his ears.

"Me and Verity had a right laugh though, we went through Linzi's Facebook posts about when she went to the Croatia house and dance music festival. I know you should be able to wear what you want abroad but the size of her arse, there is no way she should have been wearing jean shorts and a crop top. Talk about a beached whale. Look at this."

Keri picked up her phone again and studiously went through it until she came to the offending Facebook photographs. Once found she thrust the phone in Phillip's face.

He assumed that her friend Linzi was the larger of the two girls in the picture. Whilst one had a figure you normally only see in a lap dancing club or pole dancing the other girl was the polar opposite. Good figure girl had pneumatic breasts, a waif like waist and, what Christine would call, child bearing hips. She had pouting lips and a face that was completely unlined even with a posed frown. Botox filled Phillip assumed.   She wore denim hot pants and a tee shirt knotted just above the navel and nothing else. Obviously no bra and no footwear on a beach, she could have just walked off the set of Love Island. There were several lads in view, either looking on slavering or attempting to photobomb.

Linzi's shorts looked shorter than they probably were because they were shadowed by her ample stomach. At the legs, her flesh bulged out copiously and were dimpled with cellulite. Unlike her companion, her inability to tan did her no favours. Her large, pear shaped breasts were covered hammock-like by a buttoned shirt that was also knotted midriff. The buttons of the shirt were largely undone therefore there was as much flesh on display at both top and bottom.

Linzi's obvious love of food was to be seen in her face too. Porky pig eyes and full round cheeks. Having a snout of a nose was not ideal, neither was the fact that out of her thick lips protruded a cigarette that hung down like a trail of saliva from a camel's mouth.

Phillip looked at the accompanying post the picture:

"Loopy Linzi is having fun with Candy Evans at Ultra Europe"

Phillip could hardly believe that Linzi had actually posted this herself. Keri gave him her phone and said nonchalantly, "Go through them all."

Feeling obligated yet slightly guilty, Phillip did so and found that that first picture was the tamest, as there were many where the two girls wore clothes with less material and were in various stages of intoxication. Selfies grabbing each other's breasts and more with lads grabbing at them or leering at the camera. Each girl seemed to take delight in taking a picture of the other passed out on the beach or at the festival or on a bed. Legs akimbo, askew or simply very wide open. Phillip wondered whether these girls had no moral compass but decided against adding fuel to the fire by asking Keri.

Intermittently, as Phillip scrolled through the pictures, Keri would sigh heavily or tut and mutter "Drunken messes."

Phillip would look at her in the mirror and Keri would look at him with pursed lips and roll her eyes to further display her disgust. He had been here before and knew that Keri needed to vent her spleen or he would find she was going to be very busy when he came to suggest a date for his next cut.

"Linzi is a right pikey and her sister, Shelley is a fucking psycho and her Mum was sleeping with some bloke called Edgeways Callaghan. "

"What?"

"Yeah she went to Liverpool for a weekend with Shelley and they had an argument and her sister text Calvin."

"Who is Calvin?"

"He is Linzi's fiancé."

"What did Linzi tell Calvin?"

"That she beat her up, look."

Keri took the phone from Phillip and spent a couple of minutes looking for something which she found and exclaimed,

 "Here it is."

She thrust the phone at Phillip again and he read the message:

"You better reign your missus in!! She's wrecked the whole weekend because as per usual she can't handle her drink!! And before she tells

110

you I smacked her in the mouth that's bollocks!! She was saying evil things so I went for her and she hit back and I knocked my head back hard and split her lip!!

"She can't spell rein" Phillip said.

"What?"

"Nothing. Phillip decided that a lesson in spelling was as inappropriate as the message he had just read. He continued, "So, Linzi's sister attacked her and then told Linzi's husband to be. How comes you have the text?"

"Calvin sent it to Linzi the next day and said "Did she have a fat lip" and Linzi just said her sister was drunk and it was all a misunderstanding. Personally I think there are some psychotherapy issues there."

"Psychological?" Phillip said, but Keri wasn't listening.

"The worse thing about Linzi is her posts are so boring she sends me to sleep. Who give a shit about her wedding plans? Why doesn't she does get hitched to that boring fat dick Calvin, piss off to a boring married life and do everyone a favour. Sometimes she makes me want to vomit she is such a fat, dull twat, excuse my French. I look at some of her updates and I want to slit my throat."

Phillip found her use of "excuse my French," quite bizarre and wondered if she realised that her written English was usually so poor comprehension of any other language would be as likely as Nigel Farage re-joining UKIP and becoming the next Prime Minister. Brexit, Trump, Leicester City. Stranger things could happen.

Keri made a dramatic movement with her hand as she gesticulated throat cutting and then perhaps pummelling the falling head onto the ground which meant she knocked her trolley full of hairdressing utensils to the ground. The two other girls in the salon looked up but didn't comment, as Keri went to bend to right the trolley, her phone rang.

"Oh hi Linz my lovely," she said breezily, "how are you Hon, how's the wedding preps going. Can't wait for the hen you're going to look lush in that cat suit."

Phillip got up and started to pick up the utensils, he knew if he didn't he might end up staying longer than the time the call would take. As he scooped up the last perming roller he saw that Keri's one of styling scissors remained. It was razor sharp and it had long blades that glistened with intent. As quick as a flash, for why he didn't know, Phillip scooped it up and put in in his waistband making sure it was positioned so as not to cause him any harm.

Phillip stood up and looked at Keri, she had was in animated conversation with Linzi. They were talking about yesterday's meal. Keri repeated the same conversation she had just had with Phillip, saying how lush each dish was only this time she would pause, obviously allowing Linzi to reciprocate by describing every morsel she had eaten.

Added to the conversation was some bitching about "the psycho chavs on the next table."

Each time the chavs were mentioned Linzi must have said something amusing as Keri would throw her head back and roar with laughter, shrieking, "Oh Linz what you like."

To Phillip she said, "Linz has just said the three girls on the next table were so fat they made her look like Mo Farah."

To Phil she mouthed "More like Mo out of EastEnders"

To the phone she said "I've got Phil in, you know, that one I told you about" She listened briefly and then said "Yeah him."

Phillip looked at her quizzically, wondering what headnote she had given her friend of him but Keli was oblivious to his gaze instead she with the phone now perched between her neck and shoulder she began to rub gel into his hair, which she had barely touched for the last 10 minutes.

Although it would have been easier for her to stand in most places and apply the walnut and mango pomade to his right temple instead she stood by his left shoulder and pulled his head toward her so that it collided with her chest.

She shrieked, Phillip tried to straighten his head but she held it firm. To the phone she said,

"I've just had my boobs butted by Phil Linz, That's cheered him up, think I might get a bigger tip."

Even with the phone cushioned as it was, Phillip could hear Linzi shrieking on the line. What she said was inaudible but Phillip got the gist when Keri said,

"No that's about as happy an ending as it is going to be Hon." She laughed and said, "Let me ring you back in a minute babe I'm going to make Phillip a little lighter."

After the next lewd comment from her friend she said, "No his wallets the only thing that will be empty unless he is going straight into the gents for a self-service."

More laughter both sides of the line and Keri cut the connection.

She looked at Phillip and said venomously,

"She is such a bitch."

Phillip looked at her, probably longer than he should have because she raised an eyebrow but she smiled and her teeth, that were perfectly straight and stunningly white dazzled and delighted him.

"How could anyone who is so physically beautiful be as shallow inside as a pool of rat's piss? £26 isn't it?"

Phillip only said the last sentence out loud. He returned her smile.

"Yeah Phil, I won't charge you for touching me up." Keri responded.

He felt himself redden but he pulled his roll of notes from his pocket and peeled off some tens and fives.

"Wow, look at that wad." Keri teased.

Phillip gave her two tens and three fives. He did think £30 was sufficient, 12% tip extra, but a four pound tip might be frowned upon and he didn't want to look mean by adding a pound to £30 for a fiver tip.

"Thanks Phil," Keri said, "see you next month?"

She had turned her back to him so Phillip emitted a humming yes and left the shop.

When Phillip got home he read Keri's latest post on Facebook which was to follow up a post that had been put on her wall by Linzi that read,

"You're getting the FB algorithm post from me too - but just take a sec and put anything in the comments!
I don't want FB to shut you out of my news feed, so please leave a comment to let the bot know you want me to read your posts. Thanks!
Here's the explanation: The FB News Feed now shows only posts from the same few people, about 25, and repeatedly the same, because Facebook has a new algorithm. Their system chooses the people to read one's posts. However, I would like to choose for myself. Therefore, I'm asking you a favor - if you read this message leave me a quick comment, a "hello", a sticker, a dopey GIF, a snarky barb, whatever you want, so you'll appear in my news feed.
Copy and paste on your wall so you can have more interaction with all your contacts and bypass "the system.""

Keri had typed,

 "Love U babe"

on Linzi's wall, then she copied the paste and posted it on the walls of 20 of her Facebook friends, including Phillip who was on her mind because as she wrote Love U babe on Linzi's wall she was thinking "Fat dull twat."

She then responded to Marla Fishers,

"Could one friend please copy and repost? I am trying to demonstrate that someone is always listening."

#SuicideAwareness

Sending a,

"Listening Marla Honeybun"

She wished her 14 year old cousin a happy birthday with the post,

"Happy Birthday Charlotte. I literally caaaaant believe your 14. It seems like yesterday when you was a likkle bubba. Now your 14! I caaaaaaant believe it."

Phillip was seething. He didn't know why he was seething. Probably because Keri was such an idiot. Apart from being good at cutting hair, and there were probably a lot more like her, she was a complete waste of space.

Keri didn't see Phillip the next month as she had planned. She didn't see anyone she knew. She was walking along phone held in front of her looking at a video of a talking boxer dog agonising over the diet its owner had put it on. She didn't see the pregnant woman she bumped into, so engrossed was she in the video. She did manage to tell the startled lady to mind where she was going. She didn't see that the pedestrian lights were red as she stepped into the road but she did see the startled old elderly drivers face as she told him to, "Slow the fuck down you dangerous cunt." As she got within 500 yards of her flat she didn't see the person who stepped out of the shadows on that Thursday night. It was had been an unusually late 10.00pm finish due to her having a high tipping walk in. It was August, moon free, the night was dark, like a vampire's disposition. The street was made darker because the local council were cost cutting, minimising the number of street lights that were illuminated so that the town hall executives could get a 7% pay rise. The open ground common unlit on one side of street gave the scene an air of a Bram Stoker novel.

Keri was knocked toward the floor by a blow to the head. Her senses scrambled she raised one arm instinctively but this was broken by the next blow and before she had the chance to scream a third blow reduced her to an unconscious state. Four or five more blows followed and then the killer pulled her from a kneeling position, head bowed as if in supplication, so that she lay bleeding with her face upward. A pair of scissors were thrust into one of her eyes. The killer took Keri's handbag, stuffed it into a rucksack and sauntered off.

Keri Young remained there until a dog sniffed at her cold body 45 minutes later and barked excitedly until the owner came closer and the 50 year old man, looked down on the battered and bloody mis-shapen head with scissor handles still showing, and, having recently eaten a late supper promptly retched and brought it back up.

David Thompson

Phillip was looking for a hammer in the cupboard under the stairs. Normally his toolbox was immediately in front of him but was now further down the space and he had to go into the alcove to retrieve it. As he bent down he heard his mother come out of the kitchen, and slam the cupboard door shut. He quickly exclaimed "What the!"

He heard the kitchen door slam and realised his mother had, as if powered by a Formula One engine, returned to the kitchen as quickly as Lewis Hamilton on an opening lap

Muuuuuum!" Phillip shouted.

He heard the sound of the Dyson and knew that his voice would not be heard because even without the hum of her favourite contraption her hearing seemed to filter out the sound of his voice at the most inopportune times. .

He smiled to himself, however. He could quite easily kick down the cupboard door from the inside but he knew that it would be he who would have to replace the catch. The door was quite thin and it was likely that the wood would splinter if he did put his shoulder to it and then he would be faced with a bigger job than he would like.

Running the Dyson over the kitchen floor was not going to take long and Phillip thought that sitting on a toolbox under the stairs for five minutes would not be the most onerous activity he could face today. He hadn't had dinner yet so that ordeal was before him. He had his phone, he could while away the time checking on Facebook updates.

David Thompson, one of the Beal School old boys, had burnt his hand and posted 5 pictures of it with the comment

"Well that's Sunday evening I want to forget in a hurry. Just over 4 hours in A&E, after an accident in the kitchen, resulting in a badly burnt right hand. Big thank you to Rosie Watson and Gavin Watson and the lovely nurse for looking after me xxxxxxxx"

There were 22 emoji's and 68 comments.

Phillip looked at the pictures of David's burnt hand. David was afro-Caribbean and had golden brown skin, even so the injury looked like a bad case of sunburn. There were a couple of blisters on two fingers and the back of David's palm.

Reading through some of the comments, Phillip wondered whether the photographs were of David's left hand and the right one had had to be amputated.

Pru Carragher
"Oh my god are you ok"

Desmond Valentine
"Ouch Davey that looks sore"

Angela Wiggins
"Omg could have been worse hope your ok darlings"

Maureen Phillips
"wishing you better Dave, hope you've got some strong painkillers, sending lots of love"

Carlton Soul
I saw in your comments you're going broomfield,I've spent a lot of time there.the burns unit is amazing !!!
Definitely the best place for treatment.
Even though that must of hurt like mad,it doesn't look too bad compared to the burns I've seen,I reckon you'll heal up really well mate

And so the comments went on. Phillip did wonder how David had managed to slightly burn his hand to produce such an outpouring of grief.

By the time he had scanned approximately the 50th comment he got the answer from one of David's responses back,

"In a nutshell, oil in the saucepan to shallow fry, next thing its on fire, cover it with wet towel, it goes out, happy days. Move it to the window to get rid of the smoke, holding the pan I removed the towel, as I did a massive fireball went up, so lucky it could have been far worse."

To Phillips untrained eye the blister looked like it needed to coating of savlon or a similar antiseptic balm rather than a journey to the hospital to take up the times of an already strained NHS.

David was another Facebook junkie who since splitting up with his wife of thirty years, Marian, had got worse. He lived in a large house in Hertfordshire having given his now ex-wife an even larger house in Chelsea as part of the divorce settlement. David and Phillip had attended Beal School together. David had always said he would join his older brother into a career in banking, and so he had. David was less than scrupulous in his financial activities but was fortunate enough to have joined Charles Stanley Investment Company when audits, regulation and checks were less stringent and was so able to skim funds from a large number of unfortunate clients.

David was, judging by his Facebook pictures, exceptionally good at making money. Once an avid Sunday footballer player he was by now heavily overweight and a lover of lunches at fancy restaurants courtesy of the clients for whom he had earned money.

David was the owner of a Bentley Continental, Range Rover Epoque, BMW X5 and an expensive Lithuanian ex pole dancing girlfriend.

David's check-ins were as mundane as the majority of Facebook regulars. If he had to work a weekend, which happened to be one Sunday in three, to prepare for the coming weeks dealing he let it be known that

"David Thompson has checked in at Charles Stanley for another bit of weekend graft."

118

He was a season ticket holder at Arsenal which meant for every home game there was a check in and a picture of the stadium and the players as they lined up. Prior to the game he had a pie and mash which meant another check in with accompanying picture. He checked in visits to the cinema, and took a picture of the opening credits, and to his local pub where he took a picture of his first and subsequent pints. He checked in when he visited his elderly mother in the home he had shipped her off to as soon as she showed signs of senility. He checked in at supermarkets, DIY stores, Oxford Street, Regent Street. He checked in at the dentists and the bank, at home in front of the telly and in the garden before mowing the lawn.

If a hitman were hired to bump off David Thompson he would not need to tail the man. A friend request on Facebook would suffice.

Whenever it was a friend's birthday instead of posting a message on their page he posted on his and tagged them in, which meant he registered likes and comments from his friends as well as some of the recipient of his birthday wishes.

He was a lover of heavy rock music which meant for him that every Thursday night he would post a YouTube link to,

"Another Thommo golden oldie"

And wax lyrical about what he was doing, and where he was, and how much money he had, or what he was driving when the particular track was released.

David had four children Jack, Brad, Abigail and Bobbi. The two girls were at University and the two older boys at work. Abigail and Bobbi were both on course for First class honours in Chemistry and Criminal Science respectively. Jack and Brad had followed him into the financial sector having benefitted from degrees in economics.

Both boys were less academically gifted than their sisters achieving a 2:2 and Jack scraping a 3rd but David's network of friends in high places enabled him to smooth the path for entries into positions at Charles Stanley where the boys displayed their father's natural flair for financial wizardry in ways both fair and foul. David was a firm advocate of the saying that it isn't what you know but who and when

Jack made his first million at the age of 22 with the benefit of advance information and some insider dealing it proved too that the fruit does not fall to far from the tree.

David would include his children in many of his posts. Facebook knew where each had holidayed, what car Jack and Brad had bought and what car David had bought for Abi and Bobbi.

The girl's progress through University was reported with the regularity of a shipping report and their assignment marks were posted each semester under the headline.

"Proud Dad Alert. Boom Boom Boom My girls are on point again. Over 90% rating. Heading for A First #BrainsofBritain#WillSucceed#OopsYouDontItAgain#MoreRewardMoney#WhatDoYouWant#DaddyThinksYourGreat#RunningTheCountrySoon#TopPerceintileInTheCountry#BrilliantLikeYourDad

Although each of the sibling's use of Facebook had tailed off, as had their friends, they were not averse to David's simpering especially the girls, who were rewarded each time they handed in an assignment with piece of jewellery from De Beers or Bentley and Skinner on Bond Street.

David's largesse was not restricted to his children. His yearly parties were massive events. He had 32 god-children and was always one of the first names on the list for a wedding as the presents he gave were not commensurate with his acquaintance with the bride or groom. He had reached an age where wedding invites were mainly the children of friends and work colleagues.

David's Facebook post regarding his minor burn was not a one off occurrence. He reported headaches, stomach aches and hangovers. During his very toxic divorce his feelings were made known, especially as the coven of witches, the term he gave to Marian's friends had made it clear they were displeased.

When David was down, and these instances were many, social media was the first to know. One such post during his divorce process was,

"The last couple of months have been really been hard for me after hearing some sad news, I didn't want to here on Sunday night, I

120

needed some closure in my life, I messaged a few people to thank them, only to get a shedload of abuse back, the book is shut now and now looking forward to new adventures xx"

Forty comments came back each offering support and positive messages.

Garry Bennett
"Hey where ever you go there's always someone shutting the door in yeah face chin up mate keep going"

Neil Tripper
"Your luck has been terrible lately Dave, hope it's now time for it to change for the better."

Susan Higginbottom
"Believe me Dave u will bounce back it cuts u up i know but uve got good friends that will get u through it xx"

When, like a mended tap, the uplifting posts had trickled to a stop, Dave felt he needed to close off this chapter:

Thank you to everyone who sent me a kind message , I love you all to the bottom of my heart , even though it has taken a beating lately , my dream that I wanted us over now and looking forward to happier times ahead ,PLEASE c xx

When his divorce settlement was finally reached and David had parted with £9m he posted,

"WHAT A DIFFERENCE A DAY MAKES
Yesterday i can honestly say i was on a low and am thankful to my sons Jack and Brad for their contact and a close friend who popped round.
Today it seems lady luck is shining down on me as just got home after good news and this song is so uplifting
Heres wishing you all well and hope you love the song "

The good news was that Marian's friend Tabitha had come round and returned the pug that his ex-wife had taken. Marian had recently bought two French boxers having decided that pugs were no longer fashionable. Tabitha a dog lover, once in the Marian camp, was now firmly on the side of David.

The song he had posted was Aerosmith's Sunshine and the comments kept coming,

Susan Higginbottom,
"Hope you are feeling ok now my lovely xxx."

Dave replied,
"Thanks Leigh-Ann and your thoughts are much appreciated."

Kerry Bishop
"Hi Dave I am sorry to hear you haven't been feeling to good but glad today is a better day.
All my love and best wishes are being sent to you with hugs and kisses.
You keep smiling xxx"

Dave replied,
"Thanks for your lovely message and really means a lot. It's not often i have days like that and so pleased its behind me. Theres so much to look forward too and sending love , best wishes , hugs and love back at you."

Devonia Sparks,
"Glad your feeling a little more upbeat today flower! Sometimes i think people spend so much time worrying about other people that they dont have time to breathe and take some time for themselves time.....sending you humoungus huggles babbers!"

Dave replied,
"Cheers my little one and your huggles are much appreciated. I tend not to have days like that and was blown out of the water by it. Luckily im now grounded and able to be back enjoying good days Wishing you well"

It went on and on.

Phillip recalled Dave's anguish when his father had died. He knew Dave was not a Christian because of his frequent rants regarding

Muslim terrorists and Christian or Jehovah Witnesses knocking at his door or preaching in the high street.

Dave had posted, after the latest terrorist atrocity,

"Fact: Religion has been the biggest cause of war throughout history. The Governments should put all the religious people on a load of boats, set them out to sea and torpedo them. Then they can all have their seven virgins and drink milk and honey."

The agreeing responses from his Facebook friends were as rapid as the gunfire from a Gatling and just as inaccurate. Some of these were indelibly printed in Phillips mind,

Sam Crowley,
"There is no god if there was no babies would die"

Maggie Philpott,
"Moslem men do all the raping of young girls and then they go to the mosque for confessions"

Rhianna Martin,
"I know a priest who slept with all the women in his church"

Dave Murtagan,
"The trouble with those Moslem terrorists is they could live next door to you and you wouldn't know what they was thinking. Britain have never had terrorists before who could live in the same street"

Jenna Crawley,
"I'm glad I am an atheist. I don't go into churches because I don't believe there is a god, or Jesus. I only go to a church for weddings and baptisms"

Kyle Fisher,
"Its Facebooks fault, all those terrorists are in Facebook groups and nothing gets done about it and they WhatsApp each other to meet up and bomb somewhere"

Phillip had been tempted to comment that in fact around 10% of wars were started for religious reasons whilst the majority were instigated by a need for power, control, and acquisition of land or riches. He resisted mentioning the IRA, he had recalled with horror the bombing at Horse Guards parade and the Brighton incident. He kept out of these discussions because it was never worth having a debate with the irrational and ill-informed.

David's anti-religion post was in direct contrast to the annual post about his father. This year like previous,

"It's now 11 years since I lost my Dad, Derek Thompson, who now in heaven with his dear wife Glenys Thompson, my Mum, and they were both with the Lord and the angels proudly looking down on those they have left behind. "

A man that did not believe in religion had a mother and father in heaven eating milk and honey. The very thought that David was convinced of this brought on Phillip's migraine.

David's love for Gabija, his Lithuanian beauty and twenty five years his junior was a subject Phillip also found tiresome. It had started off with,

"Enjoying a great weekend in wales with my yummy new lady lovely Gabija Konstantis and new friends, the hostesses with most the mostesses Marijus and Rozalija Stanislava. Quality"

Moved on to,

"Falling the love..., I'm such a lucky man having such a sassy amazing and beautiful woman in my life, thank you lovely Gabija Konstantis, you da best innit XX"

And progressed to,

"OMG. If scallops and rump steak on a Saturday night wasn't good enough Tonight I get a beautiful duck breast in red wine and plum jus. Chez Konstantis is to die for.
Who's a lucky boy "

Gabija was showered with treats, such as,

"I'm sorry lovely Gabija, but we didn't have any 'look forward to' dates in the diary so I thought you'd like Montreux at Christmas. Its Vinces fault, he made me do it……"

On their first milestone David posted,

"Cant believe the lovely Gabija Konstantis has put up with me for six whole months. She deserves a meal…big love baby its been a blast xxxx"

As Phillip sat under the stairs he wondered whether David actually was happy. He had read numerous stories of young Eastern European women marrying Western Men and within a year the house was shared with an extended family including a male cousin in his late twenties, early thirties with whom the wife was extremely close.

Phillip felt sure that if David had split with his wife twenty years ago then he would have been with a Thai bride, he was the type who thought he could buy affection. David having an Eastern European partner wasn't a surprise even though he had voted Brexit.

Dating applications specifically catered for women from the Eastern bloc some of whom began to replace their less athletic British counterparts in lap dancing and pole dancing clubs. David had met Gabija via Tinder when he swiped right for her profile which included the caption "I will love you for 50 red roses." On meeting he was told that as well as pole dancing Gabija supplemented her income with prostitution, and for £50 he could sleep with her. For £100 she would stay with him all night and once she had had a soak in the jacuzzi of his £28,000 designer bathroom she stayed permanently.

Phillip looked at his watch, he had been scrolling through Facebook for over an hour. How the time had flown. Now it was time for him to get his mother to open the door.

Christine meanwhile was at her wits end. Of course she knew Phillip Sebastian was under the stairs when she had shut the door on him and practically run into the kitchen but now she fretted over why he hadn't blown his top and kicked his way out when she ignored his cries. Her plan to drive him mad seemed to be stalling, he seemed more tolerant than usual and this concerned her because she was more than capable of getting under his skin.

Perhaps he had had a heart attack she wondered. If he had then better she wait until there was no chance of him being revived. Going off to the Caribbean and meeting a local Jamaican, Antiguan or Barbadian for some fun was the plan she had when she had rid herself of her son. She would then return home and invite Ms Keppel over for afternoon tea and they could share holiday stories and an aperitif imbibed out of those delicate Dartington crystal glasses.

She didn't want Phillip Sebastian around judging her when she went and she didn't want him in the house if and when she returned and she was facetiming her gorgeous lover. She had it all planned out and she would outdo Bunny Stevenson who had been to Morocco the previous year and met a local businessman who had lavished her with love and attention.

The Moroccan came to Britain three times a year, he spoke good English and looked affluent, although it was rumoured that his money had come from another woman who was bankrolling him. Bunny had provided a complete new wardrobe for him in order he needed to check in no hold luggage. She was also sending him a stipend for the villa he was having built in Oulad Hassoune just to the East of Marrakesh which both would share as soon as his wretched divorce to a local woman was finalised.

Christine finally cracked, she came out of the kitchen and opened the door to the cupboard under the stairs she feigned surprise when she looked into the nether regions and saw Sebastian sat on a stack of toolboxes seemingly oblivious to her, iPhone in hand

"Sebastian Phillip," she exclaimed, "what are you doing?"

Phillip looked up nonchalantly.

"I'm sitting in the cupboard waiting for you to let me out after you locked me in."

"Why didn't you call out?"

"I did but you went into the kitchen and started hoovering, then you had the blender on so I gave up. What did you want in the cupboard anyway? You hate it under here because of your irrational fear of spiders"

"I was walking past and I saw the light on."

"So you didn't see the light on when you shut the door?"

"No, I didn't notice."

"Even though the door was ajar."

"No."

"But you noticed the light on while the door was shut."

"Yes. What is this? Do you think I did it on purpose?"

"Of course not Mother I suppose at your age you aren't going to notice every little thing. Not to worry, do you want a cup of tea?"

"I am sorry Sebastian."

"Oh that's alright, I was catching up with Facebook updates of my friends so I didn't waste my time. I see Bunny's Moroccan friend is over. He's a handsome devil isn't he, and Bunny looks so young and glamourous now. For a woman in her early 70s I mean."

Christine gave Phillip a pained look. Bunny was 79. He hadn't reacted when she had called him Sebastian, usually his nostrils flared, like a prickly stallion. Something was going on.

"He's only after her money. What are you doing on Bunny Stevenson's page, you don't even know her," she said, with venom.

"I'm sure in return for giving Mustapha some of Bunny's dead husband's estate she is getting something in return. Proper Essex cougar."

"Vulgar," Christine spat. She turned and walked back toward the kitchen.

"Haven't you just come out of the kitchen Mother?" Phillip said, "What did you come out for?" he asked, looking her deep into her eyes.

"I, I am not sure," she stammered, "I just had a feeling you needed me. Like some sixth sense I think." she tried to look bewildered, as if she was making an attempt to recall the reasons for her actions. As she walked back to the kitchen she tried to think what is was that had made Phillip Sebastian become more tolerant of her attempts to goad him. She wasn't doing enough. She would need to up her game.

Phillip walked up the stairs to his room. He was smiling to himself knowing that this latest battle of wits went to him, Phillip Anderson, the master of the mind games. It was only when he sat on his bed he realised he had forgotten the hammer. Rather than risk going back to the cupboard and have the decrepit crone lock him in once more he decided that he would put the half price planner up another time, for now it could stay on his desk.

Phillip opened up his laptop and went straight to Facebook to check out the latest statuses

David had just checked in to Arsenal v Leicester at The Emirates Stadium. As usual all his friends, who went to every game also checked in. Phillip counted. Twenty three people checking in with an activity they did every other week. How boring.

A post from Beverley Hathaway caught his eye. It read,

Can't say this will be my last post for a while, but maybe the last of significance....love you all!
Certainly, in the most difficult moments of life you realize who are true friends or the people who really appreciate you
Unfortunately, some friends will click on "like" but in reality they do not take time to read your status if they see it's lengthy.
I decided to post this message in support of a very special person to me who fought till the end with firmness and energy. Who taught us how to live each day as if it were the most beautiful day! Who has filled the world with a beautiful smile and a sweet spirit.
Now I'm watching the ones who will have time to read this post until the end.....(I reckon I will guess the first 5)
(SO SO SO TRUE).....

Phillip had started reading thinking, here was a heartfelt post but realised it was one of the many that were being duplicated and served simply to clog up the internet with traffic. He did however continue,

"Cancer is very invasive and destructive to our body, even after the end of the treatment, your body is still fighting with yourself trying to reconstruct all the damage caused by radiation. It's a very long process. (100% TRUE)
Please, in honor of a family member or a friend who died, or is still fighting cancer, or even had cancer but it's healed; copy and paste (not share) in your page.
So I will know who read my status, please write "done" in the comments.
Thank you for (reading and) this opportunity to share this x"

There were so many similar messages and however personal the message might have been to him in some ways, his father had after all succumbed to cancer, it wasn't a personal message because he could imagine probably a million people or more had posted the same. He looked at some of the comments, or lack of, that followed,

Paige Winterburn,
"Done"

Bill Smith,
"Done"

Kayleigh Hughes,
"Done"

After 19 of these he scanned to some actual, but no more interesting, comments,

Cathy Dixon,
"Done, Well said Beverley"

Beverley replied with:
"Sending you all love and hearts xx

And got back from Cathy:
"Beverley, you have a very thoughtful and caring nature! Xxx"

Phillip wondered why he had wasted an episode of his life reading these posts then looking back at the initial text he re-read the first line,

"Can't say this will be my last post for a while, but maybe the last of significance....love you all!"

It was never going to be Beverley's last post and nothing she had ever written was significant unless anyone else was interested in what her and her boyfriend Conor did on a daily basis, progress of her daughter Billie at school. Swimming, drama club or Billie eight turning eighteen conversations.

Scrolling down Phillip came to Henrietta Cavendish's latest

"So..... for those of you that don't know, Steve and I separated a good while ago now, and although we have been living together for many months since, we have finally gone our separate ways. My house is now 'our' house again as my sister Sandra, and Blade (canine furbud) will be moving in full time as soon as she gets the rest of her bits and bobs out of storage. It's a new era for all of us and time to move on with a more positive and peaceful 2018. Cheers to the past, woooo ha to the future and right now I need wine, or chocolate, or something illegal, or a gherkin. And a specialist in itchy face rashes.... love"

Riveting stuff thought Phillip, having a sarcastic conversation with himself. Henrietta was a Facebook add from his days as a regular at the O Neills bar when he was on a week long course in Cardiff Having had stirrings of attraction for her, he had taken a selfie and said shamelessly "Friend me on Facebook and I can tag you." A suggestion Henrietta, with her 2065, friends, found powerless to resist.

The usual crop of responses followed expressing sympathy, joy and wishes for love and happiness with one of,

Cathy Dixon,
"Loads of love my beautiful breath of fresh air xxxx"

Henrietta replied

"Awwwwwww you so lovely dog Mumma xxxx"

Phillip moved on.

Two people posts about dead relations:

Keith Minkham paid tribute:
"23 years today you were taken from us , RIP Mum xx"

David Thompson had also posted,

"Still cannot believe it's been 11 years already. Miss you so much Dad / Grandad, always in our hearts and thoughts."

David's post was accompanied by a picture of his father's gravestone.

Phillip wondered whether these were true reflections of feeling or blatant attempts at attracting sympathy. Probably the latter he thought.

Phillip read another post, this one from Millie Goddard,
"Happy Birthday to my stunning daughter Toni. You have grown from a beautiful baby and now a beautiful, kind independent, funny, strong young women. I am so proud you , i could burst. Love you with every heartbeat and more. Enjoy your day lots of love always mum xxxxxxxx"

Phillip never failed to understand why a birthday had to be the subject out of such outpourings these days. What happened to sending cards? He opened up a word document in which he had stored the tributes which most upset him,

"HAPPY HEAVENLY BIRTHDAY DAD
I know your all around me, to guide me through each day and that is why I'm happy and smile in many ways
Another year has rolled on and yes I do miss you and your smile could open many hearts and thats why we all loved you.
So whilst your up in heaven , please give mum a hug and all those loving people, who im sure will enjoy their hugs.
Now continue with your party, before you need a rest and remember from your loving son, I'll try and do my best
HAPPY HEAVENLY BIRTHDAY
Love Gavin X

"Happy birthday to me."

"thank you all for my pressies money and lovely cards xxxxx

It's been quite overwhelming today with all birthday celebrations, cards, gifts and messages thank you to all of you!
Made me feel very loved x

The birthday that was most documented was that of Dionne Lewis,

"My day today .. gonna enjoy it .. bring on the wine & gin & tonics"

She had followed this up with,

"Gonna party like it's my birthday…..because it is"

In response to gifts from friends,

"Thank you Lindsay & Ben for my beautiful flowers , body yoghurt & card .. lots love Dionne xx"

The end of the post day was,

"Thanks to all
My lovely friends that wished. Me happy birthday.. love you all .. I've had a lovely day xx"

Dionne had taken a screen shot of her page showing 147 friends had posted on her timeline for her birthday and posted the screen shot.

She added a message,

Thanks to all my lovely family and friends for the lovely cards and messages. Love you all xxx

The day after her birthday,

"Thank you everyone who wished me happy birthday.. all 213 of you plus lots others on my group & my family.. feel truly blessed"

Two days after her birthday,

"Thank you to all those who posted kind birthday wishes. I am touched. The rest of you will be unfriended tomorrow"

Phillip couldn't be bothered to look at the rest of the file, which was forty pages long as David Thompson had started to report in on the Arsenal game v Leicester,

"Arsenal line-up"

Cech, Holding, Elneny, Monreal, Bellerin, Xhaka, Kolasinac, Ozil, Oxlade-Chamberlain, Lacazette, Welbeck Subs: Giroud, Ospina, Iwobi, Mustafi, Coquelin, Ramsay, Walcott

"Can't believe Ozil is on the playing he plainly doesn't want it anymore"

David received no comments or likes. Phillip was mildly surprised, although the game was being televised, one would expect those watching the game would also be checking or making Facebook comments.

Two minutes in and Lacazette scored on his Arsenal debut. David checked in again and posted,

"David Thompson is feeling fantastic
Oi Oi. I knew he was going to be a steal. Watch out you Mancs and Scousers. We're coming for you"

David's joy was short-lived because after five minutes Leicester had equalised through Okazaki,

David Thompson is feeling concerned
"Fucking useless Xhaka. If he's a defender I am going to be nominated for an Oscar at the next Awards night. I said Ozil shouldn't have played he has been on five minutes and hasn't had a touch"

James Impey responded with,
"According to the stats we have 80% possession, Is it just blip? I am following it on BBC updates"

David shot back with,

"Same old Arsenal, Wenger loves us to play football outside the oppo box instead of just winning matches"

Ivan Joseph
"At the game. Early days mate"

David Thompson
"I might go at half time fed up with the same old shit every week"

James Impey
"Yeah but it's the first game of the season. Watching it on Sky!!"

David Thompson
"Its going to be rubbish"

Phillip chuckled. David's reaction to a victory was often met with negativity therefore a defeat was a catastrophe and all boiled down to Arsenal retaining Arsene Wenger.

Things got worse on twenty-nine minutes when James Vardy scored for the Foxes. David, apoplectic was straight onto his smartphone,

David Thompson is feeling angry
"This is bollocks. I'm off"

James Impey,
"Are you really going?"

David Thompson,
"Fuck off"

On the stroke of half time Danny Welbeck equalised after Ozil had played him in,

David Thompson is feeling thankful
"That got to be pass of the season from Ozil. Schmeichal could get nowhere near that one"

James Impey,
"Thought you'd gone lol"

David Thompson,

"True supporter me you twat. Surprised your not washing your birds knickers"

James Impey,
"Nah mate am round yours taking your birds knickers off ha ha "

Gabija Konstantis,
"David. Who is this man there is no-one in our house but me and Rozalija

David Thompson,
"Its okay Hun. James is a knobhead."

Gabija Konstantis
"What is this means?"

David Thompson,
"Don't worry about it I'm watching the game, can't be using the phone too, Hun see you later"

The 15th minute of the second half brought little cheer to David when Vardy popped up again, on the end of a Riyadh Mahrez corner, to get his brace and a second lead for Leicester.

David Thompson is feeling fed up
"Useless Wenger out. I'm out"

Ivan Joseph,
Its ok Dave I think we can at least nick a draw here

David Thompson,
Are we at the same game bruv? Leicester are all over us

Ivan Joseph,
Nah mate we've got all the possession. One goal and we'll be back in it

David Thompson,
"You wanna get that burkha off mate you can't see shit"

Ivan Joseph,

"Don't be a dick Thommo. Anyway he has just bought on Giroud and Ramsey. Good changes"

David Thompson,
"Do me a favour mate. He might as well give me and you a shirt. Those two are wank. Giroud couldn't score in a brothel the French twat"

In the 83rd minute, 15 minutes after the double substitution there was ecstasy at the Emirates with Dave Thompson providing the social media commentary once more.

David Thompson,
"Goooooooooooooaaaaaaaaaaaaaaaall"

David Thompson,
"Fucking brilliant. What a goal by Ramsey. Always loved him. "

James Impey,
"Do you think you or Ivan would have tucked that in then Thommo. I though you said he was wank?"

David Thompson,
 "Reverse psychology mate. I just said it so he would play well"

Ivan Joseph,
"Oh yeah, I did see him checking his iPhone before he came on. One of your Facebook friends is he lol"

David Thompson,
 "Fuck off you retardl"

Two minutes later, in the 85th minute, Arsenal were ahead.

David Thompson,
"Yeah Gooooooners....Fuck me we've scored again. Giroud. Master stroke by Arsene. What a manager"

James Impey,
"You've been slagging everyone off all game Thommo, I thought you were a Leicester fan ha ha"?

David Thompson,
"True supporter me mate. Red and white blood going through these veins"

James Impey,
"Like most people I believe if you include white blood cells"

David Thompson,
"Hark at Doctor Impey."

James Impey,
"Happy days"

Phillip commented, even though it was a while since he had interacted with David Thompson,
"Even I thought you would be gone at half time David?"

David Thompson,
"Shutup SebArsetian"

James Impey,
"You two ladies having a domestic ha ha"

David Thompson
"Bummer Anderson is probably in his house wanking over pictures of Graham Norton, Tom Daley and Alan Carr"

Phillip Anderson,
"While you are wanking over Giroud and Ramsay lol"

David Thompson,
"Great players, always said it"

Ivan Joseph,
"Didn't you say Giroud couldn't score in a brothel Thommo?

David Thompson,
"He is only interested in banging them in the back of the net mate lol"

James Impey,
"Are you going home to bang your mate Phillip?"

David Thompson,
"Jog on you twat no I most certainly will not be, I shall mainly be going home to my beautiful fiancé Gabija Konstantis for a night of post-game action"

He had tagged Gabija in the post but she would only see it later that night as she was currently in bed with her fellow Lithuanian, Gregor Jablonskis.

David Thompson.
"I'm coming for you, I'm coming for youuuuu, Gabija Konstantis.....I'm coming for you"

David's delight was crowned, like a Nigerian prince, when the final whistle blew for a famous Arsenal victory.

His final post on the subject was,

David Thompson
"All those who said Wenger was out of tune and Arsenal weren't going to qualify for the Champions League sit down now. I am sitting down lol. What a performance. To a man we were magnificent. Okay we let Leicester have a little sniff in the second half but we were just teasing them and we showed that by putting two past them in the final ten minutes. You score one we will score two. You score two we will score three. You score three we will score four. Standard."

A stream of happy messages from fellow Arsenal fans followed, and Phillip guessed that with the match over everyone was on social media of some sort to post videos or selfies and the like because a good night had been had by all.

Sean "Razor" Henderson had the final say David's Arsenal v Leicester thread, with a post which simply said,
"You soppy cunts".

Sean was a well-known ex Chelsea hooligan having written two books on his life as a Headhunter. He had also attended Beal School but failed to end in his final year, instead working on his dad's fruit and veg stall at Canning Town market or his Uncles at Romford market. He had been in the newspaper in the early eighties on a murder charge but the case was thrown out due to lack of evidence. A

138

prosecution witness suddenly had a loss of memory two days before giving testimony.

There was no other post after Sean's, David would have thought better of it. Phillip did feel a sense of jealously that he too did not command the same level of respect as Sean.

He knew that David lived in Stevenage, Hertfordshire and everything about his routine. He wondered if Sean was thinking what he was thinking, that David needed to be taught a lesson.

Two days after the match, on Sunday morning at 0600 David walked Gabija's labradoodle through the local park. Gabija had insisted he buy the dog but also insisted that walking Benji was too much for her because she couldn't bear to pick up shit and put it in a plastic bag. Besides this she didn't want to get tired walking the dog when she had spinning classes every morning at 0900 while David was with his friends at work.

David contemplated his lot and how lucky he was to have such a beautiful young wife who was doing all she could to keep her figure firm and perky for him. So much so that she didn't cook him dinner because she feared she would snack while in the kitchen and lose her slender waist or develop saggy boobs. Dave did most his own cooking on return from work and Gabija might have morsel of that. Sex was permitted on a Saturday night or after an Arsenal win because, according to Gabija, Dave's penis was so large, and her hole so small, sex made her sore. Dave was slightly perplexed at this as he knew from watching porn movies that his member was no more than an average size.

When they had first started dating Gabija was an eager and voracious lover. Dave was able to insert four fingers inside her when they were having foreplay and she would often guide one of his hands inside her knickers as they sat watching television. He knew that there was plenty of give, especially when Gabija's orifice was moist, Any program that involved a kiss or the mention of the word love, be it Last Tango in Paris, MasterChef or Shrek, Gabija would be stripped down to her bra and g string begging for her big boy to please her, and she was anxious to please him. All that ceased as soon as they were wed. After six months together they had had gone to Vegas and tied the knot and told no –one. Gabija had convinced David she

139

needed to be married as there were problems with her work visa and assured him that she agreed, they should have a lavish wedding next year. Without wearing ring but with a marriage certificate firmly stowed in the safe Gabija's drive diminished like an octogenarian's erection, and sex with David became a chore.

David reflected on how he often came home to his wife wearing skimpy underwear and no bra, sweating where she said she had been doing some high intensity training in the house to compliment the work she had done in the gym. As he pictured Gabija in his head he spotted a man in dark clothing walking toward him. The man was of slight build dressed in a long oversized black coat under which was a hooded black snood. An outfit complete by baggy black pants and thigh high combat boots.

As the person approached, and looked up David could now see dark glasses gave the person the look of a ninja assassin.

David still had Gabija on his mind when the person took a black gun fitted with a silencer from under the coat and fired twice, one bullet hitting David in the temple and the other just below his right eye. If death did not come immediately following these two shots then the two fired into the area of his chest as he lay crumpled on the gravel path would have penetrated his heart and caused his life to cease. The killer relieved David of his wallet and car keys.

Benji wasn't the most loyal or brave of hounds, with her master incapacitated and her life in potential danger she bolted back home. When Gabija heard the barking at the door she reluctantly went downstairs and was surprised ten minutes later when her partner still had not appeared. Knowing David's route from his regular Facebook posts she got dressed and hurried in the direction of the park and when she got there she saw his crumpled and bloodied body she wept.

She was still crying hysterically when the police arrived because she was relieved that, despite not being married yet, David had re-written his will for her to inherit his estate and that Gregor was probably right, his ex-wife and children probably had enough money of their own.

So unconvinced were the police officers and investigating detectives about Gabija's grief that for months they investigated every facet of her life. Once the affair was discovered they tried to pin the murder on Gregor Jablonskis and his associates, despite him having a cast iron alibi and a quite salubrious circle of friends.

Tracey King

Phillip sat in his room on his laptop eating a bag of revels. He was playing a game with himself where he guessed the centre of the chocolate covered sweet he was eating. The easiest to guess were the flying saucer shaped all chocolate or the light maltesers. When the centres were orange crème, peanut, coconut, toffee, maltesers and chocolate the orange crème, coconut and toffee could be tricky. Now coconut was replaced with coffee and peanut with raisin it was the coffee and orange crème that caused him a problem.

Alongside his Revel guessing game he was going through Tracey King's posts. She had been quiet for about two weeks and knowing that she had been expecting a baby Phillip thought she had had a problem. The problem turned out to be that the baby was severely jaundiced and three weeks premature. Tracey had not posted any pictures of the baby in an incubator, despite several beseeching messages from her friends.

The lack of posts was not Tracey's choice. The outpouring of sympathy her baby would have received if she was photographed lying helpless in the incubator of the private ward in St Marys Hospital, Paddington could have gone viral but Tracey's 32 year old Russian husband, Vasiliy Gamontov would not hear of it. He had chosen St Marys because that was where the future King of England, Prince William was born and he was a perfectly formed baby. As far as he was concerned the Gamontov blood was strong with ancestry going back to the court of Peter The Great. Vasiliy had taken over his father's property empire in Russia and expanded it to London where he now owned several rental homes on the Isle of Dogs that were let out to city professionals and a string of mansions in and around Fulham which he leased to fellow countrymen.

Tracey was Facebook friends and family with some of Vasiliy's family back in Leningrad. As Ilyana had been born with a yellow hue Vasiliy enforced the social media embargo as he did not want his mother to get any hint that she had been right and her son had married "a common English mongrel." Which are the words Ludmilla Gamontov had spat out, in Russian, when she attended the wedding and had it confirmed by a reliable source that her now daughter in law was in the early stages of pregnancy.

Tracey's social media associates were not to be disappointed when, on the day that Tracey's baby, Ilyana Conchella Beyonce, was fit and healthy enough to be photographed, mainly in Vasiliy's arms, around 200 photos were posted.

The set of photo's had the comment,

"I am so proud of our little Ilyana and how far she's come 2 months old and still way too small for 0-3 clothes but it's a long way from the tiny 33 weeker that we brought into the world"

Tracey had spent the first four days with Ilyana putting her into every outfit she had received at her baby shower and then even more painstakingly tagged the person who had provided the outfit, in the pictures. She hadn't made the album public first, instead ensuring that each accompanying caption was word perfect as was each photo. After she had checked them she sat with Vasiliy and he ran through them too, editing the comments and the order so that those snaps with clothes bought by a fellow Russian appeared first.

Ilyana was cooed over as if she were the first baby anyone had ever seen.

Toni Bell,
"Where have you been hiding Ilyana she's so lush"

Pritti Gupta,
"Ilyana is literally the most beautiful baby I have ever seen"

Martina Samanofski,
"She is gorgeous Tracey, that's because you and Vasiliy are the most amazing couple"

Penny Wright
"How have we not met little Ilyana yet?! Right, I'm on it tonight. Will text you with some dates!! Need a snuggle while she's still tiny and the girls keep asking when they can meet her! Xx"

Joanne Daley
"That outfit is tres chic. Isnt it the one I bought?"

Holly Daley
"She is stunning
#likeamodel#perfectbaby#babetastic#heartbreaker#icouldeather"

Peter King,
"Happy two month birthday Ilyana xx"

Ludmilla Gamontov
"Она здоровый глядя ребенка, где сын"

Which translates as,

"She is a healthy looking baby where is son?"

Phillip had looked at one or two of the photos, decided Ilyana wasn't adorable, a cutie, heartbreaker, or babetastic but looked like a dried up and bleached prune shaped head stuck on a raw sausage body. Everyone else loved the baby, the outfits, and the name, which was a combination of a Russian grandmother, the festival where Tracey and Vasiliy first met and slept together and their favourite pop star.

Phillip looked at how much in love Tracey seemed to be with Vasiliy, despite him looking like in photos as if he had been told his wine contained horse piss. Tracey was blatantly ecstatic to have a child, especially as she was 44 when she gave birth. Prior to meeting Vasiliy she had been taking fertility treatment and made a proactive decision that the person who impregnated her was going to be able to provide her with a good lifestyle that she had missed when she had been with her first husband.

 Phillip sat and wondered as he always did when he looked at Tracey's posts. What could have been? He pondered on whether, when he had met Tracey two years ago, after matching via the Plenty Of Fish dating website, were he younger and richer and not older and poorer it might be him on her Facebook page, married and then showing off a new born child.

Tracey had made it quite clear on the date she had had with Phillip that she was disappointed with her match.

Phillip's eight profile pictures were taken between ten and twenty years previously when he had been in his golden years. His pay at PriZSolutions was excellent and boosted by ever available overtime, a rewarding bonus scheme and share save options that were a license to print money. Phillip also had a side line of selling files of customer name, address and telephone numbers to an India based company who in turn sold them to cold call companies dealing in insurance, double glazing, pensions and funeral policies.

Investing with Barings shortly before Nick Leeson racked up $1.4bn of losses decimated Phillips savings. A loan to recover some of his debt further exacerbated Phillip's financial situation which was one of the reason why he still shared a home with his mother.

Phillip's love life was as sketchy as Leonardo Da Vinci. In his 30s he had dated Gillian Mounteagle, who was married but unhappy, Rachel Charleston, who had her own dog grooming company and Katherine Stokes who worked as a carer. Phillip was able to holiday extensively at this time, to places like Cyprus, Italy, Spain, Croatia, the Caribbean, and Miami. Being regular at the gym meant his now flaccid stomach was a washboard, his pectoral muscles as ripped as a Belarusian weightlifter's and his thighs bulged under trousers like Thanksgiving pumpkins in a canvas sack.

Phillip latest selected Plenty of Fish profile pictures were of himself striding across Jamaican and Antiguan beaches, emerging from Asian seas in scuba diving kit, hauling in barracuda in Mexico and fine dining in Bologna. His main profile picture was taken in the garden at Barry Flanagan's coastal retreat in Brighton during a party had held by the AT&T director. Back in the day, while it was still politically correct, Barry made a point of inviting the employee of the month to one of his lavish events and Phillip had gone, only because the actual winner, Ricki was away at San Francisco Pride. One picture was a selfie of him standing beside Alice Caple's BMW.

Phillip found that the number of matches that responded to his messages increased as soon as his original, up to date profile pictures were removed. These pictures showed him at Doctor Who conventions, sitting in his room with a can of Ruddles ale and doing bunny ears behind his mother as they took a selfie.

He felt duty bound to remove his original pictures after a bad Plenty of Fish experience with Connie Charlesworth. She had posted two profile pictures of a very vivacious 48 year old with a mane of luxuriant golden hair.

Phillip had thought at the time how fresh looking her face was, barely any make up, With only faint crow's feet round her eyes, Connie wasn't heavily made up and in her hair was a tribal bandana, she looked like 60s flower child. Her main picture was a head and upper body shot with a blouse showing a respectable amount of cleavage. Her second picture was quite risqué, with Sue on a beach holding a cocktail wearing a tee-shirt knotted to one side at the bottom. She was obviously bra-less as her nipples stood up like armour piercing bullets. Seeing a billboard in the background advertising the Musical Festival Cannes. Knowing the picture was taken in the South of France gave Phillip a thrill as it was a place that held fond memories for him, having gawped at the plethora of topless sunbathers as a schoolboy with Christine and Oliver in 1973.

After a week of daily conversations via POF, telephone numbers were exchanged to conduct the relationship via text and WhatsApp, Connie had arranged to meet Phillip in Frinton-On-Sea as it was a summer month. Weather wise that day it was as bad as it could get. The rain lashed down like a Chinese army marching across a trail of prawn cocktail crisps and to make it worse the satnav would not charge. Having driven twenty miles to the vicinity of the meeting place the infernal contraption cut out and would not power on.

Phillip was not familiar with the area at all and having stopped several times to ask for directions arrived at the car park 15 minutes late. Due to the conditions Phillip was obliged to wear a large mac and a showerproof hat, his golf umbrella was also at the unfurled as he scurried off to get a parking ticket. A lack of punctuality was one of Phillips bugbears therefore he was perturbed that he was late and with Connie being such a catch, he was on the verge of panic. He was almost hyperventilating searching the carpark for the woman looking like the profile picture. Ticket in hand and trembling like an English penalty taker at a shootout he returned to his car. As he reached the Ford Focus, Connie text to say she was stuck in traffic and would be another ten minutes.

Feeling vindicated and pompous Phillip sat in his car wondering why women were so inept at getting anywhere on time and why it was acceptable for them to be fashionably late. As he drummed his fingers on the steering wheel, Phillip concluded that Connie probably knew that she was one of the more attractive 48 year old women on POF and she could afford to play it cool.

In the next 15 minutes around ten cars entered the car park. Not knowing what car Connie drove Phillip was unable to determine what to look at coming into the entrance. Phillip eyed all the people who exited their vehicles and purchased a parking ticket and none corresponded with Connie's pictures.

As befitted the area and the time of day most of those who were parking were either young mothers or pensioners both male and female. He did notice a heavy set woman standing by a white van scanning the car park. She had been in one of the ten cars that had pulled in as Phillip had noticed previously the white van was a solitary vehicle. The heavy set woman that got out of it was wearing a yellow rain hat and a fitted olive coloured rain coat that made her look like Fiona from the movie, Shrek. She had yellow boots on and was leaning against an ancient Skoda that made Phillip's Focus, Bentley-like in comparison. Phillip continued to scan the car park and decided Connie had not yet arrived.

Phillip didn't like to text not knowing whether Connie was still stuck in traffic or driving but decided to show some concern. He typed,

"Hi Connie you still at a standstill, hope everything is okay. I can't wait to see you. Typical Essex traffic. Where is everyone going?" but then deleted most of this and settled for,

"Hi Connie you still at a standstill?"

Within seconds of sending the text his phone rang, it was Connie.

"Hi Phillip," she said," I'm here. As soon as I text, the road cleared and have been here for five minutes I am over by the pay machine next to a mucky white van. Someone's written on it, I wish my wife

146

was this dirty." Connie chuckled and Phillip immediately fell in love with the sound of his beauty.

He, jumped out of the car and re-scanned the carpark quickly, there must be another white van he thought. It can't possibly be the heavy set woman who did actually have a phone to her ear but was herself looking away from him at another part of the carpark.

A man walked past wearing a bandanna, long sleeved sweatshirt and a pair of khaki shorts, he smelled of stale tobacco and had large hoop earrings that made him look like a gypsy fortune teller. Given the weather was so inclement, cold and with a wind chill, Phillip was surprised at the man's attire but glancing at the man's calves he saw both were heavily tattooed. Before Phillip had the time to pontificate to himself why it was mandatory for those with a fetish for ink to exhibit the paint as if they were hung Picasso's his eyes settled once again on the single one white van over to his right, about 30 yards away. The heavy set woman was looking directly at him and to Phillips astonishment, and horror, she waved.

Phillip experienced an almost out of body experience, he felt faint and had to put his hand on his car bonnet to prevent himself tumbling over. His arm lifted, he felt as though he was trying to raise a 40kg dumb bell, and he wiggled his fingers in greeting and said faintly, "I can see ya."

With a leaden step, Phillip walked over to the woman, assessing her as he did so. Connie mirrored his stride, moving, as well as she could, toward him. She did this with the aid of a stick as she had quite a noticeable limp. She was around 5 foot four inches tall. He was no expert at woman dress sizes but he put her at around an 18-20. In her profile picture she had long curly golden hair and a size 10. The curl was still there but the length was now just above the neck and was as grey as the sky above. Her face was a ruddy, she looked slightly out of breath. This was compounded by her mouth being half open and she was panting such was the pain of the exertion of walking perhaps 10 yards. She looked around 60 if not older. Her eyes sparkled, like a fat Aunt who has just spotted the cake at a party.

"Phillip," she exclaimed, cheerfully, "how are you? Lovely to put a face to the messages we have been sending each other." With one hand still on her stick she extended her other arm toward him and up around the back of his shoulders, pulled him gently towards herself and offered her lips.

Although rather taken back by this brazen behaviour by someone who looked like his date's mother Phillip remained courteous and responded by moving his face around hers and giving Connie a peck on the cheek and when the other was presented, pecking that one too. Connie had moved her hand from his up and it was behind his head pushing his head onto hers. Her scent was refreshing, like a florists display, pleasant and natural.

He could however, hardly have put the face he was seeing to the messages and profile pictures he had been presented with but said nothing untoward to her. He felt himself smiling inside, he had been duped, but he hoped that his face did not show the smirk that should have surfaced.

"There's a pub just down the ways a bit," Connie smiled and said, "I suggest we adjourn for a drink before you ravage me. I thought I was going to be eaten on the spot." she added. Phillip smiled politely and thought to himself, Christ, this woman is mutton dressed as mutton and delusional.

"What have you done to your leg Connie? You didn't say you had hurt yourself." Phillip asked

"Oh it's a bugger Hon, I need a knee replacement but the NHS aren't the most progressive outfit in the country. Apparently I am too young at 58 for a replacement because if I get one done now I might need another one in twenty five years so they would rather I wait for another five-ten years until I am in complete agony then do the operation once and hope that will see me out"

"Your profile said you like walking and you are 48."

"I do but I can't and I'm not. I haven't been able to do that for the last two years"

"What about going to the gym?"

"I do go down the gym but I just do some yoga, obviously I can't do all the positions just the ones my knee will allow"

"First on the dance floor?"

"Oh I am always first on the dance floor, waving my stick. If I get some help I can sit down and rock to Oops Upside Your Head. Do you like that one, regular floor filler back in the day"

"Yes I am sure the floor was completely full." Phillip wondered if she caught the hint of sarcasm, he intended that Connie was so fat she would have covered the dance floor but she seemed oblivious to his comment. He groaned, inwardly. Outwardly he smiled sweetly and started to think of a reason that would cut the date short.

Perhaps he could go to the toilet, ring Ricki and tell him that he had something urgent to discuss, perhaps an upgrade that was taking place that night, then say he had to go because there was a delivery man at the door and Ricki should ring back in ten minutes. Then he would take the call, move out of earshot of Connie, and give Ricki some technical mumbo jumbo. He would keep his phone to his ear while Ricki hung up then move back to Connie saying to the phone "Look if I have to come in I have to come in but I am going to have to get the days annual leave back as I was planning on spending an afternoon with my young lady."

His smile broadened, that was a good plan. He would use it as a backup as he was going to quiz Connie on her profile which would fail any audit by a team investigating unfair trade description. With luck they might end up aborting the date.

They reached the pub, The Crooked Cow, which given Connie's condition was appropriate and went into the bar.

"What can I get you to drink?" Phillip asked.

"I'm driving so I can't let you get me drunk Phillip."

""Why don't you just have a coke or a lemonade."

"Oh twist my arm then I'll have a pint of Davy's Old Wallop."

Although he felt like drinking a bottle of brandy, Phillip ordered the pint and a Guinness for himself and sat down opposite Connie.

149

"Well here you are, don't you find dating app's a strange way to get out and meet someone. Not like back in the day, actually seeing someone you liked in a bar or club and going over." Connie beamed.

Phillip could not believe the bare faced cheek. Connie was practically lining him up with ammunition to denounce her as a fraud. He decided however to play things coolly at first.

"That picture of you on the beach. It was the South of France wasn't it. I saw a banner for Cannes, was it recent?"

Oh no," Connie said gaily, "that was twenty-four years ago."

"And your main profile picture?"

"Around 2001."

"So that is around sixteen years ago," Phillip said quickly doing the maths.

"Yes that's right. I did put some more up to date photos on when I first got on Plenty of Fish but I don't think it was the right bait." She laughed. "Then I had a bad experience with a guy I met who didn't even post pictures of himself. I expected a George Clooney look-a-like instead I got Danny Devito. It was awful, he was four foot nine. At least my pictures are of me."

"Yes but when you meet up don't you find that your date is a little surprised?"

"You're the first person I have met since I posted those pictures and the reason I agreed to meet up with you is you said, in response to my text asking you what you thought of women who wear layers and layers of make up because their partners hate to see their natural face. And these are your words." she picked up her phone and scrolled to what Phillip guessed would be one of the conversations they had had via text.

"I'm not that shallow to be all about how a lady looks I think it's more important to have a great personality and I can tell from your text you have a great personality. Beauty comes from within. I know I am over 50, but age is just a number."

Phillip recalled the text. He recalled thinking at the time that if he went out with a slim girl who ballooned in weight within six months of meeting she would be dumped. Despite being overweight he didn't want a fat girlfriend.

Connie looked at him, her brow was furrowed and she looked very sensitive when she asked. "If I posed pictures of myself now and said I had a gammy leg but that I had a great personality would you have agreed to meet or would you have just ghosted me?"

Phillip knew that he would never have agreed to meet, this question put him in a spot so he ignored it.

"You lied about your age." He said.

"Age is a number you said. I was going to tell you when we met, and I did," Connie replied, without a trace of remorse.

"You did actually say in your profile that people often take you for a forty year old."

"Poetic license. I am young at heart rather than young looking. Is this going to be a problem for us because I can just leave?"

Phillip felt slightly guilty. He loathed people, apart from himself, who made judgements based solely on looks. Connie was rather bubbly and she could potentially be a good friend if not a partner.

Phillip said "No it's not a problem. We do seem to have a lot in common from our chats and this is on-line dating after all so the rules have to be different aren't they?"

"Thank you Phillip. You have restored my faith in mankind. All those texts and messages we exchanged, we are on the same wavelength. Same sarcastic sense of humour, love of books and films and food." Connie smiled, she was rather endearing. He wished she didn't remind him of his former English teacher Miss Finch, a matronly woman who nurtured his love of reading.

The rest of the afternoon was quite pleasant. Phillip and Connie confirmed in person they did have a lot in common, a love of jazz, 80's soul music, books and quiz programs. They each had a gripe about social media, celebrity TV, and overpaid sports stars. By the time it came to say their goodbyes it was true to say Phillip had had an interesting time.

"That's was lovely Connie, we must do it again, perhaps one weekend and go to Gants Hill, re-live memories of the days of Faces nightclub.

"Thanks Phil, definitely where we don't have to drive and can have a good drink, there are some nice bars in Wanstead too."

They departed the pub, strolled to their respective cars having parted with the same kiss to cheeks that had begun the rendezvous.

As Phillip drove off he wondered how his mother would react, her being as she was very status driven. Christine would be aghast about the fact that Connie drove a Skoda or that she dressed so frumpily. He took stock. What did he care what his mother thought? His mother was the complete opposite of him as a person, he wondered how he had come to be her son they were so different. He was by no means a snob.

When he got home his first act was to ignore Connie's message which started "Hi Phil, had a lovely time....." He blocked her number on his phone, went upstairs to his laptop and blocked her from contacting him on Plenty of Fish then changed his profile pictures from the unflattering recently taken to the ones that were used to entice Tracey King.

When they met, in Hornchurch outside Frankie's Wine Bar, Tracey had looked him up and down as if sizing him up. He was wearing a fashionable pair of straight jeans and a dark blue jacket with a pale blue shirt under it. Tracey looked exactly as she did in her profile pictures. Although she was 43, she looked no older than 35. She wore skin tight black trousers, similar to those Oliva Newton John wore in Grease. Her blouse was a brown and tan leopard print and matched her high heel shoes of the same pattern. Tracey had long blonde hair but her eye leashes were jet black and as perfect as if they had been painted by stencil. Which was an accurate description as they had. Full lips with a not too vivid red lipstick and a perfume that was so appealingly rich and fruity it made Phillip salivate, visibly, which was not a good look.

Tracey said coolly,

"Hello Phillip, you have certainly aged since you had those profile photos done. I'll let that pass for now as you are dressed well, even though you are foaming at the mouth."

Phillip was grateful that he had made an effort and had brought a handkerchief that he quickly retrieved from his jacket pocket and delicately wiped his mouth. He ordered drinks, for Tracey a pornstar martini while he took a bottle of Peroni. They went over and sat at a table by the large window. Tracey eyed Phillip with the concentration of an eagle scanning a field for a mouse, and said,

"I am very intrigued about your profile pictures on POF, which I guess is why we are here now. Looks are I guess, what attracts people initially."

Phillip shuffled nervously in his seat which had suddenly become as hot Yellow Mama with current running through it. Yellow Mama was the electric chair that was at Holman Prison, Alabama. He felt a touch of déjà vu as he was now on the receiving end of the grilling he gave Connie.

"So when were you in Jamaica Phillip?"

"Eight years ago."

"Antigua?"

"Year after that."

"When did you last go scuba diving?"

"Fourteen years ago when I took three months off work to go around Asia and Australia."

"When did you catch that fish?"

"I was in Mexico in 1997 I think, or was it 1998, let me think."

"It doesn't matter it's still nearly 20 years ago."

"That main profile picture of you drinking a Peroni on the lawn of that massive house, I take it you don't live there?"

"No I was at my boss' summer barbecue. Does any of that make a difference?"

"It certainly does Phillip I thought you were a regular James Bond adventure type and instead you are more like that PG Tips monkey, Basildon Bond."

Tracey didn't laugh at her joke, she looked bored. She wasn't the slightest bit interested in Phillip's lame attempt at a joke in response.

"The monkey on the PG tips advert? I'm more of a chump than a chimp."

He laughed nervously, Tracey scowled.

"Has anyone said that to you before?"

"No but, slightly harsh I think. Fake it before you make it. Most people embellish their Match profiles don't they?"

"I am going to go before I find out anything more about you that isn't true because I am sure from your messages you said you were pretty senior at the AT&T and I guess that's stretching it."

"I am a relatively senior." Phillip said plaintively

"You were standing beside a nice BMW in one photos. Not yours?"

"My neighbours."

"And your car is?"

"A Ford Focus. It's not old."

"How old?"

"2009."

Tracey rolled her eyes. She took a last sip of her cocktail and placed the glass carefully on the plastic mat, one of a set of four.

"I won't lie, she said, "I'm looking for a husband who has enough money to enable me not to work. I want to have more children and I want to have a nice car and live in a big house. I want to go on holidays to exotic places again like the Caribbean and Asia and weekend breaks to European cities. I have done Ibiza and Malia and Benidorm and I have been out with blokes whose transport is a big fucking red bus. Been there, done that, got a few tee shirts. Did all that when I was a teenager. Thanks for the drink Phillip but I don't think we are suited in any way shape or form."

With that Tracey King flounced out of Phillips life as quickly as she entered it. He was surprised however when later that week he got a friend request from her on Facebook. He accepted it with the desperation of a teenage boy offered a dance by the last girl in the nightclub, and trawled through her photographs and activity history.

Tracey had been married young and had a son and a daughter, Conor and Anna, now aged 25 and 22 respectively. She had always been a very good looking woman but, according to some of her posts, was no stranger to the benefits of Botox and collagen. She had around thirty albums and from the titles Phillip could see that she had holidayed extensively, she had been on a large number of hen nights.

According to Tracey's Facebook posts, her son Conor, was sporty, intelligent, loved by with the girls, charitable, a proficient marksman, a comedian, housekeeper, handyman and an excellent cook. Her daughter, Anna, an Olympic level gymnast, was as intelligent as her brother, lit up a room when she walked into it, had a face that could launch ten thousand ships, was honest, caring, uber-talented on stage and off, mistaken for a model, an innovative photographer, albeit using her Smartphone and the plethora of filtering features, was funny, engaging and a natural on a dry ski slope.

There was an album for each of Tracey's wedding anniversaries and having looked through four of these Phillip deduced that Tracey's husband's name was Mick and he was an airline pilot with Virgin Atlantic.

155

They were best friends, according to Tracey because Mick, who she referred to as "Top Gun" was a marvellous father and had been a wonderful husband, providing everyone with the trappings an airline pilot was able to offer. Mick saw from the early pictures and the later ones that Tracey and Mick lived in the same large house in Weybridge that appeared to have been extended over the years. She was driving a Range Rover Evoque as well as having a convertible Mercedes S-Class cabriolet.

Tracey was the epitome of someone who was Facebook happy. Her life seemed to be a dream.

On reflection Phillip thought, she is probably out of my league, how could he compare with an ex-husband was so marvellous with children to match. Conor and Anna were pictured in front of a house which signified they had flown the nest, especially as the picture was captioned,

"What I am going to do!! My perfect children have moved out!!!"

Phillip had a look over the album names and flitted in and out of these,

"Mick and I in Antigua."
"Mick and I go Thai Island Hopping."
"King family holiday in Miami.
"Mick and I entertain Grant and Ruthie"
"New Year At Chez King"
"Holiday in Marbella."
"Dinner with the Kellett Family"
"Edinburgh Fringe with the Bambinos"
"Mick's funeral."

Slightly surprised at this Phillip dove in. Going through this album Phillip came to the conclusion that Mick had been killed rather than dying, easy enough when there were repeated comments to the effect,

Belinda Copeland,
"So sorry to hear Tracey, shocked when I got the news that Mick had been taken away so tragically"

Intermittently Tracey had responded to messages to thank friends for their support and that yes life is short and no-one knows what is around the corner.

Tashiana Morgan,
"When someone we love passes away,
We ache, but we go on;
Our dear departed would want us to heal,
After they are gone.

Grief is a normal way to mend
The anguish and pain in our hearts;
We need time to remember and time to mourn,
Before the recovery starts.

Let's draw together to recuperate,
As we go through this period of sorrow;
Let's help each other, with tender care
To find a brighter tomorrow."

Phillip with his cynical view, assumed Tashiana's message was copied from an, In Sympathy card rather than made up to suit,

Tracey King,
"Things were not all they seemed"

Tashiana Morgan,
"?????"

Tracey King.
"Inbox me"

Phillip was intrigued, he wanted to find out what had happened to Mark but did not feel he could ask Tracey direct. Having known the woman for two days if was unlikely she would want to share too much of her history with him therefore he hatched a plan. He created a Gmail account in the name of Phillipa Booth and then set up a Facebook account in that name. He listed Tracey King's school St Ursuline's as Phillipa's alma-mata and her current job as a Project Management Consultant, also the same as Tracey. He copied some

157

photos from the profile of Annabel Cummins a random Facebook user. . He sent friend requests to around 400 random people, mainly women with over 2000 friends, including 60 to Tracey and some of her friends, then waited two days.

He was pleased that of the requests 184 had been accepted, including 37 of Tracey's friends and crucially Tracey herself. Only four of the requests were met with the response via Facebook messenger saying,

"Hi Phillipa do I know you?"

These Phillip ignored.

Two weeks after creating Phillipa Booth he sent a message to each of Tracey's friends saying,

"Hiya, I went to school with Jodie Bishop and Tracey King. I don't use Facebook much, because my work has taken me to China where it is banned, coming back I was so shocked to hear that Mark had been killed. I don't want to ask Tracey what happened as I don't want to upset her. Do you know?"

Phillip knew he was treading on thin ice because he was slightly anxious someone might ask Tracey if she knew Phillipa. From the minute he hit the send button to each he wondered if he would be exposed.

He knew that personally he would be suspicious if in receipt of such a message and would check the Facebook credentials of the sender. He would ascertain that the person was new to Facebook and had added people within a short period then assume the person was either a journalist or a voyeur and publically out them.

He sat at his laptop and waited.

The responses he did get back, as his inbox pinged with regularity, were mixed

Carol Tame,
"I think you need to mind your own business"

Georgette Phillips,
"Who actually are you?"

Steve Ellis,
"I added you last week but not sure who you are. How do I know you?"

Carron Burnett,
"WTF"

Mica Thomas,
"Are you taking the piss?"

Robin Ledgerman,
"I'll tell you what you want to know if you send me a picture of your tits"

Jodie King posted on her wall.
"Who is Phillipa Booth. I don't remember her from school Have you had a message from her about Mark King, Tracey's ex?"

Phillip felt a little bit of a panic and considered abandoning his quest, then his inbox pinged again. There was message from Katie Billups which read,

"Hiya Phillipa, I believe in karma and it surely got to Tracey. Apparently Mark was a two timing bastard. He gave the impression he was a doting husband and father. Pilot with Virgin Atlantic, great job, great life great wife but he had two houses. Some of the time when he was supposed to be flying transatlantic he was shacked up with Number two. I always say you can't trust a man who doesn't use social media and he didn't have Facebook, Instagram or Whatsapp. Now everyone knew why. He got his comeupence though. He was driving his bit of stuff for a weekend in the Lake District and turned his lovely Porsche Cayenne over, hit a tree and got killed. It all came out when one of Tracey's and his mutual friends saw an article in a paper in Lancaster about Mark King and his fiancée Roseanne being in an accident and there was a photo of them both. I'm surprised you didn't know because it got in all the National papers when it all came out he had a wife and kids. Tracey used to post loads of shit about how great their life was and it turned out it was all false. The strange thing is she doesn't even blame Mark. Still thinks he is some sort of a god, says the woman he was with would have thrown herself at him because of the kudos of being with a pilot and that Mark was too nice to fight her off. If you would have seen her you could see why he was. Massive fake tits, fake tan, fake lips and fake hair. Everything about the three of them was false. What was worse was he was in debt up to his eyeballs. Gambler and always in lap dancing clubs and up whores I reckon. By the time everyone got paid off Tracey was living in a less than grand drum, driving a less than class set of wheels ha ha

Ps not sure if I actually know you"

Phillip copy and pasted the response into a word document and deleted his Phillipa Booth account.

Phillip felt a lot better about his rejection from Tracey now he knew that she too had been rejected in the past and terminally...

On another of his Face stalking evenings Phillip looked at some of Tracey's holiday albums while she was with Mick, hoping for a glimpse of bikini clad women and, with all the hen party photos thinking there might be something sexually inappropriate. He didn't fail to notice that Tracey only stayed in 5 star hotels, The Marriott was a favourite but she had stayed several times in Marina Bay Sands Singapore, Jumeirah Beach Hotel Dubai, and Hilton Los Angeles. Tracey's albums were all pretty tame so he switched to her activity.

Tracey's mother, Phyllis was also an avid user of Facebook and they shared many posts that displayed there close relationship although Phillip wondered whether they actually had a conversation or sat posing for photos to upload.

Every occasion, visit, outing was celebrated on the social media and whenever there was an opportunity to buy or accept a present it was an occasion that demanded a one hundred and twenty one gun salute.

As Phillip pored over Tracey's previous posts he saw that throughout the years she celebrated New Year's Day, Valentine's Day, Chinese New Year, Mother's Day, Easter, Father's Day, Grandmothers Day, May Day, Christmas Day, St Georges Day, St Patrick's Day, Rosh Hashanah and Diwali. With each of these there would be a picture of her handing a gift to a beaming recipient or accepting one herself.

There were days of angst, hence the post,

"To all you out there that are still chatting shit behind my back lying to me to try to get me closer to you or to try cause more shit because your life is boring. Listen I'm no fool and certainly no mug n just because I'm quiet doesn't mean I'm stupid I just don't give a shit I'm glad I'm the topic on everyone's agenda just makes me realise how even more fucking amazing I am"

When her mother was ill in hospital having caught influenza one day after going in for a hip replacement,

"Just for the record my mum is very ill don't know how long she has left but she's so frail and 8 stone and she's not eating and drinking don't think it will be long. All the selfish fuckers out there can go fuck themselves. I don't usually air my dirty laundry in public but I am fucking fuming. All my real friends are there for me thank you love u all xxx"

Shortly after this post came,

"Very happy in life.....not searching, not requiring anything from anyone, not needing attention.... Just happy and counting my blessings with so many wonderful people that are closer than close"

Tracey was another, like David Thompson, who needed to let people know she had been to the hospital, one such post was,

"Been dreading this day, heading to The Holly private hospital this morning to test to see if I have cancer on my lung"

120 comments insipid later there was the follow up from Tracey in the afternoon,

"Would love to thank everyone for their lovely messages, happy to say I am CANCER FREE, found out I had pneumonia and a chest infection and that's why I have a slight shadow on my lung"

More medical drama,

"Tracey King is feeling furious

So poorly this morning. I rang the doctors to ask for a telephone consultation, I told the receptionist what was wrong and was assured I'd get a call back this morning….well I was in all day and guess what….no phone call whatsoever!! What is this world coming to? Thankfully I'm on the mend but for all they know I could be dead in my bed! I will call them tomorrow"

Tracey was well enough to converse regularly with those that expressed concern and the thread finished with her saying,

"Much better now thanks. I am sat on the sofa with a glass of vino an some chocolate nom nom nom"

Phillip had wondered if Tracey was a bipolar. She was so ecstatically happy sometimes but more often on Facebook after Mick's demise she had moments of despair, which had been shared,

"That moment when you realise there is nothing left"

Phillip did too wonder whether it was just attention seeking because Tracey's post were always met with responses that would do away the need for anyone to use the Samaritans,

The first response to Tracey's post had been,

Kirsty Jennings
"but time. Nothing is ours but time"

Niki Clough
"This is the time when new beginnings start"

Phillip wondered what this person was talking about and whether this would have helped. He read on,

"No matter what happens in your life, as long as your breathing you can turn things around for the better. Keep smiling and stay positive xx"

Tracey may have used that one because she had surely turned things round now Phillip read through the 130 messages of goodwill. As Tracey had 1417 friends it was to be expected that a percentage of them were social media counsellors. One person was religious, which in Phillips view was rarity in a world where the mammon was money and self-promotion.

Brenda Adison posted,

"Will you join me in a group prayer for her. Our father, thank you that you are everywhere present. Thanks you for surrounding Tracey with your power and the love from all of our hearts so that she is STRENGTHENED and renewed in the name of YESHUA. Let Tracey know how much she is loved and that there is nothing too hard for YOU… Therefore she is covered and the answers she needs come to her now, and her way is made smooth and prosperous."

The last post Phillip could read before he came to the conclusion that Tracey had been in an extremely dark place was the one from her that said,

"I have been successfully keeping away from negative and nasty - one slipped through the net over the weekend and it shocked me how blatantly nasty and hateful some people can be. It seems I am not the only one to experience this person's behaviour, either! Well, I shall be taking heed of the instincts I normally listen to and will not be anywhere near anybody with these traits."

When, a year after their meeting Phillip decided, nice to know that Tracey was a lot happier with her life now that she was with a rich Russian and had his baby which meant even if she did split up she wouldn't be destitute.

A more encouraging, for her post was,

"Happy 17 week birthday to my beautiful baby"

with an emoji with the corresponding number of candles on a cake.

On a warm August afternoon Phillip sat at his computer, he was buying his mother a birthday present and decided that, for woman that had everything an air fryer would be ideal. Christine was pretty old school about fried potatoes and still used a deep fat fryer for her special home battered cod and coronary inducing chips.

Phillip had been getting concerned about his growing paunch and with the media wash with statistics on obesity and the potential for type 2 diabetes it seemed a good idea not to indulge in to many calorie bursting meals.

He settled on a £50 Kenwood not top of the range but not too cheap that his mother would turn her nose up at it. His Facebook application pinged and he saw that there was a message in his inbox. Surprisingly it was from Tracey, unsurprisingly it was a group message, which read,

"Hi all, just to let you know I am going to be doing the Walk For Cancer on June 7th in memory of my Nan and for all the brave women who fought this terrible illness some of whom have died. My Nan was an incredible woman who raised five children on her own, she had two jobs and often would go without so that her children could eat and wear clothes. She never complained she never claimed charity or benefits but soldiered on . She was a wonderful Grandmother to me and my sister and we are both going to do this walk together and make her proud. Please click on the link below to go to my Justgiving page and donate as much as you can, all money sent will go towards cancer research so that one day this evil disease will no longer exist. Thank You"

Phillip wondered if ever there would be a cure for cancer, it was after all just nature's way of limiting the population and if it were eradicated it would only mean another one would take its place or else there may have to be put into place some draconian worldwide measure of limiting childbirth.

Limits to childbirth, Phillip thought to himself. Probably not a bad idea given the number of times he had seen women crossing the road pushing prams oblivious to traffic because they were fixated on their smartphone screen. How he loathed them. How he loathed Tracey for putting him on the spot by including him on a group message. He knew that soon anyone who responded would be filling his inbox with comments and he was not disappointed. Or rather he was,

"Done that Hon"

And,

Well done Trace….you will do your nanna very proud"

He looked at Tracey's Facebook page. The same message was posted there. It was also on her Instagram feed. He recalled in her dark days she had once posted that her Grandmother was an evil bitch. He wanted to ask her about this but did not want to reply to the thread so that everyone else could see it so he sent her a private message

"Hi Tracey, just had your message about the Walk For Cancer, cant but wonder though, I recall you poste on Facebook a while ago, you said some not very nice things about her or is this another Grandmother? X"

It wasn't for another two days that Tracey responded and Phillip's message had obviously irked her,

"Phillip. How you have the cheek to bring up something I said who knows when to what I am saying now is a lot out of order. I recall when we met I spoke to you about how much you had lied on your profile. I may have had some differences with my Grandmother but she is still my Grandmother and all the mothers around Buckhurst Hill are doing the sleepwalk as is the headmistress of St Ursuline's the school I will be sending Ilyana to. Everyone does what they need to do to get by so stop being a hypocrite. Are you going to sponsor me or not?"

Phillip was in a quandary. If he further offended Tracey she would unfriend him and he quite liked looking at the pictures of her and her glamourous lady friends. Also if she had another meltdown he would be deprived of some of the posts she would inevitably make. On the other hands he didn't really want to sponsor her.

He thought he was being diplomatic when he responded

"HI Tracey, yes you got me there lol I suppose sometimes things are not what they seem. Have to tell you though I have never been one for lending money or sponsoring people. Hope that's ok"

It obviously wasn't okay because five days later Phillip found that when he clicked on Tracey's name the icon with her profile picture said "Add friend" which meant she had removed him.

165

Phillip was furious. As much as he disliked the woman he liked looking at pictures of her. He enjoyed reading her inane posts and he liked to Face stalk her many friends, some of whom were stunning. Phillip took his Swiss army knife from his drawer and began gouging a line in his desk. He was becoming to get an uncontrollable rage that could only be sated by the sight of the knife making a mark on an inanimate object. He would wish later he hadn't damaged the desk because when he looked at it later it was rather unsightly. Tracey was an inanimate object. She had no feelings. She was a rapacious, she used people and discarded those who were of no use to her with an alarming haste. Fucking bitch.

On the day before the night of Sleepwalk Tracey King was hanging out the washing in the garden of her large house in Buckhurst Hill. Vasiliy had always insisted that his smalls, and they were small, were never hung out on the line for all to see and did not see why, as he had bought a washer dryer and a dryer for the laundry room, together with the laundrette sized washing machine, Tracey insisted on hanging washing out. Vasiliy was at work and Tracey could process her laundry as she saw fit. She loved the smell of washing that had been conditioned with fabric conditioner and had dried naturally under the sun's rays. The washing line had been put up by Reggie Baxter, her next door neighbour who was also the gardener and was a very good natured, if scarcely competent odd job man.

Tracey had hung out the last item of clothing, a Dolce and Gabbana cardigan, which she had given a long smell and was now pulling on the washing line in order to wrap the excess around the hook that would leave the washing billowing in the cool breeze. There was about three foot of excess, Reggie had meant to cut this, Tracey had mentioned it to him several times and she fumed as she struggled with the line. Every time she was in this position, as she wound the line round, she said to herself she should find a Stanley knife but every time she forgot and she kept meaning to ask Reggie but there were so many things to do and Facebook posts were so much more important to her,

Tracey let out a muffled yelp when an arm shot round from the back of her and with her neck in the crook of its elbow applied a choke hold. Tracey's eyes bulged as she struggled for breath, when she came to her senses and realised that this was a fight for her life the

166

vice like grip became tighter. Her assailant was demonically strong and an expert in this particular field of competence because when Tracey lifted up one of her legs to kick back at the stranger she found she was counter attacked with a quick movement that caught that leg and flipped her face forward onto dew covered lawn.

The grip on Tracey's throat did not abate even while she pitched forward and now as she lay there, the stranger's body on top of hers she felt herself grow weaker. She could smell the grass, quite distinctly, as fragrant as freshly picked mint. The smell filled her nostrils and triggered her hay fever causing her to gag. She told herself to go limp, even before her malady was forced that upon her. Play dead and the stranger will release the grip and walk off, then she can get up and go back inside and call the police. Like a predator with its mouth around the throat of its prey that respite did not come. For what seemed like an eternity but in reality was exactly nine minutes the stranger held onto the choke hold until Tracey was not only unconscious but brain dead. To confirm death the stranger then went to the clothes line and cut a length and wrapped this twice around Tracey's neck pulling hard, gouging a furrow into the bruised flesh, face down eyes not seeing, eyes that bulged, proptosis-like with blood vessels that had burst and looked like veiny lines on Mars.

The assailant felt for a pulse, as unnecessary as this action was, then coolly prised the diamond engagement ring and solid gold wedding band from third finger of the left hand of the dead woman. A shadow left the grounds of the house the way that it had been entered.

Christine Anderson

Christine Anderson sat at her desktop computer going through the latest Facebook updates. She quite enjoyed the connection with the outside world that did not require leaving the comfort of her own home and she was also pleased with herself for being such a modern seventy-something. She was in several groups, Essex Ladies What Lunch, The Archers Appreciation, even though she didn't listen to the program. She had attended Ilford County High School for Girls and was therefore in several groups set up by former pupils. She was in every group that enthused about the Royal Family and followed several theatrical groups, Les Miserables, Oliver, Cats, The Phantom of The Opera and Oklahoma to mention but a few.

She enjoyed the everyday tittle tattle that was posted on Facebook, was keen to post an opinion and took great delight if something she said created a new thread of discussion.

The Essex Ladies What Lunch were a very supportive and vocal group of ladies who would often arrange a get together anywhere between Wanstead and Southend. Members would frequently post good wholesome advice or uplifting message, one such being,

Ethel Burnham,
"To everyone in hospital, or at home recovering, get well soon xx For those that are on chemo or radiation treatment, or those that are on drug trials, or have life threatening or life changing problems, we are with you and here for you x If you have mental health problems you aren't alone we are here to listen and support you. If you have a cough, cold or sore throat don't forget honey lemon and hot water xx"

The group was also good for seeking or giving recommendations such as,

Kelly Francis,
"Can anyone recommend a great sports therapist please? I have piriformis syndrome (very much like sciatica). Thanks Ladies."

Sammie Vickers,
"Hi ya, do anyone know where I can have my eye brows done please x."

Christine could tell from Michelle Atreed's posts that she was single and she had a house that required work.

Michelle Atreed,
"Hi.
I'm looking for someone who can fit kitchens please. Can't seem to find anyone that doesn't want to sell me a kitchen first"

Michelle Atreed,

"Hi ladies. I am looking for art and crafts activities that are wheelchair accessible for one of my clients. During the day with a carer. Anyone know of anything?"

Michelle Atreed,
"Now I'm looking for a builder who can put a window in from scratch please ie it's a wall atm thanks"

Michelle Atreed,
Morning xx can anybody recommend a good plumber please to install a bathroom from scratch

Christine Anderson,
"Hi Michelle darling, couldn't you have asked the first tradesman to give you some numbers?"

Michelle Atreed,
"Thought of that Chrissy but you know what these blokes are like, they recommend a mate then ask for 10% of the business, before you know it you are seen off"

Christine did not fully understand what seen off meant, guessed it wasn't good, and wondered but didn't ask why Michelle didn't just go to a quality builder and save any hassle of being ripped off.

The administrator of the **Essex Ladies What Lunch** group was the most active, Bunny Stevenson, enjoyed sharing her life and Christine felt she knew her intimately.

It was clear that Bunny was well thought of by the group shown by the following post,

Verity Rogers,
"I haven't been on here much this year, for various reasons, although have been silently around in the background. There are some people in life who just want the best for those around them, are gentle, kind and open. I just wanted to say that Bunny Stevenson is one of those people. Her efforts and kind words every now and again have connected people, taken away loneliness and without her knowing it, have added a sprinkling of lightness on days which for me have been very dark. Hope you are all having a fab Christmas season and when

I am more myself again, I hope I will begin to be able to meet some of you - Merry Christmas"

Bunny had replied,

"Thank you Constance for your kind words and it makes me happy to know I have helped you in some small way. I'm always around for you and others who are lonely or who have problems, just pm me and if I can sort it I will or find someone who can help, or will just listen. This works both ways as I have my own personal problems with my aging mum, MS and also the demon depression which is never far away, but I can honestly say apart from a few uncomfortable events, that this group has and is helping me so much. How, you might say, well firstly it helps with pain relief, yes really as you all distract me from thinking about it, whether it is reading your posts, thinking and putting up events or on the rare occasions actually getting to a meet up. Secondly I was slipping into depression just before the group started as I had had to give up on my open university degree which was helping with pain relief, (well I was exhausted but it was good), but mum became very ill and was never the same again and it dawned on me how few friends I had. So I want to thank you and everyone else on the group for making my life more fulfilled and the best bit was seeing my sister's face at my mum's 90th birthday party, when many of the girls turned up, she was shocked at all my lovely friends, so I do have a bad side lol xx"

When Bunny posted,

"Well not a good day, I've got to have all the felt re-done on roof as it is leaking and mum's ceiling looking dicey, so very stressed"

Replies came in thick and fast,

Lisa Phillips,
Storm damage in the wind might be covered by your home insurance... Still a pain in the bum tho could do without all that upheaval Lx

Sophie Redmond,
Oh I'm sad to hear that, always the good people that get the crap. Really hope it works out for you with as less stress as possible x

Christine sent Bunny an inbox message,
Hi Bunny If you aren't covered by the insurance I will gladly lend you the money or give you as much as I can afford to."

 Christine wasn't the most generous person in the world but she spotted an opportunity, anyone named Bunny had to be socially upmarket. Christine was quietly pleased when Bunny got back,

Hello there Christine, or can I call you Chris, Chrissy, thanks awfully for the offer that was such a sweet thing to do I am overwhelmed. When I saw your message I simply burst into tears. You're amazing. You'll be pleased to know the damage was covered by the insurance. I am so honoured to get such a generous offer. Can we meet up for lunch? I'm in Brentwood, Here's my number"

Christine did not waste the opportunity. With a head as giddy as a thirteen year old girl about to get a first date she sent Bunny a WhatsApp message and when the two ladies had come up with a mutually agreeable date agreed to meet at Tarantino's Italian.

Christine arrived at the restaurant at 12:30, she and was pleased to see Bunny was waiting at the front desk in conversation with the maître d, Gordon. Bunny was easily recognisable from her profile picture as was Christine and the two women smiled at the sight of one another.

"Hi Christine love."

Bunny was in her early 50s and her appearance matched her name. She wore a richly deep purple suit with a skirt under which was a white blouse with a frilly lace colour. At her throat was a necklace from which dangled a lump of what looked to be amethyst. Her tights covered legs were finished off with an expensive pair of calf high black and tan leather riding boots. When she extended her hand to shake Christine's a large watch caught the light and illuminated the expensive Rolex time-piece.

To Christine surprise Bunny kissed her full on the lips. It wasn't a lingering kiss just a brief touch of contact. Assuming it was non sexual Christine remained unfazed, she caught the aroma of Bunny's scent, there was a hint of lavender and it reminded her of one of the classier old ladies who used to drink in the Red Lion many years ago.

171

Christine knew that Bunny would be well presented and had done her best to ensure she was not outdone as Brentwood was certainly a cut above Seven Kings and she wanted to impress her dining partner. Christine wore a green tweed jacket and black trousers. On her feet she had put on a pair of Chelsea boots. She too wore a white blouse and accessorised with a gold crucifix.

Before they could make start a conversation Gordon said he would show them to a table.

Once seated and with a waiter appearing within an instance the ladies concluded that they both had a preference for Pinot Grigio and opted for a bottle even though both had driven.

"So pleased to meet you Christine. I was almost late I have been with one of the girls this morning, Kelly McDonald, I have got very close to her since she recovered from Hodgkin's lymphoma, I must say I was terribly touched by your offer to pay for the damage to my roof, you must be such a paragon of virtue, a veritable philanthropist," Bunny said with a voice as smooth as a Baileys liqueur. Her voice was very much London, but more Chelsea than Manor Park. Christine was comfortable with refined company and gone were the days when her aitches and tees were dropped.

"Bunny that's no problem, I look at your posts and your uplifting messages to everyone on the group and it is inspirational that you give so much of yourself to people," Christine replied. "Why do you do it?"

Bunny looked at her and for a moment her eyes moistened as though they were about to fill up but she seemed to take a deep breath and held back the flood of tears that were about to brim like an unwatched bath.

"Before I launch into my life story tell me a little about yourself Christine. Briefly though, I took redundancy from working in the Civil Service as a project manager to look after my mother who has showing signs of dementia. I was previously in an investment bank for twenty years but I got out when I split up with my husband because we worked for the same firm and it just wasn't practical, not with him getting one of the secretaries pregnant. I was bitter for nearly twenty years but I had an epiphany that made me change the way I looked at people."

Christine was somewhat taken aback by Bunny's openness but then, given some of the frank discussion that had come up on **Essex Ladies What Lunch** it was probably not surprising that Bunny felt it easy to divulge face to face what was probably out there somewhere on the social media.

Christine replied "Something in common then, I worked in computing for British Telecomm for a long time and ended up in project management when the industry changed. Married, two children. One still living, my daughter died in the 60s when she was young. My son still lives with me, he's nearly 55 if you're looking for a date. I notice you always mention being single."

Both ladies laughed.

"Perhaps if your son has a good few thousand behind him and can pay for my mother's care I'll have him. We would be more like sisters than you be my mother-in-law." Bunny said. She smiled mischievously and Christine felt she had met a kindred spirit.

Christine laughed again "My Phillip Sebastian is waiting to inherit my empire but I don't think he should be holding his breath. I have told him he isn't getting his hands on it and this lady is not for turning."

"Why is that?" Bunny asked, surprised at this revelation.

"Phillip Sebastian has no drive, he works and always has done but he hasn't made much of his life. He had a spell of holidays and adventures but now seems to have gone to seed, he's on his way to the knacker's yard. He spends most of his time on his computer these days and I feel unfulfilled. I want to sell all my assets, including the house and go travelling, explore the world until I have spent everything. I am 77 years old I want to enjoy the fruits of my late husbands and my own labours. I have a pension that keeps me ticking over, I have a little nest egg in premium bonds and my biggest asset is a house worth £600,000 that I can blow if I didn't have my son in it. I quite fancy the idea of renting it out or converting some of the equity to cash,"

"Do you ever win anything on the premium bonds? I have never heard of anyone who has won the jackpot?"

"I never win, that's for sure. I have £50,000 invested, I would have sold some of them to help you out. You seem such a lovely person Bunny. My son is draining all the life out of me and I wanted to give him a shock by offering to do something for someone. He always says I am mean but he lives in my house paying a peppercorn rent and has done all his life."

Christine realised then that her offer to give Bunny that money was not only a way of worming herself more personally into the life of someone who was, it would seem, classy but not well off, but also a way of getting at Phillip Sebastian.

"The insurance covered it but it's good to know I have someone I can fall back on."

"What is your story with your Mum?"

"Mine is a tale of woe. In short my Dad died when my Mum was in her mid-fifties and four years later she met a guy from a rough part of Birmingham, Handsworth I believe. Clem had a silver tongue and a liking for the family silver. Within a year of meeting him they were married and within six months of that he had taken a loan out using her house as equity which meant when he disappeared with her savings six months after that she was homeless. She came to live with me and within four years was going gaga which meant putting her in a residential home that cost my sister and I a fortune.

"Do you have children Bunny?" Christine asked.

"No, my husband didn't want children and so I went along with the idea of us having great holidays, it being just him and me. I came to almost hate the idea of having children. We got married after being together for four years. I hated the wedding, my husband was in control of the guest list so basically it was mainly his family in attendance. He actually chose the dress I wore and what the bridesmaids, five of his busty sisters and one of my friends, would wear which basically were the skimpiest outfits he could find. My family were placed in the worst seats at the reception, he sat down

174

with my Mum and between them wrote a speech that made him out to be the most fantastic husband I could ever get.

While we were at work he rose up the company where I seemed to have every obstacle put in my way. When I said I ought to leave the company and try somewhere else where I might get a chance to move up in seniority he said I might as well walk out on our marriage if I didn't want to work alongside him, even though were in separate departments.

He decided what we watched on telly, what we had to eat and how often I could drink alcohol. He also decided what clothes I wore and when we had sex. Whenever we went out I had to drive because he didn't want me drunk making a fool out of him while he would get plastered and leer over any woman who had a pulse. I did everything to please him because he came from such a good family, in terms of standing, his father had been a General in the army and his mother was a high court judge. Nothing I did made him happy and I often wondered why he had agreed to marry me and then he started shagging one of the secretaries and she got pregnant and he walked out. Sorry I should correct that, he told me to leave. He said his new girlfriend was moving in and he would buy me out.

What I got from a share in the house was short because the estimate was undervalued by a drinking friend estate agent of his. My senior at work, another one of his drink buddies, began to question my judgement. Some of the contracts I had were given to others and my bonus review was so poor I was asked whether I wanted to consider working for another firm. I finally realised that working at the same company as my husband was going to be a problem. Stupidly I thought that if I stayed I might win him back because he would have to see me from time to time but it wasn't to be. He completely owned me and then when he had tired of me he was ruthless.

"So you went to work for another firm?" Christine asked, she was shocked. Bunny had come across via the group as being a very strong woman yet here she was revealing a married life where she was no stronger than a child in a house where the rules were hard and fast. She did what she was told.

"So you went to work for another investment bank?"

"No. The company was scared I would leave and attract some of the clients that had specifically asked that I retain their accounts so they paid me off, handsomely, not to work in investment banking. I joined the NHS and worked at Kings Georges Hospital on the management administration side. Worked there for twenty five years. I was a very, very, bitter person. I began to hate everything and everyone. I hated children, I hated animals, and I hated my boss at work and my boss' boss at work. I hated immigrants. I hated Christmas, Easter and any other celebration religious or otherwise. I bullied my subordinates. I took time off in the school holidays just so I could piss off those with families. I surrounded myself with cronies, young girls who ingratiated themselves to me in order I would treat them better than I treated most other people. I drank two to three bottles of wine a night and smoked top quality marijuana. I was a mess but I was good at my job because a lot of my colleagues were ineffective, inefficient and incapable, in my humble opinion."

Bunny looked at Christine angrily when she said this and it was quite disturbing. That two minute statement was delivered with the vehemence of a dictator about to announce a commitment to war. Christine felt a shiver run up her spine. Was Bunny the person she thought she was?

Bunny continued, "My superiors ignored the complaints that often came in with regard to my temperamental behaviour because I delivered."

Christine noticed that Bunny had barely touched her wine and said sweetly, but nervously, "You don't drink so much now?"

"God yes, but I am finding myself unloading this so much now to anyone who will listen I don't speed drink like I used to. There was a time when I could have drank a bottle in the time we have been sat here. I am starving, aren't you my lovely?"

Bunny's face softened, as though she remembered that her persona should be Caring Essex Ladies Wot Lunch Admin not Angry Manager. She waved her arm in the direction of one of the least busy waiters and asked Christine if she had decided what to eat.

With seafood linguini and risotto pollo funghi with chicken ordered and bruschetta to share Bunny continued to share her life story.

"I had three complaints made about me. Two were from women in other departments over the way they said I spoke to and treated them and one from a guy who worked for me for 18 months. He changed things around for the project I was working on and struggling with. He had great ideas, everyone liked him. He was smart, dangerously good looking, outgoing and diligent. He got on with all the staff inside and outside the department and I made his life hell because I was jealous of him. He resigned saying he had found another job then wrote to the CEO saying he was going to sue the NHS for constructive dismissal. We ended up paying him off but I found myself less of a favourite with my boss now having been exposed by someone he liked, and more of a loaded revolver because the two other complainants were intermittently having time off with stress.

I was still a bitter person and wasn't going to change my behaviour even though less high profile work was coming my way. Then I met Ron, who became my boyfriend. Ron who was some most subservient person I ever came across. He was probably not the best person for me to be with but he had moved in down the road and was persistent on making me dinner. He could cook, he was good at DIY, he worshipped the ground I walked on, and he did exactly what I told him to do when I wanted him to do it.

He was in effect the person I was when I was with my husband and I enjoyed the power I had over him. We were going together for four years and in that time I don't think I washed or ironed one shirt, made him one cup of tea, one dinner, drove when we went out, complimented him or thanked him for anything he did for me.

"You said that in the past tense. You are not still together?" Christine asked. She was finding this all quite riveting. Her view of Bunny had changed. Behind the on- line cheery, positive persona there was a lot of angst that you could only judge when you were in the presence of the story teller. Facebook happiness was as clouded as a mist over an impressive Victorian building that turned out to be a lunatic asylum

"Ron used to do the EuroMillions Lottery. I often joked that if he won he would run off and leave me so I always got him to sign the ticket and I would too. After a while when we were winning about £3 every two months. I stopped signing it because, knowing the laws of probability like I do, Ron had no chance of scooping the pot. Which

177

turned out to be unfounded because he won £1m in the raffle part of the draw and didn't tell me until he had bought a place in Cusco, Peru, cleaned out all the money he had made from the sale of his house, I wasn't aware he had put it up for sale and left the country. He did put £1,000 in my bank account saying it covered anything I was due. He listed everything he had done for me and what I had done in return and as I spent most my money on me I wasn't really entitled to a thing. He had never rented his house out because I insisted that he keep it for the times when I wanted my own space which was quite often when he was too simpering for me to bear, like a lovesick puppy. He had always tried to hold my hand when we went out and it made my skin creep. Any public show of affection was a no no as far as I was concerned and now here I was. Publicly humiliated because he left a note at the houses of all the neighbours saying what he had done and also a cheque each for £2,500. Seventeen houses in our part of the street.

Christine mused over what Bunny had just told her. Her two longest relationships had failed, the first because she was too subservient and the next because she was too dominant. Her relationships had shaped the way she treated those she came into contact with and it would appear in a previous life she had treated others with a disdain that would make Christine's own view of anyone who shopped in Lidl, saintly.

Christine was extremely puzzled Bunny came across on Facebook as the most well balanced, most giving, most grounded, most attentive person anyone could imagine.

"So Bunny did you not try to get a share of Ken's money. Wouldn't you have been entitled to it as you were more or less partners?"

"I thought about it but decided not to humiliate myself even further by trying to get a share. My house was worth more than his and I earned more than him. I always said to him that because he didn't have a pension on his job he would work until he dropped dead because I wasn't going to sub him. When we had meals out, he would pay because he felt it empowered him to ask for the bill, the only time he showed any balls really. When he suggested selling his house, moving in with me and us using the capital for joint investments and leisure I poo-pooed it and told him what was his was his and what was mine was mine. I even wrote things down and got him to sign them because I was so worried I would find out he didn't own his house or he had an unpayable debt and I would get screwed. In the end I did get screwed and I only had myself to blame."

"You've changed. You seem to love everyone now, you can't do enough for LWL. What happened? What was the epiphany?

"My brother David, I probably didn't tell you I had one, he had a fall shortly after Ken had left me. He was on his own and slipped over and broke his hip. He was in agony and was too weak to cry out. He couldn't get to the phone or even crawl to the front door and get out so he lay there for five days. He has no friends, he is not close to our mother to me or my sister. We sort of abandoned him when he was in his 20s and into the rave culture thing. He sort of just drifted out of society out of a having any responsibility and having no money and we couldn't deal with his shit. We found out he had fallen when my sister was contacted by the police, they had found a link to her from a Christmas card or something where she had left her phone number. Apparently it was still up in his house even though he had last sent him a card six years ago. By the time she got to the hospital he was in a pretty bad way. Sandra rang me from the hospital and when I went he was on deaths door."

"The NHS is a place to go and die these days," Christine said, trying to empathise, her head was spinning. In less than an hour Bunny had gone from well-heeled to down-heeled and she was beginning to think that with her sort of family drama it made her life relatively mundane. "Did your brother get better?"

"That was the thing" said Bunny, "he did, between myself and Sandra we visited him practically every day, as did Sandra's two sons who didn't know they had an Uncle. We went to his house, which was a veritable den of iniquity. We got rid of all the drug paraphernalia and the empty beer tins and vodka bottles. We cleaned everything from top to bottom and made his flat suitable for a human being to live in. Do you know what I found one day when I was cleaning up?"

Christine hated this type of question or guessing games. How would she know what Bunny had found in her drug addict brother's flat? A dead body. A birth certificate revealing they were not related. One of the six lost Faberge eggs.

"This is intriguing Bunny do tell," was all she could muster

"It was a photo album with three newspaper cuttings. One of me getting 11 O level Grade As, there was one of Sandra representing Essex at swimming and there was one of David. He played in goal for his school and they had lost 23-0. My Dad had the pictures framed and kept in his study and we used to refer to Dave as Dopey David. We thought it was funny but it must have made him feel like a complete failure in the eyes of us all and that probably made him the person he was. That's what I think anyway."

"Did you speak to him about it when he was well?"

"Yes I did, when he came out and we had a little gathering I mentioned it to him and he said he never felt like he was really part of the family. I suppose it was because Mum and Dad had him so when they were quite old and we came along when they were in their early forties. He said he wouldn't have been surprised if he was adopted. He was always the thick one and Sandra and I were studious, model students, sporty, witty and the apples of Dads eyes"

Christine's ears pricked up, as they always did when she heard the word adopted, she asked, "How old is David?

"Oh he was 55 when he broke his hip."

The answer was of no surprise there was no way David could have been her adopted son he was way too old now but the mention of his misgivings about his parentage made Christine reminisce on the last time she had seen her first born and abandoned son.

"Well at least bringing him back into your life brought the family back together again and you all helped nurse him back to health. So that made you decide to set up a group so that people wouldn't feel alone?"

"Indirectly that was ten years ago," Bunny said, "after three months of getting to know David again, reminiscing about the good times we had, the holidays and the family gatherings and helping him to get back on his feet after having his hip replaced I was at work and got a call from Sandra to say he was dead."

"What," Christine exclaimed, "was it an accident?"

Bunny smiled, "If only it were that simple," she said. "No, David had one of his old friends over and they injected with a speedball mix of morphine and cocaine. I received an education into drug taking that I didn't really need. Morphine is a depressant and cocaine is a stimulant. Having the two together gives users a rush of euphoria. The problem is that the morphine dosage can be too high but it is counteracted by the cocaine. Unfortunately the effects of the cocaine wears off first and leaves the user getting the full effect of the morphine and has respiratory failure. David joins such luminaries as James Belushi, Zac Foley, and River Phoenix in throwing away their lives although David did live, or die up to his nickname as Dopey."

"Struggling to think of this as an epiphany Bunny. More like route to depression."

"It was. I looked at David laid on out in the mortuary and I broke. I felt like my heart had been ripped out of my chest and sliced open by a chainsaw while it was still beating. I thought that in David I had found a man who wouldn't let me down and who would love me for doing something right by him and I found he was just the same as most important men I my life, a let-down. He had a diary you know."

"Was there anything significant in it?"

"Not really. He kept writing that I had taken over his life and was controlling him like a puppet but I can't believe that for a second. Just the paranoiac doodling of a man out of control and blaming someone else. I took it, I didn't want the inquest inferring it was my fault."

"No of course not Bunny, what an awful thing for him to suggest after you helped him get back on his feet." Christine said this but felt somewhat disturbed, she wondered what else David had written in the diary but decided not to pursue that line of questioning, instead letting Bunny continue, which she did.

"I decided I needed to be a more positive person about life because I didn't want to grow old alone but I wanted to do that without a man hence creating **Essex Ladies What Lunch** and having a female network being accused of being a lesbian because the thought of a woman eating away at my vagina has never been top of my list. I do often wonder what it would be like though."

She smiled whimsically at Christine and reached out and stroked her hand gently which her opposite number withdrew quickly.

Bunny laughed and with exaggeration, shuddered, "No, don't think that's for me."

Christine shuddered too, all the lesbians she knew were almost caricatures of female oppression. Short highlighted spikey hair, Dumpy tattooed bodies. One half of the pair always dressed and looked like a man. Christine did personally only know one pair of lesbians. There was a pair down the road who fitted the description. She didn't know their names neither did she wish to, this was because they both smoked heavily and bought Aunt Bessie jacket potatoes. She had told Phillip Sebastian that anyone lazy and stupid enough to buy Aunt Bessie anything was so below her radar. Christine's radar was made in Netherlands, Belgium and Luxembourg.

"I used to be very intolerant," said Bunny, "the slightest thing would set me off. Bad dress sense. People who had garlic for dinner and then attended a social function. Shopkeepers who acted like they were doing me a favour serving them, Children misbehaving in restaurants. People who couldn't spell was a bug bear. Look at this."

She bought out her IPhone and opened the Facebook application and did a search for a name Christine initially did not catch.

"I met Deborah Ashley somewhere I don't know. She is mid-forties and I used to find her posts hilarious, not because of what she wrote but because her spelling was so atrocious. Read this."

Bunny put her phone in Christine's hand and she read,

"Sore horrifikly sad bizzar human this am, as I drove round the corner of Priddle rode to my left outside the sowing shop and by the bank in the senter of the paveman lay what can only be discribed as a Christmas terkey shaped wooden curled up Buddha covered grey hoody.
I was on my way to work so I parked up, and new I had to goe to the

182

curled up figa in the street as no one seemed to be aknowledging the person, best case scenario can buy breakfast and hot drink. No answer, so touched back, he was frozen in a cross legged ball, I phoned 999. They guided me, and a man turned up with a woman during this and told me he had been warking his dog ours before and thought it had been a black sack, he New first aid and together we uncurled what turned out to be a young man, couldn't have been older than 21. No I'd on him, he was alive thank goodness though not conshus, just frozen. I had to go work but got emurgency to take Arrans number who had helped. What the F..., hope he is ok and gets the support he needs."

The next post by the Deborah read,

"And I arrive back in Pitsea. How I ask my self, I can understand if its the wing mirror on the roadside. Then I remember a memory several years ago when I came across a young man kicking wing mirrors off the car's , when I confronted him and asked him Why, he said because he felt like it. I asked him if he new any off the people who's wingmirrors he was kicking off, and he didn't answear. I asked him did he understand how insurance worked? I explaned that often people dont claim because it puts there preminums up, and a lot of people are already struggling with there weekly bills. How people will have to take money to pay to repaire and that may mean for a family that they miss out that week on a treat, or get behind with a bill. I asked him why he wanted to make these people's lives more difficult. Then he said to me " I like braking noses too". When he said this I realised how far we had warked and sore that he was warking down a ally, I had no wish to get into a fisical scuffle. So I retreated and hoped that he had listened to some of what I had said.
Funny how triggers surface memories, was it a "why" did my wing mirror get nocked off. Guess I will never know. What a bummer, I wont be claiming on my insurance."

Christine handed the phone back, she didn't know what to say but Bunny gave her a look of triumph.

"This sort of post used to piss me off and now I don't give a damn. I don't care about anything and I try to be positive about things. I quit my job at the NHS and I am going to write some poetry or a novel. Everyone has a book in them don't they."

183

It wasn't a question, Bunny looked Christine directly in the face and once again the older woman felt uncomfortable. It was if Bunny was challenging her to disagree, which she knew would be a mistake so she didn't.

Christine responded, "Yes I have heard that. Maybe when I have got rid of Phillip Sebastian I will write a book while sitting on a desert island drinking a cocktail and having my toes massaged by a local hunk."

Bunny shot back with, "better make sure Sebastian Phillip doesn't get rid of you first."

Christine didn't know what to think of Bunny but she did find her interesting and, despite the woman's moments of despair she seemed to be as normal as anyone might be amongst fools. They shared the rest of the meal with less harrowing conversation and when saying their goodbyes Christine said she would make more of an effort to attend the lunches or dinners that were being arranged as she had stopped going so regularly lately.

Once she was home Christine went straight to her computer and sent Bunny a Facebook inbox message thanking her for meeting up. She looked at the latest **Essex Ladies What Lunch** missive,

A rather frightening looking lady with pink blue and blonde hair had posted,

Tara Callaghan,

"I'm not the most beautiful woman in the world, but I'm me. I eat food... usually more than I should. I have scars and stretch marks because I have a history. Some people love me, some hate me. I have done good. I have done bad. I go without makeup and don't always get my hair done. I'm random and silly. I don't pretend to be someone I'm not. I am who I am, you can love me or not. I won't change!! And if I love you, I do it with all my heart!! I make no apologies for the way I am.
Ladies, I dare you to put this on your status and share a picture of yourself if you're proud of who you are..."

Tara looked as though she had just had a fight, her eyes were puffy and her cheeks lined with vivid red vessels, the tell-tale sign of a fondness for alcohol. Christine put the post on her own status as a show of solidarity, and out of fear.

She noticed she had had a couple of inbox messages from a distant cousin who lived in Yorkshire but couldn't be bothered to respond. The cousin was Mariad Venables, who had found her on Facebook and intermittently posted to a group she had set up called "The Venables Family."

A quick browse of the latest message, sent to the group, revealed that an even more distant cousin had died aged 84 and the funeral was to be held ten days hence. The usual missive were to announce 21st, 40th or 50th birthday parties.

Christine tutted to herself. The Venables were to her a dysfunctional set. A family whose behaviour fell below what was acceptable but believed they were "normal." The sort of family who would drink themselves legless whilst having children in their care and allow those children to be murdered. Better to be in the group and know of their movements than to be surprised by a headline in the newspaper.

Another share filled her page,

Maxine Clarke,
"Breaking news Carole Lee Scott dies

Her niece confirmed her death on Twitter in a heartwarming tribute."

Christine had no idea who Carole Lee Scott was and decided not to read any of the heart-rending tributes from the women for whom the loss was personally felt. She did not do hysteric grief, whether the person was known to her or not. That emotion had been sucked out of her.

Christine had met different members of LWL on a number of occasions. She found that although some of them were quite interesting, mainly the ones who owned their own business or were "working from home" mothers, some were excruciating to be with. The less thought provoking were mothers of young children at school who dominated a lot of conversation by describing their child through rose tinted glasses as was the fashion it seemed. The lunches would be filled with Mother's sharing photos on phones or stories of their children's achievements, one of these was Melissa Curwen, a nice enough young girl, who had posted of her four year old,

"Evie's first parents evening at preschool. Went well very proud of my little lady, art and crafts is her thing. Cant write her name and struggles with her numbers, shes happy and very kind and caring to others but she always interrupts in group lessons and demands attention, takes her several times to do as she's told. Dunno where she gets that from lol. So happy with her progress. Love my little girl."

Reading this made Christine cringe at the level of satisfaction a parent could get from having a child who was by all accounts disruptive but then Melissa's posts were not wholly uplifting

Melissa Curwen,
"Looking forward to getting in new bed and trying out new mattress "

Seeing this made Christine think Melissa should really try devoting more time to teaching her daughter some basics but saw from a later post this would be unlikely,

Melissa Curwen,
"I've seen a few posts on here about kids home work...I don't agree with it....kids spend at least 6 hours a day at school, and the min they come in they have to work again...I know we all had to do it as kids ....but so much pressure on them nowadays, homework has got to be of a higher standard than before and parents are actually doing most of it as its too much...I don't want to work for 6 hours then come home and do even more, so why should they...to much in my opinion"

Terri Peters,
"And they start so young....totally agree"

Melissa Curwen,
"Evie will only be 4 and 8 months when she starts full time and they have homework then....I know they need to work but isn't 6 hours a day enough ..... we'll be at the beach or in the park after school not sat doing homework that's for sure"

Christine imagined that her daughter would be in the same position fifteen, twenty years down the line. Uneducated, dead end job, blaming someone else for her lack of success.

After having a run of get togethers where the company, including Melissa's was less than scintillating Christine became very selective about who she met.

She was keen to find out more about Bunny and didn't want to pass up an opportunity to be in her company, this became available with the following post,

Kelly McDonald
Right ladies I need some help. My daughter Savannah is 18 on the 25th June. We are having a meal and a few drinks in Nandos in Barking at 2pm on the 17th June which is the Saturday. At the moment there is just myself, hubby and Savannah as her boyfriend is now her ex. He dumped her a week ago What I'm asking is would a few people from here like to come as Hayley is very down and needs some cheering up. Hope some of you can help x

There were a number of replies offering sympathy but no acceptances, Christine decided she would step into the breach and it was the sort of thing Bunny would jump at as she often counselled Mum's on how to raise their teenage girls,

Christine posted,

"Hi Kelly
What a shame about poor Savannah I would love to join you all to celebrate Savannah's 18th. How about you Bunny Stevenson? Are you in?
Xx"

There was no response from Bunny and Christine assumed she was busy with something else but eventually tune in and accept the invite

On Friday 16th, having not seen a response or much activity from Bunny she WhatsApp messaged her

"Hi Bunny, am going to Savannah McDonalds 18th birthday meal, are you free. I thought we could go out for a drink after."

187

Bunny replied almost immediately,

"Sorry Hon, I am just packing to go off to Dublin for the weekend with a lady friend. I think I may be coming out as a lesbian. Tell all later."

Christine almost dropped her phone. So Bunny was a lesbian, despite her denials over dinner. She didn't look like one and she had obviously been attracted to men at some stage in her life. Suddenly her strange behaviour at lunch began to make sense. She had almost been seduced by a raving dyke.

Christine now thought Bunny's reason for setting up Essex Women What Lunch was for her to prey on unsuspecting women, the complete opposite to her statement. Perhaps Bunny was trying to groom her, sound her out and when she found Christine was a normal heterosexual, moving on.

Christine weighed up her new found knowledge and her previous opinion, that Bunny was a classy lady who could open up doors and new experiences. She decided that being an attractive, posh, well-dressed lesbian was perfectly fine.

Now Christine was deflated, she had hoped to see Bunny again but resigned herself to the opportunity to provide some succour to a girl in the midst of emotional turmoil celebrating her first big landmark birthday.

On the Saturday 17th Christine arrived in Barking, not somewhere she had been for a long time and parked in the Vicarage Field Shopping Centre. The walk from the carpark in the town centre to the restaurant had been an eye opener, Eastern Europeans, Africans and Asians were the predominant inhabitants. Christine's exposure to people like this was positive especially the Eastern Europeans, they manned car washes, seemed to be excellent baristas serving at Costa's and Starbucks in many places and the Lithuanian crew that fitted her kitchen were conscientious, polite, efficient and cheap. This was a far cry from those Christine encountered now, shifty looking, beer swilling and as dirty as an unwashed window.

Christine was glad to reach the sanctuary of Nandos which was full mainly of teenagers and twenty-somethings. The clientele were cleaner than the ones she had just seen but still made Christine as uncomfortable as she was on the street.

Almost immediately she recognised Kelly McDonald who was sitting at a table but stood when they exchanged nodded acknowledgements and a wave of hands. Kelly was a very anorexic looking 40ish year old with paper thin blondish rootsy hair and a gaunt face. Kelly was dressed in a floral dress and colourful trainers she beamed a radiant smile that showed a not so full set of brown tobacco tinted teeth. She looked like a character from Shameless.

"Hi Christine so glad you could come you're so kind." Kelly's accent was local to the area but it wasn't unpleasantly so. In fact she sounded quite sincere and polite. Christine warmed to her.

"Not at all Kelly it's my pleasure. You look fantastic."

"I fought the good fight, I overcome that dreadful illness and here to tell the tale. Didn't get many takers for the lunch but we have to look on the positive, Ron is paying so it will save him some money." She laughed and pointed to her husband who was sat down looking at his phone but peered up and gave Christine a cheery greeting. He was the opposite in terms of stature to Kelly, being a large beer bellied man with a balding head and full beard and moustache but he was equally effervescent laughingly, he said.

"Ron by name, Ronald McDonald by nature on account I have ate all the pies…..and the quarterpounders and large fries, and a couple of milkshakes followed by two muffins…..I wash it all down with a diet coke because I'm watching my figure……getting fatter."

"Shut up you daft twat," Kelly scolded humorously. She pointed to the girl who sat at the table, head down, looking at the screen of her phone, "And here is birthday girl Savannah," she said proudly.

Savannah McDonald was a very attractive girl and Christine immediately thought the lad who had split from her must have been a fool. Her unique beauty was slightly masked by her dark makeup and the Gothic look that was an increasingly predominant fashion with girls. In Christine's opinion with or without the black look alongside self-mutilation and low esteem some of the things that were fashionable for young girls was triggered in some cases by over access to social media

Christine's view of Goths was that the misconception of them all being miserable was unfounded. She often had a chat with Cherry who was an uber-goth and worked in the Sue Ryder charity shop in Seven Kings near the station. Cherry was as happy go lucky and cheerful as a cockapoo puppy playing with a toilet roll. Savannah was not so carefree, she looked quite miserable and eyed Christine suspiciously.

She was adorned in a long black dress and equally high black Doctor Martin boots. Her make up around the eyes and on her lips was as black as the look from a bull that has just tangled with banderillos. Through the flesh just above her eyes, through her nose, and through her lip were piercings with black stone adornments or rings which surprisingly to Christine seemed to work and further enhance her mysterious beauty. Both ears were pierced at least eight times each, with the same black stud type finishing on the rest of her face but it suited her elfin features.

Despite Christine's protestations Ronald insisted on paying for Christine's food. This did not make her feel entirely uncomfortable, her coming from an age when a man did foot the bill for dinner. What did make Christine uncomfortable was two hours that followed.

Once seated Ron got out his smartphone set it up so that the screen was supported by a stand he extracted from his pocket and announced that he was going to watch the football, England v Italy in a friendly. He plugged in his headphones and said, as if it made his actions acceptable that he wouldn't make anyone suffer the commentary.

Kelly took out her phone and started to scroll through Facebook and Instagram, chuckling and commenting as she came across posts that were of interest, which seemed to be everything she looked at. Savannah, whose screen Christine couldn't see, began messaging, her thumbs flying over the screen like two whirling dervishes. Every so often Savannah would pause, no doubt waiting for a response and then her thumbs would activate again and off they would go.

After ten minutes of watching their screens, after a nod from Ron to his wife all three stood up and announced they were going to pop out for a smoke before their food arrived. She looked at them as they disappeared out the door and stood huddled within view of the whole of Nandos. Ron smoked a cigarette while Kelly and Savannah vaped. From Kelly's contraption came a cloud of smoke that mushroomed over the trio like the deposit of the Enola Gay.

Inevitably no sooner had they stepped out of the restaurant their food arrived and Christine sat there in embarrassment as the numerous dishes were laid out in front of her. She became aware of other customers looking at her as if she were about to eat two plates of wing roulette, four plates of hummus with peri peri drizzle and three plates of olives.

Ron, Kelly and Savannah were gone nearly ten minutes but returned jauntily from their sojourn and were soon all tucking into their food whilst navigating whatever attraction they found on their phone. Bemused Christine picked at her food slowly, sporadically looking up hoping she might catch an eye and some conversation but all were engrossed in the world away from Nandos in Barking and present company..

Starters finished, all three of Christine's eating companions once again went out to vape and once more as they left shortly before the main courses arrived. Rather than suffer the ignomity of waiting for them to come back Christine went to the entrance of the restaurant, by which Ron, Kelly and Savannah stood and said cheerfully,

"Grubs up....again."

Mouths full, phones in hands, eyes down, only Kelly responded with a breezy "Coming right in Hon just need to get our nicotine fixes."

Christine returned to the table and sat forlornly picking at her Portobello mushroom and grilled haloumi burger with sweet potato wedges and coleslaw. The McDonalds returned ten minutes later and didn't seem to mind that their food would now be tepid. Christine did manage to get some round the table interaction from them. With the food strategically positioned so that Ron's whole chicken, sweet potato wedges, peri peri salted chips, and garlic bread, Kelly's classic burger, fries and coleslaw, Savannah's supergreen wrap, sweet potatoes and macho peas and Christine's plate together with wine and beer were looking like a Picasso. Kelly took selfie pictures with all

191

four, then got the nearest waiter to take some more and these were posted to Facebook and then Instagram.

When Kelly had taken around fifty photos and Christine was able to resume eating and the McDonald's switching between phones and food or in Ron' case robotically, as his gaze didn't leave his screen. It was noticeable that at every table in the restaurant the same scene was played out. The hum of voices was lacking, just the silence created by the swiping of fingers across screens.

It was fair to say though, Christine was pleased when the afternoon came to an end and she was able to go back home to prepare herself for whatever Saturday night had to offer.

The following week as both she and Phillip were sitting in the kitchen Christine made an announcement,

"Sebastian Phillip........I'm going to write my life story" she said as Phillip tucked into his salmon en croute, mash potatoes and runner beans.

"I don't think there is much call for a book about a page long," Phillip said dryly.

"You don't know anything about the life I have had."

"I know we lost Penny but is that something you want to rekindle mother, it's hardly going to be cathartic to bring all that up. Or is it?"

"That in itself would be a story to tell. WH Smiths is full of true-life stories with a tragedy in them."

"Why add to it with one of your own. It just feeds the appetites of the masses who revel in schadenfreude and want to feel better about their own sad lives to hear about how crap someone else had it. No-one will be interested."

"There is so much you don't know about me Sebastian Phillip but you have never been interested enough to want to find out. I need to write some things down before I go senile."

Phillip looked at her balefully. Was she having a sly dig in his ribs mentioning senility? Did she know he knew about her purposely conceived plan of behaviour?

"Going senile Mother?" he questioned, he looked her directly in the eyes as he said this, hoping for a reaction of guilt or a flush of embarrassment. He got neither.

"My memory is not what it was and they say dementia is one of the major causes of death amongst those 70 plus."

"I am sure they don't say that I am sure that. The biggest cause of death for the elderly is heart disease and lung cancer."

"Well thank you Doctor Anderson and what is the third?"

"That might be dementia,"

"Well that's what I said isn't it? Why are you so argumentative?"

"I am too much like you mother I guess, and it means it isn't the biggest cause of death then."

"You are nothing like me Sebastian Phillip, I have had a life. I have worked in pub I have had a career, I have raised you and run a house. What have you done?"

"I have put up with you, that's an achievement."

"Sarcasm is the lowest form of wit, how many times have I told you that?"

"If you've told me once you've told me one hundred times."

"It still hasn't rained has it? When do you think it will rain?"

"What"

"This heatwave. The hosepipe ban. People dying of sunstroke."

Phillip looked at his Mother and wished she or he wasn't in the room. She had always been the most random woman he had ever come across. Now he knew her behaviour lately was intentional it made things worse. She knew how it annoyed him, her sudden change of subject mid conversation she was now proactively doing it. He looked through her at the patio doors and out into the garden and picture himself sitting on the sun lounger, novel in one hand, beer in the other and perhaps a beautiful young lady in a scanty bikini sitting adjacent. He re-focussed on his Mother, took a deep breath and went along with the change of subject.

"Isn't it funny how we get an extreme of temperature in this country and can't cope?"

"What."

"We haven't had rain for ages and the country comes to a standstill. We can't wash our cars or water the lawn an there are council officers in helicopters checking whether anyone is using more than their fair share of water and people are reporting it on Facebook as if the world is going to come to an end. We haven't had rain for four weeks and all of a sudden everyone on social media did a degree in Meteorology. Do you remember what it was like when we had snow last year?"

"What are you going on about Sebastian Phillip?" Christine asked.

Phillip continued, because he was beginning to enjoy himself.

"When it snowed last February, remember, transport at a standstill and everyone was posting pictures of the snow in the garden, on the way to work, whilst off work or on their car. There was a call for Snowman Saturday, everyone was supposed to make a snowman and it seems the nation did. It was the first item on the news, it got more coverage than the update that a Swiss professor has found a breakthrough in a discovery for a cure for cancer and the poisoning of ten people in France including a British family with young children. What a kerfuffle about nothing. SNOW! SNOW! SNOW!. That man who got his kids to make him into a snowman. They covered him in about a ton of snow a pipe to breathe through, and one of them stuffed snow down it causing his Dad to suffocate."

"I thought if you were frozen your heart would stop beating and it could be re-started later."

194

"Try telling that to Captain Scott, Wilson, Bowers, Oates and Evans. Especially Oates. I am going out to make myself into a snowman. I could be gone a while."

"What!"

Phillip saw that now Christine was looking at him in bewilderment and he began to enjoy himself.

"Yes I do believe when they found Scott's body even though he had been dead for eight months they applied a defibrillator to see whether they could re-start his heart."

"Now you're being ridiculous. What's Captain Scott got to do with the snow we had in February?"

"I remember you posted on Facebook. I can't believe the snow we have had in Seven Kings. Why couldn't you believe it? It was snow. I remember when you posted five or so years ago, I can't believe my son is 50 years old. If I had been born 50 years previously, why couldn't you believe it?

"It's an expression Phillip Sebastian. Like, doesn't time fly when you have been having fun Phillip Sebastian, which I am not living with you, draining all the life out of me."

"Because Mother, your life is action packed and without me you would be doing what? Cliff jumping in New Zealand bungee jumping in Thailand, scuba driving the barrier reef, base jumping off The Eiffel Tower?"

"What is base jumping? Is it something to do with that hippity hoppity music? I would be happy just to be getting drunk and coming home happy."

"Oh what and post it on Facebook how wasted you are? Maybe take some pictures collapsed on the floor showing your knickers."

"I wouldn't get drunk every night, just most nights."

"That would be a great thing to do to your liver."

"The amount of tax I have paid I am sure I would qualify for a new liver."

"People like you would deserve to die if you drank yourself toward an early grave."

"Phillip Sebastian….what a terrible thing to say to your own mother. Alcoholism is a terrible disease."

"It's not a disease, cancer is a disease, so is Motor Neurones or Cerebral Palsy. How many people post on Facebook that they are going to get hammered, they are out getting hammered or they were hammered last night. You don't get the same enjoyment out of getting any other terminal disease."

"Alcoholism is a disease Sebastian Phillip."

"You can decide whether you drink alcohol or not. You can't decide whether you can have cancer or not. I thought we were talking about an unnatural reaction on Facebook to the weather."

"I have no idea what you are talking about Phillip Sebastian you change subject so often you confuse me. It's no wonder I think I am going off my rocker."

"You have gone off your rocker years ago Mother. You're as batty as the cat woman who you friended on Facebook who calls her 12 cats her children. You can't decide whether to call me Phillip Sebastian or Sebastian Phillip. I mean who names all her girls cats Sheila and her boy cats Dennis? She publishes a picture of all her cats every day. They wear jumpers. She videos them sleeping. Why would you share such dirge on social media?"

"How do you know about Hermione?"

"She friended me. You must know that I must come up as one of her mutual friends with you"

"Why would you friend someone you obviously have a low opinion of?"

"I didn't have a low opinion of her until I accepted her friend request and realised how mad she was. Her profile picture is of Selma Hayek."

"You thought you got a friend request from Selma Hayek? Do you realise how ridiculous that sounds?"

"I didn't think it WAS Selma Hayek, it might have been someone who looks like Selma Hayek."

"Exactly the same as Selma Hayek. Same hair same face. Same figure. Exactly the same as when she was on the billboard advertising the movie From Dusk Till Dawn. You thought you was getting a friend request from a girl who was dancing semi naked with a snake wrapped round her and could get any man she wanted?"

"I notice you shared a picture on Facebook of the new Royal baby. Congratulations Prince Edward and Kate. Do you know them? Why do you have to follow the crowd? You're like a lemming."

"Are you Facestalking me Phillip Sebastian? If you don't like what I post why don't you apply some filters or unfriend me. That's what you are always telling me to do when I don't like what I see."

"I told you that once. Because that cat woman kept posting videos of her leg with the ulcer that was being treated with maggots and you said it made you feel sick. You said it put you off cooking rice so we couldn't have curries with rice anymore."

"So you wasn't worried about my welfare and inappropriate Facebook posts you were worried about not getting a nice curry."

"Nice? Anyway, anything to avoid getting cous- cous. Who eats cous cous?"

"Alice Keppel does, she posted a picture of it on Facebook last week."

"Alison Caple."

Yes the lovely girl who drives a top of the range BMW. You are bottom of the range. Never been married. Never had children. Haven't got anywhere in your career. Never driven a top of the range car or likely to, unless I kick the bucket."

"When you kick the bucket?"

"I have told you, you won't inherit anything. I don't believe in it. I think everyone should earn their own money and not rely on someone dying to get them nice things."

"So who you going to leave your money to then? The church? The dog's home? Those nice people at the hospice you will spend your last days in."

"My other son," Christine said vehemently. She smiled as she said this but she had a look that had a sincerity to it that made Phillip's mouth dry up and his tongue felt as though it didn't belong in his mouth, like a handful of dust from a Dyson. The mouthful of fish and pastry that was just about to enter his mouth fell off his fork back onto his plate.

"Other son," he stammered, he felt cold sweat drip from the pits of his arms, "You haven't got another son. What other son?"

"I've already started my book, you can read about him in there when I have gone. He is the one I will be leaving the house to when I die."

Phillip looked at her, he felt a loathing he had never felt before but thought better of it to let her see she had riled him. In any case she was talking nonsense. Christine and Oliver Anderson had two children, a boy and a girl, and the girl had been murdered, there was only him. This was just another ruse to get him riled.

"How much have you written so far?"

"Got you interested now haven't I Sebastian Phillip? Not so cocky and argumentative now are we?"

Phillip didn't reply. He chewed slowly having retrieved his piece of pie. If he engaged in this conversation he could possibly be falling into a trap. His mother was clearly trying to push his buttons and this was just another part of her plan. If he said nothing he wouldn't find out whether this was just another step down the slope. If he entered the conversation, no doubt his mother would further infuriate him. The best thing to do would be to read her book and if there was any semblance of truth in it then so be it, he would cross that bridge. If he did have a half-brother then maybe he had some nieces and nephews too, there may be a family out there who could enhance his life.

Thoughts of happy missing families dissipated quickly. Having grown up as an only child, his life was, for him, ideal, except perhaps for a woman to share experiences with. If he did have a brother, married with children he would be forced to attend family functions. He would have to fork out for birthday and Christmas presents. He would be expected to attend school, college or university activities. What if he had a brother and there were a large number of children. This brother could have been once, twice or thrice times married. He might be an alcoholic or worse a sponge. What a nightmare this could be. He had to get access to his mother's book, he might find it hard to contest a will if there was another son."

"Well if you do have another son I guess your book will be quite interesting Mother."

"Don't you think about reading it before its finished Sebastian Phillip. I won't have it published until after my death. I have changed the password on my computer by the way."

Phillip didn't respond. He had helped set the computer up and knew the administrator password. He had also created an account for himself. Failsafe, he had told his Mum at the time. In case anything happened and he needed to access anything

"I've changed the administrator password and deleted your account too" Christine said smugly. She was the one having the fun now. A feeling of smug satisfaction washed over her."

"Were you a spy Mother? All sounds a bit OTT."

"I have had an interesting life. It would be terrible if I didn't share it and as I said, I have another son out there who might want to know more about me and why I gave him up,"

"Great," Phillip said. "Now I know you have a secret past even I can't wait to get a copy. Maybe you can autograph it. To Sebastian Phillip, my failure of a son."

"Or perhaps I can just put you in the acknowledgements. I also dedicate this book to Sebastian Phillip Anderson, without whom, I would have had a more exciting life."

Christine smiled, Phillip seethed, and they each went their separate ways to their rooms and the global highway.

Phillip had the next day off, he had a dental appointment, also his yearly health check in the late morning. Rather than stay indoors, where he had things to do, he thought he would treat himself to an iced cappuccino at Costa and spend an afternoon in the park reading a book, wearing sunglasses. The spate of good weather was accompanied by an abundance of bare flesh and not only were there a gaggle of yummy mummy's wearing skimpy shorts and low cut tops but also office staff in skirts that hugged gym fit bodies. Even some of the stouter women looked great when the sun shone and Phillip was an avid voyeur.

As he sat on a bench surreptitiously eyeing the local talent pretending to read his book he was aware that a rather shapely legged young girl came and sat on the bench next to him. He knew she was young because her skin was flawless, tanned and well-defined. As she crossed her legs, with muscular thighs and developed calves, he could see her feet bore havaiana flip-flops, these were brown. The foot suspended in the air had a butterfly tattooed on it with blue painted toenails each having a diamante mid centre. Phillip was quite entranced at the sight and stared, perhaps for slightly longer than he should have done.

"Do you want to take a picture?" The girl said.

Phillip looked away then looked back at the girl's face, the colour draining from his. He could not believe his bad luck and was so aghast all he could do was stare. He hadn't swallowed the sip of coffee in his mouth and it returned to his lips forming a pool of brown form liquid that trickled down his chin. He could feel the blood race past his neck, plunge in a globule past his chest and sit, as unmovable as King Arthur's sword. The face he saw was that of Tanya from the gym.

"Have you been following me?" Tanya demanded.

"Don't be ridiculous. I haven't seen you for ages," Phillip said indignantly, "I was sitting here first."

"Your perving me again tho incha?"

"I looked at your feet."

"I should stick one up your arse but you'd probably like that init. Like feet now then do ya, got a fing abhat young girls feet ave ya?"

"I was sitting reading my book and you came and sat next to me. I was looking down. What was I supposed to do?"

"Not look at my feet for starters. You are such a creep."

Tanya breathed in deeply and the breasts below her low cut top lifted and fell, like the rubber balloons on an old fashioned ventilator. Phillip's eyes were drawn, from her eyes, to Tanya's chest.

"And now you're staring at my tits again."

Phillip jerked his head upward then to the side determined not to make any eye or breast contact.

"Still a pervert then," Tanya sighed, "forty quid or I'll start screaming."

Before Phillip could respond Tanya added, "my mate Chelsea is on her way, she'll recognise you from last time and you'll be in more trouble."

"I only have twenty pounds," he said. He didn't want a scene in the park and he needed to get away before he had the two banshees screaming at him phone cameras in hand. He wasn't sure what came of the first incident but he was certain that when he was out children who looked like 6th formers at the local school were giving a double take as if in recognition.

.

"Ok that's a fair offer. If you had another forty I might have lobbed one out for you," Tanya smiled, she was as brazen as a two shilling whore.

"No thank you," Phillip said and pulled his only note from his left hand pocket which he knew was a twenty.

He held it put and Tanya took it, depositing it in her cleavage as she said with an even bigger smile, "You better jog on then, I might have to take a credit card payment next."

Phillip fled, he walked briskly to the park gates and scurried out. Any thought of another visit to Costa before going home was out of the question. Feeling his heartbeat had returned to normal after that nerve racking experience but oddly exciting experience. Tanya was stunningly beautiful and she had a fantastic body. He decided to head for home, he kicked himself for getting noticed. He hadn't wanted to create a stir because, there was something he needed to do.

Christine went about her usual daily routine that day. She read the Daily Mail over a breakfast of poached eggs and toast also knocking back three cups of tea before sitting for an hour scrolling through the latest Facebook updates.

It always amused her when she saw looked at the postings of some of the younger generation. English lessons obviously did not include spelling tests. She understood how Bunny had felt when she had made a similar comment. She had been friended by Carl Bishop, the angst filled son of one of the women on the LWL group.

Christine was unsure was unsure why Carl had friended her until she received a Facebook personal message asking her to lend him ten pounds. The request was ignored but Carl didn't ask again and she didn't get another message from him. The lad had had problems with the mothers of both of his children and his grievances were aired almost daily on Facebook.

It was obvious Carl was academically challenged, whenever she read one of his posts Christine would scroll through more, even re-reading those she had read previously. Although many of his posts were lad banter and re-cycled videos or pictures of the bizarre, weird or disgusting many were about the lack of access he had to his children and the fact both mothers were, in his opinion, cunts. Christine began to read,

"How can any mother stop there child seing there dad for over 2 years its discusting all I wana do is see my lil princess wat right has my ex got to stop my daughter seing her dad"

"My mum and dad or Non of my family have botherd with my lil boi this year again waste of space the lot of them all they care about is themselves"

"Cudnt sleep once again finking about my little girl to much im missing her loads"

"Its my daughters birthday tomorrow im trying to get hold of her mom so I can see my princess but I carnt get hold of any of them I wuda though sumone wud of got in contact wiv me but no so once again im probley gunna miss out on another birthday its just plain nasty"

"Its my.daughters birthday on tuesday im trying to her hold of her mom so I can see her but I carnt cuz.they have all.blocked me.so probly guna miss out on another birtthday once again horrible.cunts"

"Just went round to see my boy and ive got sum fat fuckin.mess telling me I aint seing him saying shes foning police if I dont go what a fuckin.wrongun"

"Supposed to have my boy today but once again sum ones hung over so they carnt meet me with my son to busy letting people shit stir and course shit once again.my son.misses out seing his dad all because sum.dirty piss ed wont get out of bed"

"Shit stirin cunts trying to cum between me and my son"

"Trying to keep my boi away from me worse thing anyone can do to me im gunna start putting bricks threw windows today if I dont see my ashley today"

"Woke up in a fuckin mood once again I just wana kill every cunt"

"It's farthers day and didn't even get a call of my daughter never mined getting to see her my baby mom ain't let me see my Chantel for nearly 2 years so who was I kidding her mother's a nasty piece of work just a nasty indervidual"

"My son's first Christmas today and non of my family even botherd with him we got him everythink he wanted anyway so fuck the lot of ya nasty spiteful cunts he don't nead family like mine anyway"

"I feel sorry for my lil boy he ain't seen any of my side of the family his nan grandad uncle auntie not even his sister no one's botherd wiv him its disgusting no ones even tried to see him yet he's nearly 8 months what's my son done wrong fuck all so start pulling ur fingers u selfish inderviduals"

"Off to the gym I think to let of sum anger and steam well neaded before I expload"

"Up all night with tooth ake fuckin killer I nead sum nock out pills for tonite"

"I find it so cheaky how no one in my family gave a shit before now ive got my baby here now they wana lick my ass do one u didnt wana no before so u aint nowing now"

"I feel so sorry for my daughter having a slag as a mother goin threw men like u do electric its discustin letting anyone look after my lil girl while ur out drinking getin wiv any man that will have ya having my daughter past from pilla to post making her think shes got loads of dads ur a fuckin joke sort ya self out"

Christine found it quite addictive reading Carl's posts and would have read on but the doorbell rang.

It wasn't unusual for her to get a caller, usually it was a parcel for Phillip or her, occasionally someone selling double glazing, cavity wall installation, collecting for charity or every so often the window cleaner would ask whether she wanted his services. To that particular caller it was always "No its okay my son will do it."

Christine knew there was more chance of Phillip bringing home Selma Heyek than there was of him cleaning the windows but it got that tradesman off the porch. As she went to open the front door she realised that the caller had already come past the outside door, which

204

was unlocked as Phillip had gone out. Usually callers stayed outside. Christine was ready to berate whoever had deigned to be as impertinent as she opened the door but the words never left her lips.

The caller raised a gun, fitted with a silencer and fired two shots into her forehead and, as Christine fell to the floor fired a third shot into her chest. The caller shut the outside door and walked calmly away.

John Marsh

Detective Inspector John Marsh was having a bad month. His wife Marjorie had written off the family car at the beginning of September. There was some good fortunate, no pedestrian or other vehicle was involved when Marjorie drove the family 2015 registered Jaguar into a skip. She said later that day that her attention had been drawn to a squirrel that was about to run into the road. John would say later, when his ire had abated, that Marjorie would have preferred to have killed herself than run over an animal and she was an idiot. John's father was a dour Yorkshireman and his parsimony was a family the subject of much mirth at gatherings unfortunately some of his ways had cascaded down to his offspring and John for one was not for spending brass where it could be saved. No damage to the skip but having scrimped on the car insurance the replacement vehicle the Marsh's received was a very basic Ford Ka.

Two weeks after the car disaster more misfortune followed when Frances Marsh, John and Marjorie's daughter told them that her new partner Marlon Benjamin was missing.

Frances had been married to Simon Williams, who was the offspring of Dougie Williams. Dougie was also a major player in the criminal underworld and had fingers in several pies, drug smuggling, extortion, money laundering, prostitution and people trafficking. Dougie seemed to live a charmed life. No matter how many times he came under the scrutiny of the authorities his name appearing on police whiteboard across London and the Home Counties when an investigation was under way he had a knack of disappearing under the radar like a wartime U-boat.

Frances Williams and Marlon Benjamin

Frances and Simon had no children though she had been desperate to bring one into the world thinking it might change her husband from a laddish, thuggish, boorish oaf to a loving family man. When after four loveless and childless years of marriage she reciprocated Simon's widely known extra marital liaisons by having one of her own, there were deadly repercussions.

Frances had sex with Marlon Benjamin in her hotel room after he had wooed her at a cousin's wedding that Simon deigned not to attend. For the first time for many years Frances woke up alongside someone whose first words were not, "Get up you lazy bitch and make me a cup of tea."

Frances was convinced she had been impregnated three weeks earlier when Simon had climbed on top of her and forcibly had sex with her after coming in on a Sunday morning at 5.00am from a night out in Romford. When Frances had broken the news to her family and to the Williams', Simon strutted around with the gait and posture of an African lion who had mated with the dominant lioness in the pride. The connection with Africa did not end there.

Nine months later, Simon was present at the birth. Dougie and his wife Madeline, together with John and Marjorie Marsh, were in the waiting room when the ashen faced younger Williams burst through the swing doors, his face puce, fists clenched, and spittle frothing at the side of his lips like over boiled milk.

"It's black. The fucking bastard's black," was all Simon said before he turned round and left the way he came in, leaving John, Dougie, Madeline and Marjorie staring at each other open mouthed until Madeline simply said, "Marlon Benjamin" and chased after her son, followed by an equally bewildered Dougie.

In the weeks that followed it transpired that, post the night at the wedding, Frances had been seeing Marlon who lived four houses down from Dougie and Madeline, with his divorced father Bertram, and sister Beverly. Madeline had known there was something going on but held her counsel. She had once had a brief and exciting fling with Bertram who was a colourful, fun-loving and flirtatious 65 year old Jamaican, hailing from Trelawny a parish in the county of Cornwall, North West of the island.

Madeline thought the affair would fizzle out like hers did. The Williams men were too close knit to let the women of the clan off the leash. Madeline liked Frances and thought she was obliged to have her bit of fun, she knew that her son was too much like her husband, violent, chauvinistic and happy to chase whatever piece of skirt that came his way

Frances moved out of the large house in Loughton that she live in with Simon and moved into a flat in Gants Hill owned by Bertram's brother Francis. Conveniently for Frances and Marlon the flat was vacant due to the Francis spending time in Jamaica building a holiday home in Mandeville, an ex-pat enclave in the South of the island.

Marlon was a doting father, which was unusual given he had clearly inherited his father's bad gene and had, until now been happy to lay beside any manner of girl or woman, large or small, short or tall, who was willing to share a bed. He was the proverbial alley cat and East London and Essex were awash with those for whom alcohol and party drugs served as an aphrodisiac.

It seemed Marlon had his lightbulb moment in terms of commitment the moment he set eyes on his daughter. He loved his daughter and he loved Frances. They had named the baby Ochos Rios. It was part of the current trend of naming a child according to a destination that was or was to be significant. Frances and Marlon had decided that would be their next holiday destination when the baby was older enough to endure a ten hour flight without causing distress to fellow passengers. Everything was planned

Everything about Frances struck a cord with Marlon. She was loving, sometimes painfully so, but she enjoyed his banter and could give as good as she took. He could call her fat after her pregnancy and she would respond by mocking his tendency to suck his thumb when stressed. He could call her a muppet if she had one of her blonde moments and she would attack his inability to cook and remind him that he once burnt a pot when boiling an egg. They shared the household chores, they enjoyed walking, they loved quiet nights in.

Frances was often bemused at the attention Marlon received from women aged between 16 and 60 but she wasn't the jealous type and she believed Marlon when he said that his days of laddish behaviour were over and he was determined to be a good father and partner.

207

Marlon's behaviour cemented Frances's faith in him and his reputation was a thing of the past. He got up and went to work religiously at the BMW garage where he was a mechanic. Sometimes when Ochos, or Ochi as she was nicknamed, would wake in the night crying Marlon would be up. Without disturbing his partner he would sooth his irritable child, feeding her or rocking her back to sleep, singing lullabies or nursery rhymes until she had fallen back into a slumber. Returning to bed, sometimes having only getting a couple of hours himself, before another day at the garage.

Frances was intelligent, down to earth, she was a great mother. She loved a range of food and had become experimental. Although he was fit looking unless he had a meal cooked by his father, Marlon had previously existed on pizza, four pieces and fries from the chicken shop, McDonalds or Burger King. His father and sister had stopped cooking for him because his habit of lodging with random women meant they didn't know when he was going to turn up home.

Since moving in with Frances, and with her was determined to get her figure back after the birth of the baby. Although she didn't mind his banter she longed to get back to a size 8-10 dress. The two were eating pasta, lean meat, fish, fruit and vegetables by the lorry-load. Errol was introduced to fruit and vegetables, some of which he had never heard of. Samphire, avocado, horned melon, black radish, calabash, gai lan. As much as fast foods were missed the new flavours were much appreciated.

Frances was determined to rid herself of the stereotypical Williams favourite fare, roast dinners every Sunday, meat and two veg in the week, fish and chips every Friday.

In the Williams households, only bananas lined the fruit bowl and definitely no Indian food crossed their lips.

Frances further enhanced their lifestyles by signing up at the gym and with Bertram or Beverly babysitting, the new parents would enjoy an hour workout doing a Les Mills Body Pump class or fairly fast paced 45 minute jog.

Bertram was a regular visitor to the flat as was Beverley. Marlon tended not to visit his father as he knew that his presence near the Williams' house was not wise.

Frances was surprised that her or her partner had had no physical contact with the Williams', just a solicitors letter saying that Simon had filed for divorce. Frances knew, from a Facebook post, that within two weeks of the birth of Ochi, Simon had gone to a Phi Phi.

Frances had a Facebook account but since leaving Simon it had lain dormant for posts preferring to keep her life under the radar. She enjoyed previewing the lives of others than advertising her own. Frances, like most proud mothers, did like to share pictures, she was an advocate of Snapchat and would send her friends pictures of the baby. By the time Ochos Rios was 13 months old there seemed to be a normality to the lives of Frances and Marlon.

Frances and Simon's decree absolute had, in the course of time, completed, and Simon was now back in Loughton living with a Thai girl he had met and married on the island of Ko Phi Phi Don.

Duanphen Lawan was no pushover, unlike many Thai girls with western men, she was not subservient. Her ruthlessness and resourcefulness appealed to Simon when he met her. He had witnessed her karate kick a rival seller of cocaine outside the bar he was in. She had then coerced him into buy a wrap at twice the normal rate extolling the virtue of her product and its purity and guaranteeing that he would have the best high of his life or the best ride of his life. Simon received both, one from the drug and one from Duanphen who was a skilled and attentive lover.

An added bonus for Simon was the fact that Duanphen's father was in control of the lucrative drug trade that flourished around the Phi Phi Islands. A post sex morning, lain discussing the perils of shipping drugs into either Thailand or Essex and Simon was anxious to introduce Duanphen to Dougie with the prospect of expanding the Williams empire to the East or creating a new supply line from Asia.

Duanphen found it easy to adapt to life in England and with Simon and her married this should have left Francis and Marlon to live their lives in peace.

Frances was walking along Cranbrook Road pushing Ochi's Silver Cross Wayfairer Special £800 pram when she heard her name called from across the road. It was an old, and once close, friend Naomi Hardcastle, who she hadn't seen for at least two years but with whom she had had intermittent contact on Facebook Messenger. The last exchange was when Naomi asked for confirmation that Frances was with Marlon now. Naomi was an air hostess for Easyjet, rarely spending time in the UK, therefore it was, what turned out to be, a very unfortunate meeting.

Naomi had a nomadic work and lifestyle. The work side meant many nights away, and, while in the UK, regardless of the weather, she enjoyed trips to the coasts of Britain visiting places such as Whitby, Ilfracombe, Beaumaris, Tobomory, Llantwit Major and St Mary's. Naomi's misanthropic and difficult nature meant that she rarely had a partner. No relationship lasted longer than twelve months and was usually ended by the other party, frustrated by Naomi's selfishness, bitchiness toward other women, and single-centred need for attention.

Naomi had just come back from Trogir, Croatia to find the relationship she thought was finally working, with Stevie Woodhouse, at an end. She had text him on landing at Stanstead to say she was back, he had text her back to say he didn't want her back as he was now, once again, dating his previous girlfriend. Naomi was down but not out, she knew another jaunt away from Essex was on the horizon, as would be another man, and that would give her a much needed lift. Naomi greeted Frances with a hug and a big raspberry kiss for Ochi, who gurgled happily in her top of the range pram.

"How are you babe and how is life with the exotic Mr Benjamin? Not had any death threats from Mr Williams senior or junior yet?"

"Trunky wanna bun?" Frances said, laughing as she did so. "All good Nae, so how is it going with you and your love life? Still with Stevie? You look so happy in your Facebook posts. How did you meet?"

"Same shit different day mate. Stevie is no more, as of yesterday, so I am back swiping on Tinder."

"What happened? Every time you posted when you landed either in the UK or where ever your plane landed, his messages were so cute. Must admit, didn't see one this time."

"They always start like that, like, then all of a sudden they have an issue with the fact that I might stay overnight abroad and give me grief. Then I get shit about the sort of person I am. I'm the sort of person who travels a lot and don't take no shit. My Tinder profile says like, I'm an air hostess and when I am like, chatting they say how great like, it would be to see someone who has travelled. Like, for fuck sake like, if they want to go out with someone who is a home all the time find a care worker or a shop assistant. If they can't handle a woman with an opinion go out with a fuckwit."

"I'm sure care workers and shop assistants do travel Nae but probably not as much as air hostess. I seem to remember Cam Watkins split up with you because you called his sister a dog."

"I'm not like, dissing care workers and shop assistants, yeah but like, they only go on one holiday a year because of their wages are shit, like. It's not my fault and Cameron Watkins sister was a dog man, she slept with one of my exes."

"Be hard to avoid one of your exes." Frances laughed.

Naomi ignored this remark, for her having had a number of notches on her bed post was badge of honour. She said pointedly, "Whatever Mother Theresa….Tinder is cool, at least I get to meet people outside of Essex."

"Got any matches yet?"

"Yeah got a date tonight as it goes, some investment banker from Muswell Hill, meeting him down Shoreditch like, where he works like. He might be the one."

"Naomi Hardcastle you are having more long term relationships than Jordan. Are you a serial man trap? You ought to slow down."

"Are you like, saying I'm a sket Fran?" Naomi's voice was sharp, her pitch had raised and her face visibly darkened. The anti-depressants combined with her imminent menstrual cycle meant she was easy to rile and she switched like a bulb.

211

Frances had had had a private inbox conversation with Naomi's half-sister, Grace several years ago. Grace warned Frances, as she did all of Naomi's friends that she thought her sibling was bipolar. An innocuous comment led to a catfight at a party.

"No no Nae, am joking, its only when I last saw you, you had two blokes on the go here and one in Marbella. What happened to the bloke you met off Match.com, the strawberry blonde?"

"He turned out to be a psycho. Typical ginger. Did you know he is inside now for armed robbery?"

Naomi's anger diminished as quickly as it had arrived. Like a cloud that is driven away by an easterly breeze.

"God Frances, can you imagine if I had stayed with Ginge. Can you imagine like, me visiting someone in Wormwood Scrubs or where ever it is he got banged up. Imagine if we had kids and one was a ginger? Can you imagine me walking around with a ginger kid? Mind you you've got a brown one haven't you?"

Frances couldn't imagine Naomi visiting anyone in prison, friend or lover. She couldn't imagine her with a red headed baby. She thought Naomi's comment about her having a mixed race baby was tactless, but thought best not to say so explicitly.

"Sometimes you're better off without them," was all she felt safe enough to muster.

"How is your sister Grace? Her and Paul seem to be the perfect couple. Their kids are growing up aren't they? I saw a picture of the littler one, Jordan is it? She posted loads of pictures on Facebook a few weeks ago. She posted about forty photos when the older one went to school. Mind you her and everyone else who has kids."

"No idea how Grace is. We had a fight a while back but the next day were fine because we had a bond. Anyway, I unfriended her on Facebook after my birthday and we haven't spoke since."

"Why?"

"On our birthdays like we have a tradition where we post happy birthday and a pictures of us together. I do it and we do it as sisters and with our close friends like."

"Oh yeah I noticed that, that's really sweet."

"Well that twat didn't bother and like, she reckons she didn't have time and I know she was on Facebook that morning because she liked some random post by some dickhead bird they met on holiday."

"Maybe she didn't have a good photo she could load."

"She always posted a picture like, where she looked really good and I looked like shit anyway. No excuse. I unfriended her and blocked her on Messenger and we don't speak."

"Harsh."

"So you would have just let it go like?"

"Don't know if I would fall out over it mate. Its only Facebook. Did she get you a present and a card?"

"Shit happens and yes, she bought me a card and a FitBit but that wasn't the point. Anyway, let's move on. Like, your baby is so beautiful Fran, have you got time for a quick vino?"

"I can have a quick Chardonnay Hon, need to get this one home because she can get grizzly when it's too hot."

Frances and Naomi spent 60 minutes in the local pub, catching up, mainly regarding Naomi's travels and occasionally touching on the less exhilarating lifestyle of motherhood.

Naomi was good company, she felt comfortable with Frances because she looked down on her. Divorced, the Williams' may have been bastards but they were rich. Frances wasn't glamourous, she said Marlon didn't like her to plaster make up on and she didn't feel the need to. She had bags under her eyes due to the lack of sleep and this made Naomi even more comfortable.

Naomi told Frances some rather graphic stories about the number of flight and air crew she had bedded whilst carrying out her duties for the airline. A good percentage of the men were married or attached but this did not seem to have deterred her.

Within the 60 minutes the Frances had consumed two large glasses of wine, more than she had done since she had had the baby, and she was feeling light headed.

"Marlon is so lovely" she said, her head was throbbing slightly and she needed to get home.

"Wasn't he known as Mr Busy on account he made himself busy around every woman in East London, Havering, Kent and Essex?" Naomi laughed.

"Admittedly he was Nae, but he is definitely a one woman man now. He is not going to be like his Dad, still shagging women even though he is nearly sixty. He had it off with Simon Willlams Mum."

Naomi nearly fell off her seat. She was used to drinking large amounts, the three large glasses of wine she had had, barely had an effect.

"Madeline Williams. Racist Dougie Williams' wife slept with a black man?"

Frances' tongue had slipped due to the alcohol, but even now she knew she had said too much and tried to recover the situation.

"That was in strictest confidence Naomi. You must never tell anyone. Marlon told me that Dougie was away one time years ago and Madeline knocked saying she had heard what she thought was an intruder round the back. Within about 30 seconds of her knocking at the door Mr Benjamin snr had her knickers off and had her bent over the dining room table. I think they did it a few more times after too. Do not repeat that."

Naomi let out a squeal of laughter and said, "That is the funniest thing I have ever heard. Come on let's get a selfie of me you and Ochichi"

The last thing Frances said to Naomi on parting was, "Remember Nae. I told you that in strictest confidence, don't tell anyone, you know what the Williams' are like. And don't post that picture on social media, I am trying to keep a low profile."

Naomi's reply was a reassuring, "Oh come on Fran what do you take me for. My lips are sealed."

One of the first things Naomi did when she got home was unfriend on Facebook, all the mutual friends she shared with Frances, apply settings so that her friend could not see her uploads, and posted the selfie picture on Facebook. She didn't tag Frances but she did refer to her by name in the picture and Marlon Benjamin was also referred to as the once feckless father.

Two days later Marlon was giving a BMW X5 SUV he had repaired a drive to ensure an engine problem had been cleared. Fate or subliminal homing took him near to Bertram's house and Marlon though he would swing by and perhaps pick up some of the vinyl records he had left there. He still had a key for the house and seeing no car on the drive he parked and let himself in.

Frances reported Marlon missing that evening. She had been texting him since 4pm and had no reply and when he failed to return home at 730pm she had driven to the garage to find it locked. She rang Bertram and Beverley and text a couple of his friends to no avail. When she spoke to her father he advised she sit tight and wait till morning as it was possible that Marlon had met up with someone and gone off for a well-earned night on the lash.

Morning came and Marlon had not appeared. Frances rang the garage and they said that Marlon had not been in to work and that the BMW, which was due to have been ready for the customer first thing in the morning, was not on site.

Frances had a lengthy conversation with her father who in turn, and against protocol, spoke directly to his Detective Chief Superintendent detailing the fact that Marlon had been in the past 13 months a reliable and family oriented man, the missing £100k SUV. John stressed the significance of the baby and the family relationship with Dougie Williams. He had asked for care in assigning the case as he had concerns about Dougie's influence within the force.

215

Detective Chief Superintendent Kiffer Furbank, not convinced at John's entreaties, assigned the case to Detective Chief Inspector Karen Boulding and she, in turn, when assigning two Detective Inspectors selected Detective Inspectors Nigel Maloney and Willie Patterson.

John Marsh

Right now, John Marsh was headed to the murder scene of the recently deceased Christine Anderson. He had received a call from Detective Chief Inspector Boulding and having confirmed he had the capacity to take on another murder enquiry, been given the location to which to head. As an experienced Detective Inspector it was not uncommon for his DCI to send him instead of attending herself, this was not normal practise but with an unprecedented number of murders in recent months and the country terrorist threat level being severe, resource was in short supply. He also was not given another Detective Inspector to share the load, another break from normal practise.

Once at the scene he identified himself to the police officer in charge of the scene, a man he recognised, Police Inspector Dave Blakesley

"Hello Blakey, got you off traffic duty then?" John said jovially, as he approached.

"SIO have scraped the barrel for this murder then?" came the equally jovial retort.

"What have we got?"

"Christine Anderson, aged 74, shot on her doorstep by a person unknown Two shots to the head and one to the chest that has hit her directly in the heart. I guess either of them would have been fatal but whoever did this seemed to want to make sure. My boys have knocked on most the doors and no-one who is in has seen or heard anything. As you can see it's a close with only about 16 houses and of these there were only four with anyone in."

"Who found her?"

"Her son Phillip Anderson. He is aged 53 and he lives with her. He had been out all morning, doctor, and dentist, went to and came back from the park about 1400 he said. I asked him if he owned a gun or whether he or his mother had anyone they were in dispute with and he responded in the negative."

"How did the son seem?"

"Surprisingly calm, practically dispassionate. I asked him if he needed someone with him and he said no he was ok."

"Do you think he might have done it?

"Nothing's impossible. It is rare for a domestic homicide to be done on the doorstep of the murderer without the murderer killing other people, committing suicide or turning themselves in. Until we completely rule him out I would say Phillip should be a person of interest. He might have been clever enough to stage it as if it was a stranger homicide. I had a conversation with him as to his whereabouts, like I said, whether his mother had any enemies, had appeared worried about anything or if there was anything to indicate who might be the killer. His answers were all pretty clear and give no indication of guilt but there was a distinct lack of empathy. He actually seemed rather relieved. He could have arranged for a hitman to take her out."

"Hit person? And I thank you Blakey for your expertise in this sort of thing. You don't have any previous record of empathy or understanding of body language. I am sure we will find that Phillip is entirely innocent and you are completely wrong."

"No problem Marshy I am sure that twenty years down the line some competent copper will resolve this case after its lain dormant because the bloke in charge couldn't find a fanny at a Las Vegas whorehouse."

"I don't really want to know where you went or what you did last time you was on holiday with your missus Blakey."

Both men laughed and John went into the house, had a quick look around being careful not to get in the way of the forensics team in attendance and then went back to the station.

DCI Boulding had assembled a team that would handle family liaison, exhibits, disclosure, witness, forensics, telephone, victim, CCTV, media, interview and intelligence. John ran a start-up session with the team, imparting as much information as he knew.

John decided that he would conduct an interview of Phillip Anderson. His gut feeling was that the son was not involved but he knew that the worse thing he could do was trust instinct or make presumptions. A clever murderer was often the least suspected and better to have a full statement early on in the investigations before there was time for a feeling of innocence to bed in. John also had no confidence in the interviewing skill of David Blakesley, but then John was a perfectionist and he had every faith in his own ability.

John's wife. Marjorie, said he was a pessimist. He thought she was a fantasist and thought of himself as a realist. Right now he was pessimistic about finding out why a seventy odd year old woman had been shot on her doorstep. He fantasised about being given the role of DCI when Karen Boulding had moved on but was realistic enough to know that Nigel Maloney was probably going to beat him to it.

John was a small man. Five foot four inches tall with a fleshy face that had wrinkles that would not be out of place on the hide of a pangolin. He was incredibly fit having competed in tri-athalons from the age of 28 and even now aged 49 he had stopped competing he still swam regularly.

Eight years previously, as a Detective Sargeant, he had chased down and caught a man. It was a fortuitous meeting, John was on his way to interview a witness but joined the pursuit when he heard a cry of "Stop police," and seen two bobbies hot footing it down the same road. The man he caught, was later convicted of murdering his next door neighbour. As he rugby tackled the man and brought him down, John's leg had twisted beneath him and he suffered a tear to his anterior cruciate ligament. The injury had been resolved via an operation but not well enough for John to run. John had become somewhat bitter about the injury because he had enjoyed competition. He did think that if he was not recommended for a DCI post soon he might use the injury for his get out clause from the force, get some compensation and supplement his income by becoming an odd job man.

On the afternoon of the day after the first brief, John and Detective Sargent Sangeeta Patel, knowing that the forensic team had departed, went to Seven Kings to have a formal chat with Phillip Anderson.

The pair could have not been more unlike. John, small, one hundred and forty seven pounds and fit looking, Sangeeta five foot six, one hundred and sixty eight pounds and fat looking. She had flawless brown skin and a mane of this black hair tied in a bun that sat underneath her cap at the nape of her neck. Her sclera was as white as the innocence of a virgin and beautiful brown eyes that danced with curiosity and anticipation. Sangeeta, or Pat as she was nicknamed, had a fondness for car sweets and cake. This was well known around the station, as was her ability as a DS, her lateral thinking, and her ability to coax out information that made her a useful colleague to utilise in situations such as these.

Pulling up outside the Anderson's house they saw that the forensic team had indeed departed. John had been told there was minimal evidence to gather, the house had not been disturbed and the dead woman's body contained the bullets. The shells were alongside her and with concrete paving, no footprints to analyse. The outer door was locked when they entered through the gate. Sangeeta knocked and they received no reply. Rather than stand conspicuously outside they went back to their car.

After two hours, Sangeeta suggested she pop round to the bakery for some provisions and coffees. John agreed but Sangeeta had just stepped out of the car when, to her disappointment, Phillip drove up in his Ford Focus, parked outside and went into the house.

John and Sangeeta waited ten minutes then proceeded to cross the road to the house and ring the bell. As they walked past the Focus, Sangeeta noticed that in the back window was a sticker that said, my other car is an Audi. This made her smile because she had the same sticker on her ten year old Ford Fiesta. Her father Mohan had had a philosophy that cars were one of the most over rated commodity used by mankind.

"A to B," was Mohan's mantra, "You don't need fancy car Sangeeta just one to get you from A to B." The message, imparted throughout

219

her teenage and adult life, stuck with her despite her desire to own something a little more trendy and racy.

Phillip answered the door, he looked surprisingly cheerful and was not unfazed when John introduced himself and his colleague and asked if they could come in and take some details regarding Christine's death.

As John crossed the threshold he couldn't but notice the dried blood that had turned brown but still lay on the stone tiled floor like the artwork of a five year old infant.

Phillip was still facing the two as they came in and he noticed John's glance at the blood, and said, almost apologetically, "I was going to scrub that blood off but then I thought maybe I should leave it in case the forensic team come back."

"I believe the forensic team will have enough evidence now for you to be able to do as you will Mr Anderson," Sangeeta said, as she walked with her boss, in the direction of the finger Phillip was holding up to point to the kitchen.

"I have just bought some cream scones from Marks if you'd like afternoon tea," Phillip said as he ushered the two into the room and closed the door behind them.

"Don't go to any trouble Mr Anderson." John said.

Unsurprisingly Sangeeta countered this with, "A tea would be great and I have a passion for scones."

"No scones for me though and don't feel you have to feed DS Patel either, Mr Anderson," John said as he sat down next to Sangeeta and felt her heel dig into his toes.

"I bought two boxes of two," Phillip said. "My Mum loved them and I must have subconsciously bought two because we would normally have one each after dinner and then again in the evening with a nightcap."

This was a blatant lie. Phillip normally bought two boxes for himself. He would have two by himself in the evening in his room out of sight of his mother and two he would take to work, one to have with his morning coffee and one with his afternoon tea.

"Greggs ones are nice but you've got to eat them on the day. Now if you get them from Marks they can go till the next day and be just as fresh. Waitrose ones…..don't get me started on how lush they are," Sangeeta said, exhibiting her cake knowledge, hungrily eyeing the boxes Phillip had on the work surface, "I am all for scones and tea Mr Anderson."

Phillip had no doubt that this rather rotund but pleasant looking woman liked scones, any sort of cake, biscuits, cheese, crisps and authentic curries cooked in pots of oil. He wondered if Detective Sergeant Patel was expecting to have two in one sitting. "You can call me Phillip," he said as he poured and handed out the teas with a small plate with a large scone on it for Sangeeta.

"Thank you Phillip," said John, and he proceeded with the interview.

"I know you provided a short statement to one of the uniformed police officers but as I am going to be leading this case on behalf of my Detective Chief Inspector I thought I would go over some things if I may. Just for clarity. This is just a formality, you understand that don't you?"

"I am sure if you thought I had done this you would have me down at the station now with a recorder on having read me my rights," Phillip responded.

"We just need to eliminate you from enquiries as unfortunately most murders are committed by someone known to the victim and these are often result of rage, jealousy or greed."

"I am probably a match for two of those. My mother did make me very angry a lot of the time but not angry enough to shoot her on her doorstep and greed may have been a factor as I might have inherited the house and everything she had were she to die. She wasn't charitable and she didn't really like animals"

"You said in your statement you were out all morning and you returned at 1400 on Tuesday but you have no-one to corroborate your

221

movements after the doctor visit. You could have gone straight home and shot your mother, as unlikely as that may have been."

"That's true I guess but then if I was going to shoot her why leave the house. Why go to the park? I walked, there will probably be CCTV footage somewhere along the route home to say where I was. This is all very intriguing but you will find your wasting your time detective inspector, I am not the type of person who would shoot someone, even as horrendous a person as my mother."

"There is no type of murderer Phillip, everyone is capable, given a motive, even if it is just a moment of anger. You say your Mother had no known persons who were antagonistic toward her, she got on with the neighbours, relatives, and friends?"

"Our neighbours keep themselves much to themselves though she had been into the woman next door but one and salivated over the class of the woman. Alison Caple her names is. We have no relatives. Mum was an only child and I had a sister who died when she was about five."

"How did she die?"

"Raped and murdered unfortunately. My Grandparents owned a pub and it happened in there. They never found the murderer. It was the swinging 60s I think rape, incest, child abuse, murder and free sex was the order of the day back then."

"Your mother told you all this?

"About the rape, incest and all that? Mum never stopped going on about it. The murder was never kept a secret. When my Dad was alive they used to mention Penny quite often but I didn't take much notice. When I was about 14 he told me the whole story. My Mum was more reticent about sharing the detail even after that and, to be honest, I quite enjoyed life as the only child so it never really affected me."

"Do you think your mother was the sort of person to have made an enemy?"

"The only thing I can think of is if it wasn't random then she may have insulted someone on social media because Mum can be quite outspoken. I do always think though, that even if someone is sensitive enough to get angry over a social media comment to want to kill anyone they would be a hell of a lot of killing going on. Social media definitely opens you up to a world of the uneducated, complete idiots some of the users.........in my opinion anyway."

"That's quite a thought provoking comment Phillip," Sangeeta said. "You think the most likely suspect is someone on social media. Did your Mum use, for example, Facebook extensively? I take it that's what you mean, it being quite popular still with the over 40s."

"I'm not saying someone on social media killed her, it was probably random or mistaken identity maybe but if was a targeted killing then yes maybe it was a social media thing. Mother was in quite a few groups and sometimes she says things that aren't politically correct."

"Do you know the sort of groups she was in?" Sangeeta asked.

"Women's stuff really and she went out with a few from one in particular, Essex Ladies What Lunch. She was definitely in one for bereaved parents and another for widows, I can't name the particular ones or the others to be honest."

"We have her computer and we can look at all her posts to see whether she did indeed have any malicious or threatening messages. You say you're not aware of anything?" John said.

Phillip's appeared lost in thought and John repeated the question and prompted him by adding "Phillip" at the end of the question.

"No sorry, I was just thinking, I didn't have the password for any of her accounts or even her laptop anymore and no she never mentioned any such thing to me about internet beefs with keyboard warriors. Is that the terminology they use? My Mother could talk for hours about five minute of her life so I think I would know. She was going batty and she could wind me up like one of those toy mice they used to give kids back in the day. Maybe she inadvertently antagonised someone, perhaps not even on the internet, maybe when she was in a shop."

"Why do you say that?"

"Mother was an incredible snob which is surprising seeing as how she grew up in the East End. She was the type of person who would frown at someone if they walked out of Birthdays, the card shop, or Poundland or Lidl. She had a look that made it obvious she felt distaste for such people, as she called them. A look that could curdle milk my Dad used to say. A snarl, as tough as a cheap steak was the other expression he had. Not to her face of course because she would have sent him to sit in the shed if he was ever so bold. "

"Has your mother been abroad recently? Perhaps she met someone who has come to this country for something. Money promised? A loan? Maybe she gave someone her address?"

"I don't think Mother was the Shirley Valentine type."

Apart from social media does she have any hobbies, gardening, golf, bridge, cooking, reading clubs?"

"Hobbies, winding me up. She didn't have green fingers I do the garden. No sports. I think she used to play cards when my Dad was alive but not now. She thought she was a great cook but it was either basic or pretentious rubbish and she liked reading but that not as a social activity."

"We don't have much to go on then."

No she was pretty nondescript was Mother. I don't think she deserved to be killed like that though."

He appeared wistful, but his look as sincere as a cat beside a dead mouse.

"I am sure we will be able to get to the bottom of this Phillip," Sangeeta said, offering reassurance. "We have a few contacts where you can get in touch with groups who can help you deal with this bereavement. Do you want some cards with numbers?"

"Thanks but no thanks. I don't want to sit in a room or worse go on social media, with a bunch of strangers and say Hello my name is Phillip and my mother and my sister got murdered please feel sorry for me. Then have to listen to similar stories of grief. I got the death registered this morning, I am going to sort out the probate this week and get on with things. Mother would have wanted me to move on with my life."

"We'll leave the cards and leaflets just in case and if you have any questions or you think of anything that might help with the enquiry here is my card, don't hesitate to call," John said as he stood up.

Sangeeta gave a look of disappointment when she realised that the interview was over and they would not be in the house long enough for another tea and a second scone.

As she drove away the two police reviewed the conversation with Phillip.

John asked "So what do you think Pat, you were quite quiet. Too much cream cloying your jaws together?"

"Ha bloody ha. You couldn't wait to get out to stop me from getting a second scone," Sangeeta replied. "No, I didn't think I could add much because Phillip was a first. I have never known anyone lose a close relative so recently and not appear to give a shit. He made it clear he didn't think very highly of his Mother yet he doesn't seem the type to have pulled a gun out on her."

"Maybe he is in shock."

"No he is already preparing to take ownership of the house. He has hunches about who killed her. Who would think that? Did you note what he said about it?

"About what?"

About the house."

"Remind me."

"He said he might have inherited the house. As if it wasn't a foregone conclusion. Like she may have given it to someone else but he was an only child as was she. Maybe she was going to give it to someone else."

"True. He more or less ruled out the RSPCA though."

"Did you notice something else?"

"Do tell."

"When you said that we had taken her laptop his pupils widened and he flushed red. It was as if you had said we had found a gun and it had his fingerprints on it."

"Good point."

"Given what he said about her social media use I think the laptop might reveal whether she had upset anyone. Why did he mention that he didn't have any of her passwords anymore? As if he had them once and now he doesn't."

"Better make sure the intelligence people get onto this one straight away before anyone starts to try to cover their tracks or does a runner."

Sangeeta drove back to the station, stopping off on the way to get a sandwich and some bread pudding from Percy Ingle's bakery.

Nigel Maloney

At the same time as John and Sangeeta were driving back to the station Detective Inspector Nigel Maloney was picking up an eight month old Audi TT for his wife Kim from the forecourt of Williams Quality Motors on the Bethnal Green Road. Dougie Williams was giving him the car at a more than reasonable price. Nigel had handed over £15,000 in cash and received an invoice for £35,000. Dougie needed to clean up some drugs money and this was good method.

The two went back a long way. Back when Nigel was a uniformed policeman, first as a constable, then as a sergeant before he trained for detective work, Nigel had turned a blind eye to Dougie's criminal activities in return for information on other miscreants and been richly rewarded. Dougie had provided Nigel with details of drug deals that would prove lucrative for both men. At the meeting point, the seller, buyer or both would be intercepted by two policemen, Nigel and one of his cronies. Each would be wielding official ID but both not officially on duty. When Nigel was unable to source a fellow policeman, a civilian accomplice, would be supplied with credentials. With the potential dealers given the opportunity to walk away, the drugs, and or cash would be confiscated. Nigel and Dougie would split the cash and the proceeds of the sale of the drugs, usually high grade heroin but often ecstasy or cocaine.

"Thank you kindly Douglas. Always a pleasure to do business with you," Nigel beamed as he stroked the bonnet of the red convertible. Kim is gonna love it."

"Well make sure you mention where you got it, and the discount, she might want to drop by and thank me personally,"

"I am hardly likely to tell her I got it cheap am I you half-wit," Nigel said laughing. "I am sure any gratitude she has she will express to me later tonight but I will tell you all about it if you're frustrated. Not getting any off Maddie?"

"Mad by name and by nature that bitch. The last time I had great sex she was 50 miles away." Dougie smiled mournfully, as if recalling a good memory, he then added, "Why don't you tape your gratitude, but I don't want to see your hairy arse bobbing up and down, so make sure I get a good look at Mel."

"I think I will pass on that one Douglas. Knowing you, you've probably got a hidden camera in my house already. I know you have a penchant for that sort of thing you bloody pervert."

"Maybe I should have had one in my own house Nige, or that prick down the road, might have saved me a lot of bother. Things still going ok with the hunt for Mr Benjamin?"

"No witnesses. No body. No evidence. Nothing to tie you to anything. No worries."

"As long as we keep it that way it's all good."

Just then the two men looked away from each other as a car pulled up. A woman and her two children got out. Dougie called out "Hi

227

Cheryl." The woman smiled and the two young girls, in matching school uniform squealed simultaneously, "Grandad."

As the children ran over to cuddle Dougie, Nigel reached inside his pocket and pulled out a bag of fruit pastilles and said, "How about a hug for Uncle Nigel then."

The youngest of the girls, aged six reached out to Nigel's open arms her eyes fixed on the multi coloured bag of confectionery. Her mother's voice was sharp and firm, "Chelsea, no sweets and do not go running to strangers. How many times have I told you?"

As she approached the men, she addressed Nigel directly, "sorry, can't be too careful with the little ones, no offence."

"Course not," Nigel replied, "I understand." He looked at Dougie who eyed him with a mixture of embarrassment and suspicion, then forced a smile and held his hand out.

The men shook hands and went their separate ways.

As Nigel looked in the rear view mirror at the smiling Douglas Williams, a man as dodgy as a rigged fairground attraction. He looked at Cheryl and the two children talking animatedly and then looked at his own reflection and pondered his own criminality.

Nigel was mean as a child, he hated sharing any of his toys but had no sense of fair play when it came to playing with those of his older siblings. As he got older and more aware that he was different in that sense he was less inclined to accept the words of his parents and his Aunts and Uncles who would excuse his behaviour as being typical of the youngest child. He always felt and even looked different. The Maloney's were all as fair skinned and blonde as Scandinavian mountain goats but in no way stubborn,

From an early age his thick eyebrows had been a curse. He was often call mono-brow. An unfortunate severe case of nits meant having his hair shorn off aged 12 and he was nicknamed The Hood, a villain from the Gerry Anderson children series Thunderbirds.

Nigel had self-harmed briefly when he was 12, enjoying the sight of blood running down his arm but this was tempered by a deep longing to inflict pain on others. From there he progressed to dabbling with glue sniffing but the loss of control was contrary to his persona. The next stage was shooting stray cats with his air rifle. Often not so much stray as, within the view of his telescopic lens. This latest behaviour ceased when he accidentally killed the family cat who shared the same markings as a close neighbour. So distraught were the family when Simba disappeared that even the cold hearted killer felt a pang of guilt. Nigel put away his gun after throwing the lifeless body of the cat in a plastic bag and burying it in a nearby field.

The Hood, nickname lasted two years, until an unfortunate classmate yelled "Thunderbirds are go," at him during a woodwork lesson and mimicked walking like a marionette, received a whack across the head with a mallet.

Nigel's parents were interviewed by the headmaster but they made it clear that their son was a victim too, being bullied because of his looks and ostracised because he was top of the class in most lessons. By the time they had left the headmasters office, the lad who had been hit, even when he had recovered from the blow, would not have been accepted back to the school

Nigel stole from fellow pupils at school and from the newsagent where he did a paper round. He managed to elude detection or suspicion by appearing on the surface, except his episode with the mallet, to be a model student of high intelligence and a very conscientious and hardworking paperboy.

Aged 16 Nigel was at a human biology class when the teacher imparted the knowledge that certain blood types were incompatible when determining paternity. Nigel knew he was blood type O because he had seen this written on his patient notes after a tonsillectomy three years previously.

Nigel had leafed through the folder of medical notes and papers in the house and it revealed his father was blood type A and his mother, type B which meant it was nigh impossible for them to be his natural parents.

Eddie and Babs were mortified, but somewhat relieved, when Nigel had confronted them, armed with his new found knowledge and they explained what had happened. How he had been found abandoned in an alleyway, taken to a children's home, fostered briefly, before being temporarily fostered then adopted by the Maloney's.

Nigel took the information in his stride. Eddie and Babs had brought him up in the same way they had their own and considered him their natural child but a lot of the angst he had felt but not shared fell into place.

Nigel's siblings all had traits of their parents in them, generous, fun loving, arty, fair haired and good looking whilst he was dark, brooding, avaricious and as villainous as a Victorian cutpurse.

Armed with five CSEs Nigel could have got a job on leaving school in a bank or similar white collar environment, instead opting to work as an apprentice butcher purely because they used razor sharp knives and there was a good side-line in stolen beef.

Aged 18 he then became a milkman. It was not coincidental that the butcher's takings on beef was restored to its expected level. The Maloney's own milkman had often remarked on the great perk of the job, being finished by midday, he failed to mention starting at 5.00am but Nigel was an early riser and he enjoyed the independence the job offered.

Aged 21 still working for Unigate Dairies, living at home with his parents and the one remaining unmarried sibling, Nigel felt obligated to change vocation when the house was burgled and a large number of items were taken. He was not concerned about the sum of money that was lost, the jewellery, nintendos, portable stereo players, walkmans, cameras, and the much loved camcorder. Nigel was deeply upset when he was asked to provide fingerprints. To eliminate him from enquiries they said, when the policeman asked him to press his forefinger onto the pad but he knew.

He knew that because although he had had items stolen, a camera and a Walkman, he was a prime suspect because he wasn't really one of the family. Nigel made an oath that day he was fingerprinted that he would become a police officer and be accepted fully by his so called family. He would get their approval by tracking down the perpetrator of the crime and bringing him or her to justice.

As soon as he joined the force and passed out Nigel forgot his pledge and set about moving up the tree as fast as he could making as much money as he could and greasing as many criminal palms as was required..

As he got older, Nigel wasn't without his own good looks. His face had similarities with a 50s movie star. He liked a side parting damped down with pomade and kept his dark moustache trim. Not pencil thin like French painter or bushy like a Cornish fisherman. More a seventies throw back. He had a dimple on his chin and although his smile was often forced it revealed a good set of teeth. His unusual green eyes kept him the right side of pleasant looking.

Now, Nigel sat in the Audi, he reflected on his life thus far. The nagging thought came back into his head, the one that had troubled him since his adoptive parents had revealed to him that he was not truly theirs. Who were his parents and did they have a propensity for the dark side that manifested in him. Was it was an inherent behaviour?

Nigel's mood brightened as he approached his house in the fashionable and expensive Essex suburb of Buckhurst Hill. He had divorced his first wife, Candice, fifteen years previously and having no children was able to buy her out. The settlement was amicable. Candice was only too happy to be rid of a man she had long thought of having autistic tendencies and had sucked all the life out of her. He often took jokes literally which meant he didn't appreciate her sarcastic sense of humour. He loved his own company, sometimes when there were visitors in the house. He had a photographic memory for mundane facts, statistics and numbers. He had habits that were unchangeable. One such routine was wearing his underpants in a same seven day cycle with each colour corresponding to a colour of the rainbow. This meant he did not wear black or white pants but had three sets of red, orange, yellow, green, blue, indigo and violet. With Candice an only child and her parents approaching their 80s and not long of this world she would be inheriting a £1m + pile in Effingham, Surrey while Nigel had his job and pension having disengaged from the lives of his adoptive parents and their children long ago.

He had kept the two Doberman dogs which he promptly sold to an associate, Ronnie Hagger, who had just completed a five year ban from keeping animals. He kept the furniture but compensated Candice miserably. Candice's share had been £107k but she was so relieved to be out of the marriage she would have paid Nigel to leave.

Kim Maloney

Nigel had been with his new wife Kim for three years, she was 33. After twelve years of visiting the same four prostitutes on the same days of the week once a week, Nigel decided that enough was enough and he would settle down and have a more exclusive love life. He had met four or five women via dating apps but these led to nothing long term. Fragile women who were needy and self-obsessed. Nigel had no time for those who sought solace from friends on social media and it seemed as though everyone he met was so inclined. Women who cried when they saw an orphan, human or animal. Women who cried when they received a gift or saw one of their children doing something un-noteworthy, such as writing their names, eating by themselves, the first ride of a bike or taking themselves to the toilet.

Kim wasn't much different but she had an edge. Although she was an avid user of Facebook and Instagram she was also as hard as nails, especially physically. Fiercely protective and proud of her son Brady, she became so of Nigel and to him she displayed a loyalty as fierce as a preacher to his or her bible.

Kim had lived a life on the wrong side of the tracks, both her Scottish parents were heroin addicts who lived on benefits. She often recited the Phillip Larkin poem when she looked at them.

They fuck you up your mum and dad,
They may not mean to but they do,
They fill you with the faults they had,
And add some extra just for you.

So it was that five out of eight of her siblings were welfare dependant junkies.

Kim had never felt the need to indulge instead she met through her family a big time drug dealer, Stevie Palmer, who himself also did not indulge but was happy to sell to those with less self-control. For a number of years once the drug dealing of her husband grew from wraps of cocaine to international deals with contacts in South America and Europe, Kim lived a lavish, yet not too decadent lifestyle, a four bedroomed house in Brentwood full of expensive furniture and artwork paid for by the proceeds of the drug trade. Stevie was wise enough to conduct his business away from the family home as their son Brady was a quite demanding child whose inquisitive nature and propensity to find trouble followed him like a chick that has imprinted peril as a mother.

Fortunately for Kim and Nigel due to the unpredictability caused by his special needs Brady he attended a boarding school in Southend from the age of 11.

It wasn't until Brady had reached Y5 of primary school that one of the more caring and attentive teachers suggested Kim should have her son tested for dyslexia. Kim did this and this was positive, as was the therapist's view that the lad had Asperger's syndrome and attention deficit hyperactive disorder.

The diagnosis did make Kim feel better as she had often felt a failure. Facebook helped and she often posted her feelings throughout Brady's infant and primary days,

Kim Palmer,
"Feel an absolute failure. I literally hate Brady's homework more than I hated my own.
Wish I could make it easier for him to deal with.
He could literally burst with frustration "

Robin Whitlow,
"Google no help?"

Kim Palmer,
"It's not the work Rob, just trying to get him to do. Even just to write the answers. Mission impossible "

Billie Simpson ,
"What is it? The homework I mean? Can't mum help? X"

Kim Palmer,

"It's just getting him to sit and focus for 10 mins.
Meltdown city! "

Tbumi Obama Kegugu ,
"I have it with all my four.
Turn TV off. .no tablets etc until he does 10 mins. .then 10 of TV, etc
Or he can try and do more which means he can get more TV.
If he refuses no TV. Etc. It's hard but it's worth it in the end. Sending
big hugs to give you strength. Xx"

Kim Palmer ,
"Thanks hun.
We always attempt it with no distractions but still so hard to keep calm
and understanding x"

Tbumi Obama Kegugu,
"I know it's so hard but homework is not the end of the world.
Teachers don't even look at it properly as I did a test once to see if
they paid any attention to it, guess what , they don't!! I wrote
something rude ©@π they didn't notice..... So although it's good
practice to get him to focus for small bite size pieces of time and
concentration it's not the end of the world and definitely not enough
for you to stress over. Plus if they understood ADD and dyslexia...
They won't put press on YOU or him.
At the end of the day... You know I practice what I preach.
3 of mine at university (last one to young yet)
Feme had to be retested for dyslexia as an adult as the childhood
test isn't valid for adulthood. Came back as dyslexic (very bad,) and
also ADHD.... But he's at university.
So please please don't stress, get him to learn in fun ways with you
relaxed and laughing.
Small chunks with no interruptions (no TV) with rewards like watching
a program together afterwards. It works
Love you sis xxx"

Betty Whitlow ,
"Your legal requirement is for Brady to attend school, which he does.
He is learning nothing from these extremely fraught sessions. It's just
causing unnessesary friction and distress to you both. Studies have
proven that homework is of little value to children's progress. Brady is
learning and absorbing in his own way. He's reading on his tablet and

doing Maths too. It's so difficult for him as he fazes in and out and does not remember what he is supposed to achieve. Xxx"

Kim Palmer,
"Thanks Nan"

It was with great relief that Brady was packed off to a special educational needs boarding school in Southend that provided the right environment for children who had the same problems as him and were moving to the difficult teenaged times.

When Stevie was shot in a deal with an Albanian gang that went wrong things could have gone horribly were Kim less steadfast. The underworld had become more frenetic and gangs were more fluid. Chinese, Greeks, Romanians, Ethiopians, Italians, West Indians, there was no end of nationalities vying for a piece of a very lucrative pie and collateral damage was a daily hazard. When Stevie's number was called only Kim knew where his latest haul had been stashed and only she knew where his £1.4m was secreted.

The Albanian's had put out a contract on everyone in the Palmer family, his siblings, their children and their associates. Kin was left in no uncertain terms about this when a bullet with an explicit note was delivered to the house by DPD special delivery.

A weaker woman might have fled but Kim was wily and knew that the best thing to do was negotiate a deal. Nigel Maloney was already known to her, through Stevie, as a man who could be counted on to clear things up. She was going to the police, as directed not to by the Albanians, but Nigel was a different type of police.

Stevie had pocketed a stash of money and cocaine, one of which was due to be given to the Albanians. The drugs and the money were returned together with £400,000 of Stevie's personal pile. It was an expensive payoff but it bought Kim her life that of Brady's, her Mum, Dad, grandmother and siblings although she would have happily paid less and had some of her family put to the sword.

Nigel brokered the deal for her, through his underworld contacts, and Kim showed her gratitude by first cooking him a meal then offering herself as dessert.

Not long after Stevie's funeral, before she considered herself and Nigel an item, Kim had a brief relationship with a Libyan she had met in a coffee shop.

Hatoum Al Khahuri was a pleasant enough but intense man from the city of Benghazi. He was in Essex attending an English course at the UEL that was run by students there. Hatoum had visions of deviating from his plans and thought he had secured his passport to a better life with Kim. Looking back at the relationship Kim saw it as only a need for male company and a way of coping with the absence of a man in her life post bereavement. Hatoum had been told quite firmly that she would not be making a third visit to his bedsit in Dagenham.

Hooking up with Nigel was Kim's first chance, she thought, to be able to live without having to spend any time looking back over her shoulder. Nigel was well respected in the circle of villains they both knew and she later found out, held in high regard by the colleagues to whom she was introduced. Her assumption was that however shady his behaviour was, he still did put some of the bad guys away. To Kim, child or wife killers and muggers of old ladies were far more heinous crimes than the member of the drug trade who killed one of his own.

Kim was overjoyed when she saw the Audi, with personalised plate K1 MAL, even if Nigel could be quite obtuse sometimes and secretive, often vindictive, he could always get back on her good side by an ostentatious display of affection.

This was even better than when she had told him about her recurring migraines she had experienced since the birth of Brady. A visit to the local hospital and an x ray -revealed a small non-malignant tumour. Rather than wait four months for an operation on the NHS Nigel had her whisked off to Poland for an operation that removed the offending growth. The surgeon who performed the operation Kyle Menschich gave her a watch that resembled a FitBit but it required no batteries and was waterproof. It was elegant, it allowed access to the internet, and could switch from analogue to digital display. Kyle made Kim promised not to take it off as he said it contained copper beads in the bracelet that with constant contact to her skin, would ensure she never had another migraine or headache.

236

Kyle had been insistent and spoke to Kim as if she were a child being asked to make sure she brushed her teeth nightly. Kim complied, the watch never left her wrist.

Sat now, the wheels if her new car, Kim asked Nigel to take her picture with her latest version Samsung Galaxy smartphone and immediately posted the picture on Facebook with the comment,

"He's gone and done it again, just when I thought my amazing husband couldn't get any better he has got me a TT for my birthday"

Responses back ranged from the congratulatory:

Vanessa Banks,
"Nice one Mel your Nige certainly is an amazing man"

Martin Tribe,
"Cant believe he has done that now all the wives are going to want a new motor lol"

To the jealous.

Gillian Potter,
"OMG Mel didn't you just come back from Cuba? Lucky cow some of us can only afford to go camping"

Deborah Gillmartin,
"Why do some people always post about what they have instead of just enjoying their lives. Normal people cant get new cars when the old one is falling apart. We don't all have perfect families"

Deborah was duly unfriended.

And from Phillip Anderson, who she had friended after he had stopped and helped her when her car had a puncture on the A12, a smiley face.

Most of Kim's posts were of things she had or did. Holidays, jewellery, clothes, pictures of fancy meals. Black tie events with the police force.

As she did not work, having no skill of any note. Her job was to keep the house immaculate and herself looking tidy, and this she did.

Having escaped the bedlam and dysfunctionality of a heroin racked household Kim had an obsessive need to keep things surgically clean in the houses she had shared with Stevie and now this one with Nigel. It had been slightly difficult before Brady boarded, because he had had a habit of moving things in agreement with his own feng shui, but all in all order was, the order of her day. The fridge was cleaned daily, as were all the white goods. The hoover was emptied after every use, which was every day. Mirrors and ornaments were polished.

Kim went through a phase of posting pictures of the landing toilet on Facebook, it looked as though it had never been used. This was practically a fact because the toilet was not used on a day to day basis as it was in her words, saved for best. Ken was ordered, and complied with the rule that only the bedroom en-suite should be used by them. The two toilets would be photographed then pictures posted side by side with the caption,

"Clean enough to eat out of."

Some of Kim's friends found her behaviour bizarre, some ridiculous, some were intrigued. Eventually her cleaning posts became Facebook noise ignored by many until they were no longer a thing. Kim's posts attracted little or no attention until the previous February when it snowed, as had been forecast for over a week, and she updated the community with,

"Hit the co-op before 8am to bag any bread like substance - no loaves left so wraps, brioche, fresh rolls and part baked it was, don't leave it too late peeps xx"

Sharing of that post by the lemmings that morning meant that by noon every corner shop and express store had ran out of bread and milk. Supermarkets rationed customers to one loaf and four litres of milk and fights broke out up and down the country. The police were unable to get to all the affected stores due to the lack of four wheel drive vehicles and mob rule took precedent. Anyone who had posted that they had secured a supply of bread and milk were attacked in their by angry mobs.

The bedlam had lasted for 24 hours when the temperature in the afternoon of the following day rose to two degrees and with a heavy shower of rain the snow disappeared like a white handkerchief out of the hand of a magician.

During SnowMageddon, as it came to be known, Phillip Anderson had watched the unfolding chaos on the 6pm news and felt incredibly smug as he had made a loaf of brown bread in the afternoon. Working from home due to the weather meant he was being paid to work from home doing as he chose, which was as little as possible.

Christine, deep in her campaign of attrition, made a loaf of white bread knowing her son would only eat Wholemeal. Both Anderson's watched a clip of two large ladies slugging it out for a loaf of Kingsmill Thick White Cut in the doorway of Asda.

In the present day Kim and Nigel sat, each drinking a glass of Merlot, the television was on, one of the many quiz shows, but both were browsing their own iPads.

"How's things going with that Marlon Benjamin case?" Kim asked.

"Why are you so nosey?" Nigel said laughing, "You only want to hear about the cases that might have some gossip and scandal attached to them. You could find truffles with that hooter of yours."

"Gossip and scandal are what make my world go round. Which is why I read Heat magazine. Your favourite." Kim teased.

"Nothing to report Nosey Parker. I daren't tell you anything anyway, you might put it out on one of your Facebook groups."

"Couldn't do that Nige, not unless I had some juicy pictures to go with the info."

"Why do you Facebook people feel the need to share your lives and everyone else's with the world?"

"It's not the world, it's only my friends and it's therapeutic."

"I bet half of your Facebook friends you don't even know." Nigel emphasised YOUR FRIENDS and said it with a mock theatrical lah-di-da accent.

"I know them all on Facebook. Anyway I and millions of others like it and it keeps me from going out getting hammered every day. At least I can go on Facebook and find out what's happening round here, round somewhere else, and in the world. It's like my delivered to my device newspaper."

"It's ALL FAKE news and misinformation you dozy mare. There's a team of geeks sitting there planting information that all you lot suck in like you are drawing in breath. There are robot accounts liking stuff so it seems popular and the Russians have been proven to have influenced the Brexit vote and the election of Trump."

"Change the record Mr Maloney," Kim said playfully and added "Any news on you sitting the Detective Chief Inspector exam?"

"Kon tiki."

"What?"

"The Kon-Tiki expedition was a 1947 journey by raft across the Pacific Ocean from South America to the Polynesian islands, led by Norwegian explorer and writer Thor Heyerdahl. The raft was named Kon-Tiki, after the Inca sun god."

Kim realised that Nigel had been paying more attention to the quiz show than she had thought. One of Nigel's skills was to be able to multi task and give each task his fullest regards.

A voice intoned from the screen, "What was written in cuneiform script around 500BC?"

"Babylonian mathematics," said Nigel confidently.

The contestants on the quiz show remained mute.

They did not know the answer to the names of all the heads of state in the EU countries or the name any of the Japanese emperors between the 5th and 6th centuries or whether NEFF ovens utilised read only memory. All this minutiae was stored in Nigel's brain given his prolific memory for detail, however innocuous it was to the average man on the street.

Kim admired this aspect of her husband but she had no more interest in Japanese emperors than she did the offside rule or the number of nails were used to tack down the roof of the tool shed in the garden. She repeated her question,

"Any news on you sitting the Detective Chief Inspector exam?"

"I had a word with old Kiffer Furbanks Detective Super last week, he keeps saying that with Karen Boulding going soon it will open up the spot and its between me and John The Gimp Marsh.

"You'll definitely get it then if you're up against John Marsh. I spoke to him at the last ball, as boring as a drill. You'll get it Nige I know you will," Kim said, stroking her husband's thick black hair lovingly, even though it was full of gel.

"Fucking blue eyed boy Marsh. His Dad was a Detective Chief Superintendent so that's one mark in his favour. No-one knows who my real parents are."

"They must have been mad to have given up a lovely baby like you."

"Mad…..so you're saying my parents are mad are you? Nigel snarled.

The switch from brevity to hostility was as instant as a flare lighting up a night sky. Nigel's face was contorted with rage and Kim cowered. Nigel's tolerance level was sometimes as low as a limbo dancer's pole, and as dangerous as one that had been doused in kerosene and ignited.

"Not mad. They must not have been thinking straight to give you up." Kim said, trying to extricate herself from a situation that might result in an evening sulk or worse, a fat lip.

"Not thinking straight? Temporarily mad then. They didn't give me up, I was dumped in an alley to die. Whoever did it was a psycho and they passed on their psycho genes to me. Fucking pair of cunts whoever they were."

"Sometime people do things without really thinking it through. It might have been your Mother was too young or she was married."

"A whore then?"

"No she might have made a mistake."

"In a moment of madness."

"I don't know Nigel. You don't need to worry about it though. You've done alright for yourself."

"Yes I've done alright. By being a cruel evil selfish bastard. Everything I got hurt someone else. I fell out with the family that had the compassion to bring me up. I turn everything to shit."

"Not with me you're don't. You're the best thing that ever happened to me Nige, you would never hurt me either. I know you wouldn't, and you are the most loyal man I have ever met."

"I've got bad blood. My parents gave that to me then dumped me. Fuckin hate them. How many times have I told you to stop covering yourself in fake tan? You look like an oompa loompa."

With that Nigel got up and walked out of the room, out of the house, into his car and drove off. Kim knew he would be back soon, he just needed time on his own to reflect. Nigel did not come back until the early hours of the morning she had stirred around 0300 and he was not in the bed. There was no sign of him downstairs and finding it easy to fall back into a deep sleep Kim returned downstairs at 07:30.

She found Nigel sitting at the breakfast bar in the kitchen, head on a tea towel snoring heavily. Beside him, under his elbow, was a large envopack pouch envelope which Karen prised from him and with it not sealed, peered inside, and saw it was crammed full of banknotes, and a gun. There was a plastic Tesco's bag for life by his feet and in that she saw there were 4 slabs of a grey substance wrapped in clingfilm. With her background, she knew what the slabs were.

She picked the gun up went down the large cellar and flicked a switch on the wall that revealed a large walk in chamber. In the chamber were seventy guns of various shapes and sizes that Nigel had confiscated or obtained legally. He could have handed them in but gun collecting had always been a hobby for him and Kim was happy for him to have such an interest. He had revealed to her that he had picked up a large number of weapons from a businessman for a decent price who had purchased them on the dark web. Nigel had failed to also tell his wife that he had arranged for the man's house to be burgled four months after being given this heads up. The businessman was relieved of his collection and as the purchased had been made via the dark web, there was no follow-up.

On another occasion the force had carried out a dawn raid on addresses of Ukrainian and Russian gangsters post a series of tit for tat shootings in West London between two rival gangs. In one house, where Nigel had accompanied the team, he had gone alone into the converted loft and under a bed, in a box had found two revolvers fitted with silencers. Nigel had secreted the guns in his large overcoat pocket and added them to his collection. Nigel had also sourced guns from a number of girlfriends who were holding them for their African and Afro-Caribbean gang member boyfriends.

Despite her finds, Kim's emotions were in denial. While some wives might question why her off duty husband had returned home in the early hours of the morning with such a haul she had no such reservations. As far as Kim was concerned, acting on information received Nigel had gone out and, being the dedicated police officer that he was, aborted a criminal act. Any other thought was too much to contemplate after what had become of Stevie Palmer, therefore these were shut out of her mind.

John Marsh

It was a drizzly Tuesday morning in October the sort of rain that, together with temperature of four degrees made the comfort of indoors ever more pleasant. John was given information with regard to the Christine Anderson murder that would mean a trip outdoors and a second interview with Phillip Anderson was going to be necessary. Sangeeta called Phillip to make sure he was in and was given a reply that he would be back from the funeral directors in thirty minutes time.

Forty minutes later like Groundhog Day, John and Sangeeta found themselves outside the house, Phillip's car wasn't outside therefore they gathered he had been held up. Unsurprisingly Sangeeta suggested going to the bakers. John, in his capacity as fat monitor, vetoed the suggestion and wondered if he had time to give her a lecture on obesity, the related illness of diabetes 2, and the negative effect on the NHS budget.

"I'll be back in 5 minute Guv," Sangeeta pleaded, in a childish whine. Drizzly rain gave her an appetite for sugar, as did excessive sunshine, hail, frost, snow or a wind chill.

John decided to change the subject and get Sangeeta's mind off food. "Pat, have you noticed the amount of dog shit there is on the pavements these days? I don't want to have to sit in the car with your boots covered in excrement."

"Give me some credit, I think I can negotiate output from dogs on a 500 yard jaunt up the road."

"Why do you think we are seeing a proliferation of dog do? It was never like this two years ago."

"I have no idea Guv but I am sure you have a theory, none of which will fill my empty stomach."

"I do have a theory. No point asking for an opinion if you don't have one yourself. What would be the point of that?"

"No point Guv. And your theory is?"

"I blame the popularity of pugs, French bulldogs, cockapoos and labradoodles."

"Are they known for having bowel problems?"

"Of course not, I am sure they are as regular as clockwork. Problem isn't the dogs, to be fair but the owners."

"Of these particular dogs?"

"Exactly."

"Why not Labrador owners, or Alsatians or staffs, or mongrel dogs even?"

"Owners of dogs which are fashionable are usually new dog owners who didn't realise when they saw that cute dog on Facebook or Instagram that although it looked gorgeous in a tartan jacket or with glasses, or a hat, or it appeared to be talking, telling its owner it didn't want to go on a diet. Unfortunately for Mr possibly, but probably Mrs or Miss Stupid, it was not a child that after years of potty training would eventually relieve itself in a toilet

"What?

"Pugs, French bulldogs, cockapoos etc., they are all fashionable and the owners of them don't realise that the nasty stuff that comes out of the bottoms of these dogs has to be cleaned up."

"What's your answer to this dilemma? Enforce nappy wearing? Culling? Dog poop tax for popular breeds?"

"Warden patrols. £200 to anyone who shops someone who doesn't pick up their dog do do. £1000 fine for perpetrators."

"What about the people who can't afford to pay?"

"Those dogs cost about a grand each so if you can afford to buy one you can afford the fine."

"I heard that some of these dogs are being shipped in illegally from Eastern Europe so people aren't paying top whack for them."

"Confiscate goods. TVs, iPads, Playstations."

"What if the person hasn't got a fashion dog and he or she is homeless."

"Regular dog owners are responsible people. The homeless. Take the dog off them. They only have it so they can claim an extra £10 a week in benefits, then they spend a fiver a week on the dog and a fiver on drugs. Don't get me started on the homeless."

"I didn't get you started Guv, but what about me nipping to the bakery."

"Mr Anderson is sure to come along laden with buns that you can scoff to your hearts content."

"Do you not think if we come laden with buns and he doesn't he might be more loose tongued?"

"With his mouth full of cake?"

"He was as chatty as Alan Carr last time and he had his own cake."

"Go on then but be quick and don't tread in any dog shit."

Sangeeta moved like an Olympic champion albeit a shot putter, she flicked the latch pushed open and slammed the door so hard the car rocked from side to side.

"Make sure you shut the door Pat," John muttered under his breath as his colleague scurried off.

Sods law dictated that as soon as she had reached the point of no return Phillip would return. John estimated it would take twelve minutes for her to get to and from the bakery. Four minutes after her departure Phillip drove up in his Focus. The space outside his house had been taken by someone who was visiting a neighbour so Phillip had to park further up the road. He came back to the house with a brown A4 envelope in his hand, he looked fraught as if he had received bad news and marched purposely to his front door, opened it and went in.

Sangeeta came back 15 minutes later with a plastic bag that bulged with her booty. It was obviously housing a selection of cakes and pastries and John sighed heavily when he saw her. She got into the car and shut the door so gently John thought she was either practising working under cover, or had heard his sarcastic comment. She opened the mouth of the bag as soon as she sat in the car and was about to describe her haul.

John jerked his thumb at her and said, "Don't get make yourself comfortable Pat, the Eagle has landed, so we can go and share your cake with Mr Anderson."

Sangeeta gave him a dark look and rummaged around the carrier bag and from it extricated four Greggs paper bags. "Best we hold some back. I bought us some sarnies and some cake for tea later," she said.

She smiled a beautiful toothy grin. Large, brown eyes and her thick eyelashes accentuated her look, that of a majestic doe. She was fat though and despite John wishing she took more care of her diet he knew that she was a brilliant detective and potentially one for the top. If only she didn't have such a sweet tooth. Heart attack waiting to happen.

John's train of thought was interrupted by the thwonk of the car door as Sangeeta had exited and shut it once again with such force it made his dentures rattle. He got out too, shutting his door with less venom, looked at her, shook his head and rolled his eyes.

Together with John they crossed the road, went up the path to the Anderson's front door, and rang the bell. Phillip responded almost immediately, as if he had been hovering inside, he looked less fraught.

He said as he ushered them in, "I saw your car across the road and didn't see your colleague. I wondered why you didn't come in, didn't realise she was doing a cake run. You are obviously planning on being here a while. You should be trying to find the killer and not breaking bread with me really. Do you really think we should eat so much cake PC Patel?"

"Can't eat too much cake Mr Anderson. Those two words are mutually exclusive. Much and cake. Makes me shudder."

Sangeeta flashed a smile and Phillip, like most men, melted like a snickers bar left on a window ledge in August.

"Call me Phillip and I suppose I ought to give you as much insight into my Mother as I can and yes you're right. Can never have too much cake."

If Phillip was guilty of any wrong doing he was playing the role of an innocent man impeccably.

"We thought we would return the compliment after you were so hospitable last time we were here Phillip," Sangeeta said, amiably.

"Yes and we just want to clear up a few things," John added.

Phillip showed the two, once again into the kitchen, and offered to make tea.

The three sat, like friends discussing the weather, each picking their favourite from a selection of two cinnamon buns, three ring doughnuts, a cream bakewell, a chocolate cream finger, a cherry shortbread and two toffee yum-yums.

"How are the funeral preparations going?" asked Sangeeta.

"Can't believe how much it costs. Mum insisted on a burial, the most expensive plot, the most expensive coffin but not too much to be spent on a buffet and no free drink unless it was out of my bank account. She wanted to spend a fortune on her very dead carcass but a pittance on the very much alive people attending. Not as though many will turn up. Did you want to ask something specific? You said you had some more information but needed to ask me some questions."

"Yes that's right, "John replied "On the day of your Mum's murder you said you were at the park but that no-one could corroborate that?"

"I did."

"We had some officers go to the park a couple of days later around the same time you said you were there and asked if anyone had seen you. Do you know what anyone might have said?"

Phillip drew in a large mouthful of air, not realising there were crumbs of cherry shortbread in his mouth which immediately flew down his windpipe causing him to have a coughing fit. He tapped his chest with the thumb and forefinger part of a clenched fist and red faced said,

"At the time I couldn't remember whether anyone could vouch for me."

"What about now?"

"What about now what?"

"Now you have had time to reflect can anyone vouch for you being in the park? We need to establish that you have an alibi because right now you are the only person who stands to benefit from your mother being dead. You really need an alibi."

"Something happened in the park but it was rather embarrassing."

"You'd be surprised how many things can be perceived as embarrassing but are not so Phillip," Sangeeta chimed in. "It's probably better if you can tell us as much as you can so we can pursue other pertinent lines of enquiry rather than spend any time establishing where you were."

"I wasn't going to mention Tanya because I was embarrassed."

"Tanya is?" Sangeeta pressed.

"She goes to the gym," Phillip looked at the shortbread then at his ample stomach, almost forlornly. "I used to go to the same gym. It's the second time it's happened."

"What happened?"

"Her accusing me of staring at her. I got into a bit of a debate with her and her friend down the gym about staring. They thought I was staring. I wasn't but they are the sort who, once they decide someone else is in the wrong they are the jury judge and executioner. Fake boobs, fake tan, fake hair. Fake smiles, everything about them makes me wonder what benefit they offer to anything or anyone. I had to pay Tanya to shut up. She was going on about me staring at her legs as we sat on the bench in the park. I was sitting there first, I didn't even know it was her."

"You thought it was okay to stare if you didn't know her?" Sangeeta said. An avid feminist and one who detested wolf whistles she never got, she was about to get her claws out

"What you were doing is by the by Mr Anderson. She could have offered you an alibi and saved us the trouble of digging into your afternoon," John interjected. He looked at Sangeeta as he spoke and his eyes said, not now with that don't look at me like I'm a piece of meat lecture, now's not the time. Sangeeta, to her credit softened.

"Did you arrange for someone to have her killed Phillip?" Sangeeta had quickly re-sharpened her talons.

"I am not the type to kill my own mother. On the doorstep of my house. Neither am I going to hire an assassin. Even if I wanted to I wouldn't know where to look. We bickered, but murder. Why would I do that?"

"Because she had another son, and you had a brother you didn't know about and she had said in her book if she found him she would change her will. How much do you know about your brother Mr Anderson? Did you arrange a professional hit on your Mother?"

Phillip's head was bowed he couldn't believe he was being accused of matricide even though the thought had crossed his mind on more than one occasion. He lifted his head slowly and spoke slower still.

"I did not kill my mother Detective Inspector Marsh. I did not pay anyone to kill my mother. I might not have had the best relationship with her but I am not the sort of person who would even know who to go to have someone murdered. What is this, downtown LA? I don't think she even had another son, I thought she was just being vindictive."

"We are afraid not Phillip," said John, "The team that looked at your Mother's laptop found she had a word document entitled Christine Anderson….My Life Story. She said she had a son when she was a teenager, she didn't give the name of the father but she told her best friend Kathy McGuiness. Her parents never found out. The two girls dumped the baby's body in an alley and we are still trying to follow up where that baby ended up. Your phone records have been thoroughly checked and there are no calls to numbers appear to be out of nature, you don't make many calls, to be fair. That is not to say you didn't have a burner or conduct an assignation off the grid as it were. Is there anything you feel you need to tell us at this time?"

"Not the most original names for an autobiography. What in god's name is a burner?"

"An untraceable phone."

"I didn't have anything to do with my Mother's death."

"You do have a motive though Phillip, which means we will have to dig deeper into your relationship with your mother."

"That's perfectly fine. Unless I am stitched up you will find that I did not murder my mother and you will have wasted your time with this line of questioning. I think I might need to say no more until I have a lawyer present."

"That's your right Anderson." John was now addressing Phillip with less of a friendly tone. The change was deliberate, he wanted to unnerve the man who sat before him.

Phillip sat silently, as if admonished, and suddenly the taste of the sugar from the shortbread combined with the saccharin in the tea hit his senses but left a bitter rather than pleasant feeling.

"Something else came up that was even more disturbing than your mother's death Anderson," John said gravely.

Phillip looked at John balefully. He did not like the tone John had adopted and considered walking out. His curiosity got the better of him.

"What have you found then Marsh?" Phillip said, trying to be equally disrespectful, he tried to replicate John's steely glare but found himself blinking nervously several times before lowering his eyes.

"You have a Facebook account, is that right?" said John.

"Well that would be right because there is a Facebook account with my face, my name and stuff I have posted," Phillips said, sarcastically.

"It could have been a fake account. People have been known to use other people's names and pictures to create an account for all sorts of nefarious reasons."

"I assume the account you have checked is mine I am not aware I have been cloned."

"Six people in your list of Facebook friends have been killed in the last six months."

"Some of these people may not be friends, Facebook definition of friends is very tenuous."

"Helen Tyler, Keith Huntsman Keri Young, David Thompson, Tracey King and now your mother. All dead. How do you explain that?"

Phillip looked deep in thought. He was, he thought long and hard about the names that he had been given. The names of people he detested because they used Facebook to antagonise him. No Ricki Finn, yet.

"Unexplainable. Coincidence. Am I getting a lawyer?" Phillip said flatly.

"What did you think when these people started dying?"

"Apart from Keri Young, who used to do my hair I didn't even know they were dead."

"You didn't wonder why they stopped using Facebook?"

"I couldn't care less if no-one ever used Facebook again."

"You didn't see any posts that offered condolences?"

"I am not a Facebook junkie. I am not on it that often."

"We are going to check that Anderson."

"That's perfectly fine."

"A witness saw someone in the vicinity of the location where David Thompson was killed. There was also CCTV footage of someone leaving the scene after Keri Young was killed. Although the person wore dark clothing, a hoodie, dark glasses and a dark scarf the person was about the same height as you, about five, seven. They were more athletic than you but then whose to know whether you, the man with a ju jitsu belt, has recently piled on the pounds."

"Narrows it down to a lot of people."

"We are going to have to ask you to provide details of where you was on dates we are going to give you and you need to furnish an answer as honestly as you can. If you prefer to respond in the presence of a lawyer we can arrange for one to be sent now but I do think you should let us know anything now that you feel could benefit us with our enquiries into these murders."

"I can look at my diaries and tell you where I was on some of the days but some of the information will be on my work laptop if it's a weekday and I left that in the office yesterday." Phillip said casually.

All the events occur on weekdays, some early morning some during the day and some in the evenings."

"I would have been at work."

"You work every day?"

"Obviously not. For example I was off the day my Mum was killed, but like you say, I have an alibi and I don't know any hitmen."

"So you say Anderson. Here are the dates. We will be paying you another visit though. Very shortly I would guess."

John gave Phillip a piece of paper with the dates and names of the deceased against the dates.

Sangeeta scooped up the plastic bags which held the cakes that had not been eaten. Both she and John stood up and made for the kitchen door. Phillip looked at Sangeeta wearily but said nothing, he then got up and showed the two officers to the front door.

John and Sangeeta returned to the station knowing that at 5pm an investigation briefing was to take place, they gathered around the area designated for this particular crime to get an update and to provide details of their latest conversation with Phillip. On a board in front of the seated police were pictures of the murdered victims, with names, location and date of death, it tended to focus the minds of those present.

Detective Chief Inspector Karen Boulding led the briefing. A tall dark skinned woman with a thin face and a demeanour that could be as hard as a doorman's bicep.

Karen's parents had come to England from Barbados in 1957. Donald Boulding's father had been a policeman in his home country and his son continued in that vein. Donald had had a distinguished service in the police force, of his four children, three of them boys, only Karen had followed him into service. Karen was a natural leader, she had never married, no children, and a career woman. She had always been a tenacious detective rising through the ranks impressively, breaking some balls on her way. Coming to the end of her time now she had become jaded, worn out from the increased paperwork and procedure of the present day, the constant trial by social media, the blame culture and the reactive policing, dependent on tabloid interest and hype.

Her biggest bugbear was having a Detective Chief Superintendent, namely Kiffer Furbanks as a boss. A man she could barely stand being in the same room as he had a reputation as a self-confessed old school, Neanderthal sexual predator. Furbanks behaviour he convinced himself, was simply high jinks, and friendly banter. Kiffer encouraged cronyism, tribalism and had no interest in complaints of racism, homophobia or sexism. The two were poles apart but, with pensions looming, neither was able to rock the boat of the other.

On her part Karen's biggest fault was that all her life she had an underlying desire to be desired. She liked to be flattered by men as well as by women. Never having had a pass made at her by her boss was paradoxically an axe she had to grind with him.

Nigel Maloney, with his 80s porn star moustache and silver tongue was one of Karen's favourites within the unit. When he asked if he could sit in on the briefing even though he was not involved in the case she had no issue with that, even though he had often complained about the ever increasing workloads placed on the unit with no additional resource.

"Ok team," Karen said, "who is going to go first although maybe Intel should and summarise where they are." Karen never failed to ask for an opinion and then make a decision.

Detective constable Melvyn Willis cleared his throat and took up centre stage.

"Christine Anderson's laptop has a word file on it and showed that she is writing a book about her life story and that she had a son on the 1st April 1960, she abandoned the child in an alley that same day. That story has been substantiated because she told her best friend Kathy McGuiness who was visited by a couple of detective constables and confirmed this was the case. Kathy said she believed that sex wasn't consensual, that the father of the child had forced himself on her. She said that although Christine didn't say she had been raped she seemed to suggest that the man who had sex with her gave her no choice. She wouldn't give a name, she said it wouldn't be fair if the man was alive and she was just being presumptuous. When we pressed her she clammed up temporarily, then said it could have been one of several men, then started to get upset. The child was placed in Bonner Road Children's home and adopted by a family called Fred and Myrtle Wellesley. They are now dead but we found one of their natural children, one Paul Wellesley who is living in Hackney. He said he was 15 when the child, a boy, was brought home but within a year he had gone. Apparently he cried constantly, he would barely eat and had a look that, in his mother's words, made her blood run cold. The child drove the mother to the brink of a nervous breakdown.

The child was named Nicholas by the adoptive parents but we can't find any trace yet of anyone with that name born on the date. Bonner Road have no record of him after he went to the Wellesley's. We investigating whether he was given to a relative, Fred and Myrtle each had number of siblings. Still looking into it, it's probably his name has been changed so bit of a needle in a haystack."

Karen asked, "Are we pursuing this mystery child on the basis he might have found that Christine was his mother, had been abandoned, and as such that may have been a motive for murder?"

"It is an avenue we need to explore, as rare an occurrence as it is." Melvyn replied.

Detective Constable Ursula Carpenter interjected, "One thing to update on is we already know that Christine had a daughter that was raped and killed and the murderer has never been traced. This happened on March 7th 1970. The child, Penelope Anderson was only around five at the time. The murder took place while the maternal grandparents were babysitting at the pub they ran, The Red Lion on Bethnal Green Road. There is a remote possibility that the murderer has come back for the mother of the daughter because maybe the killer is still local and Christine came to know of his or her identity? We are clutching at straws I know."

Eyes turned to Ursula who blushed.

Karen looked perplexed, she furrowed her brow and ruminated over Ursula's theory.

Melvyn said "I think we should park that one for now Urse."

Karen shot him a steely look that stopped him in his tracks. She said, with authority,

"Let's be open minded about everything Mel. Ursula, you dig up as much as you can on the child's murder. Speak to anyone who was in the pub that night, what was said, what the rumours were. Anything. If nothing else it might be a cold case we can crack."

Melvyn, suitably admonished, recovered this composure and continued,

"We have also looked at Christine's social media traffic. There is nothing on there that indicates she was the sort of person to instigate any controversy from what we have seen so far. We have analysed comments she has made yet. The significant finding on social media, or Facebook specifically is that she recently unfriended her son

Phillip. We found out that Phillip was a Facebook friend of Keri Young who was a friend of Christine's. "

"The significance of this is what exactly Melvyn?" Karen said, she found Facebook and anyone who used it, tiresome. It was however an important tool, there were many users who could not help but publicise their lives, often to incriminate themselves.

"Keri was killed in June she was bludgeoned to death on her way home from work. Handbag stolen which would indicate a robbery. There was a pair of scissors in her eyes to indicate the assailant was also quite neurotic or making a point. No pun intended. We then found that another Facebook friend of Phillips, Helen Tyler had also been killed, we dug into others of his contacts and found that before Christine there were four murders of Phillip Anderson's friends."

Melvyn held his hands up and gesticulated the quotes sign by waggling his fore and index fingers of both hands when he said friends.

"Also killed have been Keith Huntsman in Miami, Tracey King in Emerson Park and David Thompson in Stevenage."

The colour drained from Karen's face and disappeared like water down a sink. She looked apoplectic.

Detective Inspector Ian McGregor spoke up, he had a heavy Glaswegian accent, "it seems obvious to me that Phillip Anderson is a psycho who is taking out people on his Facebook list with gay abandon, and I have never met the man. Why haven't any of the other forces or investigating teams come to that conclusion. Are you onto this Marshy?"

John Marsh felt cornered, more so because this looked in all intents and purpose like a serial killer was on the loose. He reached for his top collar and undid the top button. He felt a drip of sweat fall from his brow onto the floor and used his forearm to wipe his forehead. He reddened and his throat constricted as if he were standing in front of Albert Pierrepoint. Sangeeta pitched in,

"We were given the information about the other deaths and the brother this morning and have interviewed Mr Anderson a couple of times now, lately this afternoon. One reason the murders were not connecting I assume is that robberies took place and the M.O. was different. We are following up his alibis but personally our gut instinct he is innocent or he is a very calm killer with access to a range of weapons, assassin accomplices, and or some sort of martial art expertise."

"John," Karen said, she hadn't ignored Sangeeta but she needed a view from her senior Detective, who had recovered his composure,

"Yes as Pat says we are looking into Phillip Andersons whereabouts during all the incidents but gut instinct is that he isn't the killer."

"Oh come on Marshy I wouldn't trust gut instinct mate I would check alibis and get him in and grill him." D.I. McGregor, was enjoying his moment in the spotlight immensely and he looked to Karen for approval, which was given with a knowing nod.

A low murmur filled the room as individuals began talking amongst themselves.

Someone said, "Cut and dried," and this further raised the hubbub, Karen brought order to the room simply by holding her two hands up, palms forward.

"Let's not be hasty," she said, "The fly in the ointment is we know Phillip's whereabouts when his mother was shot and he was in the park at the time."

Ian countered with, "We can't rule out that he hired someone or, our timings are wrong for the shooting."

"I think we should look at Phillip now as a person of significant interest," Melvyn said, standing up now, with a triumphant look on his face at having delivered good intel. He was waiting to deliver the coup de grace.

"Go on Melv, have you got anything else?" said Karen.

"We went to his office today and spoke to the IT security head and gained access to Phillip's laptop and work diary. When each of the six were killed. Phillip Anderson had the next day off."

The room erupted into a crescendo of noise and high fives and fist pumps were exchanged. Only John and Sangeeta remained calm. Once, more Karen had to restore order. In addition to gesturing with her hands she now also had to tell everyone to pipe down.

"Didn't you say that one of the victims was an American?"

"No not American, British, but he lived in America. Phillip and he used to work together. Phillip was there in Miami the same week training an offshore team. We have been in touch with the police department and officers handling the case over there to find out where they are in the investigation and whether they have any pointers. Currently they think they have the culprit, a black American lad."

"Someone better make sure they don't shoot him before we have spoken to our English white guy," Detective Constable Tunde Okotie-Eboh said, sardonically.

Sangeeta spoke up, "What would be the motive? He just doesn't seem the type."

Karen's patience was now as thin Japanese rice paper, "John I don't think I could be any more flabbergasted. Are you saying you have actually been to Phillip Andersons house today, armed with this information?"

"Not all of it Guv."

"In my mind he is still in his house then, probably planning another murder?

"He is very unassuming."

"So was John Wayne Gacy. I think from now on we need to focus on Phillip Anderson and accomplices and not worry about a motive yet unless someone has a theory now."

Melvyn said, "we have looked at his Facebook comments and he seems to be very intolerant of the sort of posts he sees and at one stage was quite argumentative on line. Pedantic, sniping, mocking, critical, bullying even."

Ursula said, "most people like that are Facebook warriors but wouldn't hurt a fly."

"There is a very significant thing to add," Melvyn said with a tone that signified something awesome was impending, as if he were a scientist about to reveal he had a cure for cancer.

"Which is?" said Ian, who seemed to have taken the lead from Karen.

"When the forensic team took things away from the Anderson household, the very little there was. There was a writing pad in the kitchen. It had some groceries on the front page so primarily it was used as a shopping list. Some of the pages toward the back had been written on, there were some phone numbers so it was bagged as evidence in order the numbers could be traced. It was probably also used as a telephone jot pad. Assumption here is she may have had a call from the person who was coming to kill her was the suggestion. As some of the pages had been torn out we asked the forensics to see whether they could identify anything that had been written on the pad previously."

"And."

"Someone had written the names of the murdered, plus one more Ricki Finn, in a list, and at the top of the list were the words Facebook Fucking Wanker Attention Seekers."

"I don't suppose it was Christine's writing? Doesn't seem to be her type of vocabulary."

"No, definitely Phillip's."

The room erupted, there was some whoops, fist bumps and even more high fives. This time Karen did not ask for silence, instead she breathed a huge sigh of relief. If the team had solved not one but six murders she could be going out in a blaze of glory. She could retire with more than a feather in her cap, more a tribal head dress. She could almost feel the weight of a stressful last year lifting like an upward elevator and she could feel the commendation medals being pinned to her chest.

John looked at Sangeeta quizzically. John had a feeling he knew exactly what she was thinking. Phillip was as far from being a cold blooded murderer as anyone either of them had ever interviewed.

"John, we need to arrange for a warrant and go and arrest Phillip Anderson now before he kills anyone else. In the meantime Melvyn let's keep checking Phillip's exact whereabouts when the murders were committed, the crucial one is for his mothers. Obviously ascertain where exactly his car was where he was at the time of the murders we need to pin him down with sufficient accuracy. Start getting phone data that would pinpoint him to be in the location as near as we can get. CCTV all the usual things. I know I am teaching granny to suck eggs here but it seems as though we have already dropped a ball with the fact Phillip isn't sitting in a cell right now."

John stood up looking sheepish, gave Sangeeta an apologetic nod of the head to signify she needed to come with him, and left the room with every set of eyes burning into his back.

Throughout most of the proceedings Nigel Maloney had sat in silence. He had planned on demonstrating his interest and expertise by offering advice or questioning information given but he had been unable to concentrate fully.

Ever since Melvyn Willis had given the date of birth of Christine's abandoned baby his mind had gone into a frenzy. However unscrambled his head was though, it was still cognisant enough to know that the baby and he shared the same birthdate and Bonner Road was where Barbara Maloney said he would go if he were naughty.

Phillip Anderson

Since his mother's death Phillip had become less comfortable about spending time in the house around 6.00pm. Christine and he had an established routine for dinner which was set in stone like the chiming of a church bell. Preparation always started at 5.30, this was because Oliver had been a man of routine, and he left work at 5.30 prompt and was home within the hour. No matter what Christine made for dinner it would end up on the table at 6:30 coinciding with her late husband's arrival. It was a habit Christine found it difficult to change since the passing and as often as was possible it was a routine that was maintained.

Now, Phillip would watch the clock at about 6.00 pm knowing that however bad a meal it was, nothing would be prepared for 6:30. While he had disliked his mother intensely he too was set in his ways, and change was difficult to accept. His mother's face haunted him. The look on it as she lay dead.

Phillip took to going for a walk around 6:30, it was part of his new fitness regime too, and would spend around an hour doing a route that took him along the High Road, down Goodmayes Lane, along Abbotsford or Kilmartin Road, around Goodmayes Park, back along Green Lane and then toward home. A brisk paced walk would get him home in an hour and work up an appetite for him to cook his own meal.

Before going out Phillip shared a post that amused him immensely,

How to avoid being a Facebook wanker in 4 easy steps

1. Don't check yourself into hospital and then ignore all the 'you ok hun' messages from all your fucking idiot friends. Nobody cares about your ingrowing toe nail.
2. Don't post a photo of yourself looking fantastic with the caption 'I feel so ugly.' No you don't feel ugly Tessa – you crave attention like a whore needs dick.
3. Avoid posting hundreds of photos of your children with the caption 'I love them so much'. You're meant to live them, that's the whole fucking point.
4. Don't continually share inspirational quotes about being a strong woman just because you just found out your fella has been in more beds that a gardeners spade. Here's an inspirational quote for you Alison, 'FUCK OFF.'

With that post putting him in good cheer and in a positive frame of mind, Phillip left the house. On this particular evening as he walked along, his mind empty except to take in the music from his iPod, which contained an eclectic mix of tunes from Rod Stewart to Dizzy Rascal to Queen Live at Wembley, George Benson, Joss Stone and Toots and the Maytals. He kept his eyes on the people around him, confidently making eye contact, especially if there was an attractive girl to whom he would nod a chin, if he got anything at all, it was usually get a nervous look in return.

Sister Sledges track, We Are Family, burst into his ears and Phillip considered the implications of the other child that his mother had been determined to find. If he found this person would he be forced to give up a share of the house? Christine's will hadn't been changed therefore legally he was still the sole heir. The policeman had said Christine's book had said she was going to give her other son his due if she found him. She hadn't found him so her last will and testament had him, Phillip Sebastian Anderson as sole recipient.

Phillip rued that the police knew about the other child because with his mother murdered it was likely they would pursue finding him. He had watched the program on TV where long lost relatives are found by researchers, Digitisation of records was going to make searches easier and that was not good. He wondered if his brother was a half or a full one. Whether Christine had had an affair or was just a typical silly teenager who had made a mistake prior to being in a sound relationship and found herself pregnant. Ideally the son was born to Oliver and Christine but before they were financially able to provide a home, he would be less of a problem then. Another father meant more unknown family.

As Phillip walked along Kilmartin Road, a quiet turning that led to Aberdour Road and the park opposite, as normal he crossed just before he got to the large double fronted house, semi-detached, with stone lions on the wall and lead windows and ornate front door that looked out of place amongst other less lavish single fronted terraces. A navy blue Nissan Micra car was parked on the corner of Aberdour and Kilmartin. The car had been stolen the day before from a housing estate in Harold Hill and the inhabitant, dressed in a black hoodie with a grey beanie, eyed Phillip with the intensity of a cheetah with a baby warthog within its sprint range.

Phillip crossed the road but, in the words of familiar joke, did not get to the other side. The Nissan, roared into life and picked up speed in an instant and was on him just as he looked up wondering why the sound of an engine was so close. As the impact occurred Phillip flew into the air. He was still conscious at this time, his brain functioning enough to realise what had happened but not aware enough to put his arms and hands down and cushion his fall. He lost consciousness when his head hit the tarmac with a sickening crunch. Any hope that he might have survived the dual impact was lost when the Micra reversed over his crumpled body crushing organs that had already suffered massive trauma from being struck. When the Micra drove forward, once again over his prone body, death was inevitable.

As the car sped off and around the corner residents flooded out of their houses. A young Indian girl, six months the first aider at work, Pritti Vengsarkhar, rushed over to Phillip's broken body and assessed the situation. She shouted at her brother Amit, who was standing in the doorway of the house, to call for an ambulance. Although she was pretty confident from this man's staring eyes that he was dead she began to give him chest compressions, in the vain hope she could get his heart going again.

Several of the Vengsarkhar neighbours came out of their homes armed with mobile phones. They videoed the scenes, took selfies with Pritti, still working on Phillip in the background, and went to Facebook where they shamelessly uploaded, one using the heading:

#cant believe it #hit and run #outside my front door #i think the man is dead

They went to their WhatsApp groups and Instagram and did the same. Before the police had arrived there was an almost carnival air. Friends of the residents who had seen the posts had rushed around to be part of the incident. The surrounding roads became so packed that had Pritti been able to sustain life the ambulance that arrived 45 minutes later would have been unable to get through for another 15 minutes due to the number of cars that had to be moved. A police car had to be called as an argument had broken out between the paramedics and one of those in a car. Patrick O' Toole, the occupant, refused to move saying the ambulance should have gone down Goodmayes Lane and left into Kilmartin, rather than follow him down Alloa Road and Abbotsford Roads which were much smaller.

When it was established why the ambulance took so long it transpired that this was a particular bad hour to be fatally hurt. Several down and outs had succumbed to the new Spice drug that was sweeping the country. Paramedics were busy scooping the zombies off the streets, including medics of the East of England Ambulance Service.

All in all it was a very bad state of affairs for Phillip Sebastian Anderson, and as he lay on a slab in the mortuary at King Georges Hospital. Detective Inspector John Marsh and Detective Constable Sangeeta Patel stood over the crumpled body wondering what the hell was going on.

Meanwhile Nigel Maloney was handing a phial of his blood and one of saliva over to his friend and doctor, Basil Phaseus, asking that he get it checked against the DNA sample of Christine Anderson to see whether there was a match.

Marlon Benjamin

John Marsh woke up the morning after Phillip Anderson had been killed and lay in his bed alongside Marjorie and tried to get his head around the hit and run. The prime subject to the murders was now himself dead. Was this a revenge killing or was the killer of all six victim still at large? Perhaps there was no connection.

It was likely that the phone evidence regarding Phillips movements would be available at today's briefing but given the nature of this latest incident a shadow was now cast on the likely killer.

John's phone trilled, he had an incoming text message. It was from Detective Constable Patrick Jamieson a good friend of his. Patrick and he had worked on a few cases together, they also shared a love of Essex Cricket Club and outside work in summer could be found at the County Cricket Ground Chelmsford watching a match, sinking a few pints of lager and pigging out on cheap but functional burgers, hog roasts, jacket potatoes and chips. The message was enough to make John sit up and utter an oath, it simply said,

"Marlon Benjamin's body has been found, see you later."

Marjorie was a light sleeper. She had heard her husband stir and heard the trill of the phone. She was used to the constant contact he had with regard to his work and whilst no lover of his sometimes colourful language was sanguine enough to know that the job lent itself to robust reaction. John didn't discuss his vocation with her and she didn't ask. The house was a sanctuary from the day to day world of detective work though the impact Marlon Benjamin's disappearance had on the family was profound. This was one time where Marjorie wished she knew more of what was going on for once and her laid back approach had been replaced by a more inquisitive nature, she probed,

"Language Timothy. You don't normally swear first thing in the morning John. What's up?"

"Marlon Benjamin's body has been found."

Marjorie jumped up immediately, from laying prostrate to sitting on her knees, hands to her to face to look at her husband. John rolled back, flipped the bed side lamp and looked back at her, both pairs of eyes dilated as if chemicals enhanced.

"Dead?" she said, she felt her eyes fill up with water.

"Bodies are not usually found alive love," as soon as John said that he wished he hadn't. He didn't know what to think. Did Marlon's death mean Frances could live without the fear of further retribution? Marlon had slept with a married woman, had he just got his comeuppance? His mind played a thousand songs and neither gave him peace. He rubbed his eyes. He inhaled deeply and caught the scent of the cocoa butter Marjorie rubbed into her body each night before getting into bed.

"Frances will be heartbroken. Do you know I had it in the back of my mind Marlon had gone off with someone else? I knew about his reputation. Frances showed me his Facebook page once. He had albums full of pictures with other girls, all shapes and sizes, tall, short, black, white, Indian, Chinese. He seemed to have been in every town, every city, every seaside resort from Dorset round the coast and up to Norfolk and I thought, a leopard never changes its spots, he'll be up to no good. I used to think he would sleep with anyone. When he danced with me at Roseanne and Padraigh's wedding he put his hand on my bottom. I moved it of course and he laughed and said I can see where Frances got her curves from and I said you better make sure hers is the only bottom you put your hands on or you'll have me to deal with, and he said, don't worry Mrs Marsh, your daughter is going to be the last woman I ever touch. He was right wasn't he? I'm glad in a way. That he's dead I mean. It means he hadn't run off and left them. It's definitely him?"

Marjorie had hardly taken a breath when she spoke and John was quite taken aback by her mini outburst.

He responded by saying, "Afraid so Love, I haven't got any details so don't say anything to Frances yet. When I get in I'll get some information off Perry. You're right, at least we now know he didn't run off with the car and he didn't run out on our Frances."

Marjorie didn't answer, she had turned her head into the pillow and John could see from the way her shoulders were heaving up and down that she was crying. He put a consoling arm around her.

"Don't cry Love" he said, "we'll get to the bottom of this, Ochie will grow up knowing her Dad cared for her and her mother. Frances will know that her faith in Marlon was well founded."

"Don't let whoever did this, get away John. You know it will be the Williams'. Don't let them get away John."

"They won't get away love."

Marjorie did not respond instead she sank deeper into the pillow and cried even more and John, knowing that any further attempt to pacify his wife was futile got up, showered, put on his suit and went to work.

Back at the station before he had time to discuss things with Patrick he was straight into the briefing Karen had called.

"Okay everyone," Karen said, "Yesterday's incident will throw a spanner in the works because until it happened Phillip Anderson was our prime and sole suspect. Phone records have placed him within two miles of each of the murders committed Helen Tyler, Keith Huntsman, Keri Young, David Thompson. Tracey King and his mother Christine Anderson. The nature of Mr Anderson's death means we have to conclude that either he is not the guilty party or he was and someone needed to silence him, maybe the assassin who killed his mother."

"There is a remote possibility it was a coincidence," piped up D.I.McGregor.

267

"That's right," Karen agreed. "We must NOT disregard that the possibility that this was a coincidence. It is possible he was guilty of the murders and was in the wrong place at the wrong time and it was a genuine hit and run, someone pissed or in a stolen car. I know Paul Whitman and his team are looking at all the CCTV to ascertain the make model and reg of the car that was in the incident. There are no witnesses thus far. The evidence strongly suggests Phillip was involved but the further spanner in the works obviously is most of the victims were robbed."

"That might be just ruse to throw us off the scent. It would almost rule Phillip Anderson out, he had no record of that type of activity," D.I. McGregor said, almost as if talking to himself, aloud.

Melvyn said, "The Intel team are still trawling through social media content but haven't seen any threats made, there are so many overlapping Facebook friends it is difficult to see the wood from the trees but one person of interest is Ricki Finn who shares the same Facebook link with our six dead. We are still looking into finding the son that Christine Anderson gave up but also looking into potential enemies of all the dead individuals. Is it possibly but extremely unlikely that this could all be coincidental and all the murders are un-related."

The room erupted into noise and conversations kicked off with theories being passed amongst individuals.

Karen let the conversations take their course. She decided to give everyone something else to ponder on.

"One last think as you all know I will be stepping down as DCI and it may or may not come as a surprise to you to know that John Marsh and Nigel Maloney will be undertaking the DCI exam with a view to one of them taking my place."

D.I. McGregor decided to add to the any other business before further discussion took place as to how small a chance John Marsh stood against Nigel Maloney in the race for the hot seat. He held out his hands, as if about to separate the River Jordan.

"On a separate matter, just a reminder, Pamela Gilmartin will be doing sessions every day next week at 10 am for an hour in the Silver

Conference Room on Nature versus Nurture – The Making of a Criminal. Recommend if you can attend do so, they are very interesting. I know when these were run last year they generated some good discussion and we were able to think more about the families of the people we had in, and how they may have effected future actions."

Nigel Maloney winced. He had been part of several discussions and the view of many of his colleagues and superiors was that the criminal mind was more likely to be created by a genetic defect than ones environment. He wanted his father to be a well to do businessman and his mother a woman of good stock who had had an affair and were unable to keep him due to the scandal it would have caused. Better this than to be the product of dregs of society. He did not want to find he was tainted by members of the underworld who had poisoned his blood with traits of avarice, anger, misanthrope, low compassion and low morality.

He looked over at John Marsh, his nemesis. He felt complete and utter loathing for the man. This man stood in his way of becoming a DCI and his slut daughter had cheated on her husband. The slut daughter had had the audacity to cheat on the family of one of his close criminal contacts therefore John Marsh was guilty by association. Nigel had not made too much of an effort to investigate the Williams' movements. Informing his team to take the Williams' alibis at face value. His team were asked to focus on Marlon's philandering ways, his previous conviction aged 15 of stealing a bike, and the many enemies he may have had given the spate of black on black crime in the area.

The team were pointed in the direction of Marlon's cousin, Brandon Benjamin, who was a member of the Stamford Hill Mandem, a North London gang. Marlon had, throughout his adult life, had a clean record, and had never been involved in any gang related activity. Nigel was pleased to find out though, Marlon also had an Uncle who, twenty five years ago, had been shot in a dispute over a faulty car and its sale.

The fruit does not fall far from the tree Nigel had told his team. Concentrate on Benjamin and you will probably find him holed up in the Midlands or has been done away due to a gangland beef.

Discovery of Marlon's body and the implications of this was going to be a problem Nigel didn't want to have alongside sitting the DCI exam, especially if there was a link to the Williams'.

John came over and said amiably, although each knew it was through gritted teeth, "Good luck with the exam when it rolls round, I hear you found Marlon Benjamin's body, what happened?"

Nigel could not hide his contempt "You're no better than me Marsh. I deserve to be a DCI just as much as you do. You have a family involvement with the Benjamin case so I can tell you fuckall about it." With that Nigel walked out of the room.

John wasn't surprised at Nigel's reaction, they had a mutual dislike for each other exacerbated when John reported his colleague to his superiors for falsifying a witness statement. The misdemeanour was pretty low level, the person in question was a well-known villain but John believed in fair policing which Nigel didn't. The guys upstairs shared Nigel's view, there was no repercussions but DI Maloney held a grudge. Fortunately for John any information he needed he was able to get from Patrick who he met at a desk and both men sidled off to an empty interview room.

"So what happened PJ?"

"Got a call from a member of the public out walking his dog yesterday at about 6.00pm. He was along a towpath by the River Lea at Waltham Abbey. What did you think he saw?"

"Marlon Benjamin's dead body floating in the River?"

"Pretty much. He saw a coffin up against some reeds. Why he did it I don't know but he dragged the box it to the bank. The coffins was water damaged because it wasn't made of the best piece of timber but Mr Curious found a body sized form encased in concrete."

"Jesus Christ," was all John could exclaim.

"Once a pair of plods arrived they chipped at the concrete and it evidently did contain a body so forensics were called. They have been working on it pretty solid all night.....no pun meant."

270

"Go on."

"They found that the concrete was disintegrating so it was easy to pick off. Analysed that and found it was a quick drying variety. The assumption was that if it hadn't been given time to set it would have gone off in the water and just fragmented which turned out to be a result for us. Under the concrete was a roll of carpet. Under the carpet was a large plastic bag and in the plastic bag was the body of Marlon Benjamin. He was easy to identify because although he was naked he had a tattoo with the name Ochi Rios on his arm,"

"The body hadn't decomposed then?"

"No. The plastic bag was well sealed. While it was, the gases that were released post mortem had nowhere to go so the bag became buoyant. With the concrete becoming porous the coffin became a floating tomb. Whoever did the deed was a bit too thorough in trying to dispose of the body. They should have just weighed it down with some chains."

"Be sure to advise all potential murderers of that won't you," John said sarcastically.

"You know everyone on the case thought he had done a runner don't you, including me?"

"Well I'll be damned. Even you?" said John.

He then said, rather pompously to Patrick, "I heard there was that talk of Marlon pissing off to Jamaica to be with one of his exes and the child he had with her when he was on holiday there six years ago. The other one was he was off to Florida to another of his exes who we still cannot find, or somewhere up near Newcastle to see the girl who had a miscarriage by him. All the talk from Nigel was that Marlon was a ne'er do well who had had enough of domestic life, sold the Range Rover to one of his druggie relations or contacts and was off living the high life. Instead he was pushing up water lilies."

"Just goes to prove. You can't judge a book."

"What was Nigel's reaction?"

"He thinks Marlon was involved in drugs and wanted to create a lifestyle for him and Frances and said something went wrong with a deal hence the killing. He wants us to keep looking into all Marlon's contacts, phone records, debt, spending etcetera."

"What about the Range Rovers whereabouts?"

"We know that after leaving his Dads it went up the M11, M25, and M1 and disappeared after it turned off into Luton. It was suggested he flew on a false passport and identity to Manchester or Birmingham then took a flight "

"I still think the Williams' have something to do with all this. Have they got alibis?"

"It was suggested. Given Frances had the baby while she was married to Simon Williams and until it was born it was going to be one of the clan, and considering how pissed off Dougie would have been, it was obvious they could be involved. Nigel shot that suggestion down and told everyone that it was not an avenue to go down. He said he had interviewed the Williams' and was happy with their version of events i.e. they weren't involved. It hard to do anything on an unofficial basis because Dougie Williams has his hand so high up Nigel's arse he could be mistaken for Rod Hull or Roger De Courcey. Dougie couldn't be questioned by anyone else. We know that Simon was in England when Marlon went missing but he has witnesses, cronies obviously, who have said explicitly, according to Nigel, that they were all in Lingfield at the horses on the day of the disappearance.

"Maybe, without Nigel knowing, you can get down to the racecourse and see if you can get the CCTV for that day, check whether Simon is on it"

"Might be difficult, not sure how long they keep these things and whether we will need some back up paperwork, which would mean going through Nigel. I'll have a go John."

"Cheers PJ."

With that the two men parted, Patrick to do some surreptitious digging and John to speak to the Intel guys.

Switching his focus, John felt that the link to the Anderson murders was social media and that there was something there that was being overlooked. What that something was he didn't know, but he would do his utmost to find out.

Nigel Harris

Nigel sat opposite Doctor Basil Phaseus as his contact took out a document from a white envelope, one of two he had on the desk in front of him. Nigel also had two envelopes. The first was brown and it was fully of twenty pound notes. Five thousand pounds worth.

"I'm taking a hell of a risk doing this Nigel." Basil said.

"You are getting paid pretty well just to put a drop of blood in a palette and look through a magnifying glass." Nigel replied.

"It could cost me my job and my pension. That is really important to me. Don't you realise that? The Data Protection team are getting pretty jumpy about unauthorised access to DNA records."

"Don't you realise that it is important to me I find out who my parents were and what they were." Nigel said curtly.

"You are one self-righteous bastard Maloney." Basil peered into the envelope, he licked his lips and slipped the wad of cash into his pocket. "You'll be pleased to know that, basically, there is a one in a four million chance you are not Christine Anderson's child."

"So, basically, what does that mean?"

"It means Christine Anderson is your mother."

Nigel looked Basil squarely in the face. He then looked past him. The clock on the wall was ticking and Nigel has suddenly become aware of the noise and the fact that, apart from that the room was silent. Basil was quiet, absorbed in looking down at the envelope full of money, probably thinking what he might spend it on. Nigel took a deep intake of breathe and broke the sterile stillness of the lab room.

"I guess that unless you had a sample from her late husband you can't tell if he was my father too? She might have got pregnant before they were able to afford to get married and had to give me away. Would you be able to get a sample? What about from Phillip? If I have the same DNA as him would it mean we had the same mother and father? His body is still in the morgue I could get a sample from him."

"There would be no point Nigel. I have seen details of the Anderson murder investigation. Phillip Anderson's father, Christine Anderson's husband, Oliver. He was not your father."

"How do you know? Have you got Oliver's DNA?"

"I have some information you may not like but I am willing to give you for the other five thousand pounds I mentioned. Basil's eyes narrowed and he stared at the second brown envelope Nigel had placed on the desk. Basil's long head and hawkish nose gave him an owl-like appearance. Although these birds of prey have a legend of intelligence they are not problem solvers. Basil's avian equivalent would be more akin to a magpie or cuckoo. Always on the take.

Basil began to drum his fingers on the desk, the sound of his talon like nails made a sound as annoying as a child incessantly beating a metal drum with a steel stick. His gaze never left the pile of money, so much so that Nigel became disconcerted. Regaining his aura of villainy Nigel placed his forearms over the envelope, he leaned forward and said menacingly. "I'll pay you, if the information you have is 100% bona fide because you are not going to tuck me over Basil. You wouldn't want to get on the wrong side of me."

"I know you aren't a man to be fooled with Nigel. I know how you operate. I went to the nurture v nature talk that Pamela Gilmartin held and found it very interesting"

"What the fuck has that got to do with me?" Nigel said, he was getting irritable because he felt Basil Phaseus was toying with him.

"Last year when the talks were held you got rather irate that there was a view that said a parent no matter whether present or not, could determine the nature of their offspring. I know you have a concern about your ancestry and whether it has played a part in how your personality has been formed."

"Do not fuck with me Basil I am not in the mood. I don't need you to give me a lecture on how I feel. Marlon Benjamin being found is a headache for me I don't want another headache JUST NOW."

Basil had heard about the finding of Marlon's body, he knew about Nigel's underworld connections, he knew about the Williams, he knew about the Frances and wondered whether the man sitting opposite him had a role to play in the death of the young black youth. There, the conscience of the doctor, came to a full stop. His addiction to on-line gambling and a distinct lack of luck meant that he ought not to bite off the hand that fed him. Or should he? Nigel had been good to him in the past and would be now but there were a number of others who were less unpredictable.

Basil decided, rather than drag this drama out, to pass on what he knew, get his money and distance himself from Nigel Maloney for good.

"Christine Anderson's baby daughter was raped and killed in March 1970, obviously after you were born. The police at the time had no leads into who the rapist, stroke murderer was. No witnesses that came forward, obviously no CCTV back in the day, half the people in the immediate vicinity were drunk so recollections were, at best useless, and at worst slanderous. As was common practise the lads running the investigation kept the child's clothing as evidence. Served well in the 60s and the A1 murder, if only to confirm Hanratty's guilt. Something made me wonder about criminal minds in the 1950s and 60s, how unsophisticated people were, how the death penalty did not deter people from committing horrific acts and going off to live a normal life. People who had seen the horrors of war and were desensitized by death."

"What has 1970 got to do with the war?"

"I'd say that after the war, up until around the 1980s some of the things that went on were pretty unsavoury but swept under the carpet. Incest, family scandals, divorce, murder, police corruption. All more visible now with social media and the ability to publicise any misdemeanour. Lot more inappropriate behaviour back then. Christine had her share of grief and it ended so badly."

Nigel could not comprehend what Basil was driving at. Was he suggesting that the person who had raped her child and killed her come back and murdered Christine, all these years later?

"Is there something to link the rape and murder with the death of Christine?" Nigel asked.

He was less aggressive now, his head was throbbing. Marlon Benjamin, Promotion exam, Nature v Nurture, he was Christine's son, a new inheritance.

Basil stood up.

"I got the DNA from the rapist stroke killer of Christine and Oliver Anderson's child, your stepsister Penelope Rose. I compared it with yours and there is a four million to one chance that that person is not your father. Your natural father murdered your sister."

As Basil said this he reached out lifted up Nigel's slack arms and pulled at the envelope which slid toward him as smoothly as a mouse slipping down the throat of a snake. He placed the second white envelope in front of Nigel and said "All the information you need is on the paperwork in the two envelopes. I trust now our work is concluded and unfortunately I can take no more risks on your behalf. Can you go now please? We haven't had this conversation."

Nigel rubbed his chin with his thumb and forefinger, he then took from his breast pocket a recording device, a fluorescent light signalled that the device was on. He held it up so that Basil could see that it was on but then flicked the off button.

"Thanks Basil," he said. "I need you to get your contact to run the DNA on the knickers through to see if there is a match with anyone on the police file. I need the results by the end of the week. I know there is a cold case review team but I don't want this done through official channels. We've not had this conversation. I can walk away from the force. I have made enough money to get by and I can earn a little bit more by various means. I know you can't keep away from gambling on how much rainfall there will be in China or the colour of the wedding dress at the next Royal nuptials. Until I say I don't need you you are part of my unofficial investigation team. Speak to you later."

Nigel sat in his car and considered the revelations he had just been given. His mother, Christine Anderson, was supposedly a respectable woman who had married a respectable man and had two children one of whom was raped and murdered. Prior to her period of respectability Christine had bedded a man and had a bastard child. This child, him, had been abandoned in an alleyway, placed in a children's home and then taken in when still less than six months old. The couple who adopted him were unable to cope therefore he ended up with Barbara and Eddie Maloney. His real father had returned to rape and kill Christine's young daughter.

For Nigel, this revelation confirmed to him what he already knew. Why he was wired as he was. He now knew that his criminal tendencies were a result of being produced by this rapist, murderer and who knows what else. That Nigel, a policeman, also had a sense of social justice must have come from his mother.

Nigel had a decision to make. He could allow himself to accept his lot and continue life as he had done thus far and forget about his father. In time he would be promoted to DCI, he had a mutual agreement with his criminal contacts, he wouldn't tread on their toes and they would not tread on his. His dealings with those less savoury characters had been long established, there was no shades of grey. He was paid to provide information and turn a blind eye to unethical activities. The arrangements with all his cronies had been both profitable and career enhancing. Nigel Maloney was a name in the underworld much like a made-man of The Family.

Nigel's other option was to hunt down the murderer of his half-sister and help John Marsh to bring to justice the murderer of Christine, Phillip and five other dead. He could also make a more determined effort to bring to justice the killers of Marlon Benjamin, whoever those killers were.

Which way to go? He recalled something that was said at one of the murder investigation briefings. There was one person who knew who was the father of Christine's baby.

When Nigel got home that night he was drunk. In the foot well of his car was an empty litre bottle of Captain Morgan's dark rum that he had polished off while he sat contemplating his next move. It wasn't the first time he had driven whilst excessively over the alcohol limit.

He knew that were he stopped his name and face were well known throughout the force to enable uninterrupted passage, Police stops had occurred and he had extricated himself from the situation with a show of his badge. Even tonight, stopped by a two man team who thought they might be hauling someone in for jumping a red light the police officers were as blasé as Nigel as he flashed his credentials and said, "Amber gambler boys."

As he staggered through the front door, as intoxicated as he was, Nigel felt the eyes of his wife boring into him.

"You are going to kill yourself and kill someone else one of these days Nigel." Kim said. She should have been outraged or disappointed or a mixture of both but she knew that her husband had the luck of the devil when it came to circumventing catastrophe.

"There has been a precipitation over the head of Nigel Maloney on this evening that has rendered humankind the opportunity to gaze at the perigree syzygy." Nigel slurred.

Kim wondered why Nigel found it difficult to speak to her, sober or otherwise, using layman's terms. Why did he use such clever words, she didn't care how much he knew. She had heard him use the term perigree syzygy enough to know it meant super moon. She had seen around forty photos on Facebook that night where people had posted pictures of the said moon, as if no-one had ever seen a moon before.

The same people who made announcements as if they were journalists to a blind and deaf audience, a royal baby, the wedding or death of a celebrity, the coming of summer and the announcement of an interest rate rise. Kim was part of the audience that loved the social network. She loved Facebook and she couldn't get herself away from using it and viewing every video, however banal or staged. She looked down on people whose posts she deemed boring yet she loved every post that was boring. Looking at every picture, however trivial or mundane or reading every comment, however twee or self-gratifying. Making a judgement of people because of what they said, it was part of the fun of Facebook, being a social media analyst.

"Why are you so drunk?" she asked of her husband. He didn't look too dishevelled, his eyes were slightly glazed but she could smell the stale alcohol on his breath as he stood, his face not more than a foot away from hers.

"My biological mother was murdered two weeks ago, she was compos mentis. Or at least was after she had abandoned me in an alleyway. My biological father raped and murdered my sister. A full sister because he also raped my mother. Nurture versus nature. I have the proof I need now to know the truth and the realisation of why I am what I am. I need to read my Sigmund Freud and my Lev Vygotsky. I am a rotten egg and anyone who advocates that the spawn of the most loathsome should have been put in a sack with some stones and thrown in a river probably has a point. You need to be quite cognizant about this, you are married to the child of Lucifer, Beelzebub, Belshazzar, Satan the fallen angel. I have eaten greatly of the apple."

"It must have fermented into cider Nige."

"I will be scorned. I will feel the opprobrium of my colleagues."

"What?"

"You must be obsequious. I have triumphed over St Michael and will take rule over those that would dare question my power."

"Nigel you don't have the power to walk in a fucking straight line."

"Such vituperation from one so low. Your intelligence is impecunious."

"Nigel, I don't understand your long words and you are very annoying when you are drunk."

"Such antipathy is hostile. Nature versus nurture, I am doomed. I should have been drowned at birth."

"Don't say that Nigel. No-one should ever say you don't deserve to be born. You are a good man, deep down you are the King of kings. My prince of lightness. Lots of people like and respect you. Dougie Williams for example, what a friend he has been."

"In the words of Samuel Fleet, he of The Devil in the Marshalsea, I can count all my friends on the fingers of one hand, and that is with one hand holding my cock."

With that Nigel slumped to the floor he gagged, belched and then proceeded to vomit over the fawn coloured carpet that Kim had insisted would look fabulous in the hall.

It was a sight to see. Kim was 5 foot 6 inches tall and weighing one hundred and twenty four pounds. Nigel was six foot four and weighing two hundred and three pounds. Using the technique honed during the six months she had trained with some of the gorilla-like muscle bound associates at the local gym Kim bent her knees got a purchase on her husband's crotch and shoulders and hoisted him above her head and onto her own back where, knees locked and thrusting upward lifted him and carried him to the bed upstairs.

Ken Harris

It was a damp October Monday morning. Ken Harris had celebrated his seventieth birthday on Saturday night and was in his kitchen looking at the section of work surface on which lay his presents that he had received from his four children and twenty three grandchildren, Garden tools, books, CDs, six bottles of whisky, three bottles of Malibu, twelve bottles of wine, four bottles of champagne, tickets to a West End show, a teddy bear with a bib on which was emblazoned King Ken, there was a pile of twenty and ten pound notes too. He wondered who had bought him the Malibu and decided it was Barbie's sisters Grace, Yvonne and Marnie. They didn't like him, he didn't like them, and he didn't drink Malibu.

He re-read some of the cards he had been given including one each from his two great grandchildren, Gabriel and Atlanta, although he chuckled at the way his Granddaughter, Charmain had disguised her writing to make it seem as though the ten month old twins had actually wrote out the card.

Ken's wife, Barbie was sitting by the breakfast bar reading and liking the Facebook posts that the family and friends had made that she hadn't had time to like over the weekend. Everyone had posted a picture of the cake that had been specially made. There were two dolls on it, Barbie and Ken, both clad in double denim. The two tiered circular cake was blue and white with bold red writing that said Happy 70th Birthday King Ken. The actual cake was now but a single half eaten tier. Barbie and Ken lay by its side as if they too had joined the celebrations.

Spotting the time, 10.30 am Barbara, as usual kissed Ken on the forehead and went off to work.

Barbara was Ken's fifth wife, they had been wed for three years, after the death of his fourth wife Diane in a motor accident off the coast of Spain, near Marbella, Ken and Diane had gone out for the day in a boat belonging to one of their friends and both had ended up in the water. Neither were wearing lifejackets. Ken could swim like a fish and managed to get himself three miles to land while Diane had drowned. At the inquest Ken would say that he had insisted Diane wear a life jacket as she wasn't a strong swimmer but she wanted to sunbathe without getting lines and had then proceeded to roll off the sundeck when a sudden wave lurched the boat to one side.

Why didn't he throw her a lifebelt whilst on the boat? He said he had panicked and jumped in to save his wife but she had disappeared under the waves and he couldn't see her. She had popped to the surface and when he took hold of her she struggled against him and he lost a hold on her. The undercurrent was too strong for him to keep both of them afloat and she had slipped below the surface a second time and this time did not reappear.

Diane was an only child whose parents were both from single child families. She had moved to Suffolk from Hull where she had rid herself of a long relationship with a man who was more a friend than a partner and wanted a fresh change. Hers and Ken's had been a whirlwind two month intense relationship followed by eleven months of marriage. The demise of Diane went largely unnoticed, she had made few friends since she had moved and had cut off those from the North. Ken had discovered that the initial lust for her was replaced by contempt, Diane was very bossy, she was not lacking in confidence and her initial lust for sex was replaced by a once a week rule. Ken, with his high libido decided very quickly after the marriage she was not really his cup of tea and embarked on an affair with Barbara a young looking 55 year old landlady at the Fortune of War pub in Chantry Park, Ipswich.

There were eight people at Diane's cremation including the man who delivered the scant eulogy. Five of those attending were Ken's cronies who were only there in anticipation of a free drink and buffet food.

As queer as the incident was the Spanish officials concluded it was a tragic accident and within four months of death Ken was fully ensconced with the Fortune of War overseer.

Barbara was as bubbly as a crate of agitated Bollinger but much more Ken's type. She liked a tipple but was able to keep in control when all around her were not.

Barbara was well aware of Ken's roving eye, his flirtatious banter and penchant for disappearing for days on end. She had a few irons in the fire herself but was discrete. She was not averse to Ben Bartlett, one of her regular and married drinkers sleeping it off for the night in the bedroom over the pub and her having sex with him before locking up and getting a cab home. The activity between Ben and Barbara was happening before Ken and continued after. Ben's wife Mary was one of Ken's previous conquests and when the opportunity arose was also part of an unofficial group of swingers. Both men became good friends, each unaware of the others dalliances with their respective wives. For her part she thought Ken was a good catch, he had some investments, which included the portfolio of sticks and shares he had acquired from Diane that ensured good standard of living.

Ken was the way he was. He slapped the bottoms of women, young and old. He loved nothing more than getting a cuddle from the girlfriends and wives of his sons and grandsons and his eyes were usually on a large chest more than a pair of eyes. In his defence Ken loved his large family. He was a duty bound family man, father, grandfather and great grandfather. He was generous to his own and would go out of his way to taxi, carry or babysit, and for that his sometimes outrageous behaviour was ignored. Life was going well for Barbara and Ken Harris. Until the morning that Nigel Maloney rang on the bell.

Prior to the drive up to Ipswich Nigel had asked for help from a friendly member of the detective unit, requesting someone establish the movements of the Harris'. Having learned that Barbara worked from 11am to 6pm after which the evening manager took over Nigel knew he had a good window in which Ken and he were unlikely to be disturbed. Nigel had travelled up on Sunday and stayed in a bed and breakfast close by. On Monday morning he outside Ken's house waiting for Barbara to go to work, he saw her leave at 10.30 and waited ten minutes before going to the Harris' door.

Ken was in a jaunty mood, still smiling at the attention he had recently been given, when he opened the door and saw the grey suited looking man standing there. The feeling of euphoria dissipated, with a whoosh from a fractured airship. The man, although younger, before him could have been his twin.

"Can I help you?" he asked, trying not to betray his feeling of unease, "I'm not buying anything, so don't offer me triple glazing, a new drive, new roof or cavity wall installation."

"Hello Ken," Nigel said, as if he were speaking to a long lost acquaintance. "Can you tell me if you raped Christine Anderson? Can you also tell me if you raped and murdered her five year old daughter Penelope?"

Whilst the blood drained out of Ken's extremities so fast he risked getting Raynaud's, he had the wherewithal to try to slam the door shut. Nigel had anticipated such a reaction and before Ken could swing the door toward the safety of its jamb the detective's foot was already wedged in the gap and his shoulder was thrust forward preventing it from gaining any momentum. Nigel hefted at the door, pushing it back and as he launched himself into the house grabbed Ken by scruff of the neck and propelled him back into his hall and shut the door behind them.

With Ken in a vice like grip Nigel said, between gritted teeth, "I know you raped and murdered the child, your DNA is all over her knickers. I know you fucked Christine because she had your kid. Do you remember Kathy McGuiness? She remembers you. She remembers Christine having your baby, by which time you disappeared. She didn't know you had come back for some more and because Christine was married and had two kids you decided you were going to do her daughter."

"I don't know what you're talking about."

"DNA Ken. It doesn't lie. Chances of four million to one don't lie mate."

"I want to speak to my lawyer."

Ken kneaded at his brow, his senses were so acute he felt every wrinkle on his forehead, every lump and bump and the perspiration that made his skin clammy to touch. He shut his eyes but when he opened them Nigel was still there, staring at him malevolently.

"No you don't Ken. I knew as soon as I saw you, you were my Dad. I am surprised how much alike we are but I guess the kink in the nose is a bit of a giveaway isn't it? Same colour eyes, same thin mouth, we even have the same porn star moustache. Uncanny isn't it?"

It was a rhetorical question. The two men were like peas in a pod. . Ken was two inches shorter but this was more due to that old man hunch , drawn up to his full height it was likely that their vital statistics were a match.

Ken had spent the last forty seven years in denial. By his count he had probably forced himself on around twenty women from the 1950s through to the early 1970s. His job as an auditor had enabled him to travel the country, examining books for companies that needed an independent eye. He would travel from his main office in West Bromwich and stay for as long as required during which time he would either be offered, or take what he wanted from a local woman. He had a dark past.

"Yes," he said in a matter of fact manner. "Yes I had sex with Christine. Then I went off because that's what I do, I went to the Midlands for a bit then found myself here and settled down. I found myself in East London in 1970 to do some work and I thought I would look in on her. I don't know why. I went to the pub one afternoon and I spoke to some old boy in the bar and he said Christine was all married up with a couple of kids but she stopped by every now and then. I went home and I thought, if I come back later and is in the pub she might be up for it again. She was a right one when she was in her teens. Right little tease. She was gagging for it then so I thought she wouldn't have changed."

Nigel looked coldly at the pathetic old man and said, "According to Kathy McGuiness you raped Christine." It was rape Ken, like you raped her five year old daughter."

Ken didn't deny this. In fact he acted as though he hadn't heard Nigel speak but continued on.

"I came back and it was like an open house. Doors open people milling about getting drunk and loud and groping at each other like it was chaos."

"So you decided to go upstairs and do what? See whether there was another teenager to take advantage of?"

No. I just went upstairs, I don't know what come over me. I've got this bad blood. I saw the babby and no-one was minding her so I thought well, they obviously don't care about her so I thought I'd just cuddle her a bit you know like you do she was being neglected. I was just being loving. Like I always am with all of the babbies."

"So you raped and killed her. How is that loving? She was five year old child."

"My Grandfather had raped my mother, I was brought up by my Grandmother and Grandfather as a son when I was their son and their Grandson. I was my Mum's brother and her son. I lived in a time when there was no child protection agency. My Aunts and sisters were at the mercy of my sick Grandfather's friends. That's why I did it."

"You've ruined lives Ken. Thank Christ I haven't got your urges. I've seen Barbara's Facebook posts Ken. She hasn't got much security on her account. You have a lot friends. You look Facebook happy. It is going to shock people when they find out about you Ken."

"I can't help it."

"Can't......or wouldn't. There are some things you just don't do."

Nigel took out the recorder from his top pocket and placed it on the table. Ken flinched when he saw it but quickly enough regained his composure. Enough to grab at the cylindrically shaped device. Nigel

285

was just as quick and as Ken's fingers curled around the stick so Nigel snaked out and grabbed a forearm. His grip was as firm as a cage fighter's headlock and his menace was equally ferocious. With his other hand he punched Ken's sinewy bicep causing the old man to let out a yelp of pain.

Nigel said, ""Christine is dead. She never accused you of rape, she wrote a book about it, but you don't deny that's what you did. I can get this recording put on Facebook live later."

Nigel with his hand clamped on the old man's arm felt Ken's body sag, like a crone's breast. Kens shoulders, were slumped and his eyes began to glisten with tears, he looked at the table as if he might see his reflection or a way out of this predicament in the knots of wood that stared back at him.

Ken suddenly stiffened, defiance filled his body as he spat, "you're not here official, you haven't shown me your credentials, and I bet that recording can't be used in a court of law."

"Don't be stupid. No it can't but I won't need to be official. You have become a respectable man. Barbara uses social media a hell of a lot, I have seen all her posts about your birthday and how wonderful you are. I have access to Facebook like no other person because I am what is known as a super user. I have a special access code where I can get into people's pages and post things about you even if they have not friended me. We use it in the police force all the time to get criminals to talk. You don't understand how powerful a tool this thing is. I can spread information about you at the touch of a button. I hope you know that means to all the friends and family you have that use the social network.

All the things I find out you did back in the day when you were travelling around the country raping women and killing children. I may only know of Christine and Penelope but where there's smoke. It won't take long before you'll be getting death threats. I can publish your telephone number anonymously and you'll be getting calls. Your name will be on Twitter. Something like, # KenHarris #Paedophile # Rapist #Murderer and Instagram. Lots of photos of your house, of you playing with children, outside school gates looking at them. You don't know how easy it will be to destroy your life the way you have destroyed mine. Every day since I found out I was adopted I have wondered who my real parents were, why I am the way I am and it has made me fucking mental. I keep getting thoughts about young girls. Destroyed my life."

"Destroyed your life? You're a copper. I bet you're not short of a few bob. You probably had a better life than if you were brought up with the Venables clan. Christine was years ago. My life was shit. I was abused by my Stepdad too, My Mum turned a blind eye to him coming into my room at night. She ignored me crying when my Grandad called me a cissy and teased me about my curly hair and then took me to his house so he could rape me when I was 11. They was all at me they said I was more a girl than a boy and they used me like I was a piece of meat. The only person who gave me any protection was my sister and that was because she was getting it too, off our stepdad, We used to sit together and work out a plan about how we would wait till they were all drunk, together in the house, and kill them all, set the house on fire and run off to Australia or Canada."

Nigel said, "I have an aunt then, what's she like? Paedophile like you?"

Ken ignored the jibe and continued, "Rosie. She went and got herself a boyfriend when she was 16, got herself pregnant and escaped and forgot me and left me to be passed around till I was 14 and my voice broke and I got some dumb bells, a bullworker, and put on some muscles, did a bit of judo and suddenly they minded their business and kept away from me. I had a temper then, see. My stepdad was out of work and just sat round the house being a cunt and I got bigger than him and stronger than my Grandad. When my stepdad called me a cissy that last time and I broke his jaw with one punch they knew the game was up with all that and they didn't touch me again. Five years of being molested and in five seconds it was over. My stepdad was lying on his back rubbing his chin and my Mum was fussing over him like he was the defending middle weight champion just lost his title. Fanning him with a towel and asking me to fetch him water like she thought I would feel sorry for him."

Ken reached inside his jacket pocket and took out a picture.

"I used to keep loads of pictures, of family, of girls I knew but I had to get away from some lodgings sharpish and I lost them all. All except this one of my Rosie. For years I had it in my mind I would kill her for leaving me at the mercy of all the sadistic men who screwed my life up but I came to realise that it wasn't her fault. She had to get away to keep herself sane and it was one day when I visited her and my niece and nephew sat on my lap, all innocent and loving and telling me how much they loved their Uncle Ken I knew I had to stop being the person who had become a monster but I had an urge to touch them both. I remember when I was about seven and I had cropped hair because of lice and no-one looked at me like I was a girl. I found out from Rosie that she was the one who was being raped but the attention to her went as I replaced her as the vulnerable one. I am not innocent but I am not wholly guilty Nigel."

Ken's words were coming out in a rush as if a damn had burst and it was difficult for Nigel to take in and to piece the sentences together. He thought about what Ken had just said. There were so many times when he had contemplated touching a child. Something in him had always held him back, as if there were forces of good and evil inside him battling to take control. No, the thought of raping a child was abhorrent. His mind whirled and buzzed like a hive of bees. He looked at the picture. The girl was beautiful. Unknown to him it was the same picture Christine had looked at in Ken's room 57 years ago. He felt no empathy toward this man who had just revealed the reason behind his past. He felt no compulsion to take this man in his arms and tell him it was all okay and that it wasn't his fault. The grudge he had felt over being abandoned in an alley was still there was strong as ever. Whatever Ken's reasons were, he didn't care.

If every man who had been abused as a child and abandoned his own became a rapist and a murderer what hope would there be? He tried to feel compassion but his cold heart could not summon any warmth.

Fuck Ken Harris and fuck his shit life. He got up and said, "I'm going to give you a couple of days to think about what you want to do. You can either hand yourself in to the police and confess to rape and murder or you can be outed."

Ken had expected some sympathy but as he looked into Nigel's hard eyes he could see only contempt. His eyes filled with tears once again and he felt the moisture on his cheeks. He got up and looked at his son. As they stood there, for what seemed like an eternity something happened that shocked Ken. His son, Nigel's shoulders started heaving and he started to sob, It lasted only about twenty seconds but to Ken it felt like twenty years. He breathed a sigh of relief. Perhaps his son had a heart and could forgive him.

Nigel's tears subsided and he pulled himself together. He took a deep breath. Ken waited with bated breath.

Nigel said, "You've got a couple of days or else I will destroy your life."

Nigel walked out of the house. It was going to be the last time he would look at the man who had fathered him.

Ken made himself a cup of tea. He wasn't sure whether Nigel did have all the social network access he had said he had, or whether, given the rights criminals seem to be given he was being bluffed. Ken was computer literate enough to know there was a dark web and there were people with the ability to clone accounts and to hack others. Years of looking at child pornography had kept him savvy about computing. He wondered whether Nigel would risk losing his job, his pension, whatever benefits he would have accumulated over the years.

Ken knew one thing for sure. He knew the power of social media. Barbara had often shared her mobile phone with him. Showing him pictures she had posted of the family. Posts made by the family. All the latest family news, there are the click of a button. Barbara and Ken knew who was sick, who had been to the hospital, which children had open days, book days, dressing up days and holidays. They knew if anyone had been foolish enough to take their children to school before term had started, or hadn't taken their child to school after term had started.

They knew who had a new car and whose car was playing up. They knew what the views were on the latest scandal or disaster. They knew who was affected by inclement or extreme weather and they knew what the weather was going to be like next week without having to watch the forecast slot after the evening news. They knew who was at a cricket, football or rugby match. They knew the inside of people's houses and the type of crockery they had. They knew everyone's colour schemes and plans. They knew how many barbecues everyone attended and how often they were drunk.

They knew who was dating who and who had broken off with whom. They knew what everyone's favourite food was and what they would look like if they were aged thirty years. They knew who went jogging and how long it took to run five miles. They knew who went down the gym and what they look like as they did a session on the cross trainer. They knew who had done a 12 week challenge and what they look like before and after the training and eating plan session.

They knew who killed who in the most popular soap operas even if they didn't watch them and which star was in rehab or had given their child an outlandish name. They knew what everyone's favourite drink was and how many people had had a porn star martini that day/week/month. They knew whose birthday it was, whose anniversary it was, and who had just died and what the funeral arrangement were to be. Barbara showed him more photos of gravestones than he cared to have seen had he lived in a cemetery. He expected that no-one had actually seen a concert live so busy were they in recording it for later viewing or sharing.

Ken wondered whether, had social media been available in the 50s and 60s children like him and those he abused would have been worldlier and less likely to succumb to deviants but he knew that the internet allowed more deviants' access to more vulnerable people. The world he had been brought up in and the world into which he sat were different but the same but now, everyone knew everyone's business.

As Ken stepped into his large garage with a bottle and a half of whisky and twenty Donormly sleeping tablets in his stomach he thought briefly about recording his next action on Barbara's Facebook page. She had shown him how to go live. Too gruesome.

With one end of the rope tied a clamp on the workbench and looped round the wooden beam at the peak of the apex roof, Ken kicked away the metal bucket on which he stood. He had managed, and it had taken a lot of effort, to tie his hands behind his back with a cable tie and as he thrashed around in mid-air he had the brief memory of Gabriel and Atlanta sitting naked on his lap.

Edgeways Callaghan

John sat with Sangeeta outside the Golden Fleece pub in Forest Gate and listened to the latest update on the Marlon Benjamin from his brother Police Sargent Martyn Marsh. As each fact was revealed, they became more and more astonished.

The call had been made to John by Martyn from Hackney Police station. Martyn had in his custody Billy "Edgeways" Callaghan. Edgeways has earned his sobriquet by being the chattiest villain in London and the Home Counties. He was a charmer and a habitual liar, and conman. He had grown up in a house where scamming or robbing people was the part of the family business. His Irish grandfather Seamus Callaghan had two names, one he used when he was working on building sites and was the one on his pay slips if he wasn't paid cash in hand, the other, Michael Callaghan was the one he used that matched his passport and was used for claiming benefits. His side-line was receiving and selling stolen goods, anything from radios to tractors. Seamus' sons Padraig, Conor and Jack all doormen, were all on the wrong side of the law and were heavily involved in prostitution, drug smuggling and armed robbery.

Edgeways was the son of Jack, he was a slight man with copper coloured hair, a plethora of freckles and a puny frame and buck teeth. He didn't have the aggression of the Callaghan's but he always had an eye for a deal and he was a wizard on computers. His bent was fraud and cybercrime. Phone scams were a speciality and a large number of the elderly had been convinced that they should transfer large amounts of money from their current account to a "holding account" to protect their own bank account which had been compromised. Once the transfer was complete Edgeways would transfer the money to an offshore account and close the former. Edgeways main other scam was to convince victims that their computer had been infected by a virus and that he would remotely provide a fix provided they paid him. With the number of bank accounts he had, Edgeways was able to take payments by credit or visa without fear of being traced.

Edgeways had made a fortune and had kept under the radar of the authorities by embezzling small amounts, £2k or less but made up for this by the volume of transactions. It was a full time job. Such was the scale of the work and Edgeways hyper active mouth it was a wonder that he was never caught. One glance at his Facebook and Instagram accounts, with pictures of holidays in Dubai, Las Vegas, Bali, Melbourne and Rio, together with Breitling and Rolex watches would give away the fact that the income from job he allegedly had, cavity wall installation salesman, did not match his lifestyle. His official vocation was a front for him to door stop potential candidates for his scams.

Edgeways was able to lead a charmed life, one reason was his gift of the gab, the other was he had the good fortune to be married to Dougie Williams' sister, Veronica. Dougie, with his contacts on both sides of the law was able to ensure that if Edgeways did come close to getting his collar felt, he had help that would buy him enough time to cover whatever tracks had might lead to spell served at Her Majesty's pleasure.

Edgeways luck ran out the day Veronica caught him brazenly out shopping with a twenty-five year old Ukrainian, Daryna Kopek, who he had met on a lad's weekend in Benalmadena and exchanged numbers. Whilst Veronica was wise to men in her world, her father and brother included, having the odd affair or one night stand, long-term liaisons were a taboo. The dalliances always ended quickly, the men came back to their wives or girlfriend. In the time of the fling 12 months maximum, wives and girlfriends was showered with expensive jewellery, clothing or holidays.

Veronica had been told in September 2016 Edgeways had been seen with the young girl in a restaurant in Knightsbridge. Lynn Little, a beautician, did Veronica's Botox and had been introduced to Daryna by fellow Ukrainian Cataline who was another client. Cataline was a friend on Lynn's business Facebook page, Lynn No Lines.

Cataline posted a picture of a happy foursome having lunch, her boyfriend Gregor, Edgeways and Daryna. Lynn took a screenshot of the picture and sent it to Veronica via WhatsApp. She knew that Veronica and Edgeways were married having seen Facebook posts made by her client.

Veronica at the time had passed the information off as a standard occurrence and made hay taking Edgeways on a spending spree, included an upgrade to her Bentley Coupe.

Fourteen months later Veronica, in November of 2017, found Edgeways was still dangling his beautiful young girlfriend on his arm. She saw him coming out of Dolce and Gabbana on Sloane Street. Daryna had lips pumped up like Goodyear tyres, a Botox filled forehead, that was as still as flat lemonade and massive breasts that defied gravity, perched on a size 10 waist and a five foot two frame.

Veronica knew that affairs were generally conducted with younger, fitter, women but an affair was brief and the rules had been broken. She had kicked Edgeways out of the family home. He in turn had ended his affair with Daryna because her demands on his wallet, together with Veronica's, had led to a downturn in his capital. Edgeways couldn't risk the wrath of the Williams' by not ceding to any financial demand that Veronica made which was why he found himself in a predicament.

Edgeways was surprised when he found that he was not wholly cast aside by the Williams clan. Sitting in new local pub near the flat he was in in Hornchurch he was approached by Rennie Bates, Veronica's cousin, and asked if he could be a getaway driver on a jewellery heist. It was an easy job.

As he sat in Hackney nick being interviewed by Martyn Marsh and Steve Banks, Edgeways wondered how the easy job had gone so wrong.

After Rennie and his wing man Raymond Porter had exited the jeweller in Hatton Garden they had coolly walked to the idling car on Greville Street and stepped in. Edgeways hit the gas and they were soon in Tottenham by Spurs football ground. He dropped Rennie and Raymond off, the plan was to meet with them at the end of the week once the merchandise had been exchanged for cash guaranteed from the buyer who had set up the job. Ninety minutes later, within seconds of driving into Dalston Junction, the stolen BMW318i, with a new set of false number plates was surrounded by police cars with flashing blue lights. There were old bill swarming all over him like ants on sugar.

Edgeways was confident that nothing could be pinned on him, red BMWs were ten a penny. It was probably a show of strength, police who couldn't nab a mugger stopping cars for not being taxed or with one tyre with insufficient tread. Someone hadn't squared things with the Williams'.

As he stood by his car, hands on his head, as instructed by the policeman who had forcibly pulled him from the driver's seat another policeman slid into the back seat. Edgeways was stunned when this uniform extracted from the foot well a purple velvet pouch. The policeman nodded sagely at his colleague who in turn gave Edgeways a smug grim as the contents of the pouch was emptied into a gloved palm. There were eighteen uncut diamonds recently extricated from the jewellers in Hatton Garden.

Edgeways knew that Rennie and Raymond had set him up. There was no honour amongst thieves, he had been used as a fall guy. When the deal had been made with the buyer and Dougie Williams, the latter had called in Rennie and told him to offer the driver job to Edgeways. Edgeways had been sweet talked into the job by Rennie who had said that Dougie wasn't holding a grudge regarding Veronica, she was a big girl who could handle her own love life and he was only interested in his family being part of the jewel heist.

The plan was for Edgeways to be arrested, taken to the station and interviewed by a Dougie Williams' own friendly copper, Alan Morgan, who would tell him that he had been stitched up and he should take the rap and do his bird. He would get away with being an accomplice and would be charged with possession of stolen goods.

That part of the plan fell apart when Alan Morgan suffered an aneurism just as Edgeways entered the station. Sargent Martyn Marsh, was scheduled to be on holiday all week but had cancelled due to his daughter delivering her baby a month prematurely. Martyn's wife refused to go on holiday and her husband decided to go into work and it was he who was available in place of Alan Morgan.

So it was that Police Sargent Melvyn Marsh sat with Police Constable Steve Banks opposite Edgeways and gave him the heads up.

Police Constable Banks said, "Edgeways, some members of the police force are very much aware that you have been living beyond your means all your life and that much of the reason you haven't spent time behind bars is your association with Dougie Williams. We know you are no longer with Veronica and we expect that that is because of your dalliance with the 25 years old Ukrainian girl. Yes, you would be surprised but we do keep up to speed with what folks are doing via social media. You can stay schtum if you like and do your time and when you get out Veronica will have moved on and going through whats left of your money. The Hatton Garden heist is small fish. You know things about the Williams', things that could put them behind bars. You could get a deal that would allow you to stay out, keep us from looking into your offshore accounts, the villa in Marbella, and whatever else you have stashed away."

Edgeways didn't take too long to weigh up his options. His own family connections in Ireland could be relied on to secure some safety and he was fed up with London now that his collar had finally been firmly felt.

"I know about Marlon Benjamin," he said, with the conviction of a man who was in fear of actually being convicted.

Melvyn's heart missed a beat but he was careful not to appear too excited or taken in. Edgeways ability to spin a tale was legendary. He was as likely to be about to inform the officers that Marlon had been abducted by aliens as he was to have revealed the true nature of his death. Edgeways wasn't the type to do time for anyone.

"I'm listening Edgeways," Steve said, he raised his eyebrows to the level of one about to be made incredulous.

Edgeways launched into his story. "The day Marlon got killed, Veronica got a call from Dougie asking her to come help him and do some laundry at his house. Veronica has set our daughter up running a cleaning company so she has got access to all the stuff, plus she is a germ free freak. It was a bit of a surprising call seeing as how Maddie is also OCD about cleaning and her gaff is as spotless as all the dogs that aint dalmations. I daren't sit down in the house with a biscuit in case I get a crumb on the cream carpet. I love a Flake chocolate bar but I wouldn't eat one in the house, use to go and eat them in the shed and make sure there were no crumbs on my mouth that might drop on the marble kitchen floor. After a shower I scan for hairs even though I have shaved most of mine to ensure none of them sully the plug hole. We have a cooker that has never been used because Veronica is saving it for a special occasion. Most of our meals are takeouts, micro waved or are done on the barbecue, whatever the weather. Can't get the cooker dirty. Maddie and Veronica both the same. I think they read about other women on Facebook being clean and they are like lemmings follow whatever is on shown on social media."

"Is any of this OCD with cleaning relevant?"

"Dougie and Simon were pissed off that Frances had a coffee coloured baby and doubly pissed that her and Marlon lived together but thought they were best off getting way from a family where the Dad was a prick copper who wouldn't take a back hander."

Melvyn smiled. Edgeways obviously did not know he was in the presence of the prick coppers brother because he hadn't taken much notice when Robbie had introduced them. He had actually yawned to feign boredom. That said, Marsh was a common enough surname.

Edgeways continued.

"One of France' scatty mates posted a picture on Facebook of the three of them and the half caste baby and there were loads of comments and then this scatty bird posted that Maddie had slept with Benjamin's old man Bertie. Apparently the post got removed but not before Dougie heard about it and by all accounts went ballistic. He said that if he didn't do something about it the whole of London would be laughing at him and Simon. All the time Dougie, Maddie, Simon and Veronica were cleaning up, Dougie was swearing at his old woman calling her a whore and an embarrassment and how he was a whisker from cutting her up and throwing her body over Epping Forest for the foxes to eat. Maddie just stood there apparently she didn't say a word but she was petrified, looked like she was going to pass out."

"Veronica told you all this?"

"I've been seeing some bird so I was doing my bit to keep Veronica sweet so I bought her a second hand convertible Bentley, she would have told me how big Dougie's cock was if I had asked. Him and Simon had just driven up to their house and who should they see parking up and going into his Dads? Marlon. First time they'd seen him since it all kicked off with the baby. They knew that Bertie kept a spare set of keys to the back door under a plant pot so they've legged it round, let themselves in and coshed Marlon and brought him back.

Battered him, broke his arms and his legs, done him proper, had him begging to be finished off, stabbed him up. They have always got to hand some essentials for body disposal because Dougie always used to say, you never know when you're going to have to get rid of a body. They made a mess of the rug so they wrapped his body up in that, then they put it in a massive thick plastic bag and sealed it, then put it in a coffin which they filled with quick drying cement then they chucked it in the river Lea.

There was a big panic when the boy was found but there was nothing to pin Dougie or Simon to the crime and there were enough Facebook threats to Marlon from husbands, boyfriends and women threatening to kill him for trying to dick his way through every woman in London that he was bound to get turned over at some stage I heard he was one of the most dateable men on Tinder."

"Who told you that?" Melvyn asked.

"Veronica read it on Facebook."

Melvyn wondered how many people read Facebook news and took it for gospel and were unmoved by the fact that what they read may not be accurate or up to date or pure tittle tattle.

Melvyn had met Marlon at a family barbecue once. Marlon seemed like a hardworking and family oriented young guy who was madly in love with his partner and his child. Melvyn was well aware that in a day and age of internet dating, programs such as Love Island, Big Brother, Ex on The Beach, Wife Swap, and with bars and clubs awash with cheap alcohol, sex was as common as mackerel when the sea was awash with zooplankton, copepod, shrimp and squid.

Edgeways did not know the Marlon who had turned a corner and had been a man any family would welcome with open arms.

Melvyn said, "We are going to have to substantiate your story, in the meantime I suggest you lie low for a while. I am not going to formally arrest you. We have you bang to rights with the heist but I can square it upstairs that you were set up and there are bigger fish to fry. I'll arrange for you to go. Keep under the radar and if you leave the country you're on your own because we will need you to testify at some stage after which we can get you witness protection."

Edgeways muttered, "Thanks."

The first thing he did when he left the station was book a flight to Dublin and secrete himself within the bosom of his family.

When Melvyn had updated his brother on the information received, in the days that followed John received a precis from D.I. Willie Patterson which corroborated the facts supplied.

Ian said, "Marlon's body had been found because post mortem the gases in his body had expanded. Without a means to escape it had made the rug, polythene, concrete and coffin air-filled. This might not in itself have enabled the tomb to rise to the surface except that the quick drying cement had not been left long enough to set before it was submerged. The mortar had crumbled in the water and chunks had broken away releasing the coffin from its swampy depths. The coffin was traced to a one missing from a Theatrical company that was run by Dougie Williams' daughter Carron who had posted on Facebook,

WTF some cnut has stolen one of our props two nights before we were to perform The Vampires of Bloody Island. Anyone know where we can get hold of a cheap coffin PM me.

On the day after Marlon went missing Simon Williams did a search of eBay for Axminster rugs and his Facebook advertising algorithm thereafter posted pictures of exactly the same carpet and more that had been found with Marlon's body wrapped in it."

Sangeeta said, "Seems like it all points to the Williams without a shadow of a doubt and we all know that Nigel Maloney has been directing everyone away from pursuing them as potential suspects. What do we do now guv?"

John said, "All I can do is take it up with Karen and Nigel, but those two are as thick as thieves."

"Good luck." Ian and Sangeeta said, in unison, and John went off, deep in thought.

DCI Nigel Maloney and DI John Marsh

Detective Chief Inspector Karen Boulding sat at her desk, she was depressing and releasing the nip of her pen and seemed focussed on this activity, more so than on the two men who sat opposite her.

Nigel Maloney and John Marsh had been called in and were both sitting in silence. Both had reasons to be anxious but neither betrayed anything but calm. Karen seemed in no rush to enlighten them. Finally John broke the silence,

"Are you ok Ma'am?" he said.

"Not really John we have a potential situation."

"Which is?"

"Your brother Melvyn interviewed the man who was married to the woman whose brother allegedly killed your daughter's lover."

"What's the problem?" John said, he was relieved that Karen had been given the heads up from Kiffer Furbanks.

"The problem is when, not if, this comes out the accused could say your brother coerced the information out of the witness". She looked at her notes. "Billy Callaghan. Aka Edgeways Callaghan. Former husband of Veronica whose brother is Dougie Williams. I am telling you all this and I know you both know all the detail."

John said, "I believe there is enough proof to back up what Edgeways has said for us to nail the Williams."

Nigel Maloney jumped in "Personally I don't think this is going to stick, there is no forensic evidence that proves Dougie or his son carried out the killing. For all we know someone else carried out the murder and faked the evidence to point to the Williams. He has a lot of enemies."

"He has a lot of friends." John Marsh shot back.

"The weakest link is Madeline, at the moment there is that rumour that she slept with Marlon's dad, Bertram or Bertie, we could bring her in

299

and let her know we know that Dougie and Simon had a good motive for killing Marlon and the opportunity. We can now do what we should have done a while ago and trace the movement of their vehicles on the day of the crime. The fact that Dougie was on the verge of killing her too means at the moment she must be petrified," Karen said. "Nigel, if you wrap this one up the Detective Chief Inspector role is practically yours." Karen raised her eyebrows and looked Nigel directly in the eyes, she added, "You may have to disassociate from any unsavoury characters though."

Both John and Nigel reacted to this news with mild surprise. The former thinking that it should not be possible for someone with Nigel's chequered history and fondness for bending the rules to get promoted. It was his colleague's fault that the Williams had thus far been kept out of the reckoning when they were the obvious premier candidates.

Nigel smiled knowingly. For all his reservations about his inherent behaviours he was still able to climb the ladder of success. He also knew who to have as an ally.

Nigel quickly weighed up whether he preferred to be a Detective Chief Inspector or remained in cahoots with Dougie Willams. He decided that there were any number of villians he could cosy up to, and the opportunity to tell John Marsh to jump and to be asked how high was one he could not afford to miss

"I'll make arrangements to bring the Williams in Ma'am" Nigel said, getting up to leave the office.

Without looking him in the eye Karen said "Sorry John."

As they left the office Nigel couldn't help but gloat

"So the little man beats the big man to the prize."

"How so Maloney?"

"You have a father who was a DCI and your mother was a magistrate, Your Grandfather was an officer in the commando's during World War 2. Your brother is a sergeant at Hackney. All pretty respectable. I don't know who my real parents are and it's likely they were shit because I was dumped in an alley and left to die but here I am, in line to be promoted instead of you."

"You still have a bee in your bonnet about nature and nurture and whether the sins of the father are carried through. Ezekiel 18:20 says, The soul who sins shall die. The son shall not suffer for the iniquity of the father, nor the father suffer for the iniquity of the son. The righteousness of the righteous shall be upon himself, and the wickedness of the wicked shall be upon himself."

"I don't care about that Christian mumbo jumbo. My real father was no good and my mother dumped me. Kim will be pleased to know I have overcome my past."

"How is your good wife? Still think the sun shines out of your arse?"

"Most definitely. As soon as I get promoted she will be putting my name in lights on Facebook and confirming how proud she is of me despite my setbacks."

"Another Facebook junkie?"

"Most definitely. It gets her meeting some interesting people, she went to Miami last year because one of her Facebook friends invited her there for a week."

"When did she go?"

"July 22nd last year. I know the exact date because, as you know, I have an eye for detail. She met up with a professor who had studied the science of nature versus nurture. Kim had said that her friend had written a book to argue the theory that it should be permissible to castrate all high level murderers, rapists, paedophiles, mentals, so they couldn't have children."

"Radical."

Where would I have been if that had happened, assuming my parentage is not as dignified as yours? You might be in line for Detective Chief Inspector instead of me." Nigel laughed, they had reached the men's lavatories and John decided he would take the opportunity to break off from his colleague.

"I am sure you will do a better job than me Nigel, anyway my parents are loaded and they are thinking of transferring a lot of their wealth to their children to beat some of the inheritance laws so I am probably going to retire too soon for you to be able to whip me into the sort of shape you're in." John smiled, he could read Maloney like a book and he knew that he would relish the chance of giving him the worst cases to deal with and the most paperwork to complete.

In return Nigel gave John a look of contempt, the sort of look that would refreeze ice.

As John washed his hands, post urinating, he considered what Nigel had said about his wife. There was something about Miami and the July 22nd that troubled him and he repeated the date a couple of times until he went back to a desk, opened his laptop and made a call.

Toward the end of the day John, still beavering away at his laptop received a follow-up call from Robert Royston, one of the Intel team, who said he was sending him a file of screen shots from a Facebook conversation that had been triggered by a much publicised murder where an 18 year old Scot had butchered his girlfriend and her sister when they had ganged up on him during a row over whether to watch football or Big Brother.

What had made the incident widely debated, as well as its apparent triviality, was that it had been revealed that the boy's father was serving a life sentence for killing his wife and her mother after a domestic argument spiralled out of control. To add to the family CV, the boy's Uncle had slashed a man's throat in a pub, also during an argument, this over a hand of cards.

John read the screenshots,

David Thompson,
"That girl and her sister had no chance, the kid was a low life from a low life family."

Ricki Finnegan,

"I hear ya Dave, pikey family with hair trigger tempers should have drowned the rats as soon as the Grandparents gave birth. Probably homophobic"

Tracey King,
"Get you Ricki. I didn't see anything about them killing gays but agree with Dave people like that should have been aborted."

Gavin Aitchison,
"Don't see how anyone could have known the son was going to turn out like his Dad and his Uncle and be a killer, it must be rare."

David Thompson,
"Oh come on Gavin. The Dad and his brother killed people for little or no reason. There was a link on FB to an article that said there is a younger brother who was expelled from school aged eight because he kept fighting."

Ricki Finnegan,
"Put him in a sack an drown him now."

Kim Maloney,
"Drama Queen!"

Helen Tyler,
"Even animals can be mistreated but you can re-train them. Certain humans, you just cant get the evil out of them. They said that the scroat kid killed the family pug first then done his girlfriend and the sister. He bashed the dogs brain out with a shovel. Hanging is too good for him. That poor dog."

Keri Young,
"OMG it just doesn't bear thinking about Hels, how could someone kill a little pug they're so cute."

David Thompson,
"The girlfriend and the sister must have gone through hell and back. Its proven that people with pyscho families are 90% likely to be pyschos too. It's a thing of nature."

Kim Maloney,
"Since when were you an expert on this subject David?"

David Thompson,
"I'm a professor in knowing a low-life scum family when I see one."

Kim Maloney,
"You are a professor of Smultz. How is the lovely Gabija Konstantis? Suffered any life threatening ingrowing toenail issues lately? Dad come back from the dead? If everyone whose parents did bad was killed some highly regarded people would not be with us"

David Thompson,
"Wont lower myself to respond"

Christine Anderson,
"Name one highly regarded person with a killer parent? I agree with Ricki, I think the offspring of people who have a history of perpetuating such evil should be tagged. Once is happenstance. Twice is coincidence. Thrice is enemy action."

Kim Maloney,
"Radical views."

Phillip Anderson,
"For once I agree with my mother."

Helen Tyler,
"If you don't you'll get no dessert Phillip lol."

Keri Young,
"LMAO."

Ricki Finnegan,
"Yes and Mummy wont give you any dinner money."

Kim Maloney,
"This isn't funny. Phillip are you still playing with your Star Wars toys?"

Keith Hunstman,
"It isn't funny 5 people killed by 3 hot headed members of one family. They should lock up any of the siblings before anyone else is butchered"

Helen Tyler,
"Don't forget the dog was killed as well."

Kim Maloney,
"Dog got killed. Hold the front page. You need to get a life dog lady."

David Thompson,
"I would bet money that there are other members of that family with as equally a vicious temper who would kill at the slightest hint of provocation. Its obvious."

Phillip Anderson,
"It's a good job none of us move in the circle of undesirables."

Keri Young,
"Deffo we can sleep easy in our beds knowing we aren't going to get killed arguing over dinner, T V viewing or a game of snap."

Kim Maloney,
"I am sure if you had a boyfriend he would kill you just for being annoying."

Keri Young,
"You have anger management mate, you wanna calm down."

Kim Maloney,
"You wanna or want to, learn how to speak English and I am not you're mate. No-one has anger management."

Christine Anderson,
"Your NOT you're. I shudder to think what it would be like to be connected to people like that. Lowly bred undesireables."

Kim Maloney,
"I am sure the Essex Ladies What lunch, do so in a greasy spoon and not Buckingham Palace Christine."

Christine Anderson,
Prezzo, Nandos, sometimes at Sugarhut darling but never McDonalds, KFC or the Winpy, such awful clientele ."

Kim Maloney,
"You live in Essex, its full of undesirables. You ought to move to Surrey if you're so posh."

Ricki Finnegan,
"I cant believe someone so plain looking could call me a drama queen."

Kim Maloney,
"You know sticking your cock up other mens arses used to be illiegal? Still wearing womens frocks?"

Ricki Finnegan,
"I am more woman than you'll ever be and more man than you'll ever get."

Keri Young,
"PMSL"

Keith Huntsman,
"I thought we were discussing extermination of psychos offspring and not Ricki's sexual peccadildos"

Kim Maloney,
"PECCADILLO."

Keith Huntsman,
"I know what I mean lol."

John's mind began to race. Here was a link to the seven murder victims and judging from Nigel's comment earlier his wife Kim was in Miami when Keith Huntsman was killed, there was nothing to stop her from getting to any of the others. Could she have taken vengeance on all the victims over a Facebook disagreement? Was Ricki Finnegan's life in danger?

How could Kim kill seven people and get away with it?

John hadn't noticed the note on the email at the end of the JPEG file of screen shots, the note read.

"You aren't going to believe this but the lad who killed his girlfriend and her sister, his family name was Clough. His Dad was Jimmy and his Dad's brother was Kenny. They had a much older sister called Julie who was a heroin addict along with her husband Finlay. Finlay and Julie have nine children, one of whom was Kim Clough who is now Kim Maloney. Kim came South from Glasgow and ended up being married to a drug dealer called Stevie Palmer who ended up being killed over drug money. She has seen lot of shit.

John let out a low whistle. Here was a motive, as tenuous and petty as it was and a woman who, with a bent Detective husband could find it easy to cover her tracks.

He rang D.I. Patterson, "Willie, I'm just reading some screen shots of a Facebook thread with Helen Tyler, Keith Huntsman, Tracey King, Christine Anderson, David Thompson, Ricki Finnegan and Keri Young AND Kim Maloney. They are basically having a massive slagging match about the merits of executing the offspring of people who have committed a brutal murder. Wasn't it someone's job to establish a link between the deceased and see whether anyone had a reason to kill them all? Kim is in a debate with people who are basically saying she shouldn't have lived because her family history is as criminally dysfunctional as Rosemary and Fred West's. Nigel Maloney is very sensitive about his parentage. Almost obsessive about the fact he doesn't know what they were like."

Willie replied, "It didn't seem like the sort of conversation that would lead to mass murder. Plus the fact it is Nigel Maloney's old woman we're talking about."

"Didn't anyone follow it up? Kim was in Miami when Dave Thompson was killed. Did anyone establish where she was at the time of the other murders?"

The subject was brought up. As I recall, Detective constable Ron Carpenter spoke to Nigel Maloney and mentioned the Facebook conversation."

"What did he say?"

"He said something along the lines of, are you suggesting my wife has been going around the UK and to America slaughtering people because of a Facebook rant?"

"Didn't Carpo press him or just say it was best to eliminate Kim from enquiries?"

"He did."

"And."

"Nigel said, words to the effect of, or as I recall he said words exactly like, I fucking double dare you to come and knock at my front door and accuse my fucking wife of murder."

"I believe then that Ron decided to explore other avenues."

John put his head in his hands and groaned. The Maloney's, the Williams too many roads leading to these unscrupulous people. Ricki Finn and Veronica might be in danger.

"Ok thanks Willie I may need to follow this up obviously don't say anything to Maloney."

Kim Maloney

Kim shadow boxed in the mini gym Nigel had installed in the concrete and timber shed at the bottom of the garden. With her one hundred and twenty four pounds of muscle packed into a five foot six frame, Kim, in Nike leggings and matching vest, looked awesome. She had always been a good fighter and loved to hone her skills, and her physique, at home as well as at the gym.

Growing up in Carlton, a deprived district to the East of Glasgow, scrapping, even for girls was a way of life. Having eight siblings, five of them boys meant that daily squabbles often resulted in punches being thrown to settle an argument. Male or female it did not matter, if a debate could be settled with a smack in the mouth then that was what happened. If it wasn't one of her siblings then the clenched fist of either parent was an occupational hazard of being one of the Clough's. Outside the house the Clough's together were a fearsome clan and were as lethal as, a well-trained military unit. The family of nine were often with the numerous Clough cousins or those of the McGovern's, the maternal branch.

Finlay and Julie Clough decided to move south to London when Kim was twelve, it was an opportunity for them to get away from the violence fuelled days and stupor filled nights and perhaps make a fresh start especially with some drug money owing. It wasn't a great time for Kim, she arrived at her secondary school a year after everyone else and found it difficult to make friends. For her parents, life was a breeze, it didn't take long for them to source out the local dealers and before long they had simply transferred the same existence they experienced in Carlton, down to Balham.

For Finlay and Julie life meant Netflix, smoking pot, injecting heroin, eating pizza and in rare days of lucidity, making barely intelligible Facebook posts to fellow ne'er do wells back up North about the tranquillity of their new lives. For Kim life was a case of survival until she was able to leave school and aged 17 she was married.

Kim had just turned 16 and was still in her school uniform when had met Steve Palmer, who was 24 at the time, when he was dropping off some cannabis for her parents. Kim and Steve got talking, he asked her for a date. She accepted, much to the joy of her parents, who saw this as a route to free pot. After a year Steve popped the question and the two romantically drove up to Gretna Green and spliced the knot.

Only once since she had moved south had anyone made an inappropriate advance. When she was 19, Luke Kennedy a friend of Steve's, had patted her bottom as she stepped out of the local newsagents with a Daily Sport newspaper, tobacco and papers for her chain smoking husband. Kim whipped over a straight left hand jab to the nose that straightened Luke up then delivered a thunderous right cross that broke his jaw. A two handed combination two his torso sent Luke crashing to the floor and it took the intervention of two passers-by each holding one of her arms to pull her off as she sat astride his prone body pummelling his face with metronomic and demonic intent.

When she had got home that day the feeling of euphoria knew no bounds. She sat re-living every punch. The surprise on Luke's face when he felt the crunch to his nose and the inevitable shower of blood that cascaded over the pavement like red confetti on a virginal white wedding dress. Luke's jaw had reverberated then sagged, his face looked like a stroke victim when it too had been dealt a blow. As each punch into his rib connected so the breath departed from both damaged mouth and nostrils. Kim had looked into Luke's eyes as the light went out of them and he slipped into unconsciousness.

Her bloodlust was not sated until she became aware of the men who were holding her arms pulling her up shouting "Stop he's had enough."

As she had stood she felt remarkably calm, as if she had just been carrying out a household chore, emptying the bin or drying up crockery. The two men had eyed her warily, she picked up the newspaper, tobacco and papers and sauntered off while Luke was put into the recovery position and a call was made for an ambulance, but not police assistance.

Kim was not an unattractive girl, an elfin face that suited her close cropped brown hair. Her loathing of her natural white colour meant she was a bronzy orange from her regular use of sunbeds and spray tanning. She had an edge about her that would make you think twice about asking for directions to the nearest library. She had brown eyes and lips that were often pursed, as if contemplating whether to take a glance as an insult or an offer of a straightener.

Her shoulders were broad. As well as being more intelligent than most of her siblings and parents, she was less slattern than any of the Clough's. Violence was never miles way whilst she was with Stevie Palmer but now with Nigel, life was more tranquil and Kim had sought some excitement. In the months and weeks that followed her marriage to Nigel, Kim joined chatrooms, it didn't matter what the subject was, football, cooking, education, holidays. When it became popular her networking device was Facebook. She joined several groups, including Essex Ladies What Lunch.

Kim would search out discussion that interested her and respond. Kim had in her a mood that could be as volatile as a barrel of Semtex. She could enter a conversation and respond angrily to the most innocuous response. If the person Kim viewed as the antagonist did not back down there would be a challenge for a 1-2-1 meet to further discuss or, if the debate became particularly heated a challenge to a fight.

Facebook was an easy place to find a victim because so many people used it and it was a cinch to find an angry mob of two.

A study of the type of conversation that would lead to confrontation revealed a consistent pattern,

Facebook Random 1
"I love it when I get wolf whistled, it makes my day."

Kim,
"Don't you think it objectifies you as a woman. You are basically allowing a man to leer at you and then intimidate you."

Random 1,
"Most women who don't like being wolf whistled are lesbians or mingers."

Kim,
"I am not a lesbian but of you'd like to meet me you can let me know if you think I am a minger or not. Valentines Park, Ilford over by the bandstand 7.00pm."

Facebook Random 2,
"Donald Trump has to be the most obnoxious person ever."

Kim,
"He may be obnoxious but the American people voted for him."

Random 2,
"So you would have voted for him?"

Kim,
"I'm not American but I think we should respect the rulers of other countries."

Random 2,
"A man who has nothing to change the archaic gun laws and doesn't engage his brain before he speaks half the time."

Kim,
"You speak like you live with him and know everything he thinks. Respect World leaders."

Random 2,
"If you respect him you don't respect yourself."

Kim,
"I'd like to meet up with you if you want to enlighten me on respect. Valentines Park, Ilford over by the bandstand 7.00pm."

Kim realising that given her posts and the groups she was in might overlap created 30 different aliases, social media accounts and with them different profile pictures. Although being Kim Maloney, wife of a Detective Inspector meant her route out of trouble potentially was as smooth as Roger Moore she didn't want to spoil her pastime by being outed.

Kim picked her battles wisely. She didn't pursue any battle with anyone who looked as though he, it was always a man, could match her physically. Men, she offered to meet, who accepted an invite to a face to face, were those who thought they might be able to cop a feel. The showmen were the feisty ones who thought they were hard because they had heard of the ICF, the Headhunters or Dalston Mandem. Kim had met up with eleven ladies and nine men, asked them to repeat whatever on-line jibe they had made, and knocked them all senseless with one controlled punch and walked away.

Kim did take the precaution of ensuring that if the person was out cold before they hit the floor she grabbed them to prevent any damage that would be been caused if they had hit their head on the ground. She was well aware of the killer punch phenomena and whilst beating up complete strangers was fine, murdering them was not. She only killed people she knew.

Today Ricki Finn was the last advocate left of the Drown the Murderers Children Appreciation Society. Which was how Kim had come to view Helen Tyler, Keith Huntsman, Keri Young, Dave Thompson, Christine Anderson, Phillip Anderson and Ricki.

Disguised in a hoodie, dark glasses and loose fitting tracksuit bottoms with her wiry build, Kim knew that if she was picked up on CCTV she could be mistaken for a man. Her fake tanned complexion meant that it was likely she would be mistaken for someone of mixed race, Asian or fair skinned North African, they were always the fall guys, especially if robbery was added to the mix.

The first murder had been a lot easier than she had anticipated. It was remarkably easy to slice Helen Tyler's throat. She had crept up behind the dog lover as she sat on the corner of her bed. Her task was made that much easier as the woman faced away from the bedroom door. Kim was able to move swiftly and stealthily and with her left forearm exposing Helens throat and with the eight inch knife in her right hand draw it purposely across the exposed white flesh. From behind Kim saw the blood splurt and then as she kept Helens chin in a vice-like grip the blood pump like the fitting on a rotating hose. She quickly ransacked the bedroom and stuffed some jewellery and trinkets into her holdall.

Kim had been surprised that all four dogs remained quiet. When she had exited through the patio doors the dogs sniffed at her but apart from trying to lick her to death soon shuffled off to play with toys or curl back up in their beds. They had just been fed and pugs and French boxers are not renowned for their guard dog skills.

Keith Hunstman had been dispatched in the same way. Once in Miami, Kim had rented a car but did not drive to Keith's house, instead parking several blocks away, almost three miles, and jogging to the Huntsman house. On arrival Kim had scaled the garden wall and conveniently found Keith by the pool. When she had killed him in exactly the same manner as Helen she noticed that on the table by the lounger were four lines of cocaine and a half smoked joint. Keith was a decent build and had he not been slightly incapacitated by narcotics might have been a different proposition, alert and full of fight. Drugs, never a good idea.

Keri Young had been the one she enjoyed most. Kim had an irrational hatred for the hairdresser. Probably because her Facebook photos were so obviously filtered the girl came across as shallow and vacuous. Here posts were an exhibition of wannabee famous, low intelligence and vanity. Kim had almost lost control as she rained blows down on the girl with the eight inch metal pipe. When Keri had fallen to the floor, the contents of her handbag had strewn over the pavement and amongst these were a pair of scissors. As a final coup de grace, Kim had picked the scissors up and thrust them in one of Keri's eyes. She felt a crunch as the tip of the scissor hit bone and she had twisted the weapon round as if trying to locate and puncture the small brain that may have been somewhere in the girl's head.

For variation, David Thompson was shot as he walked his dog. It was easy to get one of the guns Nigel kept and put it back afterwards. Kim had selected one of those equipped with the silencer out of the one hundred and seventy that were available.

Tracey King's murder had been satisfying from a martial art viewpoint because it was in the main completed by hand. Kim's 6 month high intensity ju-jitsu course had, amongst other things, taught her how to carry out a choke hold. Although her tutor had advised that this hold with intent should be used only in a life or death situation, where less lethal options were impractical, for Kim it was for the latter only. Tracey had gone limp well before the eight minutes Kim had planned on maintaining her grip. To confirm the death Kim had used the knife she had brought along to cut some of the washing line and use that as a garrotte. While her hands were as tough as a climb up K2 the wire enclosed nylon length was the perfect accompaniment.

Another trip to the gun arsenal and a journey out to Ilford. Kim was careful not to use the same gun but it was the second of two that was fitted with a silencer. She had parked in Forest Gate and walked the two miles east to the Anderson house. As luck would have it the outside door was open which meant that once inside the porch with the door she had entered closed she could only be seen by Christine when she opened the inner door. The look from Christine was brief because Kim had immediately shot her between the eyes twice. As Christine fell back, eyes frozen in horror, Kim fired again, aiming for the woman's heart. Kim was back in Brentwood within 45 minutes, about the same time that Phillip Anderson got home and found his mother's dead body.

Less than a month later and Phillip was the last victim. Kim had walked along 2nd Avenue, Manor Park around 0200am while Nigel was on nights and tried the front doors. There was always going to be one house where the door had to be proactively locked. The husband would have thought the wife done it and vice versa and the car keys would have been on a hook behind the front door. Christine had stolen the car and parked it on a housing estate in nearby Barking then returned the next evening and driven it to Ilford where she lay in wait for Phillip. She had flinched went he had gone over the bonnet but recovered her composure to reverse over the body, feeling the back then front wheels raise. The job was complete when she drove forward and made sure that at least one wheel went over Phillips head before she sped off. Abandoning the car in Enfield and jogging the 15 or so miles to where her own car was parked in Epping.

Just one left. Ricki Finn, the Prancing queen. She would enjoy this one the most, make him suffer. Hang him and stuff a lemon in his mouth. Bugger him with a milk bottle. Slice his dick off. Slash his arse with a Stanley knife. Stab him in the eyes. Asphyxiate him.

Kim felt she was losing control. She had acquired a vampire-like hunger for the sight and smell of lifeblood. She felt like a fox left to guard a chicken coop.

She set off for Westcliffe, in the boot of her car was a rucksack and it were the implements with which she would make Ricki's last night on this earth undeniably painful. There was the Webley pistol. No silencer. She had decided that she would break that pattern but she had also decided it was unlikely a bullet would be fired. There was a length of rope that had been used once to tow a broken down car, a knife with a serrated edge, a dildo, a large orange, a carpet knife, large plastic bag, a thick black hood, a glass cutter, small plunger and some cord.

Nigel was at work. He did a lot of nights recently. She did often wonder whether he was not actually working but was conducting a clandestine affair but she told herself this was not possible. He was a changed man, with her anyway. He might have some dark traits but he was no philanderer. She could trust him with her life and she would defend him against anyone who tried to besmirch him.

Kim parked the car on the Manor Trading Estate in Benfleet and slipped out of the car donned in her black outfit of hoodie and ski pants with asic gel nimbus 20 trainers. She had her driving license and a ready-made excuse were she approached by the police. Kim Maloney wife of Nigel Maloney Detective Inspector with the Met, currently on nights. She would say she was training for the Northern Traverse ultra-marathon, a brutal 190 mile race run over about 6 days. Training at night when it is tranquil and no pedestrians.

Kim did not encounter anyone official, the few people she had seen as she had jogged took no notice.

The run to Ricki's road in Westcliffe took 50 minutes, it was approximately 6 miles. Kim had run 10k races, the metric equivalent in 42 minutes, and was scarcely out of breath when she arrived at her destination.

Ricki's house was a garish pink. Even under the illumination of the street lights it stood out from the rest of the houses on the street. Kim walked past it just to see whether any lights were on at the front where his bedroom was, and to the end down a small alley that led to an access path that ran parallel behind the houses and their gardens.

The back of Ricki's house was painted the same hideous colour, the garden was mainly lawn, bordered each side by shrubs and flowers. Kim had seen these when she had carried out a reconnaissance three weeks previously and the same was replicated on numerous Facebook posts. Ricki was evidently green fingered and liked everyone to know.

The four foot stone wall was navigated with ease and Kim moved swiftly up the path. She had on recce spotted Ricki's solar powered night light and was pleased that just below it was a water butt. As she neared the house the light came on, Kim leapt onto the butt and swiftly plunged the garden back into darkness by placing a non-translucent hood over it.

Ricki's back door was an open invite for a burglar as it was an old fashioned type with multi windows and the key was in the lock. Kim was pleased she had had the foresight to assess her means of entry. Attaching the plunger to one of the small panes she used the glass cutter to stencil out a shape wide enough to fit her hand through and eased out the piece.

Slipping her hand through the opening she then unlocked the door and stepped into Ricki's darkened kitchen. As she moved though the kitchen door and into the hall she thought she caught a smell she recognised. It was the unmistakable waft of CK Be, the unisex fragrance by Calvin Klein, she froze, and her senses were heightened. She took another step forward and heard the unmistakable phsst sound of an air freshener releasing its own sweet fragrance in the hallway. Kim looked up and although it was dark she could just make out the shape of the box on the wall from which the spray had emitted. This smell now overcome any other and Kim quietly moved up the stairs.

She knew from Ricki's Facebook posts the exact lay out of his house because when it had been re-decorate six months previously he had posted live a grand tour, twice. The first time, with the intonation of the Lloyd Grossman presenting Through the Keyhole. Ricki had described each room and then had done the same again this time with the soundtrack, It's My House by Diana Ross, overdubbed. Facebook definitely had its benefits because Kim could have walked around it blindfold.

Kim crept into Ricki's room. He slept with a comfort light on. She did not need to see his chest rise and fall in breath as he had a snore that resembled chugging of a laboured train engine. Kim had decided to incapacitate her victim with a choke hold to render him unconscious, apply the gaffer tape to his mouth and torture him. To this end she took out the tape left the rucksack at the bottom of the bed and moved to the top and overlooked the sleeping man. As she moved her hands toward his shoulders there was a large whoomp. It was the sound of a wardrobe door being kicked open by a size 12 boot, before Kim had a chance to react a police issue Glock 22 was thrust toward her head and the warning "Kim Maloney armed police do not move." came from the person donned also in black wearing a night vision helmet

"Hands on your head. Do not move."

The room became flooded with armed officers, each similarly attired. Kim wet herself. As she felt the warm liquid cascade between her thighs Kim felt relief twice over. Somewhere deep inside her there was a crumb of morality she knew the killing had come to an end.

It seemed like an age before Sangeeta Patel stood in front of her and said,

"Kim Maloney, I am arresting you on suspicion of the murders of Helen Tyler, Keith Huntsman, Keri Young, David Thompson, Tracey King, Christine Anderson and Phillip Anderson and the attempted murder of Ricki Finn, You do not have to say anything, but it may harm your defence if you do not mention when questioned something which you later rely on in court. Anything you do say may be given in evidence."

The rest of what Sangeeta was saying was unintelligible because Ricki Finn, who had woken up with the sound of the commotion and was sobbing uncontrollably, like a hungry sea-lion out of range of a bucket of sardines.

When Detective Chief Inspector Karen Boulding was given information to the clandestine operation she was immediately able to pass that on to Nigel Maloney as was fast asleep in her bed at her Docklands flat. They had made love just two hours prior to the call she received from Sangheeta to say the operation had been a success. Karen was a compassionate as she could be.

She woke Nigel up and said, "Nigel I'm pretty certain you won't be getting the Detective Chief Inspector job now."

Mind fuddled by the recent release of oxytocin and a two hour sleep, Nigel said dazedly, "Have you decided to stay on Hon?"

"No. Your wife has just been arrested trying to kill Ricki Finn and it seems she has been on a spree killing Helen Tyler, Keith Huntsman, Keri Young, David Thompson, Tracey King, Christine Anderson and Phillip Anderson. You might want to get your clothes on and see if you can go get her a good lawyer."

FaceDead

In the months that followed Nigel Maloney resigned from the force. His lack of investigation of the Marlon Benjamin affair, his general lack of professional morality and his relationships with gangland figures, especially the Williams, were also brought to bear when he was interviewed as part of a disciplinary hearing.

Kim did not reveal how she was able to get access to the guns and Nigel's pension was not jeopardised.

Dougie, Simon, Valerie and Madeline Williams were all arrested and charged with murder and being accessories to murder.

Subsequent to Nigel leaving the force Karen Boulding retired, a feather firmly in her cap with the Facebook murderer bought to book, John Marsh was overlooked the chance to become Detective Chief Inspector, this went to Ian MacDonald instead. John celebrated that he could still work closely with her, by buying Sangeeta a tray of Krispy Kreme doughnuts.

The press had a field day. Kim was labelled the Social Media Psycho and headlines screamed, Social Murderer, Can I Be Your Facebook Fiend?

Each newspaper's agony aunt, columnist and crime journalist commented on the hazards of social media and how it had needlessly cost so many lives. Polls were conducted and it was revealed that 67% of users felt that using Facebook, WhatsApp, Instagram and Snapchat made them vulnerable to assault and 72% said they had been assaulted, verbally or physically.

When it was revealed that Kim had had a brief relationship with a Libyan some of the press latched onto this saying that the murders had been influenced by ISIS and illegal immigrants. Facebook exploded with debate and for a period Kim was the victim with some users convinced she had been part of a plan for Muslims to kill Christians,

The Moslem influence was disproved when Hatoum was killed fighting against ISIS with the Kurdish forces in Syria. Hatoum had been improving his English it was discovered, in order that he could command a unit of foreign fighters.

With a dearth of national news the debate about the murders did not abate for many months. Question Time held a debate to discuss the impact social media was having on the peaceful lives of normal people. Excerpts of the debate was played out on YouTube and was shared on Facebook and inevitably there was a movement #NotOnFacebook which soon extended to other social media platforms.

The under 30s, by now the least active users of Facebook led the way and not only stopped using their accounts but closed them down. The ripple effect was immediate because their parents and grandparents could no longer tag them in photos. Children would ask that Facebook was not used for Grandchildren photos and family photo sharing became taboo. The backlash snowballed. The over 30s began to abandon their Facebook groups and ring each other for advice. The people who used Facebook as a diary found that no-one was liking their posts therefore they stopped, instead they went back to recording their daily lives in journals to be seen only by themselves. The shameful need for attention, that did not exist prior to Facebook, ground to a halt.

Shares in stationery shops soared as people went back to paper and pen away from keyboards or keypads.

Advertisers, realising they were losing their market and wasting money began pulling out of social media, instead investing heavily in TV and radio..

Restaurants reported an upturn in profits as customers spent more time eating and less time photographing their food.

The decreased use of social media meant that instances of bullying, self-harming and anorexia similarly reduced.

Educational institutions reported that SATs, GSCE and Degree standards improved as children were no longer encumbered by the need to be slaves to smart phones. Sales of computer games did flourish which meant that for some, the need to sit in front of a screen did not diminish.

Slowly but surely Facebook became FaceDead.

Kyle Menschich

In a laboratory in Santa Clary Valley, Kyle Menschich pored through the statistics at the downturn in the use of social media and smiled as he looked through the one way mirror that filled up one wall. The robots, with a small number of human operatives were churning out the next thing in engineering.

It was called the i2uPlug. Worn on a wrist it enabled two non co-located people to hook into the physical being of the other. It meant someone in France could have a holiday in Goa by being the other person, they could go to a Rolling Stones concert in Switzerland, climb Kilimanjaro or watch the Northern Lights.

The early prototypes had proved unstable and expensive. The chip had to be physically wired to the brains of the users. Several East European Romany's, travellers, Middle Eastern or African migrants, smuggled into his European laboratory, and had been invaluable guinea pigs.

The watch version was fully tested and being mass produced. Prior to this was the one which had been given to Kim Maloney to see whether control of an individual was possible.

While Kim wore hers the body swap had been with a homeless person kept in a vegetative state while the actions of Kyle had been recorded by a camera implanted into her brain using her eye as a lens. He wanted to know that when the time came he would have at his fingertips, the lives of all wearers to do his bidding.

As Kim was sentenced to life in prison, Kyle smiled watching the news, and began to think of ways to market his device.

Printed in Poland
by Amazon Fulfillment
Poland Sp. z o.o., Wrocław
01 December 2021

a36dc30c-961f-4777-989b-26c80afe1443R01